The Hi
Scottish Romance Series - Book Two

The

Bedeviled Heart

Carmen Caine

Carmen Caine

Edited by Louisa Stephens
Cover Art by Mehrdad Azadi

Bento Box Books at MyBentoBoxBooks.com

ISBN-13: 978-0-9835240-6-9

Dedication

Mehrdad, no one encourages me more than you ... thank you

Kian, now you are stuck with me forever

Kailyn, I will always "stalk" you forever

*

Angie, I'm glad you are here ☺

Author's Note

Though Cameron and Kate never existed, the story of Thomas (Robert) Cochrane, King James III, and his brothers is based on actual historical events. In some ways, King James III of Scotland was a man born before his time, more a patron of the arts than a warrior. But it was his habit of exalting low-born favorites, among them the architect Cochrane, combined with his fascination for the Black Arts that brought about some of the first documented cases of witchcraft trials in Scotland's history.

"The Bedeviled Heart" is a slight departure in historical flavor from that of "The Kindling Heart" with "The Bedeviled Heart" being the first book in this series to cover the significant historical events of 1479. And as these events took ten years to come to a resolution, this fascinating backdrop will be continued throughout the remainder of the books in this series: "The Daring Heart" and "The Loyal Heart".

And while my goal is to weave history throughout these stories in an effort to make them all the more entertaining, these books will always be romances first and historical second. I will primarily focus on the human relationships between all of the characters in the entire four book storyline.

"The Kindling Heart" begins the story with Bree and Ruan in the Isle of Skye.

"The Bedeviled Heart" covers Cameron and Kate's dramatic romance against the backdrop of court intrigue and witchcraft.

"The Daring Heart" brings the adventure of Lord Julian Gray as he meets his match in the Italian assassin, Liselle.

1

"The Loyal Heart" weaves the spell of fated love with Merry rescuing Ewan in the events leading up to the Battle of Sauchieburn and completes the circle of how it all began.

1

THE OUTLAW

Stirling Castle

Scotland, 1479

Cameron Malcolm Stewart, Earl of Lennox, Lord of Ballachastell, Inchmurrin, and a score of other holdings, ducked his head and entered the dim interior of the alehouse, pausing for a moment on the threshold to sweep the room with a penetrating gaze.

Broad-shouldered and tall, he possessed the arresting combination of elegance and danger that resulted in a naturally imposing presence. His shoulder-length dark hair framed a devilishly handsome face with chiseled lips and a dash in the middle of his strong chin.

Unclasping the brooch that fastened his cloak, he tossed the garment at the young lad scurrying to greet him and settled with the sleek grace of a cat into the darkest corner of the establishment.

Beckoning the alewife with a long finger, Cameron waited patiently for his tankard of brew. It was not long in coming. He took a swig and winced slightly. The quality bordered on unacceptable, but he didn't come here for the ale. He came to escape court intrigue, prying eyes, and endless hours of banal conversation.

The door opened again, and a diminutive lass slipped inside, accompanied by a gust of wind and the momentary sounds of spring.

Hefting her basket to one arm, she smoothed her well-worn skirt, adjusted the kerchief capturing the silken mass of her brown hair, and subjected the occupants of the room to a shrewd eye.

The young lad greeted her with a toothy grin before scuttling through a low arch in the corner of the room. Shortly thereafter, the alewife's voice bellowed from the back, "Kate! I've been waiting for ye, lass! Give me a wee moment, will ye now?"

Wrinkling her nose in a smile, Kate leaned forward and called in return, "No need to rush! I've plenty to keep me busy."

As the muffled sounds of the alewife's cackle filtered from the back, Cameron's dark gaze followed Kate as she sauntered towards a pot-bellied man slumped over the table next to his own.

The lass was slender, shorter than most, with fine brows arching over unusually large and particularly striking brown eyes—eyes that sparkled in silent laughter, even as her brows furrowed and her full lips drew into a serious line.

Setting her basket down on the pot-bellied man's table, Kate shook the man awake. "And a braw day to ye, sir!"

The man slowly lifted his head and squinted. His eyes lit, and a smile immediately crossed his face. "Come here, ye bonny lass!" he slurred, lurching unsteadily to his feet.

Lifting her basket over her head, Kate deftly twirled to the other side of the table as she chirped with a pert smile, "A fine mariner, are ye now? How soon do ye set sail?"

"Sail?" The addled man glanced around before spying her across the table. He stumbled a little in surprise and collapsed back onto his bench. "How did ye get there, lass?"

Kate's lively brown eyes crinkled in the corners. "Ach, ye can do with a wee bit more luck now, can't ye?" she asked, dipping her hand into her basket to draw out a small round stone. "With this charm, ye'll sail with more wind than ye would have without it!"

The man grinned foolishly, nodding several times, and then a look of bewilderment crossed his face. "Sail? Lass, I sell fish in the market!"

Smoothly selecting a larger stone, Kate bent forward and whispered loudly, "Then, this is what ye need, my good man! 'Tis a charm for luck. Carry this with ye now, and ye'll sell more fish than ye would have without it!"

As the man blindly mimicked her vigorous nods, Kate leaned across the table and helped herself to his money pouch. "Ye'll be right pleased with this charm, I'm sure!" she promised, poking through the contents with a disappointed frown before making her choice.

Cameron tapped his finger on the table, a touch amused. The man was obviously a careless fool, and from the looks of the lopsided grin on his face, he was enjoying her company. Aye, being swindled by such a comely lass hardly seemed unfortunate, even for a fool.

"Thank ye for the pleasure of such fine company!" Kate bestowed a brilliant smile upon the man as she returned his pouch. And then absent-mindedly patting him on the head, as one would a dog, she surveyed the room for her next victim.

Suddenly, the alehouse door crashed back, and a rowdy bunch of men entered with hoots of laughter and a storm of curses. Calling for ale, they stumbled towards a table, overturning a bench along the way.

As they passed Kate, one particularly foul-mouthed, lanky fellow grabbed her arm. "Come here, ye fine wench, and give us a kiss!"

Pushing his tankard aside, Cameron rose swiftly to his feet.

"Thomas MacCallum, I do believe?" Kate clucked in a superior tone, shaking her head slowly and making no move to wrench free from his grasp. "What will your wife say when she hears of ye begging for kisses in the alehouse?"

The man's fingers slackened, and the silly grin left his face. With a frown, he all but pushed her away.

Placing her hands on her slim hips, Kate eyed the men up and down. "Is that really Jamie Boyd? What if your mother finds ye here, lad? And, that can't be ye, Sean Gordon? I doubt your father will be pleased hearing ye're back to swilling ale now, so soon after he paid your debt!"

"Who *is* this lass?" Jamie hissed.

They all began to back away.

"Hie off with ye now!" Kate flapped her hands at them. "And think twice afore ye foist your unwanted kisses off on hard-working womenfolk!"

Subdued, the men clustered around their table, sending her dark looks.

With a rare smile threatening his lips, Cameron sat back down and stretched his long legs out before him. Clearly, the lass was well versed in handling such men. Aye, and there *was* something rather intimidating about her. He was certain the top of her head didn't even reach his shoulder.

As he watched, she boldly met his gaze and headed his way.

She was even tinier up close.

"I've come to thank ye, sir," Kate said, dipping a pretty curtsey.

Rising to bow courteously in return, Cameron replied with a sardonic twist of his lip, "And to relieve me of my coin?"

Her brown eyes sparkled in response. Placing her basket on the table, she invited herself to sit opposite him, saying, "I couldna help but notice that ye were coming to my aid, sir."

"Foolishly so, it would seem." Cameron allowed himself to smile. It felt refreshing. He hadn't genuinely smiled in almost two months, since visiting his closest friend, Ruan MacLeod in Dunvegan.

Oddly, he had experienced more than one baffling pang of envy since Ruan had wed Bree. He had thought the feeling to be a fleeting thing, but upon seeing Ruan proudly hold their newborn son, the jealousy had returned full force.

It was a mystery.

Cameron could say with complete certainty that he desired neither wife nor bairn. Aye, several of his brides had arrived with bairns. He certainly had no desire for more. And after having suffered through seven political marriages, each having ended with his becoming a widower shortly thereafter, he had come to believe he truly was cursed and that his name alone would consign a woman to an early death. He had made his peace with the fact that it was not his fate to love as other men could.

"Sir?" Kate's lively brown eyes swam into view. "Have ye been struck dumb?"

Cameron blinked, startled at his lapse of concentration. He pushed his tankard of ale back suspiciously. Perhaps there was something amiss with the brew. Turning back to Kate, he nodded apologetically.

"Forgive me, kind lady. My undivided attention is now yours."

"Such fine words!" Kate wrinkled her nose in a bewitching smile. "I was merely pondering what a splendid gentleman such as yourself could possibly need charmed?"

Cameron tilted his head in detached amusement.

When he didn't reply, she leaned forward and whispered conspiratorially, "Or are ye needing a cursing stone? Nothing too harmful, mind ye, only a wee bit of trouble!"

If only she could give surety of tremendous misfortune, he would right gladly purchase cartloads and have them delivered to the king's court favorite, Thomas Cochrane. With lips crooked in the hint of a mocking smile, he rumbled in a low voice, "Tempting, but no."

Persistence was clearly one of her qualities. Propping her elbows on the table, she insisted, "A man can never have enough luck, sir. What is your trade?"

"Surely, such a canny witch as ye would know?" He issued the amused challenge and settled comfortably back on the bench.

Aye, the lass was proving a charming diversion.

Pursing her lips, Kate studied him thoughtfully. "Your clothing is fine, and your manners are well-bred, but no noble would deign to enter such a humble establishment as this ..." She held out her hand, indicating the alehouse as her laughing brown eyes swept him from head to toe.

Cameron enjoyed her bold scrutiny. It afforded him the opportunity to study her in return. He was quite unused to deviously impudent women, but he was finding it surprisingly invigorating. Instead, he was familiar with the women of the court, and they were of the flirtatious, retiring, and duplicitous kind.

Slamming a palm on the table, Kate exclaimed, "I have it, sir!"

Tilting his head to the side, he waited.

Leaving her place to slip onto the bench next to him, she whispered in his ear, "Ye've come upon grave misfortune and have turned to outlawry! And ye must be among the daring sort to sit so fearlessly beneath the shadow of Stirling Castle in the broad light of day!"

At that, Cameron found his lips bending into a genuine smile. "And ye seem to be wickedly clever, lass."

"Then buy a stone from me for good luck, sir." She lifted the corner of the cloth covering her basket in a tantalizing manner. "There are many wonders to behold here! And surely a man in such a perilous trade as yours can use all the luck he finds in his path!"

Cameron eyed the spirited lass at his side with a deepening interest. Tossing a shilling onto the table, he lowered his lashes and murmured suggestively, "Aye, I'll buy something from ye."

Her brown eyes widened in shock at the shilling, and in a flash, she tucked the coin away, once again wrinkling her nose in the catching smile that he found quite delightful.

"And which charm would please ye most, sir?" she asked. "To be swift fingered, fleet of foot, or perhaps glib of tongue?"

The corner of his lip twitched in amusement. Fires of Hell, but this young witch actually possessed an uncommon ability to make him relax. With his dark eyes smoldering a little, he leaned close and replied, "A kiss." A mere kiss wouldn't hurt anyone.

Never had he seen such expressive eyes. Even now, as she rolled them, they were gleaming with mirth. "My kisses canna be bought, sir!"

"A pity," Cameron murmured with a twinge of disappointment.

Placing a smooth stone on the table—of the most common kind he had seen in countless numbers on every riverbed and loch shore—Kate announced with a precocious grin, "But since ye paid me good coin, sir, I'll grant ye my luckiest stone. With this, ye'll have far more good fortune than ye would have had without it!"

Cameron captured her hand in his long fingers, bantering lightly, "Surely, such a bonny lass as ye could not begrudge a weary traveler a kiss?"

She didn't move her hand from his, but leaned closer, brushing against him as she whispered a warning, "Beware, sir! I've a noble, jealous lover who would avenge my honor, even on the likes of ye!"

Cameron was not surprised to find her taken, though he deemed the man rather despicable to allow his mistress to walk around in such bereft attire. She obviously deserved better. Still, he had only wanted a kiss. Mildly curious, he inquired, "And who might this dreaded lord be?"

Sliding her fingers from under his, she swept her arms in a dramatic gesture. "He is none other than Cameron, the Earl of Lennox … the Dreaded Earl of Death *himself*!"

Cameron stared at her blankly.

With a sly twinkle in her eyes, she nodded in satisfaction. "Aye, now ye really *have* been struck dumb!"

Dismayed to hear his own name upon her lips, he repeated stonily, "The Dreaded Earl of Death?"

"Aye, his touch alone can curse!" she promised brightly.

The words were hauntingly familiar and Cameron winced, no longer enjoying the exchange. "If his touch is cursed, then he is a poor choice of lovers," he observed in a cutting tone.

"He is a most skilled lover, sir!" Kate responded with a haughty toss of her head. "But I'm of low birth, and I'll never wed the man. I'm in no danger!"

The kerchief binding her hair slipped askew, freeing the heavy mass to spill over her face and shoulders in the most appealing way.

Inexplicably, Cameron's annoyance fled.

Catching her wrist, he pulled her close and imparted a sound kiss full on her lips. His intention was to tease, or so he told himself as he felt her lips freeze in surprise beneath his. But then she returned the kiss with such an unexpected burst of enthusiasm that he was swept into the enjoyment of it all until a wild hunger threatened to rise in his blood.

With great difficulty, he tore his lips away and stared down at her, startled.

A moment later, he found himself roundly slapped across the face.

"How dare ye take the liberty, sir!" Kate jumped up, her cheeks flaming.

Cameron blinked and held still. He had stolen countless kisses from whomever he pleased his entire life, and none of the lasses had ever slapped him for it.

"The Dreaded Earl of Death does not allow others to fondle his mistress, ye lout!" Kate planted her hands on her hips, taking him to task.

None had ever dared to name him a lout before, either. Affronted, he rose to his feet. As he had thought, she didn't even come up to his shoulder. "Have a care, lass," he advised in a chilling tone. "I only took what ye named mine!"

Kate's eyes flashed dangerously. "Ach, ye must be drunk! I've half a mind to send the Dreaded Earl to knock some sense into that thick-witted head of yours!"

"Then, do so!" Cameron replied in a soft, chilling tone. But then again, his annoyance vanished, and even though his cheek still stung, and he was less than pleased to discover his own reputation as the Earl of Death, he found a perverse amusement in the situation. With a cynical gleam in his eye, he added, "I confess that I'm quite anxious to meet the man!"

He stood close, towering arrogantly over her in a manner that had oft before intimidated many a man, but the lass merely jabbed his chest with her finger.

"Surely, ye aren't such a muckle fool?" She clucked her tongue. "He's a jealous lover and canna bear another man to even gaze upon me! Just be off afore ye're never seen again … alive."

Folding his arms, Cameron replied dryly. "Ach, lass, I do believe I've nothing to fear from your *Dreaded Earl of Death*."

Clearly irritated, Kate's voice took on a storyteller's lilt as she splayed and theatrically wiggled her fingers. "Ye should be quaking in your boots! The man has slain countless men and even his own seven wives, each on their wedding night, and the first he killed when he was a wee lad of eight!"

His humor dissipated.

He hadn't expected her to speak of his ill-fated marriages. And she wasn't even accurate.

Icily, he felt compelled to correct. "The first wedding was at the age of eleven, and 'twas purely an arrangement of titles and land. The English lass was ill on her deathbed, but she lived a week." Because of the massive amount of land involved, the church had overlooked his young age and blessed the union under the pretext that since the bride was from England, the marriage should adhere to English church law.

Kate's lips parted in surprise. "Then, ye *have* heard of him!"

"Perhaps." Cameron lifted a long finger, signaling that he no longer cared to continue the conversation. He was not inclined to discuss his past wives with the lass, no matter how pleasurable he found her kisses. And even though he thought of his past often, he simply never discussed the matter.

She didn't take his hint. In an exaggerated tone, she continued, "Then, ye know that he murdered the next wife, a poor innocent wee bairn, not even five years of age!"

Of all his wives, the murder of Anna still haunted him. He closed his eyes, unable to prevent the memory from returning full force. He had only been eighteen when political interests sent him off to England once again, to a child-bride named Anna. He had given her a doll and had straightway returned home to Scotland. Several years later, he found himself once more at her estate, standing at her funeral.

"Some say 'twas poison—" Kate was saying.

"The Keiths murdered Anna!" He raised his voice in displeasure, his fingers clenching imperceptibly. No one dared to speak of Anna in his presence. They all knew better.

"Ach! Why would that be?" Kate snorted, piqued at the interruption.

With his lips tightening in a thin line, he replied curtly, "To bolster their claim for the land! They argued the marriage was against church law from the start." Aye, he was still fighting some of them on the matter to this very day.

Kate slapped her palm on the table, clearly aggravated. "Ach, ye must have a different tale to tell of Elizabet and Cecilia, then?"

At least she had the names right, though he doubted anything else would be.

"Beheaded, both of them!" She inserted before he could stop her.

"Nonsense!" Cameron roared, striking the table with his fist.

He blinked, taken aback at his uncommon loss of control. Rarely did he lose his temper, and why he was doing so now, he was at a complete loss to understand. Perhaps it was because he simply never discussed his unfortunate marriages with anyone, save Ruan, and even then, only when he was drunk and on the verge of being traded yet again, like a horse at the market.

Quickly composing himself, he replied in a restrained tone. "Elizabet fell victim to the plague, and Cecilia died of milk fever!"

"Only a fool would believe that when the poor bairns he got on them have been locked away in dungeons ever since!" Kate disagreed stubbornly.

Taking a deep breath, he answered evenly, "The wee lassies are safe in Inchmurrin." They certainly weren't his children. He'd never shared a bed with any of his wives, yet Cameron had claimed the bairns as his own in exchange for land, titles, and political influence. It had seemed a fair bargain at the time. Now, he wasn't so certain.

"He hung the fifth wife!" Kate was clearly enjoying herself.

"The fifth ran off with her lover, and their horse plunged over a cliff in the darkness of night." Cameron differed in a cool tone.

"I know not where ye heard such tales!" Kate snapped.

In the interests of ending the conversation quickly, Cameron continued impassively, "The sixth drowned." Aye, she'd been so terrified to wed him that upon hearing of his impending arrival, she had thrown herself in the loch. Clenching his jaw, he finished, "And, lastly, the seventh wife, Heloise, died in childbirth last year."

He had agreed to wed Heloise, at the behest of the king to ward off the queen's wrath, but also at the request of his peers to prevent Thomas Cochrane from acquiring a title. At the time, it had seemed an irrelevant decision. Now, with the rumors of Cochrane's growing power, he wasn't so sure.

He winced to find himself thinking of court intrigue in the very place he had come to escape from it.

Kate had been watching his face with her dark eyes flickering in annoyance. "Well, ye've listened to the wrong folk," she finally insisted. "*I* should know the truth! Ye'd best tread carefully. The earl is a jealous man who will have your head if he hears ye dared kiss me!"

With a huff, she stepped away, but there was something in the way she moved the made his blood run hot. His hand snaked out and he rose to twist her around, pulling her close against his chest.

"Then perhaps ye should not let him know how ye responded, Kate," he whispered in her ear. "'Twas almost as if ye enjoyed it!"

The color rose high in her cheeks. Jerking free, she snatched her basket from the table and sailed to the back room, not once turning back to look in his direction.

Cameron watched her go with a riotous mix of frustration and desire, and then with an aggravated growl, he ordered the lad to fetch his cloak.

Not in the best of moods, he quit the place and strode through the trees to where his man had waited with his charger the entire afternoon. Informing him that he would return to the Brass Unicorn Inn on foot, he sent them away and wandered through the town of Stirling, hoping the fresh spring air would clear his mind.

High above him, Stirling Castle perched on the rocky outcrop overlooking the town like a hawk. Soon, he would enter its walls to engage in the inevitable scheming trickery required of him. He detested court life. It always left an unpleasant taste in his mouth.

Closing his eyes, he took a deep breath and inhaled the crisp, clean smell of spring. A soft, warm breeze blew gently on his face, carrying with it the scents from the highlands. He sighed, wishing he could mount his horse and ride away to gallop for miles through the heather and hills.

Grimly, he opened his eyes and made his way through the gray stone houses hugging Stirling's cobblestoned streets. Ach, but that lass was a meddlesome one! He'd much rather be thinking of her kiss and not the pain of the past her words had summoned. Perhaps she truly was a witch, sent to remind him that by merely keeping company with a woman he would dispatch her to a speedy death.

Aye, perhaps he should take to calling himself *The Dreaded Earl of Death*. He wondered how many had called him that and for how long.

It took some doing, but after wandering through the bustling town for a time, he finally succeeded in driving Kate and her wild tales from his thoughts as concerns of court rose to take their place. He wasn't so sure that was an improvement. He eyed the great gray castle above him. He had yet to step foot in it and he was already weary of it.

He would have to announce his presence soon.

He had been at the inn for almost a week, secretly meeting with select nobles, listening to the latest tidings and court gossip, and plotting the most advantageous time for his return. He never arrived at court without knowing what he was stepping into, but this time, what he had learned caused him grave concern.

In the past years, the king had handpicked artisans from low birth to attend him at court and had engaged in ever increasingly scandalous conduct with them, but the men came and went in quick succession. But not so with the mason, Thomas Cochrane. The nobles had thought he would soon disappear as the others had. But he had not only remained, he had succeeded in garnering a considerable amount of power since Cameron's last visit to court.

The shadows had grown long when Cameron finally turned down the lane that led to the Brass Unicorn. The dying sun cast a golden glow on the ivy-covered walls of the buildings clustered around him, and he eyed the scene spreading out before him with a twinge of longing. Moss and ferns grew on the slate roof of the stables. An ancient tree huddled in the center of the courtyard, the early buds of leaves dusting its branches in a fine green mist.

Often times of late, he dreamt of leaving his wealth of titles and land, to become a humble innkeeper of such a place.

He stood there, savoring the peaceful simplicity for several long moments before the sounds of merriment drifted through the open door, beckoning him, and he entered the modest establishment to find a traveling minstrel regaling the common room with a tale.

The low-hanging sun slanted through the window, and the air was already growing chill. Taking a seat next to the fire, Cameron stretched his long legs and listened, not to the minstrel, but to the chattering of the people about him. Closing his eyes, he savored being a nameless face in the crowd with no one begging favors or showering him with false compliments for their own purposes.

"I've saved ye a fine trout, sir." The Innkeeper's wife broke into his thoughts. "And some of that fine Rhennish wine ye favor."

Cameron's long lashes fluttered open. The old woman knew quite well who he was, but she knew how to keep a secret. And he made it worth her while, paying her a princely sum to keep her most well-appointed and spacious lodgings free for his personal use.

"And I thank ye, Morag," Cameron replied, lightly brushing his lips over her wrinkled hand.

"Ye should be saving yer kisses for lassies, lad," the old woman protested, but she was smiling and her green eyes gleamed as she threaded her way through the crowd.

The mention of kissing brought unbidden thoughts of Kate. Cameron turned his dark gaze to the fire, recalling her soft lips under his. The passion in her response had startled him, but he knew he would never pursue it. He had little time for women and no desire to tempt Death's hand yet again. No, his lot was with the king and his court, not in a wife and son like his friend, Ruan MacLeod. If he were honest, he would recognize the wave of loneliness that swept over him, but he was adept at ignoring it, and the bottle of Rhennish wine that Morag was carrying his way would only aid in that pursuit.

Morag set the wine and a wooden platter of fish down on the table. Pursing her lips with a sly grin, she said, "Why dinna I see ye here with a fine lass on your knee, lad? A brawny lad like ye should nae be alone!"

Permitting his eyes to smile, Cameron deepened his voice and replied easily enough, "And, why would I have need of such when I am in your company, fair Morag?"

"Ach, now, ye foolish lad." Morag cackled. "Ye'll make these withered old cheeks blush." With a laugh, she moved away.

The crowd parted and Cameron spied a richly dressed figure lounging against the far wall, watching him like a hawk. And any semblance of peace he had managed to gain fled in an instant as he recognized the long and narrow face of Thomas Cochrane.

Thomas Cochrane was a young man with brown hair, a sleek beard, and a wiry frame, but with the bad coloring of one who indulged far too often in wine and other vices. Sporting a fancy hat with a blue feather and an embroidered satin mantle lined with pearls, fit for a king, he was clearly out of place in such a humble inn.

The crowd milling around him paid little heed, knowing he was just like them, low-born and holding no real power. But Cameron knew that was changing. The rumors from court clearly indicated that Thomas was moving from a mere nuisance to a potentially formidable enemy.

As the man approached, Cameron pushed his food away untouched. His meager appetite had disappeared entirely.

"My lord!" Thomas bowed before him. "'Tis surprising to find ye in such a lowly place."

Keeping his face outwardly composed, Cameron nodded cordially. "A good day to ye, Thomas. Pray join me."

The man took a seat opposite him, and even though his thin lips smiled, his green eyes held a glint of anger. "I have been remiss in offering ye my condolences for the loss of the Countess Heloise. I confess I'm still astounded at her passing. She was so young, filled with life, ere her fate, and I canna help but think I could have done something to prevent ..." He allowed his voice to trail off suggestively.

Years of court experience allowed Cameron to conceal his annoyance. It had been almost a year since Heloise's untimely death. Obviously, Thomas still regretted losing the chance to gain a title. Aye, the man had grown bolder since their last parting, or else he would not have dared to utter such words in his presence.

"Aye, 'tis unfortunate." Cameron inclined his head slightly. "And I thank ye for such kind words, but tell me what brings ye to the Brass Unicorn? 'Tis not a place ye are wont to frequent."

Thomas eyed him, absently stroking his sleek beard, and then with obvious pleasure replied, "Aye, I've come on the king's business."

Cameron eyed him with a detached curiosity and gave an indifferent shrug. "And what business would the king's Mason have with me? I know naught of building castles."

Thomas' long face adopted an almost gleeful expression. "I've come to speak of your impending marriage, my lord. We've decided to forge new bonds with France, and ..."

Cameron drew back, greatly displeased.

Royal affairs had clearly deteriorated far more dramatically than any had thought, if Thomas brazenly spoke using *we* in forging bonds with France. And it was beyond preposterous that the king had allowed a low-born mason to discuss the marital affairs of an earl and his own cousin, a Stewart no less.

By the Saints, the evening was worsening by the moment!

The man was smirking. "Ye look a wee bit upset, my lord. Allow me to pour ye some of this fine Rhennish wine."

Accepting the offered mug, Cameron drained it in a single draught.

It was wiser than speaking.

The man was clearly engaged in some unsavory plot of power and revenge. A prudent course of action would be to befriend the man, but Cameron knew he was incapable of it, at present, when all he wanted to do was reach across the table and throttle the pompous fool's neck. Coolly reminding himself that allowing anger to guide a decision was the hallmark of a fool, he cleared his throat and remarked in a reserved tone, "These matters are best not discussed outside castle walls. I will see the king on the morrow."

Clearly disappointed with his reaction, Thomas gave a reluctant nod.

And then unable to bear the man's company a moment longer, Cameron rose to his feet. "I've a matter of the most pressing nature to attend. I pray ye forgive such a hasty departure from your company."

Rising to his feet as well, Thomas nodded, but there was a sense of gloating about the man that Cameron found intolerable.

Aye, so Thomas thought to match wits? Adopting his most benevolent expression, Cameron clasped the man's shoulder and pulled him close in a brotherly embrace. "And I've weighty matters to discuss with ye as well. Of late, ye've proven to be a trustworthy man."

The man's brows furrowed in momentary confusion.

Aye, Thomas had grown in the ways of the court, but he hadn't been steeped in it since birth as Cameron had. He couldn't mask all traces of emotion. Let him remain confused, unsure if Cameron was his friend or foe.

Striding away, Cameron ducked into the kitchens and made his way to the back door of the inn to stop in a small, walled herb garden.

Aye, if Thomas was now meddling in an earl's marriage prospects, it was time to discover what he was dabbling in.

Marriage.

Cameron closed his eyes and swallowed.

He could not allow himself to be wed off again. Kate was right. He *was* the Dreaded Earl of Death. He shuddered. He could not watch another woman die. A kiss in the alehouse was as far as he would go.

Suddenly, the herb garden walls around him seemed to be closing in.

Pox and Pestilence, but he wasn't going to stay there and smother!

Quickening his stride, he kicked the back gate open and, pulling his hood down over his face, once again restlessly wandered the streets of Stirling.

2

CAN A MAN BE CHANGED?

Kate bid the alewife a hasty farewell, and clutching the shilling tightly in her hand, ran through Stirling's cobbled streets. It was difficult to do. Her worn shoes offered little protection from the uneven stones.

Why the brawny outlaw had given her a shilling for a charmed stone that he hadn't even bothered to take with him was far beyond puzzling.

The sudden thought that he had likely stolen the shilling gave her a momentary pause, but only for a moment. She was in desperate need and using the coin for the benefit of the poor was a worthy destiny, particularly for a stolen shilling.

Upon reaching a tiny cottage on the edge of town, Kate paused before a gaily-painted red door. Taking a deep breath and willing herself to remain calm, she gave it a sharp knock.

After a moment, the latch rattled, and she heard a woman grumble, "Ach, what is it now?"

Maura was a young, creamy-skinned, charming lass with bright blue eyes, dimples in her cheeks, and an amply curved figure. Having recently inherited the cottage from her aunt, she had moved to Stirling a short time ago and had found work as one of Stirling Castle's chambermaids.

Knowing that Kate was searching for an affordable room, the alewife had introduced them a fortnight ago. Feeling her heart would burst before Maura could reply, Kate blurted, "Tell me quick! Is the room still to be had? If it is, I'll take it now!"

"Aye, 'tis still free." Maura nodded, frowning. "But ye haven't the shilling, and—"

"I have it now!" Kate fairly danced, pressing the coin into Maura's hands. "I've had the most blessedly fortunate day!" Closing her eyes, she hugged herself in excitement. Perhaps her father's health might strengthen, now that they could move into the tiny back room of Maura's cottage, away from the rank, dismal almshouse that presently served as home.

The woman stared at the coin in surprise before snatching it and stuffing it down her bosom. "Then I'll borrow the Fletcher's cart and we'll get your father right here, but tell me first, where did ye get a shilling? 'Twas only two days ago and ye had nothing!"

Kate grinned foolishly, thinking of the outlaw in the alehouse. Pressing a finger to her lips, she could almost feel the warm touch of his kiss. With a secretive lift of her brow, she only replied, "From someone most generous!"

Maura's eyes lit with interest. "'Twas a man?"

Kate hesitated. While she didn't know Maura well, it was obvious that she was the jealous type, particularly where men were concerned. The woman desperately wanted a husband. "Aye, a man, but not a braw one," she lied. Maura didn't need to know the outlaw had been exceptionally handsome, broad-shouldered, and tall with the most compelling dark eyes.

"If he's wealthy enough to hand out shillings, it matters little if he is pock-marked and long of tooth!" Maura eyed her suspiciously.

"Ach, but he was an outlaw, not to be trusted," Kate replied truthfully enough.

The woman was a bit surprised at that, but shrugged it off, muttering, "If he can hand ye coin, then I still say it matters not." Grabbing her cloak from its hook, she tied it under her chin. "Let's be off to the Fletcher then."

Unable to contain her exhilaration, Kate found it difficult not to run there, but Maura did not share her enthusiasm and would only walk. She had other concerns on her mind.

"Now that ye'll be living with me, Kate, ye can share some of those secrets of love," she said, broaching the sorest subject between them.

Kate stifled a sigh.

Maura was under the impression that she truly knew how to make charms, and even though Kate had promised her, time and again, that she truly knew nothing of such arts, Maura refused to believe her. "I wish I had knowledge to share." She sighed.

"How can ye expect me to believe ye?" Maura twisted her lips in a scowl. "Ye clearly bewitched the outlaw into given ye a shilling, didn't ye now?"

"'Twas only luck." Kate expelled a long breath through her nose. Living with Maura wasn't going to be easy, but anything would be better than where they lived now.

Maura dropped the subject because they had arrived at the Fletcher's house, but Kate knew the conversation was far from over.

The Fletcher's home was a tiny place, but well kept. The man's wife was less than pleased to see them. When asked, she pointed to the cart readily enough, but with dark looks that made Kate nervous.

Maura rudely brushed past the woman, pulling Kate along to the small courtyard where the cart stood under a scraggly pear tree. With a smug laugh, she assured, "Ach, Kate, no need to worry! The harridan is just jealous of me. Think nothing of her!"

"Jealous?" Kate repeated apprehensively.

"Her husband fancies me," she replied proudly, vainly patting her own cheeks.

Kate suppressed an uneasy feeling. Was it a mistake to rent the woman's room? But the thought of her weak father still battling his long illness reminded her that she had no choice. Maura's room was the only one she could afford. If her father remained much longer in the foul environment of the decrepit almshouse, she was certain he would die.

Shrugging her worries aside, she grasped the handles of the cart.

As Maura babbled about the many men of Stirling who swooned at her feet, swearing that she had the finest complexion of any woman in Scotland, Kate strained to lift the cart handles with a loud humph.

It was too heavy. She cleared the cobblestones by only a few inches.

"The men of Stirling are mad for me." Maura was saying. "But I've not the eyes for them now. I've set my sight upon the Earl of Lennox. They say he'll be at Stirling Castle, mayhap even on the morrow!"

Kate dropped the cart with a crash.

Mention of the earl brought back her lies and about the mysterious outlaw in the alehouse. He had clearly been annoyed at her conversation, but then, he was probably angry over her reaction to the kiss. He must have felt cheated, paying an entire shilling for only a kiss and a stone. Though ignorant of how much kisses were worth, she had thought it to be a remarkably thrilling one. But then she'd never kissed anyone before, either.

"What is it, Kate?" Maura eyed her with suspicion.

Flustered, and not quite sure why, Kate lifted the cart and wobbled a few feet before letting it fall again. "I dinna think I can do this alone, Maura!"

She wasn't about to tell Maura of the outlaw's kiss.

"Dinna look to me! I've done more than my share in getting ye the cart!" The woman flicked her fingers in irritation. "I've errands to run. Ye'll have to get your father to the cottage on your own." Drawing her cloak about her, a bit indignantly, she hurried away into the gathering darkness.

Kate watched her go with a frown but also with a small measure of relief. The woman was difficult to be around for any length of time.

She gave the cart a rueful look, wondering how she could push her father back to the cottage when she couldn't even get the empty cart to where he lay to begin with.

Heaving a sigh, she strained to push it forward, cursing under her breath and vainly wishing herself taller and stronger. By the time she had made it down to the end of the lane, she was sweating and short-tempered. Kicking the cart with her worn shoe, she cursed at the top of her voice, "Ye fobbing loggerheaded motley-minded barnacle! I've had enough of ye!"

A dry chuckle sounded from the shadows nearby.

Kate whirled, assuming a stern expression to cover a ripple of panic. "Who goes there?" she demanded harshly.

To her utter astonishment, the outlaw from the alehouse stepped forward to tower over her. In the darkness of the deserted street, he was even more intimidating than before. He stood, tall and proud, with a fine cloak clasped about his neck by an intricately wrought silver broach. She eyed it sourly. He must have been busy pilfering things since their last meeting.

Clenching her fingers tightly, she adopted a fierce look. "If ye want the shilling back, 'tis too late. I no longer have the thing!"

The man's lips twitched in what could have been amusement, but she wasn't entirely sure. As his dark eyes roved over her and the cart, his deep voice queried, "Ye bought a cart?"

"Ach, this isn't mine, and it is worth far more than a shilling!" Kate rolled her eyes, amused by his ignorance. Of their own accord, her lips cracked into a smile.

His chiseled lips momentarily curved in response, and they stood there in the street as Kate wondered what it was about the man that made her heart flutter. She knew the man was an outlaw and that she should not keep company with such men, but it did little to still her beating heart.

Suddenly, the evening church bells tolled.

Kate tensed. It was late. Her father was most likely fretting over her this very moment. Worrying would not help him recover. With a polite curtsey, she nodded a farewell. "'Twas a pleasure to see ye again, sir, but I've places to be."

Grasping the handles, she hefted the cart with all her might. A sharp jab ripped through her side, and she abruptly doubled over to gasp aloud in pain.

"Ach, Kate!" She felt the man's strong hands about her waist, steadying her. "A wee lass like ye can't wield this thing! What are ye up to?"

Sucking in her breath, it was some time before she could reply, "I'll be fine, sir. I've need to hurry now. I canna cause my father to fret. 'Tis not good for his health."

"Then, allow me to assist ye," the man suggested, placing a hand firmly on the handle.

"'Tis quite a valiant offer, but I must refuse," Kate replied, impressed by his kindheartedness. "Ye've done plenty for me this day, in the payment of the shilling for the charmed stone."

He laughed softly at that, and leaning close, whispered in her ear, "'Twas a fair trade for the kiss, lass."

Kate blushed. Turning her head away, she was grateful for the darkness as she gripped the cart handle once again in determination, stubbornly refusing to acknowledge the pain still burning in her side.

To her surprise, the man planted both hands firmly upon her waist and lightly tossed her into the back of the cart. And then with a gallant bow, unclasped his cloak to throw it over her shoulders, and said, "Pray tell me where ye wish to go, kind lady. I am your humble servant."

With a grateful sigh, Kate quickly gave in and smiled widely. "I dinna know what I did to deserve ye this day, kind sir, but I'm grateful.

What with the shilling and now your brawny arm, I would think ye an angel if ye weren't an outlaw."

Easily lifting the cart handles, he shook his head in disagreement and commented wryly, "I am far too cursed to be an angel."

"What might I call ye?" she asked, unable to stop herself from admiring his rippling muscles.

"Cameron." There was a hint of arrogant amusement in his tone as he dipped his head gracefully in yet another bow.

Kate blinked, taken aback.

Apparently, he had a wicked sense of humor.

"I won't betray ye. Ye can tell me your true name," she promised, drawing her brows into a frown.

His lips twitched a little as he asked, "And why do ye think that is not my true name?"

"Ach, man!" Kate replied with an insulted huff. "I know well that ye only chose the name of Cameron because I told ye this very afternoon in the alehouse that the Earl of Lennox was my lover!"

Cameron's dark eyes lit with laughter even as his lips thinned into a line. Jiggling the cart a little, he rumbled deeply, "The only name I'll give ye, lass, is the one I was given, and that is Cameron. Now, tell me where ye wish to go afore I take ye to the Brass Unicorn for another kiss."

Feeling herself blush at the thought of a kiss, Kate burrowed into his fine cloak and ordered, "Then, hie ye off to the almshouse, and be swift of foot, *Cameron!*" The man was obviously intent on keeping his identity secret. Not for one moment did she believe that he shared the same name as the Earl of Lennox.

As he set off, she settled back into the cart to enjoy the unexpected respite. She had slept only a few hours that night, rising before dawn to care for her father, and then taking to the streets to sell charms. The past few weeks had been particularly harsh. She'd only earned a few pence before stumbling upon the brawny thief now pulling the cart. Her gaze flickered over him appreciatively. Ach, but she couldn't help again admiring his broad shoulders and hard muscles.

It was a good several minutes before she noticed they had gone the wrong direction.

"Dinna ye even know where the almshouse is, Cameron?" she asked, astonished. "What manner of outlaw are ye, man?"

"Apparently an ill-taught one," he replied dryly. Setting the cart down, his dark gaze ensnared hers.

Ach, but he was handsome. His lips seemed carved of stone, and she found the dash in the middle of his chin remarkably distracting.

Slowly, he propped his elbow on the edge of the cart, reaching back to playfully pinch her cheek as his deep voice suggested, "Perhaps ye should tell me where it is then, lass."

Blushing still more, Kate pointed to the opposite street.

She watched in silence as he hefted the cart and moved forward, all the while searching for a witty response but finding none. His touch had caught her off guard. Ach, but the man was disturbing in the most delightful of ways.

Once they had achieved a steady roll, she couldn't resist asking, "So, why did ye become an outlaw then, Cameron?"

"Why do ye think?" he responded evasively.

Pursing her lips, she mused aloud, "'Tis always over coin, but how did ye lose yours? Gambling? Ill fortune? Are ye seeking revenge, or did ye commit a crime and were forced to flee—"

"I've done no wrong!" He interrupted strongly, but then added in a voice much less sure, "Intentionally, that is. Though mayhap I am cursed ..."

The thought of a curse tugged at her heart, and she couldn't help but say, "Ye'll only make it worse with the path ye've chosen! 'Tis never too late to turn back."

He gave a laugh, if she could call it that. There was little mirth in the sound.

She watched him curiously, wondering what heartache he was hiding and if it were over some lass. That thought took hold, and she found it impossible to resist prying further, "Surely, ye have some reason to live a better life, or womenfolk who care if ye lose your head?" Foolishly, she wanted his answer to be no.

The line of his head and shoulders tensed, and his tone sounded reserved. "Are ye asking if I've a lass waiting for me somewhere, Kate?"

She blushed that he had seen to the heart of her question, but she was scarce one to shy away. "I would think a man like ye would have a lass safely tucked away in each town ye pass through," she replied pertly.

She expected him to laugh, but he answered quietly, "I've no one waiting for me anywhere, and I'll keep it that way, Kate. I was not jesting when I told ye that I'm cursed."

Finding that response far more intriguing than any other could have been, Kate leaned forward in the cart. "Ach, now, have ye turned to thievery for the lack of another soul caring for ye? 'Tis a poor choice! A braw man like ye could even sail the seas! Surely, anything would be better than finding a noose about your neck if ye be caught wearing such stolen finery as ye have on your back right now!"

Cameron set the cart down carefully and faced her. The moon was bright enough that she could easily see that his dark eyes gleamed with mirth. "Are ye trying to save my wicked soul?"

"I'm not sure that ye can be saved," she teased, impulsively tapping the crease in his chin with her finger.

His hand lifted instinctively, as if to brush her away. It was a gesture of someone unused to being touched.

Kate found her heart tugging even more. While never wealthy, she had always lived in a family filled with an abundance of love and laughter. "In faith, Cameron, but ye seem to be a poor, lonely soul," she said with a sympathetic smile.

"Nay, not so much," he replied distantly, drawing back. With a shrug, he took the cart back up and continued down the hill.

She tried several more attempts at conversation, but he remained silent, and she lapsed into silence herself until they finally arrived at the almshouse.

The bright moon illuminated the long, low building in a flood of light. Once, it had been a fine charity under the care of monks, but some years ago, a resurgence of the plague had slain them all. Now, the almshouse struggled to handle the destitute, the ill, and the elderly within its walls. The roof was in poor repair, and there was little to eat.

Setting the cart down, Cameron swung Kate down with an easy

arm, but he was distracted, his dark eyes locked upon the almshouse in dismay.

"Aye, 'tis right glad I'll be to sleep elsewhere this night." Kate shook Cameron's cloak from her shoulders, folded it neatly, and handed it back to him. "Though my heart hurts for those I'll be leaving behind."

Cameron lifted a querying brow.

"Come!" Kate crooked a finger and beckoned him to follow.

Stepping through the low doorway, she led him into the dark interior and familiar rank stench, watching as he ducked his head and followed. In the corner of the room, a single candle flickered on the windowsill, revealing dark forms huddled on the floor around it.

Allowing a moment for her eyes to adjust, Kate picked her way over the sea of coughing, hacking, and snoring forms to the adjoining room.

"Is that ye, Kate?" a weak voice asked from the shadows.

A rat squeaked nearby.

"Aye, father!" Kate replied brightly. "I've come to take ye away now, as I swore I would!"

"Ach, lass, what foolishness is this?" Her father's voice shook.

Stepping over several sleeping figures, Kate knelt next to him. "I've a room at Maura's now, and I've a cart here to take ye there."

Her father struggled to sit up, and she hurriedly slipped her arm under his thin shoulders, helping him to rise. The moonlight streamed through the cracks in the roof, lighting his face.

He had once been a strong, hearty man. His shoulders had been broad and his hands steady. A fisherman by trade, he had often taken his young daughters with him in his tiny boat. Kate could still remember the countless, pleasurable hours fishing with her father and younger sister, gliding over the shiny loch that reflected the blue sky and white clouds like a mirror. It seemed a lifetime ago before the fever had struck them all, taking the life of her mother and sister, leaving her father weak and blind, but Kate untouched. She still didn't understand it.

"Who is that with ye, my sweet bairn?" Her father shifted his head to the side.

Shaking off her sad thoughts, Kate gripped his hands tightly. "'Tis an angel sent to help us. His name is Cameron."

"Hardly an angel," Cameron disagreed softly from behind her. "But I am at your service, sir."

"The Saints be praised!" Her father's voice trembled with unshed tears. "Then, ye spoke true?" He began to cough, covering his mouth with the back of his arm.

"Can ye stand?" Kate asked when his coughing fit subsided. "Ye'll have to walk to the cart, father."

He tried, but he was far too weak. Kate was on the verge of tears herself to see this once proud, strong man reduced to such a state, but she had little time to indulge in sadness. Pursing her lips, she frowned and forced a strong voice. "Ye'll have to stand. I canna carry ye…"

"Step aside, lass," Cameron's deep voice ordered kindly.

In one swift movement, Cameron scooped her frail father up in his strong arms and threaded his way through the sleeping forms on the floor to the door.

Hurriedly, Kate scrambled to collect their possessions. They didn't have much, only a few bits of ribbon, her mother's hairbrush, and a candlestick to evoke the cherished memories of their former life. By the time she had finished tying the bundle and hurried out of the almshouse, Cameron had finished tucking his fine cloak about her father's feeble form.

"Are ye ready, Kate?" Cameron looked down upon her with unreadable dark eyes.

Clutching her precious bundle close, she nodded, and giving the almshouse a long, last look, straightened her shoulders and marched up the street with Cameron pushing her father closely behind.

The journey back to Maura's cottage was a silent one, each comfortable with their own thoughts. Maura's stone cottage looked inviting, even in the moonlight. Several fruit trees flowered on one side of the tiny stone building, while an herb bed graced the other. It was untended, still tangled with the dry brown weeds of the year before, but Kate already had plans to make it ready for planting on the morrow. Soon, the hedges, trees and the brown herb bed would be bursting with life. She felt it was a sign. Perhaps she and her father were finally emerging from their ill luck and on the verge of a new life.

The cottage was dark, signaling Maura had not yet returned. Strangely relieved, Kate lifted the latch and pushed the door open as Cameron once again gathered her father in his strong arms and carried him over the threshold.

Kate proudly led them to the back room. A small window allowed enough moonlight to filter through to show the straw pallet on the floor, a three-legged stool, several woolen blankets, and a small hearth. Aye, the room was tiny, but it was free of fleas and rats, and smelled only of spring, not the rank odor of the almshouse.

As Cameron gently set her father down on the pallet, Kate slipped into the main room for coals and peat, returning to coax a fire on the hearth. In moments, meager flames licked the peat, and Kate sat back on her heels with a contented sigh.

"Ye did well, my wee one." Her father laughed weakly from behind her.

Turning, she found him comfortably settled, clutching the top of the woolen blankets with his swollen knuckles. Sweat rolled off his brow. He was still clearly unwell.

"Ye shouldna worry so, lassie." He nodded his head in her direction. "I may be blind, but I can still see ye worry too much, my wee bairn."

Kate's lips split into a smile. Her father knew her well.

"And, Cameron, bless ye, lad." Her father dipped his chin to where Cameron leaned against the wall. "Ye've been a godsend this day. How can I ever repay ye, lad?"

"I've done naught that requires it, sir." Cameron shook his head.

As they began to murmur, Kate returned to Maura's room to borrow a kettle and a handful of oats. She'd repay her in the morning, but her father needed to eat now. Placing the kettle on the hook over the fire, she bent to kiss him on the forehead.

"I've the cart to return to the Fletcher now, and I'm not of the mind to make enemies with the man's wife," she said. "By the time I return, the gruel will be ready."

"I'll take the cart back for ye, lass, if ye lead the way." Cameron stepped forward. With a slight bow to her father, he bid his farewell.

"'Twas an honor to meet ye, sir."

And then she stood, once again, in the moonlight as Cameron lifted the cart. For a moment, she was oddly shy. But only for a moment. She was not the retiring sort, and the air of intrigue about the man was fascinating. As they set off to the Fletcher's, she shook her head. "In faith, Cameron, but I wouldna be pleased to find ye dangling from a tree, ye've been far too kind this day."

His lips twitched in amusement. "I swear I'll not allow myself to be hanged."

"There's honest work to be had in Stirling," she continued. "And even more in Edinburgh."

"I'm afraid I must stay in Stirling, at present," Cameron replied with a bitter lift of his brow.

"Ach, well, that is good then," she said. Skipping to keep up with his long stride, she couldn't resist prying. "So, 'tis revenge that brings ye here, then?"

He gave a slight humph and murmured in a restrained tone, "If only it were that simple."

"Oh?" Her eyes lit with interest.

"Nay, I'll not unburden my sorrows on ye, lass." His voice was gentle. "Ye clearly have enough."

His voice was so soft and kind that Kate caught her breath. Staring straight ahead, she found herself saying, "My father was a brawny sailor once, sailing the seas until he met my mother. She was so afraid to lose him that she forced him to turn to fishing, and a fine fisherman he was! He often took us with him to the lochs ..." She blinked back tears, stubbornly refusing to shed them.

"Us?" Cameron asked quietly.

"Aye, my mother and my wee sister, Joan," Kate replied gruffly. "'Twas the fever that took them both and stole my father's strength and eyes. I'm the only one who didna take ill." She clenched her fists and forced herself to continue. Perhaps it would be easier to forget if she said the words instead of keeping them locked in her heart. "We had to leave … we lost everything and the villagers didna take kindly to the fact that I wasna taken ill like the rest. They swore 'twas the devil's work."

"Fools!" Cameron growled in a low voice.

His response made Kate smile. "Aye, but there is some perverse amusement to be had." Her smile broadened. "We fled because they accused me of witchery, simply because I didna fall ill. And here I've earned our keep by selling charms as I find I'm still named a witch, but 'tis a respectful title here."

He didn't share her amusement. "While the highlands may still hold witches in high esteem, lass, matters are shifting in the lowlands. I'd not let others name ye as such."

"Ach, now, I've hopes to find other work." Kate blithely shrugged her shoulders and pointed to the Fletcher's house. "Just set the cart down here, and ye'll be free of me, sir!"

She watched him roll the cart to its place under the pear tree, feeling a twinge of disappointment. He would go now, and she would probably never see the man again.

He strode back to tower over her, and silence fell between them.

Finally, she dipped a curtsey. "I canna thank ye properly for all that ye have done for me this day."

"There is no need, lass." He bowed in reply. It was an elegant, courtly bow.

Giving into impulse, she stood on her tiptoes and pulled his head down. She meant to give him a friendly kiss on the cheek, but he turned his head at the last moment and covered her lips with his.

His kiss was soft and tender, sending a shiver down her spine. She was lost in the sensation of it until the light touch of his hand cupping her jaw jolted her to her senses. Abruptly, she tore her lips from his.

He drew back warily, but with a glint of humor in his eye, he asked, "Are ye going to slap me again?"

Ignoring the pink tingeing her cheeks, she rolled her eyes. "I shouldna have anything to do with the likes of ye!" She placed her hands on her hips. "I'm an upright, hard-working lass who knows better than to keep company with outlaws!"

"I've no dishonorable intentions …" he began with a wry expression.

But she was no longer listening to his words. His lips were extraordinarily fascinating, finely chiseled, begging to be touched. And, oh, the dash in the middle of his chin cried out for her fingertips. Unwilling to think, lest she lose her courage, she gave into her desire and burying her fingers in the cloth of his cloak gathered about his throat, roughly pulled him close and kissed him fiercely.

He melded his mouth to hers at once in a wildly passionate, deep, and feverish way. Emotions she had never known to exist exploded through her, and this time, he was the one to wrench away, breathing hard.

"Ach, lass … 'tis …not a wise thing …" He cleared his throat, apparently finding it difficult to speak. "Women do not ... thrive in my company."

He looked almost angry.

Ashamed, she covered her reddening cheeks with her hands. She had been too brazen. "I canna think what came over me—"

And then, all shame and embarrassment fled as this time, it was he to sweep her close as his lips claimed hers once more but with a softer touch and a tenderness that she wanted to last forever. His hand moved lightly down her back, pressing her close, and then all too soon, he lifted his head and pushed her gently away. Sliding his long fingers down to catch her hand, he brought it to his lips and kissed the inside of her wrist.

"Aye, I'll be leaving now, while I still can," he said in a deep voice, still holding her hand.

"Will I see ye again?" she asked breathlessly. She almost didn't want him to answer, afraid he would say no.

"Aye, I think we both know that I'll not stay away," came the soft reply. "But ye should run the other way the next time ye see me."

The desperate words pulled her heart as she watched him stride away into the darkness. But then her spirits took wing, and with a light step, she ran back to the cottage and slipped inside.

Maura had returned.

Sitting on a chair before a tiny mirror, the woman brushed her long blonde hair. "There's to be a feast at the castle soon," she said. "And I promised Charles that I'd find him several serving wenches. The work is yours, if ye want it, Kate."

"Oh, Maura!" Kate's eyes danced as she ran to smother the

woman in kisses.

"Enough now!" Maura laughed, pushing her away. "Ye can come with me on the morrow. Tend to your father now!"

Feeling as if she would burst with joy, Kate slipped into her room to find the gruel ready and her father awake. Whistling a merry tune, she slowly spooned the mixture into his lips.

"And why is your heart so light, my sweet Kate?" her father asked with a weak grin.

"Oh, father! We are gone from the almshouse, and I've work at the castle. I do believe our fortune is changing at last!" She was so happy she wanted to sing.

"Are ye sure it isn't that lad that has ye singing?" Her father laughed. "His voice was kind."

Kate smiled. She didn't want to speak of Cameron. Not yet. She just wanted to think of him and to hold the memory of his kisses close to her heart. But then her heart gave an odd flop and she sighed. If only the man wasn't an outlaw but a good, honest fisherman like her father. Lifting her chin, she wondered if it were something she could change.

3

THE COURT OF THE KING

Cameron returned to the Brass Unicorn Inn, walking slowly, lost in thought.

Something about Kate lightened his heart. Aye, she was precocious, lively, and given to chatter, but that was her charm. The lass was warm-hearted, filled with life, and the loving tenderness with which she cared for her father was moving.

He had no business seeking her company.

Grimly, he turned up the lane, hearing the sounds of merriment drifting from the inn long before he saw it. The noise was comforting. It was the precise reason he kept rooms there. The continual commotion distracted him from his heavy thoughts.

One of his men waited outside the door, and Cameron hailed him. The dismal conditions of the almshouse had appalled him. He meant to fix it straightway. Dipping his head, he murmured his orders into the man's ear, and then betook himself to his chambers.

On the morrow, he must announce his presence to the king in Stirling Castle. It was a miserable thought. He didn't want to think of court intrigue. He'd much rather think of the lively lass with the sparkling brown eyes who wouldn't stop talking, but 'twas difficult to do without a twinge of guilt.

Settling before the warm, crackling fire, he focused on Thomas, wondering what the man was plotting, but Kate continually intruded upon his thoughts.

Ach, she was a temptation! He hadn't been tempted in quite some time, but he knew better than to give into his baser instincts. Ach, before, with just one thought of his deceased wives, any impulse he might have had would have died in an instant, but strangely—this time—that customary deterrent was oddly ineffective.

He found sleep long in coming.

* * *

After spending a restless night, Cameron rose with the sun. Bidding Morag the Innkeeper a fond farewell, he mounted his charger and set off through Stirling's winding, cobblestoned streets with his men riding behind.

The early morning sun cast Stirling Castle in a warm glow as it rose majestically above the belt of trees clustered at the base of the cliffs. He eyed the massive structure with reluctance as he urged his horse up Castle Hill. Below him, he could see the River Forth glistening, swans gracefully gliding under the stone bridge spanning its width. Bright green fields led to the entrance of the Royal Deer Park, and to the west, he could see the jousting arena with the highlands climbing behind it.

He grimaced.

Clothes fittings, banquets, and games of treachery would now occupy his day.

'Twas far worse than a good honest sword-thrust.

The sound of hooves caused him to glance over and see Archibald

Douglas riding forward to greet him.

Cameron raised his hand in acknowledgement and reined his horse. "Well met!"

"Aye, well met!" Archibald flashed a grin, leaning over to clasp Cameron's arm in a warm welcome.

Archibald Douglas, the Fifth Earl of Angus, was a great bear of a man, square-jawed, ruddy, and stern with a small scar under his left eye. His rumpled red hair, bushy beard, and warm hazel eyes gave him an unassuming, friendly air, but Cameron knew him as one of the craftiest noblemen in Scotland.

"Ye've been a long time in coming, Cameron." Archibald wiggled his bushy brows. "We've missed ye sorely."

"Aye." Cameron nodded, offering nó further explanation. He didn't need to. While not particularly close friends with the man, their sense of mutual respect ran deep.

"Word has already been sent of your arrival," Archibald informed him. "The king will see ye within the hour."

"And Thomas?" Cameron raised a curious brow.

"Aye, it isn't easy to get the king's ear of late. Thomas stands in the way. He never strays far from the king's side." Archibald growled. "We've need of your silver tongue, my friend, and that of Lord Julian Gray. I sent for him nigh on two weeks ago, and I expect him this day."

The news gladdened Cameron's heart. Lord Julian Gray was as close a friend to him as Ruan MacLeod.

With a curt nod, Cameron raised his hand, signaling the conversation was over, and in companionable silence, they rode up the street to the castle gates.

At the entrance, Cameron again paused, eyeing the great castle of Stirling rising above him. Green moss and lichen clung to the base of the outer walls, standing out in stark contrast against the dark gray stones. It was an ancient fortress and one of Scotland's finest.

"Aye, 'tis time, my friend. Ye can delay it no longer," Archibald murmured in a tone somewhere between understanding and amusement.

With a grimace, Cameron spurred his horse forward.

He dismounted in the courtyard, eyeing the newly finished, ornate tower house with its great vaulted chamber, the work of Thomas Cochrane. He'd heard the man had studied in Italy, and his work clearly demonstrated a fine skill. But in architecture only. He had no place seeking titles and attempting to govern the land.

"Follow." Archibald raised a hand and led him through a side entrance towards the royal apartments.

As a Stewart, and cousin to the king, Cameron was entitled to rooms in the west wing of the royal apartments. As he passed the Great Hall, he caught a glimpse of the immaculately carved wooden ceiling.

"Aye!" Archibald snorted in disgust. "Our king is only interested in cavorting with his painters, tailors, and masons. I've not seen him on the back of a steed since he moved his court here, nigh on three months ago."

King James III had always favored the fine arts over all else, neglecting the governing of the realm in the pursuit of gratifying his own pleasure. In recent years, his behavior often carried into excess, with endless banquets and the continual bestowal of lavish gifts upon a parade of favorites.

"What of Hommil the tailor?" Cameron asked. Last year, the man had never strayed from the king's side. The king had openly caressed him with the fondest affection at every banquet. Thomas Cochrane had been there but hovering in the background. The entire situation had been scandalous.

"He's been traveling with the previous castoff, Leonard the smith, spending their ill-gotten gains," Archibald replied gruffly. "Of late, even Torphichen the fencing-master has been scarcely seen with the king. It has only been Thomas Cochrane receiving fond kisses and all favors."

Climbing a spiral staircase, Archibald led him through several chambers to a suite of apartments that looked out over the highlands.

A velvet carpet graced the floor in front of a high, curtained bed, and nearby stood a writing desk with a vase of flowers, a feather quill pen, and a large candelabrum with eight tapers. Several carved chairs with crimson velvet cushions sat before a fireplace with a fire already crackling on the hearth.

Situated to allow the morning light to filter in, the window of the bedchamber afforded him a view of the surrounding forests and wild expanse of the moors spreading across the horizon.

He moved to the window and breathed deeply of the chill breeze sweeping down from the highlands.

Closing the door soundly behind him, Archibald leaned against it and folded his arms. "There are strange doings afoot, my friend. 'Twas at the feast last night that the king received tidings of Mar and Albany's arrival within the week, but he fell into a fit of anger at the news, and began shouting they were coming to unseat him."

Cameron drew his lips in a thin line.

Alexander, Duke of Albany, and John, Earl of Mar, were the king's younger brothers. Rumors always circulated that both sought to seize the throne. But Cameron knew this to be untrue. The three brothers shared an unusually close bond.

The king's tirade smacked of some ill doing. Was Thomas Cochrane responsible?

"I'll see what I can discover, Archibald." Cameron gave a curt nod.

He was back at court only a few scant minutes and already found himself engulfed in treacherous plots.

The man sent him a wide grin. "Then, I'll be on my way."

As the door closed after him, Cameron wearily rubbed the back of his neck. He had found precious little sleep in the night. He took a deep breath, inhaling the fresh spring air blowing through the window, ruffling his raven hair.

He longed to return home to Inchmurrin Castle, standing tall on the most southerly isle of Loch Lomond. And he would straightway, he promised himself, as soon as he had overturned any marriage plans the king might have made and once he had insured all was well between the king and his brothers.

There was a knock upon the door.

Wincing at the intrusion, Cameron murmured, "Pray enter."

The door creaked open, and Thomas' nasal voice snaked through the room. "Greetings, my lord."

Expelling a silent breath, Cameron composed his features and graciously inclined his head. "And what brings ye here, Thomas."

The man wore velvet breeches and a jeweled doublet. A heavy gold chain glittered about his neck, and he fingered it fondly as he replied, "The king would see ye now in his supper room, my lord. I've been tasked to escort ye there." He watched Cameron closely.

Seeking to disarm the man, Cameron sent him a pleasant smile. "I would discuss the matter of Heloise that lies betwixt us first, Thomas."

Thomas tensed and his eyes narrowed.

"If truth be told, her lands and title were not of sufficient worth for a man like ye." Cameron continued softly. Aye, he'd twist this current situation to his own advantage, even though such court games of flattery were becoming ever more distasteful. "'Tis your marriage we should be discussing with the king, not mine, and I'll tell him such words."

Almost imperceptibly, Thomas' eyes flickered in pleasure.

"Aye, let us speak of this to the king." Cameron clasped the man's shoulder. "Lead on, my good man. I will follow ye."

The way the man postured and strutted importantly as he led Cameron towards the king's apartments was disgusting. Upon entering the outer guard chamber, Thomas pointed to a chair, asking Cameron to wait until he had assured the king was truly ready.

Relieved to escape the man's company, if only for a moment, Cameron folded his hands behind his back and moved to stare out of the tall, narrow window looking out over the town of Stirling.

Idly, he wondered what Kate was doing.

Was she sweet-talking more victims into buying her charmed stones?

His lips thinned in a disapproving line.

He'd have to find her some other form of work. He hadn't been jesting her concerning the dangers of being named a witch. Of late, there were increasingly disturbing reports of witch burnings in Germany. Times were changing.

And then Thomas reappeared to guide him into the king's private supper room.

The chamber was a small one. A carved, wooden table stood before the blazing fire, set with gold-inlaid goblets, a platter of sweetmeats, and a silver bowl of spiced oranges. Before the window stood a long, low chest with leather-bound books neatly stacked on its surface. Tapestries from Flanders hung on the walls, along with several portraits of the king.

Cameron moved to inspect them.

"My dear cousin, the Earl of Lennox."

Cameron turned to see the king entering the chamber from the opposite door.

King James was young, nearly the same age as himself, but he looked much older. His pallid face was long and oval, his lips thin, and his eyes heavily lidded. His pale red hair clung to his forehead in thin, wispy locks.

As he moved closer to extend his hand, the faint odor of whisky eddied about him.

Cameron's dark eyes narrowed faintly. While the king he knew cared greatly for wine and whisky, he had rarely allowed himself to become drunk. And never so early in the day. Bowing low, Cameron kissed his ring and murmured, "My sovereign lord."

"Ye've been long in coming, Cameron." The king moved to the table, selected a sweetmeat, and popped it in his mouth.

"I crave your pardon, sire," Cameron replied dutifully.

"We ordered ye here last winter," the king admonished with a petulant smile.

"I beseech your forgiveness, your majesty," Cameron repeated in a respectful tone.

The king paced towards him, placing a finger on his jaw and looking deep into his eyes for a time before smiling. "Aye, we shall never doubt ye, Cameron. Ye've proven your loyalty time and again. Ever have ye supported the throne."

Aye, I've rescued ye time and time again from the wrath of the queen over your scandalous passel of bastards, Cameron commented in his mind. But he knew the king was referring to his brothers this time and not the queen's ire. Seizing the opportunity, he skillfully inserted, "I am a Stewart, your majesty, and I, along with my cousins Mar and Albany, will ever sustain your throne."

The king jerked a little and Thomas gave a sharp intake of breath.

Ah, so Thomas *did* have a hand in this. There was a clear flicker of guilt in the man's eye.

Moving away, the king selected another sweetmeat, indicating that Cameron help himself, and said, "Thomas has brought the most disturbing matter to our attention."

"And that is?" Cameron inquired politely.

"How can ye not know?" The king's face appeared paler than usual. "The Flemish astrologer Andrews prophesied the Lion of Scotland would be devoured by its own whelps! Surely, ye have heard of it?"

Cameron had never before heard such words nor of the famed astrologer. Doubtless, from Thomas' tense expression, this was also part of the plot. Aye, it would be most helpful for the Lord Julian Gray to arrive soon. He could aid in uncovering it.

"We have sent for Andrews," the king was saying. "We shall prevail upon him to reside here forthwith until a deeper insight is gained into this divination!"

At that, Thomas cleared his throat and bowed from his place at the door. "My lord, the feast is ready. The musicians from Spain await ye, sire."

The king's eyes softened as he looked upon the man and then he turned back to Cameron. "We shall speak of Andrews at a later time. But afore we attend the feast, there is the matter of your next marriage, fair cousin. We can't have ye unwed."

"I beg to differ, sire." Cameron lifted a mocking brow before nodding discreetly in Thomas' direction. "'Tis Thomas ye should send in my stead. The man is clearly ready for the honor of a marriage—"

"No," the king interrupted tersely, greatly displeased.

Cameron eyed him with a measuring look.

"Come!" the king ordered, throwing his arm about Thomas' shoulders, he exited his supper room, leaving Cameron to trail behind.

Cameron followed them thoughtfully.

Aye, there was something unholy about Thomas' relationship with the king. And this business of a prophecy was clearly Cochrane's work. And by the man's tense reaction, he wasn't pleased for Cameron to know of it. Clearly, it was a plot of the nefarious kind.

Strains of music floated above the din of voices as they entered Stirling's magnificent Great Hall, which boasted intricately carved wooden panels on the ceiling and a fireplace on each end. Richly decorated with the finest of tapestries and the high table set with silver goblets and gold inlaid spoons, Cameron could well understand the complaints that the king had grown excessive.

Painters, poets, and sculptors thronged the hall, mingling with the highest nobles in the land. But the dissatisfaction of the gathered lords and their ladies was readily apparent. It was in the looks, the unsaid words, and huffs of breath. It was surprising that the king blithely chose to ignore it. It was foolishness for a monarch to do so, and doubly more so when the common people were suffering from poor harvests and plague.

Waiting for the king to take his seat, Cameron stood by his customary place at the high table. Suppressing a yawn, he lowered his long lashes to observe the king and Thomas Cochrane. The king scarcely spoke without darting quick glances, seeking Thomas' approval. When had he become the man's puppet?

Finally, the king sat and as the Spanish musicians strummed their lutes, the feast began.

Cameron reluctantly took his place. He would be banqueting for hours, dining upon dish after dish amidst the glittering merriment and nervous titters of laughter as nobles and court favorites clamored for the king's favor, a king that they did not even respect. The whole thing made his head ache.

To Cameron's right sat the tacit, stern Lord Hume, a man intent only upon eating. The place to his left was empty. He hoped it would remain so in the coming hours. He was scarce in the mood to talk.

And then the courses began to arrive. Roasted swan with the feathers carefully replaced upon the carcass to resemble the live bird, fish in aspic, and partridge with greens.

It was tasteless.

His thoughts wandered to Kate and he did his best to resist for a time, but it proved nigh impossible. Thinking of how she tenderly cared for her ailing father, he decided that the man would do well to eat better.

Raising a hand, Cameron waved for one of his trusted men waiting nearby.

"Send a basket of eggs and partridges to Kate," he ordered and then hesitated with a twinge of conscience. He had no business in sending her gifts. Yet, what harm could there be in a gift? Shrugging the guilt aside, he continued, "But let her think it comes from the thief, not the earl."

"Aye, my lord." The man nodded with a serious expression.

"She lives near the—"

"We know where she lives, my lord," the man interrupted with a glint of humor in his eye.

Cameron winced as a sudden wave of embarrassment flooded through him. Aye, they would have followed him. How could he have forgotten? His men were loyal and they watched over him continually. Ach, was nothing secret?

Subdued, he returned his attention to the feast, striving once more to clear his thoughts of Kate, but as more courses arrived, he thought of no one else.

He wondered if her nose would wrinkle in a delighted smile upon receiving the eggs. He shifted in his seat. He would much rather have delivered the basket himself than sit through this torturous affair!

Surveying his trencher with growing distaste, he discovered he had toyed with his food the entire course. Signaling for a serving wench to take it away, he took a long draught of spiced wine instead and began searching for any excuse to quit the place when a distinctive laugh carried across the hall.

There was only one man with a laugh such as that.

Lord Julian Gray stepped through the parting crowd, a tall, slim form with blond hair and searching gray eyes. A smooth-spoken courtier, he was also a formidable and daring warrior, but only a select few in the land knew him for what he truly was: the boldest spy in all of Scotland, England, and France. His courage was matchless.

But most saw him as he wished them to—as the irresponsible, reckless young lord who held vast estates in the north of Scotland, but spent his time drifting from court to court in pursuit of pleasure.

With his lips curving into a smile, Cameron rose to embrace him. "It has been far too long, Julian!"

"And what dire circumstance brings me to Stirling at the muddiest time of the year?" Julian drawled in a light tone. "I pray it does not concern ye?"

Cameron winced but answered readily enough, "Nay, I'll not be wed off again. Speak with Archibald. 'Twas he who summoned ye, though I have things of more than a passing curiosity for ye to unravel."

"Ah!" Julian's gray eyes lit with interest. "And the queen?"

"In Edinburgh," Cameron replied. The queen, expecting the king's third child, had retired to Edinburgh months ago, weary of her husband's preoccupation with court favorites. This time, the rift between them seemed permanent.

Shoving the chair next to Cameron with his boot, Julian draped himself upon it and observed languidly, "Little has changed, then."

"Perhaps not." Cameron allowed his gaze to shift to where Thomas sat fawning over the king.

Julian followed his gaze and nodded once. And then spearing a partridge with his dagger, he helped himself to wine and turned his attention to greeting others in a light and merry tone. It did not take long before an enthralled circle of admirers surrounded the man. He entertained them with many a jest and wild tale, whilst reaching to pinch any serving wench that wandered nearby. They didn't mind. In fact, it was obvious they sought any excuse possible to wander within his reach.

Finding his thoughts once again dwelling on Kate and her sparkling brown eyes, Cameron played with the idea of paying her a visit, and with the aid of spiced wine blithely ignored all thoughts of curses. Ach, and since when had he turned into a believer in curses and black arts anyway? And what did it matter? 'Twas not as if he planned to wed the lass!

Simply seeing her and stealing a kiss or two would cause no harm.

Downing his last draught, he rose from the table, bade his farewells, and excused himself from the merriment, acutely aware of Thomas' eyes upon him as he exited the hall.

He would deal with Thomas Cochrane later.

Right now, it was far more important to see if the lass had gotten the eggs.

Quickly, he lay aside his court clothing and chose his simplest attire before making his way to the wide, arched gates leading into Stirling Town.

One of his men hailed him as he stepped through. "She's at the Thistle and the Pig, my lord," the man whispered conspiratorially.

Had his intentions been so readily apparent? Oddly embarrassed, Cameron dismissed the man with a cool nod, and wondering if he were a fool, set off for the Thistle and the Pig at the bottom of Castle Hill.

It was a rather disreputable place, serving more as an alehouse with bedding on the floor of the kitchen than a proper inn. The common room was dark containing only a single man drinking his ale with a scowl upon his face.

Kate was nowhere to be seen.

Grimacing in displeasure, Cameron turned back to the door when he heard her warm laughter sounding from the back. Suddenly, his heart grew light and he found himself striding to the low door and ducking to peer inside.

Kate stood with her back to him, laughing at a young lad as she pressed a small bundle into his hands. "Ach, ye wee ruffian, I'll not tell your mother what ye just said, but be careful with these eggs now!"

Catching sight of Cameron, the lad's eyes widened, and clutching the bundle, he bolted out of the back door without a moment's hesitation.

Turning, Kate's brown eyes sparkled at once upon seeing him. "Ach, 'tis Cameron!"

He stood there, grinning like a fool in a manner quite unlike himself and saying nothing.

Kate didn't seem to mind. She clearly enjoyed chattering. "Aye, your eggs have made many a smile this day, Cameron," she said, throwing a faded plaid over her shoulders and stooping to pick up her basket. "I'll not ask ye where ye got them, or the partridges, though I'll have no more such fine gifts. 'Tis not worth your head!"

"Did ye keep any eggs for yourself, lass?" he asked mildly.

"I'm not a saint!" Kate wrinkled her nose and added with a sheepish smile, "I ate three, and my father ate two. But wee Donald's mother is taken ill, and she canna leave the almshouse to find work, and 'tis difficult to heal eating only the weak gruel that is made there."

"She'll be fine," Cameron murmured in assurance. In fact, he knew she would be eating right well. He had ordered his most trusted man, Sir Arval, to set the almshouse to rights, but Kate didn't need to know it. "Perhaps fortune will yet bestow blessings upon the place."

Kate rolled her eyes. "'Tis a nice thought." Then, looping her basket over her arm, she grabbed both of his hands in hers and swung them exuberantly. "I've thrilling news! Maura found me work at Stirling Castle!"

"Stirling Castle?" Cameron repeated, flinching in displeasure at the thought.

"Aye! I'm to be a serving wench! I spoke to the Chamberlain of the Great Hall just this morning, and I'm to start on the morrow!" She was ecstatic, but then her brows furrowed. "What is it?" she asked. "'Tis written bold upon your face that ye aren't pleased to hear this!"

"A serving wench … in the Great Hall?" Cameron's lips thinned in a grim line. 'Twas appalling news.

Kate frowned in bewilderment, but then began to laugh. Standing on her tiptoes, she reached up, pulled back the hood of his cloak and asked, "Do ye fear that I'll see the Dreaded Earl?"

"Aye," Cameron replied in a reserved tone. It was exactly what he feared.

"Ach, I was not telling ye the truth, man." Kate nudged him in the ribs and sliding her arm through his, pulled him out of the kitchen. "I've never met the man."

"And I pray ye do not," Cameron murmured, clenching his jaw. He wasn't ready to give up playing the part of the outlaw. Not yet. Her company was far too intoxicating. He would enjoy it just a wee bit longer first. But only a wee bit longer.

The door to the inn burst open, and a middle-aged woman swept inside. Spying Kate, she blew her a kiss as she hurried into the back room, calling over her shoulder, "Thank ye for minding the place, lass!"

"'Twas an honor," Kate called back. Then, smiling up at Cameron, she invited in a warm, cordial tone, "Come with me! I've something that will put a smile upon your lips!" Grabbing his hand, she pulled him out of the inn and down the street.

"Where are ye headed, lass?" he asked, not particularly caring for secrets.

Sending him a mischievous look, she refused to answer. Still holding tightly onto his fingers, she tugged him up a familiar street and turned down the lane that led to the Brass Unicorn.

Stopping in front of the vine-covered inn, she reached into her pocket and drew out a penny. Dangling it before his nose, she said brightly, "Allow me to buy ye supper with a hard-earned, good honest coin! 'Twill taste like a king's feast!"

He had no doubt it would taste far better, but he shook his head. "I'll take nothing from ye, lass—"

"Pah!" Kate rolled her eyes, yanking him into the place and pointing to an empty table. "Sit there, ye lout. I'll be back shortly."

Cameron eyed the place that he had only just left that morning.

From the corner of the common room, Morag straightened curiously and watched Kate sailing toward her with purpose.

Reluctantly, Cameron made his way to an empty table, jostling and bumping elbows along the way. And then moments later, Kate joined him with a meat pie filled with pork fat, a dish of stewed hare, and a tankard of ale. Seating herself by his side, she took a big bite of the pie before holding it up to his lips, nodding for him to do the same.

He watched her tongue lick her lips and then all thoughts fled, save ones of pulling her close and exploring her mouth with his own tongue. Quickly averting his gaze, he swallowed and murmured, "I thought 'twas the lord's duty to see the lady's trencher filled first."

Kate snorted. "What fine words, but ye aren't a lord and I'm certainly not a lady!"

Cameron tensed, wincing at his lapse and expelled a breath, relieved Kate had taken it as a jest. But then he noticed she was watching him, her brows drawn in a puzzled line.

"Ach, but ye always appear to be fighting some inner battle, Cameron," she said, laying a compassionate hand on his arm. "I wish I could be of aid to ye."

Covering her hand with his long fingers, he squeezed it and answered truthfully, "Ye are, my sweeting, for I find ye a warm welcome in an otherwise inhospitable place."

She smiled at that and leaned her head against his shoulder.

For a moment, he was tempted to bury his face in her hair.

He drew back a little.

It was a mistake to be here with her. She was quite unlike any lass he had ever met, and if he were honest, a temptation he would fail in resisting. He should be an honorable man and leave while he still could.

The traveling minstrel from the night before took out his recorder and began to play a lively tune, and the folk gathered in the room began to clap. Several women picked up their skirts and began to dance.

Springing to her feet, Kate grabbed his hands and pulled him up. "Dance with me!"

Holding the tankard in one hand, she slipped her other arm through his and tried to reel him around, collapsing into laughter when she failed miserably in the attempt.

Her merriment was contagious and his lips began to twitch in amusement. It was hard to worry in her company. She knew how to distract him from his dark thoughts.

Tingling with excitement, he caught her about the waist, twirled her around and bending her head back, kissed her full on the lips. It was a quick kiss, but a vibrant one. Her lips were sweet and eager.

And then Kate moved away, her merry eyes teased his as she danced a moment and then she stepped close to whisper ruefully in his ear, "I should have nothing to do with the likes of ye!"

"Aye," Cameron agreed, looking steadily down at her. If only he *were* a thief instead of an evil bane to womankind.

"What is it?" Kate asked softly, laying a light hand upon his chest. "I wish I could unburden ye."

With a deep breath, he replied darkly, "'Tis dangerous to be with me, lass. Ye should go." Losing interest in dancing, he returned to the table.

"Then, dinna be such a fool!" Kate followed him and slammed her palm on the table surface. "Walk away. Ye aren't bound to live a life of ill repute as an outlaw!"

He glanced up, a little startled at her misunderstanding.

She stood close to him, too close, with a fierce expression on her face and her hands upon her hips. And he found himself falling under her spell once again. It was impossible to think morose thoughts when she was standing so close. Her lips were compelling. Everything about her was a temptation.

She was giving him an earful about mending his criminal ways and then, in spite of it all, he found himself smiling.

He rarely smiled.

Why was he doing it so often in her company?

Aye, she was the lively talker, but he knew one way to stop her chattering.

Succumbing to his desire, he slipped an elegant finger under her chin, tilted it up, and slid the pad of this thumb gently over her lips before touching her mouth lightly with his in a slow, lingering kiss. She responded at once, sliding her hands up his chest to lock them behind his neck, and making soft sounds in her throat, opened her mouth eagerly to his.

But then hoots of laughter from the surrounding folk in the inn shattered the moment and, feeling her smile against his mouth, he reluctantly lifted his head.

"My mother warned me to stay away from men like ye," Kate accused breathlessly with her brown eyes dancing. "But she didna say 'twould be so hard!"

His dark, smoldering eyes locked with hers and the corner of his lip curved into a smile, but then he caught sight of the tall, black velvet-clad figure of Lord Julian Gray stepping into his field of vision.

Cameron straightened, noting the wicked gleam of mirth in the man's eyes.

"A good evening to ye, Cameron." Julian winked, folding his arms to observe Kate from under half-closed lids. "And, who might this sea-siren be?"

"Sea-siren?" Kate burst into laughter. "I would think ye must be speaking of Cameron, good sir, for I know ye canna be speaking of me! But then I would remind ye that only a lass could be a sea-siren."

A smile creased Julian's cheek as he eyed her with a curious interest.

Leaning close, Kate whispered in Cameron's ear, "I'll leave ye to your fellow thief now. I've errands to run afore I go home, but we'll speak on your choice of trade the next time we meet!"

She turned to leave, but Cameron caught her fingers and gave them one last squeeze before she disappeared through the throng of merrymakers still dancing to the minstrel's tunes.

"'Tis a curious thing to find ye here with a lass," Julian drawled, lifting a long leg over the bench to settle across the table from him.

"Aye, 'tis foolishness that must halt," Cameron murmured. Clenching his jaw, he began tapping the table with a long finger.

"If ye speak one word claiming ye are a bane to womankind then I'll have little patience with ye this night." Julian rolled his eyes. "Ach, I'll never understand the Stewarts and their penchant for superstition! 'Tis a warm-blooded lass ye have in your arms, lad. How can ye even think of curses at a time like this?"

"And I've not said a word of curses, Julian," Cameron replied in an aloof tone. He couldn't admit that he had been *thinking* of them. Deliberately switching the subject, he asked, "What brings ye here?"

But Julian was just warming up to the subject. "Ye never even slept with your wives, Cameron. How could ye have cursed them?"

Cameron sent him a cold look of disapproval. "I'll not speak of this now, Julian."

A merry glint entered Julian's gray eyes. "But I've solved your problem, lad! Your ill luck with women lies in the fact that ye *dinna* bed them. Just bed this one, and you'll find your curse broken!"

With a scathing look, Cameron rose to leave.

When it came to women, Julian had never understood him. Aye, he'd never understood Julian, either. Though neither of them had ever formed a true attachment to any lass, Cameron hadn't out of fear of harming them with his ill luck, aye, perhaps even a curse. Julian merely lost interest after a few short weeks.

Julian caught his forearm. "Ach, dinna be such a fool. I meant no slight on the lass. Wed her first, if ye must," he growled in apology.

Withdrawing a rolled parchment from the folds of his cloak, he pushed it across the table and then helped himself to the tankard of ale and added, "I came to deliver ye that most pressing missive."

Sitting back down, Cameron slid a long finger along the crease of the parchment, breaking the wax seal. It was a letter from one of the stewards of his holdings stating that a certain Lady Elsa MacRae was now his ward. The newly-made heiress had recently lost her father in a border skirmish and had fled her tiny castle in order to seek his justice and protection.

He tossed the letter back onto the table and murmured, "I'll send a man to see to her protection straightway."

"Ah, but the lady is already here." Julian set the tankard down and wiped his mouth with the back of his arm. "She delivered the message herself. And, if I might add, she has the look of a woman on the hunt for a husband."

Cameron raised a brow. "Then, as my ward, it is my duty to find her one."

They fell silent then, each lost in his own musings, and it was not long before Cameron's thoughts returned yet again to Kate. He missed her already. Her presence alone made his heart light. And it was nigh impossible to think of curses for long when in her company. Her lips were far too distracting.

"I dinna like the way ye look at me, Cameron." Julian lifted a wary brow, his mouth shifting into a suspicious smile. "I've no inclination to wed your ward!"

Cameron's lips twitched in amusement at that. Recognizing Julian's unspoken apology, he replied in a lighter tone. "'Twould be an uncommonly cruel fate for the both of ye."

Julian grinned and stretched. "Aye, there is not a lass walking this Earth who could ensnare me into marriage," he swore good-naturedly, but then his face grew serious as he abruptly switched subjects. "I'll do what ye ask and look into the doings of Thomas Cochrane. Already, I dinna like what I see."

"Aye," Cameron tapped a finger thoughtfully on the table. "He has changed. He's up to some devilry concerning the king's brothers, of that I am certain. And if he has the backing of a noble then I fear for Scotland herself."

"And he dresses overly rich, even for the favorite of the king." Julian snorted. "His wardrobe is worth a king's ransom. I have no doubt the path of his coin will lead us to his supporters."

At that, they mused on possible supporters and their motives for a time, but Cameron still found it difficult to concentrate with images of Kate dancing in his head.

4

EIGHT SHILLINGS A YEAR

Kate left the Brass Unicorn Inn with a spring in her step.

The strong presence of the man was overwhelming, and the air of intrigue about him made her heart flutter, but she knew she shouldn't associate with an outlaw.

Why couldn't she walk away?

Saving him from a life a crime was a feeble excuse. Few people changed. And if truth be told, when she was with him, she quickly forgot such noble thoughts in favor of admiring the man and his chiseled lips.

Ach, his chiseled lips made her blush.

Hurrying through the streets of Stirling, she made her way to the almshouse, continuing to war with herself.

Why couldn't she remember he was an outlaw? A cutpurse! And the fellow at the inn was clearly disreputable as well. He was dressed far too fine to be an honest commoner. Cameron must be involved with a band of them.

The thought was a dismal one, for it meant he was likely entrenched in his misguided ways. And only tales portrayed thieves as heroes. Aye, the Englishman hero, Robyn Hode, had given alms to the poor, but he was the only outlaw known to have done such a thing. The rest were brigands preying upon their victims.

With a sinking heart, she knew she must resolve to avoid the man. 'Twas best that way.

Depressed, she charged down the lane and turned toward the almshouse only to stop abruptly in surprise.

The warm glow of many candles flooded through the windows. A cartload of slate roof tiles stood to one side. New timber stretched across the gaps in the roof, and several men were climbing down, apparently just finishing their work for the day.

The cheerful hubbub of voices, laughing and singing, emanated from within the almshouse, as in stunned amazement, Kate slowly stepped over the threshold.

A crackling fire blazed upon the hearth with a large cauldron bubbling over the dancing flames, releasing the delicious aroma of what smelled like mutton stew. Several monks distributed wooden bowls and blankets to those gathered around.

"Kate!" exclaimed a voice. Donald, the young lad from the Thistle and the Pig, rushed forward to tug her arm. His peaked face split into a wide grin. "We've a benefactress now! She's hired us to fix the almshouse!"

Kate laughed as everyone babbled at once, but it only took a few moments to piece the story together. A noble highland lady had decided to fund the almshouse as her private charity. She had hired the able-bodied to repair the building, establish a kitchen, and tend a garden on the plot of land she had purchased a short distance away. She had also bestowed a yearly stipend to the monks from Cambuskenneth Abbey to manage the effort.

"And her name is Kate!" The young Donald laughed, still tugging her sleeve. "Lady Kate!"

Kate blinked sudden, grateful tears from her eyes. "Aye, 'tis a fine name for a lady!" She laughed with him, grabbing his spindly arm and twirling him around. "I'm honored to share her name!"

After spending some time with them, and after convincing the monks to bring eggs, herbs, and a higher quality blanket on the morrow, she quit the almshouse with a pleased smile upon her face.

Aye, she was grateful to Lady Kate for her charity, and she'd personally see that the monks properly tended the almshouse on the lady's behalf. "Aye, maybe one day I'll meet her and let her know another Kate saw it done aright!" Kate mused aloud, smiling at the thought.

A gentle breeze, perfumed with the flowers of spring, ruffled her hair as she made her way back to Maura's cottage.

And once again, in spite of her resolutions otherwise, her thoughts wandered to Cameron.

Ach, wasn't the man worth saving? If she *could* guide him from his wicked ways, 'twould not only benefit them both but society as well.

Torn, she pushed open the door and entered.

The main room was dark, indicating that Maura had not yet returned. She expelled a silent breath of relief. The soft glow of firelight poured from the back room, and she tiptoed inside to find her father sleeping.

Silently kneeling by his side, she cradled her chin on her knees and stared at his pale face.

His breathing had improved dramatically, and there was a bit of color on his cheeks.

Aye, he would likely recover now.

Tears of relief threatened, but she scowled, brushing them away in annoyance. She had little time for tears, even happy ones.

The Chamberlain had ordered her to report to Stirling's Great Hall before the sunrise. She tossed her faded plaid in front of the hearth and settled down to sleep, but it was nigh impossible. So much had happened in the past few days. Since meeting Cameron in the alehouse, the evil in her world had unraveled at an extraordinarily rapid pace. Such rare good fortune was astounding.

And Cameron.

How could she not think of the man?

Gradually, her eyes grew heavy as she again and again relived the memory of his chiseled lips upon hers. But her last conscience thought, before she fell into a deep slumber, was the one hoping he had eaten all of the meat pie and the hare stew. It was decadent to waste such fine food.

It seemed like only a moment had passed before she heard the cocks crowing.

Rubbing her eyes, Kate rose, shook out her plaid, and fanned the coals of the fire into life. As the flames licked the peat, she set the small room in order, humming a little tune and surveying her father's sleeping figure with satisfaction.

He was much stronger. Perhaps even his eyes would heal!

If she could only travel to the Pilgrim's Well at St. Fillans, she had heard in the almshouse that the water was healing to the eyes. She sighed. It was not far, only in Dunfermline, but it might as well be in

France. She could not think of how to get there.

Her father's voice startled her. "I can tend myself, lass. Be off with ye, afore ye try the Chamberlain's wrath!"

"Ach, but I haven't made your gruel yet, and—" Kate protested.

"I'm blind, my wee bairn, not helpless! And I've gained such strength these past two days!" He demonstrated by swinging his thin legs over the edge of the straw pallet. "Hie off with ye, now!"

Grinning widely, Kate kissed him a farewell before slipping into the main cottage room where Maura rose sleepily from her bed.

"Ye canna wear that tattered dress!" The woman swept her with a critical eye. "Not at Stirling Castle!"

"'Tis all I have," Kate replied, drawing back but raising her chin stubbornly. "The Chamberlain said naught of it!"

Growling, Maura opened the wooden chest next to her bed and searched a moment before drawing out a suitable brown dress. Tossing it at Kate, she snapped, "Ye can pay me next week. I'll not have my reputation ruined by the likes of ye! I canna let myself be seen in the company of a ragamuffin!"

Not knowing whether to be grateful or insulted, Kate quickly slipped into the dress as Maura made ready. Neither spoke as they left the cottage a short time later, hurrying through the dark streets to the castle high above them.

The sun had just painted the sky a faint pink when Kate stepped into Castle Stirling's Great Hall, her heart beating wildly with excitement. Looking around in awe, she spied a cluster of women huddled in front of a wide fireplace and hurrying to join them, gave a cheerful greeting, "And a braw day to ye all!"

The women eyed her, curious.

Several smiled.

One timidly replied, "And the same to ye, lass."

"Are ye waiting for the Chamberlain as well?" Kate asked, drawing her plaid closer about her shoulders and eyeing the Great Hall with wonder.

It was mostly dark, but what she could see was beyond magnificent. The kings' high table stood on a dais, rising high above the other tables lining the length of the chamber. Neat rows of ornate, carved chairs with velvet cushions lined the walls bedecked with fine tapestries of unicorns. Suits of armor graced each entrance, casting ominous shadows in the flickering firelight.

As Kate surveyed the place in awe, she found her gaze drawn to several dark forms huddled on the floor. Squinting, she peered closer. Apparently, some of the servants had fallen asleep there the night before. She frowned, wondering why they had not yet risen.

"They'll pay for their folly," someone murmured, noting the direction of her scrutiny.

Kate pursed her lips. "Can we not wake them?" she asked. "'Tis an act of kindness."

The women eyed her suspiciously.

After a tense moment of silence, Kate made up her mind. Straightening her plaid, she marched over to the sleeping servants.

In the dim light, she could barely make out three men, snoring on their backs. Prodding them with her shoe, she flapped her plaid and hissed, "Away with ye now! The Chamberlain's to be here soon!"

One of the men stirred and looked around sleepily before shouting at the others. Scrambling to their feet, they bolted out of the hall without a backward glance.

Pleased, Kate smoothed her skirt and moved to join the others only to find the Chamberlain already there, watching her with a scowl.

The Chamberlain of the Great Hall was a gray-haired, lean man with a bulbous nose and penetrating green eyes. Dressed in a fine blue plaid and leather boots, he looked very distinguished.

Kate hurriedly returned to the fireplace under his skewering gaze.

"Your name?" He asked, scowling.

"Kate Ferguson, sir." She dipped a quick curtsey.

"A Ferguson!" The man's brows drew into line of displeasure as he pointed at the cluster of women. "Heed me well, all of ye! Ye do as I order, and if ye don't, ye'll pay for it. Kate, ye can serve as a warning to all. Ye'll spend this day mucking the stables with the lads!"

Kate frowned. She hadn't disobeyed the man. He hadn't even been there, but she knew better than to point that out to him.

Several of the women smirked in her direction.

"The rest of ye can work to set the hall to rights!" The Chamberlain eyed them critically. "Ye'll bring the peat, set the tables, and fill the salt cellars. Ye'll keep your heads uncovered at all times. All of ye are to be gone afore the nobles arrive. Ye aren't fit to be seen! Ach, what a poor lot!"

As he continued berating them, Kate took a step back. Aye, mucking the stables was looking finer by the moment. The man hadn't been nearly so cantankerous when she had met him the day before. She wondered what had happened.

Signaling for the higher-ranking servants to take charge of the new ones, the Chamberlain eyed her once again and barked, "Off with ye to the stables, Kate!"

Raising her chin in a slight gesture of defiance, Kate curtsied and sent him a sweet smile.

He didn't miss her challenging response, and his brow cocked upwards as a middle-aged woman in a blue dress approached him. With his eyes never leaving Kate's face, he bent an ear to listen as the woman tugged on his sleeve.

All at once ashamed, Kate dipped a contrite, deeper curtsey and headed for the door.

She was right fortunate to have this work. After months of scraping by she now, at least, felt somewhat secure. Ach, she had no cause to be ungrateful or to match wits with the man.

She had taken only a dozen steps before the Chamberlain's rough voice ordered her again, "Kate, ye'll be working in the scullery instead. They've need of extra hands this day."

Turning to bow at the man yet again, Kate kept her eyes focused on the floor as the middle-aged woman swept into view.

"Follow me, lass," she ordered in clipped tones, guiding her from the Great Hall to the North Gate housing the castle kitchens. "Ye can help the lads unload the fish from Leigh harbor and the vegetables from Cambuskenneth, but only those two carts, do ye hear? The others are nae my concern. And then ye'll wash the pots. Many have taken ill this week, so ye'd best be quick afore the cooks start grumbling. 'Tis a murderous affair when they do. Ach, I feel chill. I fear I've the fever myself now! I'll show ye the carts first, be quick now!"

Kate followed her into the courtyard and hurried across, the wind whipping her hair unmercifully. She burrowed deeper into her plaid.

Spring was slow in coming this year. The bare branches on the trees were only now budding with life. Soon the fruit trees would bloom in the countryside and flowers would spring up along the riverbanks. For a brief moment, she felt a twinge of longing, remembering the many springs that she'd spent with her father fishing on the lochs. Spring was her favorite time of year, filled with hope and the promise of a new life.

She couldn't resist a smile. Fortune was favoring her at last. Aye, she had been punished, but working in the castle kitchens, 'twas hardly a punishment. Even mucking the stables was better than tricking drunkards into buying charmed stones.

A line of carts waited outside the kitchen doors, and the woman pointed out two of them, repeating firmly, "Only those, lass! And have a care, 'tis for the king's table. See the lads treat them gently!"

Half a dozen lads scurried about, unloading kegs and crates, bumping and jostling with each other as the woman waded through them, boxing their ears. She then disappeared into the kitchens.

Rubbing her hands together, Kate bustled through the lads, grabbing two of the sturdier ones by the ear and pulling them along. "Be quick and have a care! Ye heard the woman! These are for the king's table!"

"Ach, 'tis all for the king's table," one of them grumbled, but they both heeded her well enough, and in short order, she saw the baskets of greens, roots, and fish safely stacked against the kitchen wall.

The kitchens of Stirling Castle bustled with life. To one side, a row of kettles bubbled over a great turf and peat fire casting a ruddy glow about the room. To the other side, several fireplaces spanned the width of the chamber, each with a large roasting spit and a lad on both ends, turning the spits while wiping the sweat from their brows. She could feel the heat from where she stood.

Torches flickered on the walls between shelves that were stacked with bowls and pitchers. A variety of waterfowl and rabbits hung from the ceiling, mingled with braids of garlic and ropes of onions. Through one doorway in the back, she saw bakers sliding fresh round loaves into large baskets. The other doorway revealed the scullery.

Taking a deep breath, she marched into the room, prepared for the same frosty welcome she had received in the Great Hall but found herself greeted warmly instead.

Divided in half, one side of the scullery scoured the dishes and pots, while the other prepared the vegetables, fish, and fowl for the cooks.

Kate found herself sent straightway to pluck the geese, joining several others who welcomed her with broad smiles and a stream of gossip.

Time flew quickly. She lost count of the geese she had plucked. Indeed, she scarcely noticed she was even working. The work was easy and the company of the women entertaining.

Suddenly, a scullery maid dashed into the room, holding a large, slightly-burnt meat pie over her head. "'Tis time to eat!" She grinned widely. "Harkin napped a wee too long again!"

They began to cackle and file out of the door, beckoning Kate to join them. "There's plenty here for all, lass! And, ye have to taste Harkin's meat pies!"

Kate followed them out into the bright spring afternoon, to a patch of new grass growing next to the castle wall. As the others settled down, leaning against the stones warmed by the sun, she stared in the opposite direction.

Never had she seen such a view. She could see for miles. This side of the castle overlooked the valley and glens, leading into the highlands beyond. At the base of the hill, the great stone bridge straddled the majestic River Forth winding into the distance, towards the sea, and towards Dunfermline.

Dunfermline.

She stifled a sigh. If only she could find some way to get to the Pilgrim's Well and to heal her father's eyes. 'Twould be a miracle. She closed her own eyes, wrinkling her nose, and wished for a miracle.

"I've been looking for ye everywhere!" Maura's voice sounded from nearby.

Kate turned to see the woman striding purposefully her direction.

"Where have ye been, Kate?" Maura asked, a scowl marring her comely face. "Were ye not to be in the Great Hall? Why are ye here with the scullery wenches?" She spoke the words disdainfully. As a chambermaid, she was placed far above those in the scullery.

The scullery maids clucked, mimicking her grand gestures behind her back in such a way that Kate found it difficult to remain straight-faced. "The Chamberlain sent me here. 'Twas a misunderstanding..." Kate trailed off in the attempt to swallow a laugh that came out a gurgling kind of snort instead.

Maura raised a disparaging brow. "I'll not have ye ruin my reputation! 'Twas my good name that got ye that position! Remember that ye owe me the love potion, and 'tis only fair that ye give it straightway!"

The scullery maids stopped their mimicry to eye Kate with interest.

"I told ye, time and again, Maura!" Kate frowned, allowing annoyance to riddle her tone. "I've not the knowledge or skill for such a thing!"

"Ach, but aren't ye the wee, crafty one!" Maura reached over and pinched her cheeks in what looked like an affectionate gesture but was far too hard to be anything but a warning. "I've no longer the time to waste! I've need of the potion this day!"

Kate expelled her breath. The eye of every woman was upon her. Pursing her lips, she replied, "Ye've no need of a potion, Maura. With your fair hair and fine looks, ye can have whatever man ye wish."

The women were still watching her with interest, and Kate sighed inwardly. She could tell by the sudden, hopeful expressions on their faces that the lot of them would soon pester her for potions. If she couldn't convince them of her inability to make them, convincing them that they didn't need witchery to heal their hearts would be her only option.

"Look at ye now." Kate moved to the nearest girl to straighten her gown and to brush a goose feather from her red hair. "Your hair is bonny, any lad would tell ye so."

The girl blushed.

"And ye!" Kate turned to the girl's companion. "Your green eyes could beckon lads from even Edinburgh!"

The girl giggled in response.

With a bright smile, Kate moved onto the next, a careworn woman wearing a gray patched dress. She was rigid, tense. "I do know of a tea that will help ye sleep," Kate offered, and then ordered, "Close your eyes and think only of spring flowers while I knead the muscles of your shoulders. Ach, ye are as taut as a bow string!"

The others laughed and the woman smiled ruefully, but did as Kate bid, closing her eyes as Kate firmly pinched the woman's tight shoulders. She massaged them as the monks at Cambuskenneth Abbey had taught her, in order to help ease her father's suffering.

"I'll speak with the lass mothering the others. Bring her here at once," a low, melodic voice ordered from close by.

Kate whirled.

The speaker was a young woman of stately bearing, dressed in a wine-colored silk gown with a pearl-encrusted headdress upon her russet-brown hair. Her delicate coloring, posture, and proud carriage announced her as a member of the nobility.

She stood a short distance away with her blue eyes locked on Kate as she motioned to the gray-haired, stern-faced woman at her side.

The scullery maids, including Kate, gasped and bowed deeply as the stern-faced woman glided forward.

Kate held her breath as a pair of fine leather shoes stopped in front of her.

"Rise, lass," the woman ordered in a peppery voice. "And let me see your face."

Cool fingers cupped her chin, pulling her up, and Kate lifted her gaze to stare into the woman's unreadable, brown eyes. After a moment, she nodded, and then said, "Lady Elsa would speak with ye, lass. Follow me."

Biting her lip, Kate did as she was bid, curtseying low before the lady in the wine-colored gown.

"You may rise," Lady Elsa said, waiting before continuing. "And your name?"

"Kate, my lady," Kate replied, taking a deep breath.

Lady Elsa was quite young, scarcely older than herself. She was beautiful, with fine white skin and an exquisitely slender neck, but the manner in which she inspected Kate, with fluttery almost nervous gestures, suddenly reminded her of a bird.

The thought helped to Kate relax immediately, and she smiled.

The lady's eyes narrowed. Tilting her head to one side, she looked deeply into Kate's eyes before she said, "Walk with me, Kate."

Keenly aware of Maura's black looks, Kate fell into step behind Lady Elsa, following as the noble lady ordered the stern-looking woman away and moved further down the castle wall. When they were alone, she turned to Kate. "You look to be the fine, trustworthy sort."

Kate dipped her head in thanks.

"I've just arrived in this place, coming from the Borderlands." Lady Elsa looked away, grimacing a little. "And I've need of a maid."

Kate nodded politely, wondering why Lady Elsa spoke to her of such things. The touch of sadness about her face made Kate feel a surge of sympathy, and then she understood all at once. Ach, the lady's heart was heavy. She felt the need to unburden herself.

Kate sent her an understanding smile.

Lady Elsa paused and frowned. "And why do you look at me so?"

"Forgive me, my lady." Kate bowed again. "But ye seem sad, and

I know what sadness feels like."

The lady raised a finely sculpted brow. After several long moments, she murmured, "You seem to be an observant lass."

Again, Kate nodded a polite thanks.

"I've survived an attack upon my castle and have fled here to the arms of my protector," Lady Elsa informed her and then added, "It was an attack in which my father was slain."

Kate's brown eyes flooded with sympathy.

"My father told me many a time, when in a strange land you must form allies, and true allies are best found among those you lift from the mire." Lady Elsa blinked rapidly, fluttering her lashes in a very birdlike way as she turned her full gaze upon Kate. "I've need of a loyal maid, one I can trust, and I think I like you, Kate. Your eyes are open and earnest, and your manner is kind."

Kate blinked, embarrassed. "I can only give my thanks for such generous words, my lady."

"Well?" Lady Elsa tilted her head to one side. "I can offer eight shillings a year, but you must go where I go, and sleep at the foot of my bed." Sweeping Kate with a critical look, she added, "And, I will include two suitable dresses a year."

It took Kate several long moments to understand. She gasped. The woman was offering her the position and at *eight* shillings a year? The Chamberlain had only offered three, and Maura, as chambermaid, received five. If she made eight shillings a year, she could even pay one of the women from the almshouse to look after her father.

"What say you?" Lady Elsa's lips were twitching in amusement.

"Oh, I am honored, my lady!" Kate breathed in astonishment

before she began to frown. "But, I have no knowledge in the ways of a maid. My father was a fisherman, and I spent my days mending nets and selling fish in the markets."

"I have little doubt you will learn quickly." Lady Elsa laughed in a silvery laugh. "And I am not a fine lady, but a poor one, most likely to be hastily wed in an unsuitable match if I do not have a trustworthy maid at my side to spy on my behalf and assist me in such important matters."

"Ah, it sounds most thrilling, my lady!" Kate tingled with excitement.

"Then, let us try each other's company this month, Kate," Lady Elsa suggested. "Are you willing?"

"I am right willing, my lady!" Kate bowed, unable to believe her good fortune.

"Then, follow me at once," she ordered, moving down the gravel path towards the castle.

Obediently, Kate slipped behind her, wondering if she were in a dream.

Directly below, Kate could see the castle gardens. A man stood alone there, swathed in a great black cape that billowed out behind him in the wind. His hair was dark and his shoulders broad. She shaded her eyes and looked closer. He seemed familiar. For some odd reason, he reminded her of Cameron, but she had little time to wonder as Lady Elsa had moved too far ahead, and she had to scurry to catch up.

Lady Elsa's chamber was of moderate size, containing a curtained bed, a massive wooden chest, a red carpet in front of the fireplace, and a small table with a chair by the window.

Moving to the window, Lady Elsa took out a small purse from her sleeve and selected a coin. "I've need of yarrow, lovage, and pearlwort."

Kate frowned. "'Twill be difficult to purchase them in the market this time of year, my lady."

"Then, can you find them?" she asked, a bit nervously.

"I believe so," Kate murmured thoughtfully. "I believe I saw the yarrow last week, whilst searching for herbs in the forest, my lady." She had been seeking herbs to aid her father's recovery.

"Then, go. I trust you will be as quick as you can." Lady Elsa drew her lips in a worried line.

"Yes, my lady." Kate bowed and turned to leave but then a thought crossed her mind. "My lady, may I have permission to see my father? He has only just recently recovered from an illness that took his sight, and still lies abed most of the day. I would see that he has enough food for the evening and hire someone to see to his needs, afore I return here to sleep at the foot of your bed."

Lady Elsa's face softened. "I am a charitable woman, Kate. You may tend your father, but be quick. I would see you back here afore the sun falls and with the herbs in your hand."

"Yes, my lady, you are most *generous*!" Kate smiled brightly, and with another curtsey, bolted out the door.

Descending the spiral stairs of the castle to the courtyard below, she thought her heart would burst from her good fortune.

Aye, the thief's shilling must have been a blessed coin. From the moment she had held it in her hand, her fortune had brightened.

The afternoon sun was bright as she hurried across the cobbled courtyard of the outer close of the castle. She had nearly reached the main gate when she heard Maura call, "Kate!"

With an excited smile, Kate whirled to greet her, holding out her hands. "Ach, Maura! I've been blessed with the most unexpected luck! I'm to be Lady Elsa's maid!"

Maura tripped and stumbled to a halt. A look of pure outrage flitted across her face before her expression went stony all at once. "What nonsense are ye speaking?" she asked at last.

Hesitating, Kate replied, "Lady Elsa … I'm to be her maid."

"Her maid?" Maura repeated, walking slowly to join her. Her blue eyes were cold. "How can ye be a *lady's* maid? Ye know naught of it!"

"Aye, she knows that well!" Kate shrugged, wishing in vain that she had kept her lips sealed. "'Tis luck, Maura. That is all."

"A lady's maid?" Maura was plainly angry. "How can ye expect me to believe there is no witchery here, Kate? Ye have uncommon luck!"

"Aye but only after uncommon mischance, Maura." Kate frowned. She and her father had struggled for months, nearly starving in the process.

"And how much is she paying ye?" Maura demanded, crossing her arms and scowling.

"Not much more than a chamberlain." Kate evaded. "She's not a rich lady, Maura."

Maura tossed her hair and rolled her eyes. "Still!"

Not wanting to anger the woman further, Kate stepped back and dropped a friendly curtsey. "I must be going! I've errands to run, and the lady has kindly permitted me to check upon father and—"

Maura's eyes narrowed and took on a dark gleam. "Your father? Aye, well, now that ye'll be sleeping next to your lady, I'll be tending to him, is that it?"

"No! Not at all, Maura." Kate shook her head. "I would never do that to ye! I'll have Fiona come stay in my stead, to tend to him and—"

"Then, that 'twill be another shilling for the rent. Nay, let's make it three shillings." Maura lifted her chin in challenge.

Kate stared at her, open-mouthed. The entire cottage would only cost five shillings a year to rent! She knew that well. "But that is more than half the rent for the entire cottage, and we only ask for one tiny room of it! 'Tis not honest, Maura!"

Maura gave a derisive snort. "Ye be the strange one to speak of honesty! I've only politely asked ye to share a love potion, and ye have refused, time and again, keeping your secrets to benefit only yourself! Well, pay the three shillings or ye'll see your father in the street. I doubt any other will rent ye a room after I'm done telling them that he has a catching illness and they'll go blind if they help the man!"

Kate caught her breath, astounded at the vindictive change sweeping through the woman. Aye, already she was regretting that they had moved in with her, but 'twas too late now. Fearing for her father, she replied quickly, "I'll pay ye the shillings, and I'll find ye a love potion. There is no cause to spread rumors."

A satisfied gleam entered Maura's blue eyes, and she gave a nod of satisfaction. "'Tis a good thing ye have finally come to your senses, Kate. Well, be off with ye then. Ye canna have the lady upset with ye! Go!"

Taking a few steps back from the woman, Kate whirled and

almost ran through the main gates of the castle.

Aye, Maura was proving to be more spiteful than she had first thought.

She would have to find someone who knew something of love potions.

Perhaps, then, the woman would leave her and her father alone.

5

THE PASSIONATE BLOOD OF THE STEWARTS

Pacing the wind-ravaged castle ramparts, Cameron lifted his eyes to the highlands spreading across the horizon. Above his head, great hawks soared lazily in the bright blue sky.

Resting his chin on the palm of his hand, he leaned against the cold, stone walls and wished he were on the back of his favorite charger, racing across the heath with the scent of damp heather in the air. And if Kate were with him, her arms clasping him firmly from behind, laughing, and wrinkling her nose in that delightful manner he found captivating ... 'twould be paradise.

Thoughts of Kate summoned memories of her fiery kisses that made him ache with longing, but the usual twinge of conscience quickly followed. He was growing far too fond of her company. He should walk away before his touch robbed her of life.

Wincing, his gaze dropped to the gardens below, and his stomach turned sour all at once.

The king strolled along the gravel paths on his customary afternoon walk. Thomas staunchly trailed him like a dog.

Cameron shook his head in disgust.

How had the commoner gained such control over the king?

As he watched, the king bent over to whisper in Thomas' ear.

After a moment, both men laughed and continued down the garden path with the king's arm circling Thomas' shoulders in an intimate gesture.

Cameron expelled a pent breath.

By failing to understand the complex webs of loyalty among the nobles of the court, both Thomas and the king were inviting disaster. A shadow was falling over Scotland. The king had never been popular, but his behavior of late only threatened to make matters worse, for himself and for Scotland as a whole.

In a rare break of the wind, the sound of hooves clattering in the courtyard below caught Cameron's attention. Turning, he spied Julian dismounting a red roan. Raising his arm in greeting, the young Lord Gray sprinted toward the nearest tower with the obvious intent to join him.

Julian clearly had discovered something of value. The man truly was a spy unmatched. With a nod of satisfaction, Cameron folded his hands behind his back and resumed walking the ramparts.

After a moment, Julian's deep voice hailed, "'Tis as ye thought. The man does indeed have backing of nobles." He fell into step beside him.

Cameron thinned his lips. Years of habit kept the rest of his facial expressions in check as he waited patiently for Julian to continue.

"The golden chain he sports on his neck is not the king's gift, and he will not tell from whose hands he received it," Julian informed him with a disgusted shake of the head. "The king was sore angry upon discovering it, just a fortnight ago. From what I've been told, I'm fair sorry to have missed witnessing the event. Some say 'twas a lover's quarrel."

A gust of wind tore through the battlements, ripping further words from his lips and rendering conversation impossible.

They walked in silence for a time.

From what Cameron could recall of the chain, the artistry had been notable. It was clearly worth a substantial sum. These unknown supporters were wealthy. What had they desired from Thomas in return?

The wind died down at last, and Cameron said, "Then we must find from where this golden chain comes."

At his side, Julian paused and stared off into the distance, absently fingering his dirk.

Cameron followed his gaze to where Thomas still walked the gardens with the king.

"I would welcome better days for Scotland." Julian growled. "And for a king who is a warrior, not a perfumed courtier. Scotland needs a king, not a woman skulking in the garden, reading books, and consulting the black arts for clues to the future! Aye, and any fool can see 'tis not a long walk afore Thomas is granted a title. Take a look at how the man simpers and fawns over your cousin!" He pointed to where Thomas was bowing over the king's hand, covering it with kisses.

Both Cameron and Julian arched a brow and exchanged a long look.

"Aye, but Thomas is a rash, overbold fellow, and prone to error." Cameron's lips formed a scathing smile. "He will undo himself in the end."

"Aye," Julian agreed. A concerned glint entered his gray eyes. "I grant that is true, but we both know he can wreak havoc along the way."

"There is that," Cameron conceded.

They watched as the king left the garden to hurry across the courtyard and into his apartments with Thomas still in tow.

Folding his arms, Julian said, "I've word out amongst the goldsmiths. We'll find who paid for the thing to be wrought and have our answer soon."

Cameron nodded.

Then Julian's countenance shifted and his tone turned light and teasing. "I spied a bonny, brown-haired lass quitting the castle as I entered. She was quite fetching, with the most astonishing brown eyes. Aye, a high-spirited beauty that I just might have to know better, if she's not yet entangled with another man …"

Cameron eyed him in amusement. Even the thought of seeing Kate brought an unbidden smile to his lips.

"Be gone with ye, man!" Julian laughed, rolling his eyes. "I've often wondered if ye were meant to be a monk, but for the first time I can see that ye aren't!"

Cameron's face clouded, and he looked away. "I care for the lass too much to see her again," he said grimly.

Julian snorted. "The hordes of other lasses ye've kissed still walk this fine Earth." With a chuckle, he strode away.

For a time, Cameron resumed his stroll on the wall, but Kate's dancing eyes and sweet, promising lips grew more distracting by the moment until he finally followed Julian's suggestion and, against his better judgment, strode through the castle gate and into the town of Stirling.

Turning down the lane to her tiny cottage, he hesitated briefly upon the step before knocking purposefully on the red door.

Dimly, he heard her father's voice calling from the back, "Pray enter!"

Stepping into the cottage, Cameron made his way to the back room.

"Cameron? Is that your step I hear, lad?" The man sounded stronger. He sat on a three-legged stool before the hearth, appearing younger than Cameron had first thought him to be. Though streaked with gray at the temples, his hair was dark. Lines still creased his face, but more had been from the illness than Cameron had known. With closed eyes, Kate's father tilted his head to the door, straining to hear, as a warm, welcoming smile graced his lips. "Well met, lad."

Cameron bowed. "Well met, my good sir."

"Have ye come for Kate?" The man chuckled. "Ach, of course ye have, lad. She's nae here."

Feeling a twinge of disappointment, Cameron opened his mouth to ask after the man's health when the cottage door banged open, and Kate's cheerful voice sent a shiver of pleasure down his spine.

"Father! I've the most splendid news!" Kate sailed into the room, panting. She pulled up short to see Cameron, but her face lit with joy. "Cameron, I've the most wonderful news!"

"Catch your breath, Kate." Her father laughed.

Grabbing her father's hands, she danced with him as he sat. "I'm a lady's maid, father! Eight shillings a year! *Eight!*"

Her father's jaw dropped open as Cameron raised a curious brow.

"'Tis the most fortunate day!" Kate laughed. Dropping her father's hands, she grabbed Cameron's and squeezed them in excitement. "I met the most gracious lady, and she asked me to be her own maid!"

"And who might this lady be?" Cameron lips crooked into a smile as he looked down into her sparkling eyes. Her joy was catching. Slipping an arm about her tiny waist, he lifted her up and twirled her around.

Laughing, she replied, "Lady Elsa! She's just come from the Borderlands!"

Cameron stumbled and nearly dropped her. With a sharp breath, he quickly regained his control and set her lightly back upon her feet.

"Are ye ill, Cameron?" Kate gripped his arm and shook it. "Ye suddenly look pale!"

"Lady Elsa?" He cleared his throat. Surely, it couldn't be his ward, Lady Elsa MacRae? Couldn't there be more than one Lady Elsa in Stirling?

Kate watched him closely. With furrowed brows, she eyed him up and down a bit suspiciously. "At the castle this morning, I swear I saw a man that looked just like ye, Cameron."

"Oh?" he asked guardedly. There was no doubt now. It had to be the same Lady Elsa. As always, fortune played cruel games with him.

"Surely, 'twasn't ye now, was it?" Kate folded her arms, her brown eyes locked on his.

"And why would I be at the castle?" he evaded.

Casting a glance at her father, Kate shook her head and placed a finger upon her lip. Moving to her father once more, she said, "The wee Donald will bring Fiona here to stay with ye now that I must sleep at the castle with my mistress. He'll bring her within the hour, but I must run errands now for the lady. I'll be by as often as I can, to check on ye both, and the wee Donald will come here three times a day to fetch whatever ye need!"

"Ach, my sweet bairn, dinna forget to breathe!" Her father laughed and then added, "And dinna worry overly much of me, lass. I'll be hale and hearty soon!"

A wistful expression entered Kate's eyes as she bent to place a quick kiss on his forehead. "Mayhap I'll have enough coin soon to get ye the water from the Pilgrim's Well."

"Ach, lass." Her father shook his head but sent her an indulgent smile. "My sight is gone for good, and there's naught to be done if it. Do ye not recall the good monk's words? Dinna waste your coin on a fool's dream!"

"Miracles, father, not dreams!" Kate frowned stubbornly in disagreement.

Squeezing her hands, her father ordered, "Be gone, Kate, afore ye try Lady Elsa's patience! And take this young lad with ye. He can aid ye in the lady's errands."

Blushing, Kate waited as Cameron said his farewells before pulling him out of the cottage to stand on the step. Placing her hands upon her slim hips, she took him to task with a frown. "I'll be stern with ye now, lad! I swear that was ye at the castle, and if it was then ye are a fool! If ye dinna care in keeping your own head, think of me! I care that ye keep it! There is honorable work to be had! And now that

I've eight shillings a year, I can help ye—"

She continued berating him, but Cameron was no longer listening.

Had he just heard the wee lass correctly? Did she really just offer to lend him coin on eight shillings a year? The estate of Inchmurrin alone sent thousands of pounds into his pocket each year, and he had countless other holdings.

His dark eyes swept her from head to toe.

He had never met a more generous, sincere, or kind-hearted lass in his life.

Nor one as fetching.

It was then that he knew she wasn't a passing fancy. If he stayed in her company he would genuinely fall in love. He didn't want to think he already had. Surely, it took longer, but even as he wondered, he was certain it was already too late.

Inexplicably, he had fallen for the lass.

He had never been in love before. Aye, the women of the court pursued him incessantly, tempting him to their beds in countless ways, but he was too wise to fall into court traps. And though he'd been wed seven times he hadn't touched a one of his wives. If truth be told, even though he'd kissed many a lass, even an ungodly number, he had never bedded a one of them. His curse had overshadowed his life.

"Listen to me, ye lout!" Kate reached up, jiggling his chin to focus his attention. "There's no cause for vengeance, if that is what drives ye! 'Twill only eat your heart and leave ye dry and bitter in the end!"

He should run, disappear. He could not allow his curse to affect such a pure heart. But her sweet lips were beguiling, and her passionate, brown eyes took his breath away.

She had bespelled him. There could be no other answer.

Suddenly nothing else mattered.

Uttering an unintelligible oath, he caught her close and pulled her lips to his, plundering her mouth with his tongue. His kiss was a claiming one, a statement of intent. Aye, he wanted her in a way that he had never wanted any other.

Her warm lips hungrily sought his, driving him mad with desire for all too short a time before her palms slid up his chest, and she pushed him away.

She was speaking but he didn't hear her words. He eyed her kiss-swollen lips possessively and with satisfaction. Aye, he'd make the lass his. He wanted her, all of her. A kiss was not enough.

"Are ye listening to me, ye oaf?" Kate's dark eyes sparkled with mirth even as her brows furrowed deeper. "I said if ye expect kisses from the likes of me, ye'll have to prove yourself worthy of them! I'll not kiss an outlaw!"

And then his hot blood cooled.

He was a fool for blithely ignoring the facts and letting it go this far. What would the wee lass say if she discovered he truly *was* the Dreaded Earl of Death.

"Cameron?" Kate's eyes filled with concern. "What is it?"

For a moment, he was tempted to tell her the truth, but only for a moment. Placing his hands over hers, he caressed her fingers and heaved a sigh. "I cannot tell ye the truth of it, lass, but when ye see me, run away as fast as your feet can carry ye. I've nothing but ill fortune to bring to ye, and I do not have the strength to stay away."

That was certainly true enough.

She eyed him sympathetically. Sliding her arm through his, she guided him down the lane. "I've had nothing but good fortune since meeting ye, Cameron, and whatever curse ye think ye might be under … well, mayhap we can break it together!"

Ach, he was a weak fool. Within minutes, she had him feeling at ease and even playful, and tossing all concerns aside yet again. Aye, the wee lass had some unholy power over him.

At the bottom of Castle Hill, she paused and pointed to the castle high above them. "I've herbs that must be gathered for the kind lady up there, and ye can lend me a hand. 'Twill heal your heart to feel the good earth under your fingers, Cameron!"

Permitting himself to enjoy her company, he allowed her to lead him to the banks of the River Forth and over the wide stone bridge, weaving through the crowd of carts, peasants, and the occasional monk crossing into the town of Stirling.

As they strolled down the tree-bordered road, Kate chattered of her dreams, childhood, and her father. "And now perhaps I can journey to Dunfermline, to the Pilgrim's Well at St. Fillans. 'Tis said the water can even heal blindness!"

"Truly?" Cameron murmured, tracing his thumb over the tips of her fingers. 'Twas pleasant to hear the soothing sound of her voice while enjoying the warmth of the sun upon his face. He couldn't recall the last time he had felt so at ease.

"'Tis worth trying, is it not?" she asked.

There was hope in her voice. "Aye, it cannot hurt to try." He caressed her hand in a comforting gesture.

With a fierce smile, Kate slipped her fingers out of his and pointed to the edge of the road. "Last year, I'm told that lovage and pearlwort grew here. We might find some new leaves. Follow me, lad, and be quick!"

The next hour was the most enjoyable that Cameron could recall in some time. He climbed as Kate directed, nipping tender leaves and pulling roots, caking his cloak and boots in mud as the spring sun shone on the ancient forest bursting with signs of new life.

Kate was lively and filled with spirit. Artfully slipping away each time he tried to steal a kiss, she tossed her hair and sent him secretive smiles, until at last, standing on a muddy bank, she beckoned him close. "Give me a hand now, will ye? I canna slip and ruin this dress more than 'tis already!" Ruefully, she lifted the muddy hem of her gown, but higher than was truly necessary and enough to playfully flash her ankle.

Lowering his lashes, he reached up and yanked her roughly into his arms. With his heart pounding with desire, he planted another kiss full upon her lips, and as ever, she responded enthusiastically. Dropping her basket to the forest floor, she entwined her arms firmly about his neck, returning the passion in full measure, her heart beating rapidly against his chest.

Aye, he was a fool.

The passionate blood of the Stewarts ran through his veins.

He had no power to walk away, and apparently, neither did she. He caught his breath and tore his lips away as a hideous thought crossed his mind.

Had he cursed her already?

An unpleasant chill ran down his spine.

"What sadness do ye hide?" Kate's soft voice broke into his tortured thoughts. "I wish ye could share your burden."

He hesitated, and then allowed the bitter words to fall from his lips. "My touch is death, lass. I was wed afore and ... they died ... untimely deaths."

"They?" Kate stepped back, dropping her gaze to her feet.

"Aye, one or two ..." Cameron cleared his throat uncomfortably. How could he say seven? Suddenly, it was important to add, "But I never loved them. I never chose them. The marriages were arranged and—"

"Arranged?" Kate drew her brows into a frown. "What band of outlaws are ye involved with, Cameron?"

At that, he couldn't resist a perverse smile. "Outlaws of the worst kind, Kate." Aye, now that she mentioned it, the nobles in the land were indeed far worse than any band of outlaws he knew of. His smile widened.

"But 'tis no laughing matter!" Kate did not share his mirth. "Ye must run from them!"

He shook his head with a touch of annoyance. "'Tis not possible. I've tried. They always find me, lass."

"But ye canna have them rule ye so!" Kate insisted. "Surely, ye can escape! Is your master the outlaw I saw at the Brass Unicorn?"

"Julian?" Cameron's lip twitched. Suddenly, it was difficult not to laugh. "No! Julian is a ... friend. My master is ... a fool ruled by a treacherous lapdog, and I'll not rest until I unmask the cur for what he is."

She stared at him, and then her eyes sparkled. "Ach, I knew it. Ye *are* an honorable thief, just like Robyn Hode! But will ye leave after ye reveal this lapdog's wicked ways for all to see?"

"Aye." Cameron sighed. For a moment, he allowed himself to dream of galloping away to Inchmurrin with Kate at his side, but the thought brought the habitual twinge of guilt. And then as Kate grabbed his shirt, pulled him close, and devoured him in a wildly passionate kiss, the guilt mysteriously faded away.

Even if he had tried, he could not have resisted her and when he did pull away, he knew it was hopeless. Curse or not, he would have her. Her eyes were mischievous, inviting, and her moist lips made his blood surge. He wanted to bury his face in her thick, luxuriant hair and kiss the creamy, soft whiteness of her neck.

Catching her to his chest, he slid his hands along the soft lines of her waist and hips as his mouth traveled down her neck. He could feel her heart fluttering wildly against his chest and then she gave a little moan of delight that caused the last shreds of his control to desert him.

Pressing her back against a tree, he intended to make her his right then and there when the sound of a horn split the air.

They sprang apart.

Kate filled her cheeks with air and blew them out in exasperation as Cameron suppressed a groan.

Through the trees, a short distance away, they could see a party of horses moving along the road.

"Let's see who comes!" Kate's eyes lit with excitement. Locking her fingers around his wrist, she pulled him through the hedge and burst onto the road just as the first horses rounded the bend.

Cameron recognized the royal party at once.

Alexander, Duke of Albany and John, Earl of Mar, rode upon silver-bedecked chargers in the midst of their entourage. Nobly attired in crimson velvet, they looked every inch the princes that they were.

"Let's go!" Cameron hissed, attempting to pull Kate away, but she slipped free.

"Oh, 'tis Albany!" she whispered breathlessly. "And Mar!"

Frowning, Cameron covered his head with the hood of his cloak just as Albany's penetrating green eyes turned his way.

"Let's go!" Cameron grated in a low voice.

He had taken only a single step toward the hedge when Albany's dark brows rose in surprise, and he called out in a loud voice, "Cameron?"

Startled, the man's steed suddenly neighed and reared, but Albany mastered the unruly beast with ease. Aye, he truly was the prince that everyone wished was king. Even Kate watched in open admiration as the prince laughed effortlessly, his sharp green eyes shifting to lock on hers. Sweeping his hat gracefully from his head, he gallantly bowed in her direction.

Frowning, Cameron yanked Kate through the hedge.

Kate turned upon him, wide-eyed. "Did Albany call ye by name?" she asked, astounded, looking back over her shoulder in shock.

Clenching his jaw, Cameron willed Albany to keep moving, holding his breath as the horses filed by in a jingle of bits and creak of leather. To his utmost relief, no one stopped. Instead, they pressed on for the town on the far side of the River Forth.

"I swear I heard him call your name!" Kate insisted, shaking his sleeve.

Composing his features, Cameron gave her a disarming smile, "Ach, now, why would a royal prince call the likes of me, lass? Surely, Cameron is a common enough name." He shrugged.

She scowled and folded her arms, but then adopted a sheepish expression. "True enough. My father is always reminding me that I'm too fanciful of a lass. And Cameron is not even your given name! Ye have yet to tell me what your true name is!" She raised a brow, challenging him, but when he did not respond, she sighed. "'Tis growing late, and I must be off to my mistress afore she regrets her choice in maids!"

"Allow me to fetch your basket." Cameron offered smoothly, desiring to escape her piercing gaze. Retracing his steps, he found the thing where she had dropped it, and returned to find her standing on the road once again, watching Albany and Mar make their way to Stirling Town.

Reaching down to capture her hand, he trailed the royal party at a safe distance as she offered a wealth of advice on how he might escape the clutches of his fellow outlaws.

Cameron simply listened, enjoying the soft lilt of her voice, and slowed his pace even more, not to avoid Albany, but to prolong the joy of her company.

Ahead on the road, a crowd pressed around the princes, slowing their progress. Children ran alongside their horses, dancing and singing, and from somewhere distant a band of pipers played until midway across the bridge, the royal party came to a complete halt.

Cameron hesitated, resisting Kate's tug upon his sleeve.

"I canna be late, ye oaf!" She frowned at him. "I must prove myself to my new mistress!"

"And I'm sure ye will, lass," Cameron murmured. Bringing her fingers to his lips, he kissed them softly. Aye, he'd speak with Lady Elsa right quickly. He would see his wee Kate treated well and paid more than a mere eight shillings a year. He had no idea what a good wage was for a maid, but eight shillings was a beggarly sum. Kate deserved so much more.

"Oh, look!" Kate shaded her eyes, peering at the bridge. "The nobles have come to greet Mar and Albany! Let's go see them!"

Glancing over, Cameron spied a group of horsemen trotting down Castle Hill towards the princes on the bridge. Even from this distance, he could see the flaming red hair of Archibald Douglas. He couldn't resist muttering bitterly, "Surely, ye'll see enough of their ilk now that ye work at the castle."

Kate turned a sharp eye on him as her face flooded with sympathy. "Did nobles wrong ye, ye poor lad?"

Cameron winced and looked away. He should tell the lass the truth, but the words stuck in his throat.

"I hope someday that ye'll trust me enough to tell me." Kate sighed.

Ach, but she knew how to worsen his guilt.

"When will I see ye again, Cameron?" she asked, leaning her head against his shoulder. "Where do ye sleep at night? Are ye safe?"

Clenching his jaw, he stared at the castle, high on the hill above them.

Kate sighed and her lively brown eyes clouded. "Why do I feel ye have some dreadful secret that I'll not like, Cameron?"

He remained silent. He felt like a fool. He'd never lost the power of speech before.

"Are ye still wed?" she asked suddenly, skewering him with a suspicious look.

"Ach, no!" The words ripped from his throat.

Satisfied that his response was genuine, she slipped her basket from his arm. "Then, what is it?"

After several long moments, he promised softly, "I'll tell ye soon, lass." The farce had gone on long enough.

Gently, Kate cupped his hand in hers and raised it softly to her lips. "I won't judge ye, Cameron," she swore. "I swear I'll understand ye."

Reverently, he bent down and kissed the top of her head.

"I must be gone now." She smiled warmly, but a shadow of worry played about her eyes. "Will I see ye again, soon?"

"Aye." He nodded.

With a bright smile, she gathered her plaid close and ran toward the bridge, turning back several times to wave before disappearing into the crowd.

Cameron watched her go with a heavy heart.

He didn't want to think. Woodenly, he watched as the princes finished their prolonged greetings. Archibald motioned his fine company of men forward to join the princes' entourage, and the procession up Castle Hill resumed.

The onlookers followed them, and Cameron pressed forward, slipping through the crowd and Stirling's side streets to enter the castle ahead of the procession.

Retiring quickly to his apartments, he cast his muddy cloak aside and raised his voice, calling for his man to pull off his boots as he took his seat in the carved chair before the crackling fire.

Sir Arval, the gray-haired, grizzled Frenchman who had served him from birth, entered the chamber. Eyeing the mud-caked leather boots, he raised a brow at the dirt on Cameron's breeches. "Did some ill befall ye, my lord?"

Suddenly shy, Cameron turned his head to the fire and did not reply.

The Frenchman merely smiled. Removing his boots, the man stepped into the adjoining chamber and returned quickly with fresh attire.

Rising to his feet, Cameron stretched, prepared to don the black and gold velvet when he found himself struck with a sudden thought. "Arval, send straightway for water from the Pilgrim's Well in St. Fillans and send the fastest horse. I would have it on the morrow."

"Aye, my lord." The man bowed.

"And send word to Lady Elsa. See that she pays her maid well." He'd see Kate well cared for. "Eight shillings is not enough. See to it yourself. I would think a more decent wage should be eight pounds, do ye agree?"

The man's eyes lit in humor, but his face was grave. "I will see her paid exceedingly well, my lord."

With a satisfied nod, Cameron shrugged into his fresh, white shirt, before remembering to ask. "The almshouse? Have ye seen to the monks?"

"Aye, my lord. Father Herrick will see ye in the morning."

Cameron nodded, lacing his velvet breeches.

He wanted to give the lass something, but he knew not what an outlaw might give a lass. As an earl, he had bestowed many a fine gold necklace with precious stones upon those who struck his fancy, but he knew Kate would not accept such gifts.

"Might I suggest ribbons for her hair, my lord?" Sir Arval's quiet voice held a distinct note of humor.

Cameron stiffened. Aye, his men knew him well.

He grimaced.

He had no business courting her.

With a grim shake of his head, he replied in a reserved tone. "No. 'Twould be a mistake."

Sliding into another pair of fine leather boots, he strode out of his apartments and to the courtyard where Albany and Mar had just arrived. Quickly descending the spiral stairs, he reached Albany's side as the man dismounted.

"Cameron!" Albany clapped him warmly on the shoulder. "I could have sworn I saw ye on the road not an hour hence!"

Muscular and tall, Albany looked Cameron directly in the eye. A skilled warrior with his reddish-brown hair cropped short, he was a handsome man, and his green eyes and engaging smile had won him the hearts of many.

"Well met, my lord." Cameron bowed.

"Ach, couldn't have been ye, I suppose." Albany shook his head. "I was fair hoping 'twas. The man was with the bonniest lass I've seen in many a day! I would know her better."

Cameron straightened. As a fierce, protective wave surged through him, his dark eyes narrowed of their own accord.

Albany's brows twitched upwards. With his eyes glittering, he leaned forward, and whispered, "So 'twas ye on the road now, was it not, fair cousin?"

He remained there, his face planted mere inches from Cameron's, and for several long moments, their gazes locked in challenge before Lord Julian Gray's silky voice inserted itself, "Might I escort ye to your chambers, my lord?"

Albany turned away, greeting Julian with a fond punch on the arm as Cameron took a step back.

Perhaps he should send Lady Elsa and her wee maid to Inchmurrin.

Aye, the more he thought on the matter, the more attractive it sounded.

6

LOVE POTIONS

Kate slowly opened the door to Lady Elsa's chamber and peeked inside. The room was empty. Taking a deep breath, she tiptoed to the table and set the basket down.

She still found it hard to believe she had the right to be in a lady's chamber and harder still to believe *she* was truly a maid in Stirling Castle. And paid eight shillings a year! *Eight*!

Closing her eyes, she hugged herself, reveling in pure joy at the thought. But only for a moment.

Eager to please her new mistress, she surveyed the chamber with a critical eye. The chambermaids had done their job well, but she plumped up the pillows anyway, moved the chair in a more inviting angle, and added a touch more peat to the fire.

With a pleased sigh, she glanced about the room, smoothing her skirts, and then returned to the table. She found the view from the window breathtaking—the river, the ancient forest and the moors were covered in green, bursting with signs of life.

The afternoon had been delightful. She could think of nothing better than to have wandered through the woods with Cameron, stealing kisses, while gleaning tidbits of information about the man. He revealed more each time she saw him. Ach, he was such a mysterious man, and such a charming and caring one.

For a time, she absently shuffled the herbs in the basket, wondering how she might help gain his freedom before permitting thoughts of quite a different nature. He had kissed her with such raw hunger, crushing her passionately against his hard chest, and she relived the moment, again and again, until her cheeks began to burn.

The door rattled, and she dropped into a deep curtsey as Lady Elsa swept into the room.

"You have returned!" With a pleased nod, Lady Elsa joined her at the table and reached for the basket. "Did you find it all?"

"Aye, my lady." Kate nodded. "Though 'tis early in the season, I found roots and some new leaves."

The woman's lips quivered and she clasped her hands over her heart. "Well done! Now, you may prepare the potions."

"Potions, my lady?" Kate repeated, surprised.

Averting her gaze, Lady Elsa explained with a demure smile, "Love potions."

Kate blinked in dismay. Love potions? Why were all the other women she knew so infatuated with love potions? And before she could stop herself, she blurted, "How could such a bonny lady like ye need a potion?"

Lady Elsa tittered and clamped her hand nervously over her mouth. With cheeks turning a slight pink, she replied, "'Tis an important matter, Kate! I've made my decision. I shall have my protector, the earl, as my husband and none other. The man is right handsome and strong, but he does not even look my way. He has yet to speak with me, and I've been here days already! These potions will change that." She pinched the pearlwort and added in a wistful tone,

"They *must* change that!"

"Aye, my lady," Kate replied, striving hard to mute the skepticism in her voice.

"Then, start at once." She picked up the basket and placed it in Kate's arms. "I must carry the yarrow with me at all times. The lovage must be eaten, and it would be best if the earl ate it as well." She twisted her lips in thought, as if wondering how to accomplish that before pointing to the pearlwort. "And boil this, so I may wet my lips with it. All it takes is a kiss, and he will be mine."

Kate eyed the tiny plants in disbelief.

"And be quick, the earl is not an easy man," Lady Elsa added, picking up her needlework to sit primly on the edge of the bed. "Off to the kitchens for a pot then, Kate. You can boil the pearlwort here. And keep your lips sealed. I'll not have the other ladies gossiping about this."

Dropping another quick curtsey, Kate ran down the stairs as fast as her worn slippers allowed, still astonished that a beautiful lady such as Elsa would find it necessary to resort to potions. But it was a blessedly fortunate event. Aye, she would keep her lips sealed, but she could make extra pearlwort to satisfy Maura's demands. She had no choice. Surely, it wasn't a betrayal. Using pearlwort was apparently common enough knowledge in the Borderlands. At least, Lady Elsa spoke of it so. Ach, if only Maura hadn't forced her into such a predicament. She was whole-heartedly beginning to resent the woman.

Aye, since meeting Cameron, her fortune had improved by the hour. How could the man think himself cursed? Surely, the plague had taken the two wives forced upon him, no doubt, the very same plague that had robbed her of her mother, sister and so many more.

Her heart ached as she recalled the pain in his eyes, but as always, thoughts of Cameron quickly shifted to thoughts of his hard muscles under her fingertips, his chiseled lips, and ardent kisses. Ach, but he made her blood hot. Fanning her reddening cheeks, she placed her hand on the latch of the door leading to the courtyard.

Suddenly, a nasal voice ordered, "Halt, wench!"

Kate whirled to find a tall, long-faced man descending the spiral stair behind her with a deliberately slow step. Finely dressed in yellow velvet, he wore a thick, golden chain about his neck, and his expression was one of outright disdain. He was clearly a nobleman.

With her heart beating rapidly, Kate cast her eyes to the floor and curtsied. "My lord."

"Rise!" the man ordered harshly. "Let me see your face."

Holding her breath, Kate lifted her eyes to meet his, unable to suppress a shiver.

Stepping close, he gripped her chin and slowly turned her face from side to side. "Aye, 'tis clear what the earl sees in ye."

"My lord?" Kate swallowed.

He studied her face for several, long moments, and then said, "Ye can tell the earl that Thomas knows his weakness now, and that ye'll be the first one to get hurt if he continues probing into my affairs." He smiled. It was a cold, hard smile, and he leaned closer to add, "He'll not want to see ye hurt. He's not a man to share his affections lightly, don't ye agree?"

Kate held still. What was the man speaking of? Was he drunk?

"Aye." Thomas nodded slowly, apparently pleased. "I see the fear in your eyes. 'Tis good. Be gone with ye now and deliver the message!"

For a moment, Kate hesitated. Should she tell him that she had not understood a word of it? Clearly, he had confused her with someone else. She opened her mouth to point that out, but as his eyes narrowed, she changed her mind and fled out into the courtyard, the door banging shut at her heels.

Drawing her plaid close, she cast several glances over her shoulder, to ensure he had not followed, before making her way to the kitchens.

He must have been drunk.

Aye, he'd mistaken her for another. Now that she worked at the castle, she would probably encounter many such peculiar situations.

"Ach, 'tis the same as the alehouse!" She laughed outright before quickly subduing her mirth to mutter under her breath, "Drunken nobles are no different than drunken sailors!"

Brushing the matter aside, she secured a pot from the kitchens and hurried back to find an agitated Lady Elsa waiting at the door.

"Make the pearlwort with haste!" she cried, wringing her hands. "And bring me the yarrow. I must speak to the earl at once!"

"What is it, my lady?" Kate asked, concern flooding her face.

"The Earl sent a messenger, instructing me to leave for Inchmurrin on the morrow!" Lady Elsa paced nervously in front of the fire. "A messenger! Why does the earl shun me so?"

"Away?" Kate repeated with a sinking heart. She had only been a maid for a day.

"The yarrow! Tie the roots to my skirts! Oh, leaves would have been better!" Lady Elsa wrung her hands as she stood in the center of the chamber. "Be quick, Kate! I must change the man's mind!"

Selecting one of the roots and a green satin ribbon, Kate tied the bundle to the hem of Lady Elsa's fine shift. "What does it do, my lady?" She couldn't resist asking.

"Yarrow brings love. It will draw him closer to my heart." Lady Elsa ran to the basket and crushed one of the pearlwort leaves against her lips. "And the pearlwort should be boiled, but mayhap this will serve as well! I've naught to lose. Stay here and finish the potion. Be quick!"

Kate eyed the distressed woman with sympathy, watching her flutter around the chamber like a bird before hurrying out the door, intent upon seeking the earl's company.

Moving to the table, Kate eyed the plants with a bit of disgust.

Ach, she'd never wear roots on her shift or rub leaves on her lips to catch a man! But then she scarcely needed to. With a dreamy expression, she pulled the tender pearlwort leaves from the stems, settling in to think of Cameron once more when the door opened again.

This time, Maura shamelessly entered. "Good evening, Kate."

Maura was dressed in a red gown and her fair hair tied back with a black velvet ribbon. Her cheeks dimpled in a stiff, little smile, but her eyes were hard as she asked, "I'm sure ye recall my words at our last meeting, Kate?"

With a surge of annoyance, Kate turned back to stripping the stems. "Good evening to ye, Maura."

"And?" Maura pressed, joining her at the table. "Are ye making my potion? Because I swear if ye aren't, I'm off straightway to toss your father on the street—"

"'Tis a pearlwort potion," Kate interrupted, her anger rising at the woman's threatening ways. How had she ever been so foolish as to trust her? Ach, she assumed the woman was good-hearted far too fast. She should have listened to her father. He was ever reminding her to think twice.

Maura's lips formed a pleased smile. Picking up a leaf, she raised a fine brow. "And how is it to be used?"

"Ye have but to kiss the man and he is yours, or so 'tis said." Kate frowned. "But I canna promise ye that 'twill work. I have no knowledge of such things."

"We've already seen it works very well!" Maura's cold eyes swept her up and down. "But I'll not foolishly waste it on an outlaw. I'll have the Earl of Lennox as my lover afore the week is done!"

Kate rolled her eyes. "The Dreaded Earl of Death?"

Moving to the bed, Maura threw herself down upon it with a sensuous, growling sound. "Ye clearly have yet to see the man. He is so tall, and brawny, and his lips beg to be savaged! And his eyes, Kate! Each time he looks at me, I know he's already undressed me, and—"

"Maura!" Kate interrupted, half in shock and half in displeasure at the wrinkled bedcovers. "Hie ye off the bed! 'Tis the lady's and ye'd best not ruin it!"

"Ach, but ye make a fine maid, Kate!" Maura slipped off the bed. "'Tis all ye'll ever be."

Kate sent her a disparaging look as she smoothed the coverlet and plumped up the pillows.

"Aye, make sport of me, if ye will!" Maura tossed her head. "But

I'll have a man in my bed who'll spirit me away from a life as a chambermaid! Aye, he'll shower me with trinkets and gowns, and muckle more should I bear his bairn!"

"Ach, Maura!" Kate expelled her breath and returned to the table. "A bairn is not a path to riches!"

With a scathing snort, the woman replied, "I dinna want the comfortable, ordered life ye seek, Kate! Even if ye change your outlaw's ways, at best ye'll have a boring and sensible life, but more likely ye'll end up with hungry bairns and no coin after your man is hung on a tree!"

"He's not that kind of thief!" Kate slammed the pot down and faced Maura with flashing eyes. "He's a right honorable man!"

"So the wee Kate has a temper? Does she think to stand against me?" The woman smiled coolly before hissing, "How has your father been feeling this fine day?"

Her veiled threat was impossible to misconstrue, and for the first time, Kate felt the icy cold fingers of fear clutch her heart. This woman would not stop at one potion. Aye, she would have to find another place for her father forthwith, but until she could, she would have to keep Maura happy. Forcing a smile, Kate turned back to the potion. "I'll give this to ye on the morrow. 'Twill take some time to finish it."

"Very well." Maura nodded in satisfaction. "I'll expect it first thing. I must have it afore Albany's feast. I've switched places with one of the serving maids at the high table where the Earl of Lennox is sure to be. Ye'd best not disappoint me, Kate."

With that, she turned on her heel and glided out of the room.

Kate twisted her lips in a tight line, a cold pit of fear growing in her stomach. How could she find a new room for her father when she had no coin? She'd given Maura everything she had. And should she remain lucky enough to remain Lady Elsa's maid for longer than a day, she wouldn't receive any coin for it for at least a month. The task of keeping Maura happy for a month would likely be an impossible one. She moved about, preparing the pearlwort, fretting, until the door opened and a much calmer Lady Elsa reappeared.

"'Tis most fortunate that I ran into Thomas Cochrane, Kate," she said with a relieved smile.

Kate stiffened at the name of *Thomas*, thinking at once of the man dressed in yellow velvet.

"He gave me an immediate audience with the king, and I'll not be sent away!" Lady Elsa sighed thankfully. "The king insisted that I stay here at Stirling Castle."

Shaking off her concern, Kate allowed her lips to break into a wide, exuberant smile. Her position was safe! Ach, there were probably a dozen men named Thomas in the castle. "'Tis the most wondrous tidings, my lady!" she said.

"I kissed the king's hand." Lady Elsa frowned, taking her seat by the fire. "But I wiped the pearlwort from my lips first. I'm sure I've no cause to think that he might fall in love with me."

"I'm sure there is naught to fear, my lady." Kate agreed with a lighter heart.

"I shared sweetmeats and oranges with the king, and the earl has left the castle with lord Gray, so I've no reason to attend supper this night. And I will be glad to miss it, now that the king's aunt, Princess Annabella has arrived. The woman is harsh and difficult to please. I'll not be the one to try her patience this night." She yawned and then held out her hand. "My needlework, Kate."

Kate rushed to give her the basket, and then stood at the foot of the bed to watch as Lady Elsa carefully measured lengths of silken thread.

Time passed.

The shadows grew longer.

The occasional cracks of the fire were the only sounds to break the silence as Lady Elsa dreamily pulled her needle through the cloth for what seemed like ages.

It did not take long before Kate had trouble holding still. Ach, she felt like a caged canary! How could the woman endure such a stifling existence? How could she just sit there, stitching, hour after hour? Surely, she did not do this every day!

Suppressing a sigh, she looked longingly out the window, but it was dark, and she couldn't see a thing.

A sharp knock on the door startled them both.

Kate ran to open it and discovered two lads standing before a wooden chest, with another boy holding a large red bundle of satin.

"Gifts from the earl to Lady Elsa and her maid, Kate," one of them mumbled tiredly, dragging the chest inside before Kate gave him permission to enter.

The third lad thrust the satin bundle into her arms. "I was told to give this one to the wee maid named Kate." He eyed her for a moment and stretched out his hand as if to snatch the bundle back. "Ye are Kate, aren't ye?"

"Aye." Kate frowned. She eyed the red satin, perplexed.

"What is this?" Lady Elsa rose gracefully to stand before the chest. "Open it, Kate."

As the lads scampered out of the chamber, Kate set her bundle aside, knelt in front of the chest and lifted the lid.

The delicate scent of lemons escaped into the air as the firelight cast a warm glow over the shimmering contents.

With a cry of astonishment and a little clap of her hands, Lady Elsa sank on her knees before the chest. Lifting an exquisite gown of garnet-colored satin, she gasped, "This is the finest Spanish lace! And this hooded mantle—I've never seen such fine stitching!"

There were gowns of satin, velvet, and fine wool, several mantles, and silken slippers. Lady Elsa exclaimed softly over each one, until finally emptying the chest, she sat back and sighed. "Oh, Kate, the yarrow is already working!"

Kate smiled, amazed at the treasures in the chest, but less inclined to give credit to the yarrow. "Your protector is very kind, my lady."

"And generous!" Lady Elsa pointed to the satin bundle. "Do open yours!"

Kate didn't need to be told twice. Excited, she untied the ribbon and caught her breath to see a gown of rich green silk, another of blue wool, trimmed with gold braid, and one of yellow velvet edged with fine lace. Under the gowns, she found a soft mantle of black wool and a finely made pair of leather shoes.

"Surely, there must be a mistake." Kate drew back with a frown. "These are much too fine for me."

"No, the earl is most kind." Lady Elsa smiled, though she appeared quite surprised herself. "He even wishes my maid to be finely dressed! You must change at once, Kate. Your brown dress is truly not fitting for my company."

Feeling strangely shy, Kate selected the green silk and retired to the corner, quickly shrugging out of Maura's brown dress. To her utmost surprise, the dress was the correct length, and the shoes fit perfectly.

Lady Elsa had returned to her needlework, daintily adjusting her skirts, but looked up to smile as Kate reappeared in the new gown. "'Tis a fine gown, Kate. I will wear the garnet satin on the morrow for Albany and Mar's welcome feast. I must look my best when I thank the earl for his fine gifts. You will attend me."

"Aye, my lady." Kate dipped a curtsey.

The silence in the chamber resumed as Lady Elsa once more focused on her needlework, but this time with a private smile playing upon her lips.

At first, the green silk and the shoes kept Kate occupied. She had never touched such fine material, and the shoes made her feel as if she walked on clouds. Her good fortune was astounding.

She couldn't wait to show her father, but the thought that he couldn't see the colors dampened her mood. She clenched her fingers into a fist. If only she could get the water from the Pilgrim's Well. She did not believe in magic, but perhaps the water had properties yet unknown that would cure her father's eyes. There was little harm in trying.

The evening progressed and the moon rose. And as sounds of laughter and music filtered through the window, Kate once again couldn't resist the temptation to inch closer in order to hear the beautiful melodies.

"The musicians are from Spain," Lady Elsa informed her quietly from the fire. "They play to welcome the king's aunt."

Kate jumped guiltily and returned at once to the foot of the bed. "The music is lovely, my lady. I've not heard the like before."

"Aye, they are most accomplished, but I'm sure Princess Annabella is greatly displeased. Even Albany and Mar fear the woman!" Lady Elsa rose to her feet, hiding a yawn behind her fluttering fingers. "I will retire now, but you may step outside and listen to the music, Kate. Just stay within hearing, so I may call out for you if I desire."

"Oh! How kind of ye, my lady!" Kate's eyes sparkled in excitement. "I swear ye must be the most generous lady in the castle!"

"Thank you, Kate." She smiled in return, and then her eyes clouded. "I am but a poor lady, so poor that the others here scarcely speak to me. I'm really no different than you."

In short order, Lady Elsa was ensconced in her curtained feather bed, and Kate carefully folded her dress, laying it on top of the new ones in the wooden chest.

After banking the fire with ashes, she carefully tiptoed out of the chamber, leaving the door open a crack. She moved closer to the music, to a window overlooking the courtyard and leaned forward, resting her head against the cold, gray stones.

The lively tune reminded her of days gone by, fishing on the lochs with her father, and her wee sister, Joan. She sighed softly, lost in memories, and losing track of time until she gradually became aware of two tall figures standing in the darkness of the courtyard below.

They stood close, heads bowed, as if whispering to each other, and then one stepped back and laughed a deep, rich sound that sounded very much like Cameron's laugh.

Curious, she craned out of the window.

The men moved across the courtyard, pausing under the flickering light of a torch, and her heart leapt into her throat.

There was no mistaking him.

It *was* Cameron!

He stood in the dim light, speaking with the fair-haired man from the Brass Unicorn. The man he had called Julian.

She watched in horror.

Surely, he was not half-witted enough to steal from nobles?

They would hang him straightway!

Praying that Lady Elsa still slept, Kate flew down the stairwell and out into the courtyard, arriving to see both men entering a side door to the royal apartments.

She hesitated for only a moment.

Angrily cursing Cameron under her breath, she darted past the guards, expecting them to stop her. She was astonished when they didn't, but she had little time to ponder the matter as she entered the royal apartments.

Torches flickered in their wall sconces lining the narrow corridor, shedding a soft light on the tapestries covering the cold stones. She could barely make out the dim forms of Cameron and his companion moving slowly ahead of her, heads bowed and murmuring in quiet voices.

Ach, Cameron was a fool! Did he not care one whit about keeping his head? He wasn't even looking around to see if he had been followed! Angrily, she wondered if he even cared one whit about *her* and how *she* felt!

Aye, she was going to take him to task!

From somewhere behind her, a door slammed, and at the sound of approaching feet, she panicked.

Ach, she couldn't see the man get caught, no matter how angry she was at him.

Picking up her skirts, she flew down the passageway. Catching up to them, she threw open the nearest door, grabbed Cameron's arm as he whirled in surprise, and yanked him through it.

As an afterthought, she reached back and pulled his companion in for good measure.

She slammed the door shut, leaning against it and breathing heavily as she quickly glanced about the dimly lit chamber. She was relieved to find it empty.

"Kate! What—" Cameron began but she cut him short with an angry frown.

"Hush!" She nodded her chin at the sound of footsteps outside the door. Lifting a finger to her lips, she glared at them both to remain silent.

Cameron towered over her with an expression she could not interpret as his companion, Julian, slouched against the wall, folded his arms, and slowly began to grin.

When the passageway was quiet once more, she placed her hands on her hips and hissed, "What are ye doing, ye fools? Can ye not know 'tis dangerous here for the likes of ye?"

Cameron's lips thinned.

Julian's grin widened.

At that, Cameron graced the man with a dark glare of disapproval.

"'Tis not a jest!" Kate snapped at the fair-haired man. "Ye could both lose your heads, ye lout!"

"Lout?" Julian snorted in outright amusement. "Are ye naming me a lout?"

"Aye, but 'tis plainly too fine a name for ye!" she retorted fiercely. This man was clearly a bad influence on Cameron. Cameron had said he was a friend, but what kind of friend would incite another to thieve at the castle? "Why canna ye leave Cameron be? Surely ye can find others to corrupt! Let him free from your band of outlaws, ye onion-eyed varlet!"

Julian blinked and then threw back his head and laughed.

"Enough, Julian," Cameron warned grimly.

As Kate watched, the fair-haired man bent down and planted his face inches from hers. Ach, he was a wickedly handsome man. She'd never really looked at him before. His beautiful, long-lashed eyes locked on hers with an open gleam of interest.

"My wee, bonny Kate." He grinned with a roguish lift of his brow. "I swear I'm half tempted to court ye myself!"

"'Tis enough, Julian!" Cameron warned again.

Kate lifted her chin and answered truthfully, "I've no interest in ye, man!" Aye, he was a braw man, but nothing compared to the seductively dark Cameron standing at his side.

"Ach, but Cameron's a possessive lover—" Julian began in a light, mocking tone.

"Julian, be gone," Cameron interrupted sternly.

With a shrug, Julian lazily dropped an arm about her shoulders and bent his fair head to kiss her on the cheek. It was a brotherly kiss. "Then as ye wished, sweet Kate, this onion-eyed varlet will take his leave."

With a mischievous wink, he slipped through the door and shut it quietly.

"Will he be safe?" Kate whispered anxiously, suddenly torn with concern. "'Tis dangerous here, and though he is an unsavory character, I'd wish him no harm!"

"There is no cause to fret, Kate," Cameron reassured in a strained tone.

He stood close, swathed in a dark, finely made cape with a silver brooch at his throat. She eyed it in consternation, and her anger returned full force. "I swear ye'll drive me to an early grave, Cameron! Did ye come for the brooch? Put it back, man! I canna bear the thought of ye losing your head—"

He moved suddenly and his elegantly long fingers grasped her by the shoulders. "I'm not a thief, Kate!" he swore.

She frowned in confusion. "We canna speak here! If we're caught—"

"We are safe in these apartments!" His strong jaw clenched and his dark brows furrowed into a line. "These rooms ... are ... not used. No one will look here. We're safe, lass." He seemed to have difficulty speaking.

Kate glanced around, taking a closer look this time. The room was dark, illuminated only by the dying fire, but she could see enough to discover it was a finely furnished one, so fine that she'd never seen the like.

Suddenly, she turned white. "Ach, ye fool! We must be in the king's own rooms! Look at the tapestries on the wall, and there is even a rug on the floor! We'll hang—"

"Kate, no one will come here this night. I swear upon my life's blood that we are safe, lass!" There was something odd about his voice, and he almost looked ill.

But their safety was her most pressing concern. "Are ye sure no one will come?" she asked. "How could ye know?"

For a moment, it appeared as if he would not answer, but then he replied in a voice so soft she scarcely heard it, "These apartments belong to the Earl of Lennox, and he is not here … at least … not … now."

Kate sucked in her breath in shock and shivered. "The Dreaded Earl of Death?"

He winced. "I thought ye claimed the man as a lover! How can ye name him such a thing?"

"I told ye that I lied." She frowned sourly. "I've never seen the man."

Inexplicably, his lips curved upwards and his voice deepened. "Are ye sure of that, my sweeting? 'Tis a fine dress ye wear this night, Kate."

"'Tis a gift from my lady's protector!" Kate replied with a puzzled look. "He's a right generous man."

His dark lashes lowered, roving over her figure in a way that made her heart skip.

"And what does he expect from ye in return?" he asked in a suggestive tone.

Astonished at the implication, Kate's lips parted in surprise. "I've never met the man, Cameron!"

He moved closer, so close that she could feel his breathe on her neck.

"Are ye sure, lass?" he asked.

His behavior puzzled her a moment, and then the understanding dawned. He was jealous! Secretly pleased, she frowned outwardly. "Are ye calling me unfaithful?"

As soon as she said the words, she blushed. He had never promised himself to her. Why was she acting as if he had?

Cameron laughed. It was a deep, rich, rumbling sound.

"Ach, but ye are acting right strange, Cameron," she retorted and averted her eyes. Once more, the room caught her attention. The earl must be decadently rich. She'd never seen such luxury. But then her momentary interest faded, and she glanced back up into Cameron's eyes once more, insisting, "We'd best go. The earl might return straightway and find us here!"

"He'll not return this night." Cameron shook his head. "I swear upon my life, Kate. Trust me!"

"Ach, but 'tis getting harder to trust ye, Cameron." She sighed, shaking her head. "Ye've no reason to be here, and—"

"I've something for ye, lass." He interrupted, moving across the shadowed chamber to return holding out a small earthen flask. "'Tis water from the Pilgrim's Well."

In that moment, Kate forgot everything else.

She stared at the flask in his hands, speechless.

"Take it, lass." There was a warm smile in his voice.

Wondrously, Kate lifted her eyes to his face. "Is ... this why ye came here, Cameron?" she asked, her voice thick with emotion.

He hesitated. His eyes seemed tortured. "I've other matters to attend to here, Kate, but this is the one I enjoy the most." Gently, he placed the flask in her hands and cupped her fingers around it.

Heaving a deep sigh, she confessed, "I worry for ye so."

"Kate, I ... have words that must be said." He frowned, clenching his jaw tightly once again. "I should have told ye long ago..." He struggled for words a moment, but then fell silent and lifted his hand to stroke her cheek softly with his thumb instead.

"I *do* trust ye, Cameron," she whispered, overwhelmed with a flood of compassion. "Ye dinna have to tell me your true name. I trust your heart." Throwing her arms about his neck, she meant only to give him a comforting hug, but he was so distractingly handsome.

Ach, no man should be that handsome.

She couldn't resist pressing against his hard chest and as the desire flared in his dark eyes, she parted her lips for his kiss. He pulled her mouth to his, seizing it in a manner that all but took her breath completely away. For several splendid, intense moments, time stood still, and then he let out a ragged moan.

Tearing himself from her embrace, Cameron stepped back and struck the wall with his fist. "'Tis perilous for ye to stay here, lass," he swore, swallowing hard.

Dazed, it took her a moment to collect her thoughts, but then panic returned and she gasped, "I thought ye said the earl was gone for the night?"

She whirled as if to flee, but he caught her arm and pulled her against his chest.

"Forget the earl, lass. I meant 'tis dangerous to be here … with me," he groaned against her throat. And then he was nuzzling her neck, his chiseled lips burning paths of fire.

Sliding her hands up his muscled arms, she ran her fingers through his raven hair and whispered, "Ach, ye aren't dangerous, ye fool!"

"I'm cursed," he said huskily, and then drew back grimacing, dropped his hands as if to push her away.

The man's presence was overpowering, and she suddenly thought of nothing but the desire to feel the heat of his skin under hers. As he moved back, she locked her arms about his waist and swore fervently, "I'll break your curse! I'm not letting ye go, Cameron."

For a moment, she thought he would still push her away, but then he brought his lips to hers once more in a devastating, ravishing kiss, a kiss with a dark and rough edge to it. She gasped in surging desire and he stopped his exploration of her lips at once.

"I cannot indulge in these sweet imaginings!" He inhaled bitterly and cursed under his breath. "Ye'd best leave, lass, afore I go too far and make ye mine."

"I already am yours, Cameron. We both know it," she confessed. With a fingertip, she traced the dash in the middle of his chin and melded her body against his.

She felt him shiver against her, and then finally his chest heaved, as if he had laid down some great burden. With his dark eyes burning hers, his lips slowly descended, brushing against her cheek in a touch as soft as silk before capturing her lips in tender caresses.

Her breath quickened and his own matched it as the kiss deepened, and he plundered her lips with a raw, urgent hunger, and then crushing her against him, he lifted her in his strong arms and carried her to the adjoining chamber to lay her down on the magnificent, curtained bed.

Once again, he seemed to hesitate, appearing caught in some internal battle, but she would have none of it. Unleashing a wild passion that she had been aching to set free, she pulled him down and confessed, "I do believe I love ye, Cameron."

With a hoarse cry, he caught her close, his lips once more claiming hers in a masterful way that swept all other thoughts aside.

7

WHAT HAVE I DONE?

Kate stretched languorously, reveling in the softness before slowly opening her eyes.

She squinted in the darkness of the dimly lit chamber and frowned, unable to place herself. Heavy velvet embroidered bed curtains blocked the view of the window, but she could see enough of the pale pink dawn to know she had overslept.

Suddenly, she became aware of an arm curled lightly over her hip. Drawing back, she caught a glimpse of Cameron sleeping peacefully at her side.

Jolting bolt upright, she half screeched, "What have I *done*?"

Cameron sprang to his feet, his raven hair falling to half cover his face. The hard angles of his fiercely muscled chest and the masculine perfection of his powerful thighs posed bare for her to see.

Quickly, she averted her gaze, gasping in shock. "Ach, ye haven't a stitch of clothing on, Cameron!"

"Look to yourself, lass!" He swallowed visibly, turning pale.

Kate glanced down, and then the memories of the night flooded her all at once. Blushing furiously, she covered her blazing cheeks with her hands and gulped, "*What* have I done!"

Cameron's eyes flickered with dismay. "What have *I* done?"

Gathering the coverlets about her, Kate scrambled from the bed, searching for her shift and gown on the chamber floor.

"And Lady Elsa! How could I be so foolish?" she wailed. "She'll banish me for certain! What will become of my father now, and what if they catch us here, Cameron? We must leave at once! How could I have fallen asleep?" Close to tears, she wriggled into her shift. "My mother was right! I never stop to think! I'm such a careless, foolish—"

"We won't be caught." Cameron's voice sounded oddly muffled.

Glancing over, she saw him shrugging into his shirt. Ach, but the man was a brawny one, and his clearly visible, well-defined muscles succeeded in making her pulse quicken once again.

"Ye've naught to fear, Kate," he said in a restrained undertone, his head emerging through his fine, white shirt.

His dark hair stood on end and Kate smiled. And then nothing else mattered. In a slow, teasing manner, she approached him, walking her fingers up his arm and playfully tweaking his nose, before letting her finger trail down his cheek and along the dash in his chin. Suddenly, she pulled his head down and caught his lower lip between her teeth.

He responded at once, and the kiss was timeless, lingering, and sensual.

But then he pushed her firmly away and swore, "No more kisses! My touch is death!"

Astonished at his response, she frowned and stepped back. "Ach, ye fool, what has ye so worried? 'Tis not like ye are the Dreaded Earl of Death now, is it?"

She expected him to laugh, but he turned white. His expression was grim and his lips drawn into a thin line.

Confused, she slid into her wrinkled gown with a growing sense of dread but then spied the rumpled bed. "Ach, we've ruined the bed!" she gasped as her panic resurged. "We must tidy the chamber! And Lady Elsa—"

His strong hand caught her wrist and she looked up, startled.

"Ye've naught to fear, Kate," he said tightly. "At least from Lady Elsa and the like … ye have every right to be here with me. 'Tis your own doom ye must fear now…" His voice trailed off and he shuddered, closing his eyes.

Kate scowled at him, bewildered. "Ye make little sense, Cameron! And ye seem rightly displeased!"

"Aye, I am," he grated. "Last night should … never have happened."

At these words, a wave of shame and anger washed over her, and she found herself strangely silent.

As the silence between them lengthened, she tied her gown and slipped into her shoes. Glancing again at the bed, she repeated, "We canna leave the chamber so untidy—"

"I will see to it," Cameron whispered, abruptly moving to peer out of the window.

She could see the tense line of his jaw outlined in the dim light, every muscle in his body was taut as a bowstring.

"Ye must forget me! Do ye hear?" His tone was commanding, aloof. "I'll never wed ye, Kate."

Kate gulped at the unexpected words.

"Forget last night. It never happened," he continued. "I'll never touch ye again. Aye, I'll never see ye again, I swear it!" And then his voice broke.

Covering her ears, she whispered, "I canna understand ye now, Cameron."

Not knowing what she should think, she fled the chamber, grabbing the small container of water from the Pilgrim's Well on her way out.

Mercifully, the corridor was empty, and she quickly ran down the length of it, encountering the guards only upon exiting the royal apartments.

They scarcely looked her way.

Apparently, it was a common enough event to witness a maid scurrying away from the royal apartments in the light of the early morning. And, she thought bitterly, for precisely the same reasons she herself was flying across the courtyard.

The magic of the night now seemed only a dream. Cameron's riveting dark eyes and his rich, deep voice that had warmed her very soul had already faded, replaced by memories of his cold anger. Now, she could only hear his words over and over again in her mind. *I'll never see ye again, I swear it!*

The night had been a precious one, and she recalled Cameron's lean, hard body and tender kisses with a pang. What ailed the man? And his kiss, just moments ago, belied the words he had uttered only a moment later, and oh how harsh his words had been!

Confused, she made her way to Lady Elsa's chamber and stood staring at the latch, her courage failing her. The woman was probably furious. Most likely, she'd toss her out of the castle, or have her beaten for disobeying, or both.

Biting her lip, she took a deep breath and timidly pushed the door open.

The chamber was dark, the weak gray light of the morning unable to penetrate the shadows.

"Kate?" a voice queried sleepily from the bed. "Is it morning already?"

Could it be that Lady Elsa hadn't noticed her absence? Cautiously, she cleared her throat and murmured, "Aye, my lady."

Lady Elsa sat up slowly and stretched. "Did you enjoy the music?"

An enormous sense of relief washed over Kate. She expelled a grateful breath and knelt before the fire, stirring it into life as she meekly answered, "Aye, my lady."

She should feel guilty in deceiving the woman so, but she could scarcely confess she had spent the night in the Earl of Lennox's chamber rolling on the bed with a brawny outlaw. She blushed, scarcely able to believe it herself even as she felt a deep ache in her soul for how it had ended. Aye, and the end made little sense. She'd have to speak to Cameron, to understand what ailed him. Something was not right.

But first she had duties to attend to.

Yawning, Lady Elsa sat down in her chair, allowing Kate to brush her soft, lustrous hair with a fine, silver-handled brush. After a time, she eyed Kate critically. "You shouldn't sleep in your dress, 'tis far too rumpled for the feast. You'll have to change."

"Aye, my lady." Kate dipped her chin.

Unbidden, the sudden recollection of Cameron unlacing the green silk and tossing it over his shoulder paraded through her thoughts. She blushed, jerking the brush a little, but Lady Elsa didn't appear to notice. The woman chatted lightly as Kate arranged her hair, pinning a modestly adorned headdress to the silky mass, and assisted her in stepping into the fine garnet silk gown edged with the Spanish lace.

Smoothing her hands over the fine material, Lady Elsa gave a pleased, dreamy sigh. "The earl will not be able to resist me, Kate."

"Aye, my lady," Kate agreed obediently, kneeling to tie yarrow to the woman's shift. She felt strangely weary. As Lady Elsa chattered nervously about her earl, Kate's thoughts shifted to Cameron. Why had he kissed her so, and then, just moments later, pushed her away? Was love that cruel?

With a heavy heart, she watched Lady Elsa douse her lips in pearlwort and retire again to her chair before the fire, taking up the needlework once more to wait for the feast to begin.

It suited Kate well. She was oddly reluctant to talk. She stood at the foot of the bed, wading through her bewildered thoughts when a sudden knock at the door startled her. Lifting the latch, she discovered Maura standing on the threshold, holding out a small flask.

"Not now!" Kate hissed, glaring.

"I'll have what is mine!" Maura hissed back, her blue eyes icy cold. "Fill it, Kate. At once!"

Gritting her teeth, Kate grabbed the flask, casting a sidelong glance at Lady Elsa, but the woman was staring into the fire, lost in thought, a smile playing about her lips.

Turning her back so that she could not be seen, Kate hastily filled the small container with the pearlwort all the while sending dark looks Maura's way. Aye, her patience was wearing thin with the greedy woman. Returning to the door, she thrust the flask into Maura's outstretched hands.

The woman's eyes lit. "Aye, the Earl of Lennox will be mine afore the night."

"Aye," Kate muttered doubtfully.

"Ye'd best pray he is!" Maura threatened softly and then hurried away, humming a tune under her breath.

Kate watched her go with a feeling of trepidation. If the earl did not fall for the woman, she was in trouble. She heaved a sigh, hoping that he would. Her thoughts were interrupted as Lady Elsa announced it was time to attend the feast. After a last minute checking of the yarrow, and a dab more pearlwort upon her lips, Lady Elsa set out for Stirling's Great Hall with Kate trailing in her wake.

The day promised to be a beautiful one with not a cloud in the sky, and for a moment, Kate closed her eyes, enjoying the warmth of the sun on her skin. She hoped it would lighten her increasingly heavy heart, but it did little to ease the burden.

Her head was beginning to ache.

Ach, she'd never expected the day to turn so sour.

They were halfway across the courtyard when the door to the royal apartments opened, and a tall, stern-looking woman dressed in a blue silk gown and a pearl-encrusted headdress stepped out into the bright sunlight. Three grandly dressed women, one carrying a small gray dog with long silky hair, followed her closely.

"'Tis Princess Anabella!" Lady Elsa squeaked under her breath, coming to an abrupt halt.

Immediately, the tall woman's cold gaze turned their way. After a moment, she lifted her hand and slowly beckoned them to join her.

With noticeable reluctance, Lady Elsa complied.

"Princess Anabella." She bowed deeply before the woman in greeting.

Princess Anabella was a thin, middle-aged, red-haired woman of such unusual height that Kate found that alone intimidating. But there was so much more about her that inspired fear. Her eyes were sharp, intrusive, and her thin lips etched in disapproval as she towered over them, demanding, "And ye are?"

Remaining deep in her curtsey, Lady Elsa licked her lips nervously. "I'm Lady Elsa MacRae, of—"

"Cameron's ward?" The princess interrupted, raising a critical brow.

"Yes, my lady," Lady Elsa whispered in a wavering voice.

Kate blinked. Cameron? Surely, Lady Elsa's protector was not Cameron Stewart, the Dreaded Earl of Lennox? Ach, why had she not bothered to find out which earl protected her mistress? A ripple of horror washed through her, and she eyed the hem of Lady Elsa's skirts in dismay. What a fool she was! She'd given two women love potions for the same man! Sweet Mary, but she prayed the potions truly didn't work.

"Enough simpering!" The princess sniffed disdainfully. "Rise!"

Lady Elsa straightened, fluttering her hands nervously.

"Attend me at the high table, then," the princess ordered, adding, "Only because ye are the ward of my beloved kinsman." Whirling on her heel, she proceeded to the Great Hall with Lady Elsa submissively in tow.

Worried and biting her lip, Kate joined the other maids. If only she had heeded her mother's advice, and her father's, too. If only she had thought twice! The day was turning into a disastrous one, and she strangely wanted to weep.

Clenching her hands, she stepped into Stirling's Great Hall.

Lit with the light of a thousand candles, the Great Hall was a magnificent sight to behold. The tables lining the great chamber were already set with the most elaborate assortment of delicacies that Kate had ever seen. Silver bowls of oranges, braided loaves of bread, and platters of almond cakes already graced the tables as servants poured fine Rhennish wine from ornate flasks into silver-inlaid goblets.

Lads moved through the hall bearing pitchers of water, basins, and towels to wash the hands of the finely dressed nobles. Musicians attired in green embroidered satin played softly on recorders and lutes as jugglers and poets entertained small clusters of nobles near the massive fireplaces.

Princess Anabella grandly made her way to the high table to pause behind the king's empty chair. It was a massively carved chair with velvet cushions and a blue canopy, embroidered with the royal crest.

"Where is James?" She huffed, scowling deeply.

A man detached himself from a group of nobles nearby. It was almost comical, the way he strutted and postured as he made his way to the princess, but then Kate recognized him and all humorous thoughts fled. He was the nasal-voiced Thomas, the man who had threatened her with the erroneous warning for the earl he thought she knew.

Bowing low before Princess Anabella, he stretched out an elegantly ringed hand. "Your highness—"

Deliberately turning her back upon the man, Princess Anabella repeated, "Where is James? Why doesn't anyone answer me?"

Thomas straightened. His long face flushed darkly.

Spying a burly man with a red, bushy beard and a friendly, welcoming face, Princess Anabella waved curtly to him. "Archibald Douglas, come here at once!"

As Thomas stepped back, his cold eyes fell upon Kate, and a sudden smile flickered on his lips.

Kate swallowed uneasily. The man appeared to remember her. What if he hadn't been drunk that day? Worriedly, she stepped behind the woman carrying the princess' dog, but the sudden fanfare of trumpets announcing the arrival of the king distracted them all.

Rising on her tiptoes, Kate peered through the crowd to see the king making his way to the high table, his arms flung about the shoulders of his brothers, Albany and Mar. They were followed by an entourage of musicians, poets, and nobles.

The three brothers closely resembled each other, but with several contrasting differences. They were all tall and red-haired, but Albany and Mar were rugged, possessing an easy self-assured grace. The king was pale, edgy, and had an unhealthy look about him.

Kate watched them with interest.

She had never seen the king before. He rarely left the castle. She had only heard the rumors that most thought him an ill fit to be king and preferred Albany or Mar to rule the country in his stead. If she were to judge by appearances only, she was inclined to agree. However, she felt a twinge of shame at the thought. Simply because the man appeared weak, it did not mean that he was, and besides, what did she know of such weighty matters? She was simply a maid and grateful that she still remained one after her recent folly of the night.

Not wanting to think of Cameron, she moved closer to where Lady Elsa still hovered in the company of the princess.

"The mason, Thomas, is hardly appealing," Princess Anabella was saying tartly to the red-haired Archibald Douglas. "I fail to understand James' fascination with him. 'Tis scandalous."

Archibald laughed congenially, muttering to the princess in reply, but his eyes had locked upon Lady Elsa with open interest.

Lady Elsa, however, was looking elsewhere, and Kate guessed by the way the woman suddenly began to twitch that her protector was nearby.

With a rueful twist of her lip, she sighed.

Ach, how could she have given two women potions for the same man?

The thought suddenly brought a worrisome one to mind.

Maura had traded places with a serving maid so that she might meet the earl at the feast. Apprehensively, Kate searched the faces of the crowd, but when no sign of Maura appeared, she allowed herself some sense of relief.

It was short-lived.

A stone's throw away, a blonde head wove its way through the hall and Kate grimaced.

Maura.

Wearing a gown of red silk, Maura approached the high table with a provocative sway of her hips. Her lips glistened with pearlwort.

Kate held her breath, not knowing whether to feel pity, distress, or exasperation, as Maura stalked toward a tall man clad in black velvet bowing before the princess.

The man must be the earl.

"Maura!" Kate hissed as she walked in front of her, but if the woman heard, she gave no indication of it.

Biting her lip, Kate glanced back at the earl.

He stood with his back to her, inclining his head towards Lady Elsa now, but something about his movements caught her attention.

Frowning, she peered closer, but several musicians strolled by, affording Kate only a glimpse of a blushing, giggling Lady Elsa. And then the musicians were gone, and she could see the back of the earl's broad shoulders and dark hair.

Ach, but he seemed familiar.

Learning forward for a better look, she nearly collided with a group of servants bearing a roasted swan upon a silver platter.

"Back, wench!" one of the men growled as someone shoved her back against the wall.

Embarrassed, she stepped away, finding a new vantage point just in time to witness Maura touch the earl's arm and declare in a husky voice, "What a strong sword arm ye have, my lord!"

By the Saints, she prayed the plants did not work!

She eyed the man for any signs that would indicate that he was bespelled by either woman, but found herself immediately distracted.

There was truly something familiar about the man.

Had she seen him before? She couldn't place her finger on it. Was it the set of his shoulders? She wished he would turn around, so that she might see his face.

Lady Elsa was frowning at Maura, but Maura was so intent upon the earl that she hadn't noticed.

It would have been wickedly humorous if it were someone else's doing that both women were wearing pearlwort for the same man, Kate thought wryly. Holding her breath, she continued to eye the man curiously when it struck her.

His dark hair and unusual height reminded her of Cameron. She smiled, surprised at the similarities, when he turned.

Kate's heart stood still.

There was no mistaking the strong line of his jaw.

And only one man possessed those dark, expressive eyes.

Cameron stood there, tall and proud, clad in fine black velvets with the silver brooch he favored clasped about his throat.

Kate couldn't move.

She couldn't even think.

She could only watch as Maura lunged. He sidestepped her easily, moving back with a sinuous grace as she sprawled at his feet. He stared down at her with a flicker of annoyance.

The maids around Kate tittered.

Lady Elsa clutched her skirts and gasped as Maura scrambled to her feet, her cheeks staining a dark red, and it was then that Cameron turned his head and casually glanced back in her direction.

His face went blank and he froze.

Time stood still as their eyes met and locked.

Kate did not know how long they remained that way before the fair-haired Julian stepped into view. Clad in a white shirt with a fine plaid, the man leaned close to murmur in Cameron's ear.

Cameron did not respond.

Frowning, Julian followed his gaze to Kate, and then he went still, his lips parting in surprise.

It was then that a cold, nasty jolt of realization struck Kate.

They were both nobles.

Cameron *was* the Earl of Lennox, the Dreaded Earl of Death.

She couldn't breathe.

She watched with horror as Cameron shook off Lady Elsa's restraining hand and approached, his dark eyes boring into hers.

She knew she should run, but she was strangely rooted to the spot.

"Kate!" Cameron's long fingers grasped her shoulders, giving them a little shake. "Kate!"

She stared, unable to speak.

And then fair-haired Julian appeared. With a warm, sympathetic smile, the man dipped into an elaborate bow. "I am the Lord Julian Gray, my sweet Kate, and I am most pleased to make your acquaintance."

It had to be some horrible dream. "No!" she heard herself whisper.

Cameron winced and clenched his jaw, murmuring, "Forgive me, Kate."

Nodding at Cameron, Julian said the dreaded words, "And this, unfortunately, is Cameron Malcolm Stewart, Earl of Lennox, Lord of Ballachastell and Inchmurrin."

Kate closed her eyes.

Fate was cruel.

Ach, but he must have been amused at their first meeting. Her heart felt torn asunder. He had merely been playing her for the fool! And she had fallen for it, given herself to him, and even foolishly dreamt of wedding him and giving him bairns!

Now she understood his reaction only a few hours ago. Aye, an earl would never wed a mere maid. He'd used her for bed-sport and she'd blithely welcomed it. A deep anger rose, dispelling her stupor. Of its own accord, her hand reached up and slapped him across the face.

He didn't move or try to avoid the blow. He stood there. His hands clenched into fists.

Julian folded his arms and winked at her with an understanding smile. "Aye, I'd say he deserves more than that, Kate."

Then suddenly, Kate became aware of Lady Elsa shrieking and the gasps of those circled around her, and the full horror of what she had done struck her.

She had just slapped an earl. And not just any earl. One with blood ties to the royal family—a Stewart.

Swallowing bitterly, she forced her wooden lips to apologize, "Forgive me, my lord…"

The words stuck in her throat.

It was nigh impossible to think of him as a noble, but she had only to look at him to see that he was. How had she missed it? Why hadn't she stopped to think?

"I must have amused ye right well!" The words tumbled from her lips. "And I even swore that I loved ye!" She gulped back sudden tears.

"Forgive me, Kate," he whispered hoarsely.

She eyed him fiercely and vowed, "Never!" And then

remembering his station, belatedly stammered, "M-my lord."

"Kate, ye swore ye wouldn't judge me." He swallowed, his dark eyes radiating distress. "Mind ye, Kate, that ye swore that day in the woods, that ye would understand! Whatever it was—"

She blinked, and then retorted angrily, "I lied, ye fool!"

Again, the onlookers gasped.

Clapping her hand over her mouth, she gulped, "I-I meant to call ye my lord earl, my lord!" Tears threatened.

Cameron blanched, and dragging a hard breath, asked bitterly, "Is being an earl so unforgiveable? Is it worse than an outlaw?"

How could she answer the man? She longed to disappear, to run far away.

"What is the meaning of this, Kate?" Lady Elsa was asking.

Suddenly, it was all too much. Not knowing what else to do, Kate gathered her skirts and bolted.

A flurry of voices called after her, but she heard Cameron's rise above all others, "Let me go! I'll not lose her like this! Not like this! Leave me be!"

More voices erupted, but she paid them little heed.

Somehow, she reached the courtyard. She kept running, the commotion from the hall fading behind her as she stumbled on.

"Kate!"

She whirled.

Cameron had followed.

Angrily, she hoisted her skirts higher and flew down a flight of twisting, narrow steps but at the bottom, she came to an abrupt halt, barely retaining enough presence of mind to recognize the fact that she had stumbled into the royal gardens.

She could not proceed. She could not risk the severe punishment. She whirled to leave just as Cameron barreled around the last step and collided into her, slamming her back against the garden's stone wall.

They stood there, breathing heavily. Feeling his chest pressed against hers summoned unbidden memories of the night before. His voice had been soothing, gentle, and his lips had teased her into a multitude of pleasurable sensations.

How had it suddenly gone so wrong?

A gust of wind swept through the garden, snapping the royal pennants above them and breaking the spell.

Cameron stepped back. "I told ye to forget me, Kate," he said hoarsely, his dark eyes snaring hers. "Now, ye surely see why!"

Raising her chin, she replied tightly, "Aye. You are an earl. Ye'd never wed a lass such as me."

"Aye." He curled his hands into fists. "I'll not be responsible for another death." His voice was strangely thick.

At that, she paused. Everyone knew the Earl of Lennox had wed seven times, and three of his wives had given him daughters. She had not realized she could hurt even more. Closing her eyes, she whispered, "Ach, ye have bairns."

He didn't respond.

She took a deep breath, unsure of what to feel.

"I'll not see ye again, Kate." He finally broke the silence between them. "But I'll see ye taken care of. I—"

Tossing her head, she shoved him back, hard. "I'll not take a coin from ye. I'll pay ye back the shilling, and for the water from the

Pilgrim's Well." Glancing down at her gown, she suddenly realized exactly where it had come from. Yanking at the fabric, she added almost hysterically, "Aye and I'll be happy wearing my own clothing. I canna be rid of this accursed gown fast enough!"

He went white.

She turned her back on him then, and fled up the stairs, letting the tears flow unchecked down her cheeks.

Aye, she was done with Stirling Castle.

Once inside Lady Elsa's chamber, she quickly changed into her brown dress and tucking the water from the Pilgrim's Well in her sleeve, turned to leave only to find Maura and Lady Elsa standing at the door.

"And what potion have ye there, Kate?" Maura's sharp eyes were livid. "Is that how ye bespelled the earl?"

"Silence!" Lady Elsa ordered haughtily. Stepping close, she whispered through trembling lips, "Aye, the earl is a man, Kate. While he might happily bed a wanton like you when you strike his fancy, he'll never make you respectable. He'll choose a fine, upright lady, such as I, to stand by his side, someone of breeding and distinction. He'll never choose a whore. You are ruined! No good man will want you—"

"Silence, ye thoughtless lass!"

All three of them jumped back, startled to see Lord Julian Gray duck his head to step into the chamber.

"Come, my sweet." The fair-haired lord gently extended his hand to Kate. "Shall we quit this foolish place?"

Numbly, she allowed him to guide her out into the courtyard even as she heard Maura pleading desperately from behind her, "Don't go, Kate! Don't leave me! I want that potion! Ye have to make me bonny, Kate! Please, just make me bonny!"

Snorting at the woman under his breath, Julian pulled Kate along by the wrist through Stirling's gates to the town outside its mighty walls. Towering over her, the man kindly brushed a curl behind her ear before leaning down to plant a brotherly kiss on her forehead.

"Cameron loves ye, Kate," he said softly. "The foolish lad fears he's cursed and that his touch will cause ye harm, even death. The fool thinks to drive ye away to protect ye. Be patient with the man. He's given ye his heart."

Overwhelmed, Kate simply stared at him. Only the day before, those words would have made her heart sing. Now, she glanced away, disbelieving. And even if she were foolish enough to believe, the man was an earl. There was no hope in it.

"Ach, this story is not yet finished, lass," Julian said with an amiable chuckle. "But tell me where might I escort ye this fine day?"

Kate looked up into the bright sky. Only a day ago, she had thought the world to be turning into a fine and promising place. Now, she could see little promise anywhere.

"Thank ye kindly, my lord." She bowed into a deep curtsey. "But I'll take no more of your time. May ye have a good day."

With that, she turned on her heel and strode down Castle Hill.

Aye, she'd treat her father's eyes with the water from the Pilgrim's Well, and then they would both leave at once for Edinburgh. There was plenty of work to be had there. She'd pay the earl back his coin and then, as he had asked, forget him.

Aye, she had no choice but to forget him.

Hot tears threatened, but she slapped her cheeks, forcing them away. "Ach, ye are such a fool! Ye canna weep over this. Ye willna weep over this, ye fool!"

Finally back at Maura's cottage, she kissed her father in greeting and silently bathed his eyes until his gentle prodding finally induced her to speak. She had scarcely said three words before he asked her what ailed her and his understanding, tender hug unleashed the torrent of tears that she swore she would never shed.

With her head upon his lap, she confessed her folly, leaving nothing unsaid. Her thin shoulders shaking with despair.

"Ach, my wee bairn." Her father compassionately ran his palm over her head. "'Tis a tale as old as time—the love betwixt a lad and a lass."

"But he doesna love me," she whispered.

"If ye say so, my wee one," he replied. "But know ye this. I'll always love ye, and I know 'tis only your warm heart that led ye down this path. 'Twas the same path as your mother before ye, my wee bairn."

Surprised, Kate lifted her head.

"'Tis why she asked ye to think so often. She saw so much of herself in ye. But I never regretted that ye came to us only several months after we wed. My ship was months late, and 'twas a fair surprise to see your wee mother waiting for me on the docks with a burgeoning belly." There was a smile in his voice.

Kate froze.

Not only because of her parents' secret, but more so from the fact that she'd never once thought of the possible consequence of the night before.

Surely, it took more than once to make a bairn?

"Whatever the future brings us, my sweet wee one, we'll find our path together, I promise ye," her father was saying.

Overwhelmed, Kate held her father's hands tightly. They were prematurely aged, dry, and wrinkled. With a pang, she remembered they had always been strong, brown, and smelling of fish from the many hours on the lochs.

How could she take care of him?

And now she had a new concern.

Sweet Mary, she prayed she did not carry a bairn. How could she feed it?

Bowing her head, she clenched her fists.

Aye. This was a lesson she would never forget. She would not only think twice, but thrice from this moment forward.

8

THE PROPHECY

Cameron stood in the door of his chambers, unwilling to enter, staring at the freshly made bed with a sense of loss that threatened to undo him. Images of Kate danced through his mind. Aye, she had been the purest pleasure he had ever experienced.

How had he forgotten that fate denied him such pleasure?

What had he done?

He closed his eyes, filled with horror at his lack of control.

Never had he felt such a love. Aye, his time with her had been short, but he knew he loved the lass more than he loved anything.

What if he had already condemned Kate to an untimely death? There would be no penance for that crime.

He struck the door with his fist.

His behavior was unforgiveable.

And even if fate spared her and he had not consigned her to a life of imminent doom, he had most certainly broken her heart. He would never forget the look on her face when she had realized his identity. She had seemed lost. Forlorn. Betrayed.

While he wanted nothing more than to hold her in his arms for eternity, he loved her too much to deny her the best chance of a long life. Aye, he must love her enough to let her go and to never touch her again. Such a life would be an endless torture for him, but for Kate he could endure such loneliness.

Mayhap her broken heart would heal over time.

It was his lot to stand, watching from afar.

He drew a long, dragging breath and closed his eyes when a horrifying thought struck him.

No one in the Great Hall had missed the exchange. Now, his enemies knew his weakness. He wasn't a fool. In court, he knew those who willingly kissed his cheek in greeting would hardly hesitate to knife him or poison his food if it suited their purposes.

Now, Kate was a target.

Fear rippled through him, along with the sinking realization that it was already beginning. Already, he had set in motion the fate that would rob her of life.

Swearing loudly, he whirled and strode purposefully through the royal apartments to the chambers of Princess Anabella. He did not wait for her ladies-in-waiting to announce him. Shamelessly, he opened the door, waded through the shocked, gasping women, and entered Princess Anabella's privy chamber.

The princess sat at a large table, feeding her precious dog bits of waterfowl. She glanced up as he stood boldly before her.

"Aye," the woman said, taking one look at him. "Now ye have seen what ye've done, ye foolish lad."

He had always shared a special bond with the princess. Upon occasion, she had played the role of mother after his own mother had died giving birth to him. He winced. Even then, his touch had been death.

Stooping to place her dog upon the floor, the princess commented harshly, "I always warned ye that love was the worst danger of all."

Her expression was bitter. She had suffered two ill-fated marriages, both having ended in annulment. And she had loved each husband, only to experience the court intrigue that ripped them both from her side.

He suddenly found his voice. "Kate must join your household."

The woman pursed her lips and replied with a severe scowl, "Though 'tis dangerous for ye both if she remains outside the castle, having her here with me will be even more so if ye cannot keep your hands off the lass."

"I will never touch her again," Cameron whispered hoarsely. "I swear it!"

Princess Anabella rose from the table. She was an imposing figure and considered by many to be the most powerful woman in Scotland. She was definitely the most politically astute. "'Tis the only chance the lass has. If our enemies believe your heart lies elsewhere then she cannot be used as a tool against us."

Clenching his jaw, Cameron nodded.

"But after your spectacle this morning, 'twill take much convincing, and it may never be done, ye foolish lad." She shook her head in exasperation, sweeping her hands over her skirts as a hard expression entered her eyes. "Ye'll have to wed again, Cameron. And right quickly."

Cameron felt the color drain from his face.

"Ye'll wed your ward, Lady Elsa," Princess Anabella announced starkly.

"No!" He answered in a chilling tone. He'd never touch another woman but Kate. Aye, if he couldn't have her, he would turn monk.

"'Tis not your touch that is cursed, lad," the princess retorted, misunderstanding him. "'Tis your blood. Ye'll never love as others can. You are a Stewart. Ye'll wed your ward and suffer whatever fate has in store for ye."

"I'll not do it," Cameron replied. It was a vow never more fervently felt.

"Ye haven't a choice." The woman shrugged.

He watched her move to the window, stubborn and resolute, and then he replied with soft authority, "No. Ye haven't a say in this. Ye'll take Kate into your household this day. I'll never wed again. Not even Lady Elsa. Send for Kate at once and be swift."

Princess Anabella turned a shocked expression his way as he strode from the chamber, pushing through her ladies eavesdropping at the door.

"Cameron!" the princess shouted after him. "Love is only for fools! Ye must prove that ye no longer care for the lass or else 'twill be used against ye, if not us all!"

He paused, his hand on the latch, to whisper, "I'll never stop loving Kate."

Making his way to the royal stables, he ordered his charger to be made ready with haste, and shortly thereafter, pounded through Stirling's gates and down into the town.

Kate had refused his aid. He understood her anger. Ach, he deserved more than a slap on the face, but he would not let her suffer. He would take care of her, whether she willed it or no, and he knew right well how to do it.

Spurring his horse on, he galloped through the cobblestoned streets and down the tree-lined lane to Maura's cottage.

Dismounting, he entered without hesitation.

"Cameron?" Kate's father stood in the door of the back room, leaning heavily on a cane. "Kate isn't here, lad. She's gone to the almshouse to ask for aid—"

"The almshouse?" Cameron snorted contemptuously. Ach, but she was a wee stubborn lass. Did she truly imagine he'd allow her to throw herself at the mercy of an almshouse? Who did she think him to be? Setting his annoyance aside, he cleared his throat. "I've not come to speak to Kate, sir."

"Ah!" The man nodded once, moving back in invitation and holding out a shaking hand. "Pray enter, lad. Ach, forgive me! I should address ye properly, my lord."

Cameron caught his breath and flinched. "Then Kate … has spoken to ye?"

"Aye, my lord." Her father sat down heavily on the edge of his straw pallet and placing both hands upon his cane, leaned wearily against it. "The lass told me the truth of it."

"Then know that I'll never allow her near the almshouse, sir. I've come to see ye both well taken care of," Cameron swore in a strong, sure voice. "Princess Anabella will see to Kate, and I've come to ask what ye wish for yourself and I'll see it done."

The man sat still, his head cocked slightly to the side for several long moments, and then he questioned mildly, "Are ye trying to buy me, lad?"

"I am protecting Kate, sir," Cameron replied firmly.

The man nodded thoughtfully, and then asked, "I've one question for ye, my lord. And I beseech ye to answer it truthfully."

"Aye," Cameron promised with a firm nod.

"Do ye love my wee Kate?"

Cameron took a deep breath. Clenching his jaw, he whispered the truth, "More than life itself!"

Her father smiled. "'Twas in your voice from the beginning, lad, and it warms my heart to know that my Kate will be safe, even if I were to leave this world."

Cameron clenched his fists. "She'll never be safe with me." He could not lie to the man. "For my touch is death. I am a cursed man. Surely, ye've heard of the ill fate of my seven wives, and 'tis not for naught that I am named the Dreaded Earl of Death. But I swear upon my life that I will never touch her again." His voice shook with emotion and he paused a moment, and then finally managed to whisper, "I will pay for my sin by seeing her well taken care of the remainder of her life and ye in yours. I vow I will never lay a hand upon her again."

Leaning heavily on his cane, the man rose shakily to his feet and gave a snort. "'Tis a foolish vow, my lord, look around ye. Ye aren't the only one to encounter loss and misfortune. Life is harsh and 'tis only the love that makes life worth living. Once ye find it, dinna be so hasty to throw it away."

"Perhaps that is true," Cameron murmured, and then added darkly, "… for others."

Kate's father smiled a little, feeling his way to the tiny cottage window. His hands trembled as he fumbled with the latch. After watching him struggle a moment, Cameron reached over and gently pushed the shutters open.

The man stood there, taking several deep breaths of the fresh air before speaking softly. "I lost my sweet wife and youngest bairn, my livelihood as a fisherman, and I am now no more than a blind beggar, but I dinna call myself cursed. I have my wee Kate. I can still smell the fresh-turned earth. I can feel the heat of the sun and hear the call of the birds. Life is pain, lad, but life is also joy. Only ye can choose which way ye want to see it."

Watching the blind man stand there, leaning heavily upon a stick with shaking hands, Cameron suddenly felt ashamed. Aye, others suffered. There were many ways of suffering, he supposed, and clearly some had suffered far worse tragedy than he had.

He was not in the habit of considering that.

Feeling his way to the door, Kate's father smiled. "Aye, I'll accept your kind offer, my lord, and become your reminder."

"Reminder?" Cameron repeated, frowning a bit uncertainly.

"Aye, my lord, ye'll bring me into your personal household so I may sit on your hearth and remind ye daily that life is to be lived." The expression on the man's wan face was calm and self-assured, as one with deep knowledge of life. "Ye aren't living, my lord, if ye let the fear of loss keep ye from love."

"Mayhap it is not my fate to have love," Cameron responded bitterly.

The man shrugged. "'Tis a coward's answer, my lord."

Cameron's head snapped back. "Did ye just name me a coward?" he asked, astonished. No one had ever dared to name him a coward before. The man was just like his daughter.

"Aye." The fisherman's lips quirked in a half-smile. "My Kate has suffered much, yet she lives each day, cherishing the joy that comes her way. If such a wee lass can stand in the face of uncertain destiny, surely a man as powerful as ye can forge his own fate?"

Cameron blinked and opened his mouth to retort, but the man lifted a hand. "I've one last wish, my lord."

"Aye?" Cameron responded slowly, unsure of what to expect.

"Ye say ye love my Kate, enough ye would lay down your life for her, aye?"

"Aye." Cameron agreed. Why did he feel a net had just snared him? The fisherman was proving to be exceedingly crafty.

"Then, for her, can ye lay down your fear instead, lad?" her father asked softly.

Inexplicably, Cameron smiled, and it gave him pause. He hadn't thought to smile again. But though the man's request was a provoking one, he didn't believe the answer to be so simple. Still, he eyed the man curiously and asked, "Might I know your name, sir?"

"My name is John." The man bowed respectfully. "'Tis best we leave afore Kate returns from the almshouse to find me now your man whilst she is still hot with fury towards ye."

"Aye," Cameron agreed, imagining her passionate, brown eyes flashing with anger. Ach, how could he stay apart from her? 'Twas a cruel fate. "I've brought my horse for ye to ride, sir. I thought to bring ye away before she could flee with ye."

It was not long before the man was in the saddle and ready and Cameron led his charger back up the hill in a companionable silence, pondering the words they had shared as he eyed the outline of Stirling Castle somberly.

Once in the castle courtyard, he assisted the man to a nearby stone bench and sent for Sir Arval, ordering him to place Kate's father under the care of the royal physicians at once and that he be given quarters befitting a place of distinction within his household.

He left them there and made his way to the gardens, pacing for a time, deep in thought, amidst the peacocks wandering along the gravel paths.

Already, his heart longed to hold Kate close in his arms once again. The vows he had so passionately sworn that morning already seemed impossible to keep.

"Ach, I've been searching everywhere only to find the lovebird keeping company with the peacocks," a mirthful voice mocked, shattering his thoughts.

Cameron glanced back to find Julian standing behind him, arms folded, observing him in merciless amusement.

"'Tis too late, Cameron," the muscular young lord announced. His lashes lowered in a teasing look before he continued, "Even if I were to believe ye cursed—and I most sincerely do *not*—'tis too late with your wee Kate. Ye've already claimed the lass as yours. Turning from her now will not stop the hands of fate. Wed the lass and be done. She'll make a stunning countess."

Cameron expelled a deep breath.

It was true. He was behaving foolishly now. It no longer mattered if he were cursed or not, a coward or a fool. His feet were already upon the path.

Closing his eyes, he took a deep breath and whispered, "What have I done?"

"Ye've fallen in love." Julian shrugged and then admitted, "Ach, I'm half in love with the wee, feisty vixen myself."

Cameron turned his head away, looking out over the green grass swaying in the wind. What was to be done now?

"But I did not come to speak of love," Julian's deep voice continued. "I came to escort ye to the king's privy chamber. The Flemish astrologer has arrived, and we've both been summoned."

Lost in thought, Cameron followed him in silence as they returned to the royal apartments and made their way to the king's privy chamber.

It was a luxurious room with tapestry-lined walls, ornate chairs, and finely crafted rugs. The princes, Albany and Mar, were already present, standing before several portraits hung next to the fire, and as Cameron and Julian entered, they briefly glanced over their shoulders with grim expressions before returning their gaze back upon the portraits.

Cameron joined them to see a freshly painted portrait of the king in a gilded, golden frame. Hung next to it was a slightly smaller likeness of Thomas Cochrane.

The four men exchanged glances.

After a few moments, they moved to the table set with platters of almond cakes, a silver bowl of nuts, and several flasks of fine Rhennish wine.

"Aye, so 'twas your mistress I saw upon the road then, Cameron." Albany broke the silence after tossing back a goblet of wine. "'Tis clear now why ye wished to hide her from me. If her passion in bed is anything like—"

"Mind your courtesy," Cameron warned coolly.

Albany snorted and there was a cold glitter in his eye. Taking a nut from the bowl, he cracked it. "Are ye so protective of your whore then?"

Mar slammed his goblet on the table and eyed his elder brother with open disapproval. "Do ye have no honor left? Beseech forgiveness from our cousin at once!" the youngest prince demanded.

Cameron blinked in surprise at them both, at Albany, for his surprisingly coarse conduct and at Mar for his sudden strength. Mar had always lived in the shadow of his brothers and though loved for his honor and renowned for his skill as a warrior, he had always been the quietest of the three.

"Must I beseech forgiveness for telling the truth?" Albany sniffed with an indifferent shrug. "Aye, she is fetching, though she is of low origins. But origins matter little in the bed." He laughed, as if expecting the others to join in, but his mirth faded when only silence met his words.

"Ach, but the Borderlands have changed ye." Mar turned away in disgust. "I scarce recognize either James or ye anymore. And to think the three of us once stood so fast, vowing our life's blood to keep Scotland strong and free."

"Scotland is strong and free the last I heard tell." Albany smiled, but the smile was hard, cold. "We are not yet minions of England's king."

Cameron moved to stand before the fire, casting a side-length glance to where Julian had retired to lounge lazily in the windowed recess, giving the appearance of outright boredom. But Cameron knew well enough he was listening acutely and had not missed one word of the exchange.

A melancholy voice broke the tension in the room.

"What ails the Stewarts that they only find love in the baseborn?" the king questioned mournfully as he strode into the chamber dressed in a heavy brocade doublet with gold thread and a linen collar trimmed with lace in the fashion of the French. He moved to lay a hand upon Cameron's arm in a comforting gesture. "What do ye need from your king, dear cousin? Shall the wee lass be made a lady?"

"Ach, the way ye dispense titles to the riff raff of Scotland, we'll soon be a land of nobles with none left to swing a scythe!" Albany pounded his hand on the table in a flare of anger.

It took Cameron a moment to quell the anger rising in response to Albany's indirect insult of Kate, but he accomplished it with no outward sign. He could not allow emotion to cloud his sight. He eyed Albany with unease. Never before had he seen this side of the man. Aye, as Mar had said, becoming Warden of the Marches had changed him.

Mar stood with his arms folded, feet planted widely apart and a flush of anger staining his handsome face. "I find your conversation this evening ill company, Albany." The young prince eyed his brother contemptuously.

"Silence!" The king frowned at both of his brothers, but more so at Albany. Adopting a slightly guarded tone, he asked, "Would ye see Scotland ruled differently, Albany?"

"Aye." Albany tossed his head, nodding his chin towards Thomas' portrait hanging on the wall. "And I am not alone."

The brothers glared at one another.

"And ye, Mar?" The king turned to the youngest of the three.

"I will ever be mindful my sworn duties to my sovereign king, your majesty." The red-haired prince bowed deeply but then straightened to add, "But there are some matters that should be … dealt with, for the sake of Scotland." He pointedly stared at the portrait.

The king's jaw clenched.

Cameron held still.

The three Stewart brothers had always shared a close bond, unusually so, and while there had been rumors upon occasion, that both Albany and Mar were better fit for the throne, and in fact seeking it, anyone that truly understood them thought the rumor a preposterous one.

Suddenly, Cameron was no longer so certain.

The nasal voice of Thomas Cochrane cut the silence. "My liege lord, it is time."

Thomas Cochrane stood in the door of the king's privy chamber, wearing a strikingly similar costume to the king, but with a rich cape trimmed with fur flung over his shoulder and the heavy gold chain about his neck.

A smile hovered on his lips.

It was a calculating smile and one that caught Cameron's eye. The man was clearly pleased at the rising tensions between the brothers, but he turned with an elegant sweep of his hand and announced, "May I present Baldric Andrews, the most esteemed Flemish astrologer, your majesty?"

Baldric Andrews was a stocky, muscular, middle-aged man, with thin gray locks clinging to the sides of his balding head. His piercing gray eyes swept over the faces in the room as he sank into a low bow before the king, kissing the hand imperiously offered to him.

"Rise," the king commanded. "Take refreshment ere we speak of your prophecy. Come."

Leading him to the table, the king flicked a finger at Thomas in a silent bidding to pour the wine, and as Andrews nervously sipped it, Cameron joined Julian in the windowed recess.

"A most entertaining evening," Julian scoffed ironically. "And methinks 'twill only become more so."

Cameron did not reply. Leaning against the wall, he tapped a thoughtful finger as Thomas glanced his way.

Setting the wine flask aside, the man strolled over to join them.

"And a good evening to ye both, my lords." Thomas bowed respectfully before raising a brow at Cameron. "If I can be of service to ye, my lord, ye have but to ask, and it will be done."

There was no doubt he was referring to Kate. That Thomas might weave Kate into some ruthless, vengeful plot made his flesh crawl, and Cameron found himself uttering, "The pleasure of the lass has already past. I confess now that she knows my true name, I have quite lost interest. My concern lies with Lady Elsa." Ach, let the man think that he intended to wed Lady Elsa.

Julian stirred.

Thomas blinked, unable to hide his surprise when Albany's rough voice inserted itself into the conversation.

"So ye've lost interest in your wee mistress, have ye?" the prince asked with a slow smile. "Then ye should care little if I play with her now."

"'Tis too late for the likes of ye, Albany." Julian rose to stretch lazily and then stared coolly down at the man. "I've had quite the busy afternoon with the lass, and I'm not the kind to share."

The vein on Albany's temple throbbed.

"Come," the king ordered, interrupting the exchange and taking his seat at the head of the table. "Let us hear the ominous words of this most esteemed astrologer."

Reluctantly, they moved to the table as Andrews, looking very much like he would rather be anywhere else, took the chair appointed to him.

"Speak more of your prophecy," the king commanded. "And leave naught unsaid."

"I am most honored to speak, your majesty," the astrologer replied in heavily accented words. "But I must first have my books."

Albany snorted with impatience as a lad entered, carrying several large, leather-bound manuscripts and placing them before the man. And then Andrews began to flip through the pages, providing a detailed explanation of the signs and labors of the months to the attentive king.

Paying little heed to the prattling astrologer, Cameron focused his attention on Thomas.

The man stood behind the king's chair, at times laying a hand upon his majesty's shoulder and applying pressure. Each time, the king responded by questioning the astrologer further, oblivious to Albany and Mar's rising impatience.

"And that represents the lion, to be devoured by its whelps during the month of hay threshing, your majesty." Andrews tapped the manuscript illustrated with stacks of hay, indicating the month of June.

"Then there is time yet!" The king heaved a sigh of relief. "Nigh on a month to gain clarity."

"There is a viper in our midst," Thomas murmured with a frown of displeasure. "A month is precious little time to the deal with weighty matters such as this."

"Pah!" Albany slapped his hand on the table, rattling the goblets and startling them all. "Must we sit here and listen to these fools babble?"

"Send for Bonatti and Roger at once, Thomas. And Andrews must stay here at court until this danger has passed." The king deliberately ignored his brother. "We shall seek further divine guidance before taking any action. We will consult for deeper meanings to this prophecy."

"Ach, ye turn to more witches and sorcerers for wise counsel?" Albany scoffed in outright disdain. "Ye seek to lock yourself in your chambers, reading books—"

"Hold your tongue, knave!" King James shouted an interruption. "Leave us, at once!"

"Right gladly, ye fool!" Albany thundered. "If ye could only see what a laughing stock ye've become! If ye really thought ye stood in danger, ye should be raising arms, not slavering over manuscripts by candlelight!"

He marched out of the room, slamming the door.

Mar rose to his feet, his lips drawn in a thin line. "I will take my leave, your majesty," he respectfully addressed his brother but shot a look of disdain at Thomas. "But I would ye remember the oath we took as brothers. If there is indeed a whelp to rise against ye, it comes not from the litter of Stewarts. I will begin searching from whence it comes."

Thomas paled.

The king watched his youngest brother go, and then turned to Thomas and Julian. "See to the needs of our esteemed astrologer. Cameron, tarry a moment, we would speak with ye in private."

Cameron remained seated as the king waited for the chamber to empty.

He was clearly troubled, repeatedly clenching his fingers into fists and licking his lip, and when they were alone, he turned at once to Cameron. "Tell me truly, fair cousin. Do ye believe Andrews speaks the truth … that the king of Scotland will die at the hand of his own brothers?"

"Brothers?" Cameron repeated in surprise. "And why would ye think it were your brothers, your majesty? Andrews speaks of whelps, surely more akin to offspring than a brother?"

The king rose to his feet, pacing nervously before the table. "Thomas has pondered of late if the true meaning refers to Albany. Our own issue is yet too young to rise against and slay us in but a month."

Cameron could not prevent a sound of exasperation escaping from his lips, but it was so soft that the king did not appear to have noticed it. Clearing his throat, he replied in a cutting tone, "And I would ask why Thomas is so quick to lay blame at your brother's door, your majesty."

The king's response was an unexpected one.

"Ye, too?" His eyes narrowed in anger. "Thomas is ever unjustly ridiculed and treated unfairly. We would have thought that ye would have understood, having love for a baseborn lass. We would have thought ye could see that all men are very much the same, in love and loyalty at least."

Cameron eyed the king, surprised. "Then your loyalty lies more with Thomas than with your own brothers?"

King James turned cold all at once. "Leave us!"

The sun was low in the sky when Cameron stepped out of the royal apartments to find Julian waiting for him with his favorite chestnut charger, saddled and ready to ride.

"What is this?" Cameron asked, taking the reins.

"Ye'd best see to Mar," Julian informed him gravely. "He just left, ordering his retinue of attendants to remain behind."

"And they let him ride alone?" Cameron raised a brow, leaping into the saddle.

He didn't wait for an answer, touching spurs to his horse's flanks, he sprang away, galloping down Castle Hill. At Stirling Bridge, he caught sight of Mar hurtling towards the moors, riding low over his horse's neck.

Cursing under his breath, Cameron urged his steed after him.

The clouds above grew darker, heavier with imminent rain, as he flew over the heather moors after the prince. He pounded inexorably closer, until upon the rise of a hill, Mar suddenly jerked the reins of his horse and wheeled around.

In a moment, Cameron was at his side.

"I knew it would be ye, Cameron." Mar greeted him quietly, almost sadly as he stiffly dismounted. Facing the chill wind sweeping down from the highlands, he pointed to the River Forth winding below them. "Do ye recall the summers we spent as children, sailing the river, fancying to be the Knights of the Round Table? We swore then to uphold honor and duty above all else."

"Aye," Cameron agreed softly, alighting from his charger to join the prince.

"It seems my brothers have forgotten," Mar murmured, shaking his head as if he were bewildered. "I would we were back in times gone by, when as lads we stole the royal hounds from the kennels and falcons in the mews to hunt stags in the forest and hawk on the moors."

"Aye." Cameron expelled a heavy breath. "But those days seem gone forever, Mar. Now, I fear we tread upon paths once deemed impossible."

"Meaning?" Mar asked, training his eyes on the desolate expanse of moor rising before him.

"I fear Thomas and his power over the king," Cameron answered truthfully. "I fear both ye and Albany are in great danger. He's all but convinced his majesty that his brothers are the whelps of whom Andrews speaks. He seeks to turn James against ye both."

Mar did not reply. He stood silent, staring unseeing over the gathering gloom as the weather turned foul and rain began to fall. Finally, he spoke. "I do not fear my own brother, Cameron. He was born a poet, not a warrior. His heart is true, both Albany and I know it."

"Aye, I do not doubt your brother's heart." Cameron wiped the rain from his face. "But I fear the trouble that Thomas is stirring. He may bring about events where the king has no choice but to obey the laws of treason."

"Treason?" Mar shrugged. "I've done naught to bring about that concern."

"Thomas will not need the truth," Cameron warned. "'Tis best ye stay out of his sight, at least until June has past. Perhaps ye should visit France?"

For a moment, it seemed as if Mar entertained the suggestion, but then he gave a short laugh. "Thomas is ridiculously fond of finery, do ye not think?"

Cameron arched a brow.

"What do I have to fear from a mason intent only on gathering gold trinkets?" The young prince pointed ahead in the gloom. "Do ye see the stag, Cameron?"

Turning slowly, Cameron caught sight of a stag a short distance away, watching them from beneath the shelter of a lone tree. Mar clapped his hands and it started, bounding away.

"I'm that stag, dear cousin. Have ye ever witnessed a mason slay a stag with a brick? Thomas is no match for me." With a soft chuckle, Mar mounted his horse and pointed back towards Stirling Castle. "I've lost my taste for riding in this foul weather. Shall we end this night with wine and fair maids?"

He didn't wait for an answer. With a cry, he spurred his horse back down the hill, charging across the moors to the castle rising in the distance.

Cameron heaved a sigh and slowly mounted his charger, murmuring, "And so the folly begins. I would I had none of what is to come."

9

THE PRINCESS

Kate entered Maura's cottage, expecting to see her father but finding two messengers in his stead, one dressed in the livery of the Earl of Lennox and the other wearing the crest of the Royal Stewarts emblazoned upon his tunic.

"Princess Anabella summons ye at once to her chambers," the princess' man announced formally.

The other man stepped forward. "The most esteemed John Ferguson has joined the household of Cameron Malcolm Stewart, the Earl of Lennox, and kindly requests your company at the castle forthwith."

Kate stared at the second man in utter shock. "Joined … the earl's household?" she gasped.

But the men did not repeat their messages. Anxious to return to the castle, they spun on their heels and exited the cottage, leaving her to return on her own.

Astonished, Kate sank down on the straw pallet.

What had her father done?

Outside the cottage, darkness gathered and the wind rose, driving the rain against the shutters. She did not know how long she sat there, dumbfounded, staring at the cobwebs on the ceiling and listening to the beating rain.

She didn't permit herself to think of Cameron.

It hurt too much to know that she would never again caress his face or trace her fingers along the dash of his chin.

Aye, she was furious with the man. Or she was desperately trying to be.

Then she stomped her foot.

Ach, if she were honest, her anger had already faded but it had been replaced by a hurt too deep to bear.

It was simply too painful to see him again, and her father knew that. His gentle, understanding words had proven he truly understood.

They had made plans that very day to move to Edinburgh forthwith. And she had gone to the almshouse to see if any traveling that way might provide her father with transportation.

So why had her own father betrayed her?

Picking up the empty flask that had contained the water from St. Fillans, she idly twirled it in her fingers, but then it reminded her of Cameron and his dark, passionate eyes.

She dashed it to the hearth, hoping to be angry once again, but experienced only a deep pang of sorrow.

How could her father join the earl's household?

He was *her* father, not Cameron's!

She might fail in finding her anger for Cameron, but she could summon it for her father. Aye, she'd make her way back to Stirling Castle and have a word with the earl's new man, the new one named John Ferguson, and she'd remind him that his loyalty lay with his devoted daughter, the one who had struggled to bring him back from the brink of death these past long months.

Irritably, she threw her worn plaid over her head and stepped out into the darkness, squeezing her eyes shut against the fierce sheets of stinging rain.

She had scarcely taken a dozen steps when hooves thundered behind her, and she found herself swept upon the back of a massive chestnut charger and encircled by an arm of steel. Before she could respond, Cameron's deep voice rang in her ear.

"Allow me to escort ye to Stirling Castle, lass."

At once, her heart fluttered, and a lump rose in her throat. She couldn't have replied, even if she had desired to, the relentless wind and rain rendered conversation impossible.

The ride proved a bittersweet one.

Though his touch reminded her that he wasn't hers to keep, wounding her heart even more, she closed her eyes and leaned against him anyway, vowing to cherish each moment as the horse struggled up Castle Hill battling the wind and rain.

Aye, she would burn every second of this into her memory forever, to keep her company in the long, lonely nights ahead.

All too quickly, the horse trotted through the gates, across the courtyard and to the stables. As the stable lads sprang to open the doors wide, a warm, welcoming light greeted her along with the comforting smell of hay and horse.

It was only after Cameron swung her down from the back of his massive beast that Kate allowed herself to glance up into his dark, passionate eyes.

It was a mistake.

At once, she wanted nothing more than to throw herself into his arms. Bitterly, she grimaced and whispered, "I liked ye better as an outlaw."

"Well, now ye must deal with me as your dreaded lover!" Cameron's dark eyes narrowed in a thunderous expression. His gaze turned suddenly hot and intense.

Aye, she was defenseless against the sensual power of the man. He didn't even have to speak. His mere presence alone melted her resolve to flee. She couldn't let him make her stay, there was no future for her in his life. She knew that too well.

Averting her eyes, she turned her head, but he reached out and lightly traced the line of her jaw before moving his thumb to smooth her frown away.

"I love ye, Kate," he confessed, his voice soft and husky.

She sent him a wounded look. To speak those words now was entirely unfair. "Much evil is done in the name of love," she said, her voice shaking with emotion.

He pulled her close, holding her head against his shoulder, and she could feel his hot breath upon her neck. "I've never loved afore, and I'll never love any again as I love ye. Julian was right. It is already too late. Mayhap we should—"

She pushed him away, afraid of what she might do should he continue his sweet words. "Well, ye clearly loved enough to father three bairns," she interrupted, seizing upon the first thought. It was a jealous one, but the subject of bairns had been uppermost in her mind the entire day, ever since her father had brought the possibility to her attention.

A startled look crossed his face, but he answered readily enough. "The wee lassies ye speak of are not mine, Kate. I've given them my name, but the king is their father, and 'twas an arrangement that suited us both at the time." He tilted her chin up with an elegant finger and then planted a reverent kiss on her forehead. "I've never bedded a lass afore ye, and I'll never bed another."

Kate blinked in surprise as a healthy blush dusted her cheeks. It took her several, long moments before she managed to tear her eyes away from his. "'Tis impossible to believe," she said finally. "The tales of your exploits are well known and spoken of even in the alehouses."

"Aye, well, wagging tongues aren't necessarily the best sources for truth," Cameron observed drolly. "'Twas ye who proved to be the thief, lass, for ye quite stole my heart."

Tears threatened. "Dinna say such sweet words to me," Kate whispered hoarsely. "I'll have none of them!" She couldn't let herself. It would only hurt more, and the pain was already unbearable.

He drew a long breath and then murmured, "The princess is expecting ye, Kate. Stay with her until I've sorted this matter. I'll not have ye suffer for my sake. There are those here that would use ye cruelly to reach me. And I cannot bear that."

The words jolted her back into the harsh reality she now lived. Stepping away, she curtsied and whispered, "Aye, my lord."

She could tell that he regretted the words the moment he heard her response, but she suddenly wanted to be gone. This path could only end in heartache. She could not knowingly let her emotions guide her into folly. Ignoring his pleas to stay, she gathered her plaid close and fled the stables.

She would see Princess Anabella first. She could not yet face her father. Within three words, he would hear the pain in her voice and offer sympathy that would be her undoing.

She had no time for tears.

Frowning at herself furiously, she slapped her cheeks and ran through the cold rain to the royal apartments. The guards let her through and pointed the way. In moments, she stood dripping at the door of Princess Anabella's chambers, cringing under the critical gaze of her ladies-in-waiting.

"Ach, ye canna see her highness in such a state!" one gasped in shock.

"How can the princess speak with a ragamuffin?" Another pursed her lips, her fine nostrils flaring.

"Then fetch her one of your gowns, Mary." A dark-haired, sultry-eyed woman with wide, pouting lips and an arresting presence stepped through the others. "I am Lady Nicoletta di Franco, and I am most honored to make your acquaintance, Kate."

Kate sank into a deep curtsey, but the woman caught her elbow.

"No, you shall not bow to any in this room," Lady Nicoletta ordered in a husky tone and smiled, a secret sort of smile, as the other women gasped, affronted. Turning to them, she raised an amused brow. "Have a care! You are fools if you cannot see that soon you will bow before *her*. Bring her your finest gown, Mary, and give wings to your feet!"

"Then ye be the fool, Nicoletta!" The one called Mary rolled her eyes spitefully. "'Twas only this evening the earl himself swore to wed Lady Elsa. 'Tis the talk on everyone's lips!"

The words cut Kate's heart like a knife, and she suddenly could not breathe.

"And you, Mary, can never see further than an inch afore your nose," Lady Nicoletta responded coolly. "You would do well to understand the hearts of those you watch. Mark my words, the earl will make this one countess or turn monk the remainder of his days. Have I ever been wrong?"

Apparently, she hadn't because the women of the chamber fell silent and Mary cleared her throat. "Shall I bring the gray gown with the pearls or do ye think the blue satin would suit her better?"

Kate was grateful the women had moved away. She closed her eyes and took a deep breath. Of course, she knew she could never wed the man, but had he already promised himself to Lady Elsa? She wanted to run away and weep, but Lady Nicoletta gave her no opportunity.

"Do not listen to rumors, Kate," the woman advised softly. "And do not doubt your earl."

Kate frowned. It made little difference. Cameron could never be hers.

Leaning forward, Lady Nicoletta placed a finger on Kate's lips. "You have much to learn. Silence will be your friend until you understand the game. Be silent and watch."

Perplexed, Kate sealed her lips and allowed the women to dry her hair and clothe her in a fine gray gown with pearls sewn in the bodice. As Lady Nicoletta brushed and arranged her hair, she began to dispense advice in a firm, imperious tone. "In court, there are rumors and truth. The truth is seldom heard. You must watch for it in fleeting looks and false laughter, in who speaks to whom—"

"And who beds whom!" Someone giggled.

"Ach, *she* knows that!" another hissed spitefully.

Kate felt her cheeks redden with shame.

"And you must never betray what you feel." Lady Nicoletta searched her face with a raised brow.

Kate sighed and answered with heartfelt sincerity, "I'll never be a creature of the court, my lady. I am a lowly fisherman's daughter, and 'tis far too late for me to learn such wily ways."

Several of the ladies murmured soft sounds of sympathy, and even Mary suddenly fell silent.

With a knowing smile, Lady Nicoletta leaned close and whispered in her ear, "Some are born with the skill. Already, you have begun to melt their icy hearts. I pray you will remember me, my lady, for I may one day beseech a favor from you."

Kate frowned in confusion.

"What secrets are ye sharing?" someone complained as Lady Nicoletta slipped her arm around Kate's waist, and guiding her to the adjoining chamber, announced her to the princess.

Princess Anabella sat at the table, poring over a manuscript with her small dog upon her lap. She glanced up as Kate entered and absently began fingering the diamond brooch on the bodice of her jeweled satin gown. Her dangling gold earrings glittered in the candlelight.

"Your highness." Kate sank so low that she lost her balance and slipped to her knees.

The princess burst into a startled laugh.

With her ears flaming red, Kate struggled to her feet. "Forgive me, your highness," she said through dry lips, wanting nothing more than to cry. "I truly belong in the kitchens and not in your presence bedecked in such finery."

Rising to her feet, the princess advanced, still holding her dog. "Ach, ye foolish lass." The austere woman's voice sounded mildly annoyed. "Ye have placed my beloved kinsman in the greatest danger. How could ye not know?"

"I thought he was a thief, your highness!" Kate whispered in her defense.

"A thief?" The princess paused mid-step. Frowning a moment, she scowled. "I have asked how ye failed in knowing your outburst would only place him in great danger! Why do ye speak of a thief?"

Kate swallowed, wishing herself anywhere but under the woman's critical eye.

"Speak!" The woman ordered sharply.

In halting words with eyes averted, Kate recounted her first meeting and the resulting misunderstanding of Cameron's identity. When she was finished, she cast a side length glance to discover, to her utter astonishment, that the woman's lips held the hint of a smile.

"'Tis an entertaining tale," the gruff woman admitted, returning to her chair to lean back in it comfortably. "But ye are a fool if ye think to change a man's heart."

"Aye, your highness," Kate agreed, keeping her gaze focused on the floor.

"And what would ye say, if I were to tell ye that Cameron will wed Lady Elsa by midsummer?" The princess looked directly at her.

Kate swallowed, striving to choose her words carefully. "I … would wish him well, your highness," she finally said. Her heart felt heavy, and she closed her eyes tightly, refusing to shed tears.

"Ach!" The princess expelled an exasperated breath. "I am not as hard-hearted as I may seem, lass. I would ye could share your lives, for I can see ye truly love the man, but only tales have happy endings. A man of his position must wed as politics require. There is little room for love. Such is the ugliness of life."

"Aye, your highness," Kate whispered. "I willna stand in his way. I was on my way to Edinburgh when I received your message." She clenched her hands to give herself strength. She absolutely would not weep and especially not in front of this woman.

"I am prepared to take ye into my household, to protect my kinsman," Princess Anabella stated briskly. "But ye'll see naught of him from this time forth. His time of dallying with ye is over. Others could use ye against him, and 'tis too dangerous for us all should that happen. Do ye understand?"

Her words reminded Kate at once of Thomas' warning. It seemed so long ago. Ach, but the man hadn't been drunk. He'd sent a warning to Cameron and she had blithely tossed it away. She had been naïve! She had no business being involved in court affairs.

"What is it?" the princess asked, watching her face.

"I understand, your highness." Kate licked her dry lips. She could never place Cameron in danger. She still loved him. She always would. "I'll not bring harm upon him, I swear it."

The princess nodded firmly, apparently pleased with her answer. "Each of the ladies who serve me comes from the finest of families in

Scotland, France, and Italy, and each possesses talents that I find useful. Are ye skilled with the needle?"

She had no skill that a princess would find desirable, and by the sharp glint in the woman's eye, it was obvious the princess knew it as well.

Were court games always so cruel, so humiliating?

With a twinge of anger, she curtsied again and replied honestly, "I fear I have no talent to offer ye, your highness. I am a fisherman's daughter who has only her father left in this world, and I live to enjoy what beauty I may each day for I have seen it taken away in the blink of an eye."

Princess Anabella's gaze hardened. "'Tis a folly of the young, to believe there is beauty in the day. When ye have lost enough, ye'll see there is no more beauty to be had."

"Then I will remember what I have encountered thus far, your highness." Kate murmured, thinking of the days she had spent sailing on the lochs with her sister, the laughter she had shared with her mother, and the glorious night with Cameron. Aye, she would live in memories, if she must.

"'Tis your pure heart that is your talent, child." Princess Anabella's voice cut through her thoughts. "But few hearts are strong enough to resist power and greed. I shall be most curious to watch how ye fare at court."

Unsure of the expected response, Kate curtsied again.

"Nicoletta!" The princess called, waving a dismissive hand. "Take her away."

After showing her where she was to sleep and giving her a chest, several fine gowns, and a silver-handled brush, Lady Nicoletta permitted her to slip away to visit her father. But by the time Kate finally found him, he was snoring soundly in a soft, feather bed.

Kate stood quietly by his side, looking down upon him.

Clad in fine clothing and sleeping peacefully, her father already looked younger. Several flasks of water from St. Fillans stood on a nearby table, along with the remains of a roasted chicken and a goblet of wine. The chamber was small but finely furnished with even a rug and a silver candlestick.

A wave of emotion rose to engulf her. Her father looked so comfortable. She could never provide for him so. And then her anger evaporated. If being Cameron's man afforded him the opportunity to be well, then how could she deny him the chance?

Glancing around the room, she knew she was viewing Cameron's handiwork, and the tears she had refused to shed slid freely down her cheeks.

Why had she found Cameron only to lose him?

Why was fate so cruel?

Slowly, she backed out of the chamber and softly closed the door. Resting her head upon the door a moment, she wiped the tears from her cheeks and took a deep breath.

Returning to Princess Anabella's chambers, she ignored her pallet spread next to the sleeping Lady Nicoletta and instead spent a sleepless night, sitting at the window and staring out into the darkness.

The princess did not call for her the following morning but instead set out for the daily feast with her dog and two other ladies in tow, leaving the remaining ladies-in-waiting to stay in her chambers.

Time crawled.

Kate moved about restlessly, listening to the women gossip as one played the lute, and the others labored over their needlework.

Kate suppressed a sigh.

This was hardly an existence.

Again, she felt like a caged canary, but she was less inclined to grumble this time, comforting herself with the fact that by remaining thus, she was helping to keep Cameron safe.

She wandered to the window, at first trying to resist all thoughts of the man, but it was nigh impossible. At last, she succumbed to the temptation and let herself relive their wondrously passionate night, only occasionally fretting over the possibility of a bairn.

A sudden knock sent them all in a flurry.

Nicoletta opened the door and stepped back as Thomas Cochrane strutted importantly into the chamber.

His eyes went straight to Kate.

With a falsely benevolent smile, he held out a small, silver dish. "I've come to welcome ye, Kate, and to gift ye with the finest honeyed-pears from the king's own table."

A soft cloud of appreciative "ahs!" circled through the gathered ladies. One of them squealed outright in delight.

Smoothing his trimmed, sleek beard, he extended his hand in invitation. "Walk with me a moment, will ye, Kate?"

Kate hesitated but knew she had little choice. She'd learned enough to know the man was the king's favorite, though she failed to understand what the king saw in him. He was hardly appealing.

Ach, she was cornered, with no choice but to keep the man's

company.

"Allow me to fetch a mantle," Lady Nicoletta inserted skillfully, drawing Kate to the side to throw a soft, velvet mantle over her shoulders and to murmur a warning. "Step carefully, Kate. There is danger here."

She hadn't needed to be told, but Kate nodded her thanks just the same.

Shuddering at his touch, she allowed Thomas to guide her from the royal apartments, out into the open air and down the winding stair to the king's gardens below.

At the foot of the gravel pathway, she hesitated.

"There is no place denied me, Kate," Thomas boasted, noting her reluctance. "The king denies me naught. In his eyes, we are equal."

Kate blinked at his arrogance.

He extended his arm, but she pretended not to notice and stepped onto the path as the wind rippled through the fresh green grass and rustled the tender leaves of the trees lining the garden's edge.

"We share much, Kate, and could be of great service to each other." Thomas' nasal voice took on an almost wheedling tone as he fell into step beside her.

So the man sought to beguile her? She resisted the temptation to laugh in his face, and instead forced her lips to flatter. "I fear ye are mistaken, my lord. I share little with a man of your esteemed position."

"We both are baseborn." He shrugged her comment aside. "And both hold the heart of a Stewart in the palm of our hands."

Ach, but he sought to endanger Cameron! She would be no party to it. Lifting her chin, she replied in what she prayed was a disinterested voice, "Perhaps ye do, my lord, but my time is already done. His lordship already looks to others and will not see me. Surely, ye have heard of Lady Elsa?" She selfishly prayed the rumors were false, but either case suited her purposes if it insured Cameron's safety.

Thomas eyed her in disbelief. He opened his mouth to speak when a light-hearted laugh startled them both.

Lord Julian Gray strolled their way, impeccably clad in the white shirt and plaid that he seemed to favor.

"Ach, my wee Kate." He grinned, his gray eyes slowly raking her from head to toe. "'Tis your favorite onion-eyed varlet come begging for more of your pleasures."

Before she could respond, he caught his strong arm about her waist, crushing her close and kissed her hungrily.

The kiss lacked passion.

His fingers dug into the small of her back in warning, but the sounds he made in his throat would have convinced any who watched that the throes of passion had all but consumed him.

Idly, she wondered where the man had gained such consummate skill in deception.

Dramatically tearing his lips away, Julian stepped back, panting in a masterful touch.

Thomas Cochrane's already narrow eyes turned into slits.

"Ye'll excuse me if I steal this fair rose away from ye." Julian's words were polite, but his tone was imposing. "Come, Kate." He grabbed her arm.

"My lord!" Thomas raised his voice, extending his hand to catch Julian's sleeve.

Julian paused. With deliberate slowness, he dropped a chill gaze upon Thomas' fingers and absently allowed his fingers to stroke the hilt of his dirk.

Thomas quickly removed his hand, viewing him in alarm.

"Yes?" Julian's deep voice queried.

"I … wish ye both a good day." Thomas cleared his throat. Stiffly, he turned on his heel and resumed his walk of the gardens.

Chuckling under his breath, Julian pulled her up the stone stairs and back to the courtyard.

Once there, she curtsied deeply. "When I named ye an onion-eyed varlet, I thought ye were an outlaw, my lord." She found it necessary to explain.

Julian threw back his head and laughed. "I find the title most endearing, lass," he admitted with a merry glint in his eye.

A door slammed shut, and several finely dressed ladies scurried across the courtyard.

As they passed by, Julian tilted his head, allowing his eyes to rove over them with an overt flicker of interest.

Kate found herself smiling. "If ye truly wish to convince others that I've ensnared ye, my lord, 'tis best not to find your attention so easily distracted," she couldn't resist murmuring.

Julian shot her a mischievous look, and looping her arm through his, patted her hand in a brotherly gesture. "There is naught that I wouldn't do for Cameron," he said. "Though kissing ye is hardly a nuisance."

At Cameron's name, she flinched and looked away.

"Ach, Kate." Julian squeezed her hand. "Ye are a wee fool if ye think that Cameron will truly let ye go. Already, his faith in his own curse is shaken. Ye have an unholy grip on the man, and there's naught he wouldn't do for ye, lass. And, regardless what ye hear, he'll never wed that one, I assure ye. He only said it to convince Thomas his interest in ye had waned."

Following his gaze, she spied Lady Elsa watching her from a doorway across the courtyard. Their eyes met, and the woman crooked a beckoning finger.

"Only speak to her if ye wish it," Julian rumbled softly.

"I must, my lord." Kate pressed her lips firmly together. "She was kind to me."

He raised a skeptical brow but leaned down to kiss her cheek, murmuring, "Then I bid ye farewell. Send for me, whenever the need arises and I will be there."

Flashing a grin, he sauntered through the same door the ladies had disappeared into just moments before.

She smiled and watched him go. Then suppressing a sigh, approached Lady Elsa.

"Join me," the woman ordered tightly. Fluttering a hand over her breast, she pursed her lips and led the way to her chambers.

Kate followed in silence, a wealth of emotions racing through her heart. Regardless if the rumors of Lady Elsa wedding Cameron were true or not, it mattered little. She must accept the harsh reality that the man would wed as suited his position. She had no real place in his life.

Standing just inside the door, Kate watched as Lady Elsa moved with stately and serene grace to sit unhurriedly in her chair before the fire. With equal slowness, she picked up her needlework and leisurely pulled the threads.

"I'm sure you must have heard that I am to wed the earl," she said at length and without preamble, looking up to search Kate's face.

Kate nodded uncertainly, willing her heart to slow its frantic beating.

With narrowed eyes, Lady Elsa abruptly asked, "Does the earl still bed you, Kate?"

"No, my lady!" Kate gasped and averted her gaze. Her cheeks flamed red.

"And what would ye do, should he approach ye with the intent once again?" Lady Elsa pressed with an uncharacteristic callousness, but her hands were shaking. "Would ye deny him?"

"Aye, I must," Kate whispered. "I canna let his enemies use me as a weapon against him, my lady."

A series of expressions crossed Lady Elsa's face and among them, Kate recognized sorrow and displeasure.

"Go, Kate," the woman ordered tersely, waving her needlework in the direction of the door. "Please go."

With a respectful curtsey, Kate slipped outside the chamber, strangely wanting to weep.

"Ach, ye fool!" She pinched her cheeks, stubbornly refusing to let the tears fall. "Ye canna be so weak! He was never yours to have!"

Taking a deep breath, she stepped forward, intending to return to the princess' chambers at once when a flash of red caught her eye. Instinctively, she pulled back and peered cautiously out from the doorway.

It was Maura, wearing her red silk dress as she hurried down the passageway, head bowed.

Kate felt a wave of aggravation, but something about Maura's movements caught her attention.

The woman halted, hovering in front of a door, nervously glancing from side to side and behind her back several times before finally pushing it open to disappear quickly inside.

Kate frowned.

The Maura she knew pranced about with an air of superiority, wearing a permanently smug expression upon her face and speaking every word as loudly as she could, so that she might draw as much attention to herself as possible. She wasn't one to scurry and hide.

She was clearly up to nothing good.

Hesitating only a moment, Kate stole down the passageway and placed her ear against the door.

She heard nothing.

Cautiously, she pushed it open with one hand, waiting a moment before peeking carefully behind it and finally stepping inside.

She had entered a small antechamber. She had thought it empty, but as the door thudded behind her, she heard harsh voices rising in the adjoining room.

Suddenly losing her courage, Kate moved to leave when the latch jiggled underneath her fingers.

Panicking, she sought a place to hide and spied a desk with a chair placed near the window. She had barely managed to wedge herself behind it when the door opened again, and Thomas Cochrane strode purposefully into the room.

"Did ye find the chambermaid?" he bellowed as he approached

the table.

Kate bit her lip as he placed a booted foot on the edge of the chair, inches away from her knees. Ach, surely the man could hear her pounding heart!

"Aye," said the voice of a man she did not know. He came closer, pulling Maura along with him. "She's the chambermaid I spoke of and will have no difficulties in doing what ye want. Ye can trust her."

"Can I?" Thomas moved to circle Maura, lifting a lock of her blonde hair and twisting it around his finger. "Do ye know what happens to those who betray me?"

Tossing her head, Maura's cheeks dimpled in a haughty smile. "No, my lord, nor will I ever learn."

Thomas laughed and exchanged an amused glance with the man. "That is well, then." Reaching into his velvet doublet, he pulled out two letters and placed them in her hands. "Put these in Albany's writing desk within the hour. There can be no mistakes, do ye hear?"

"Aye, my lord," Maura promised. "I'll see to it straightway!"

"Then go." Thomas ordered, pointing to the door and motioning for the man to remain.

In moments, Maura was gone.

When they were alone, Thomas lifted his lip in an arrogant sneer. "I'll see the Earl of Lennox hang by Albany's side before the week's end. Once the king reads those letters, he'll have no choice!"

Kate froze.

"Then, I'll be off to keep Lord Hume informed," the other man replied. "Ye'd best go. The king will soon join Albany in his chambers."

"Aye, soon we'll be rid of the thorn in our side." Thomas laughed in anticipation, clapping the man on the shoulder as the door closed behind them both.

Kate jumped to her feet.

Ach, she'd not let Thomas endanger Cameron!

Gathering her skirts, she rushed to the door and peeked outside, relieved to discover the passageway empty.

She had to warn Cameron immediately.

Without hesitation, she made her way to the royal apartments, but once inside, realized she could not recognize the way to Cameron's chambers. With rising panic, she fled down several corridors, searching in vain. Ach! Why could she not recall the way? Surely, there were not that many rooms. Why couldn't she find it?

Her heart jumped to her throat in despair, and she had almost given up hope when she caught a flash of red from the corner of her eye.

Darting under an archway, she peered down the corridor to see Maura moving with swift purpose to open a large door at the far end, enter, and close it softly behind her.

Kate's heart pounded loudly in her ears as she waited. Should she follow? What if she lost her?

Suddenly, the door opened again, and Maura sailed away with a smug smile.

Kate expelled a pent breath and willed herself to calm down.

The letters were in the chamber.

Should she seek Cameron out and warn him?

But she knew there was no time. She had wasted a good amount of time getting lost in the royal apartments. She had to retrieve the letters herself, before the king found them.

Making her mind up swiftly, she fled down the hall and burst into the chamber.

There was only one writing desk, an ornately carved one placed beneath the window. Flying across the chamber, she yanked the drawer open and, to her utter relief, found the letters at once. Tucking them into her bodice, she turned to flee when the chamber door opened, and Albany himself stepped inside.

The prince's eyes immediately found hers, and his brows lifted in astonishment, even as his lips spread slowly in a lascivious smile. "What a delightful surprise, Kate."

10

A FOOLISH VOW

Cameron paused on the threshold to Albany's chambers to witness Kate rising from a deep curtsey before the prince. Protected from view by the door, neither she nor Albany saw him, and he took advantage of the moment to let his eyes slide over Kate appreciatively.

The fine gray wool gown she wore suited her well, accentuating her slender figure in delightfully distracting ways. Aye, she was quite stunning. Standing slim and straight-backed with her mouth curved in a composed smile, she possessed a natural air of grace and power that made one pause and take note.

A wave of desire rippled through him.

Her presence was more intoxicating than the finest of Rhennish wines! Already his blood turned hot from simply looking at her.

Wrinkling her nose a little, Kate looked Albany directly in the eye. "Forgive me, your highness, but I seem to have lost my way to Princess Anabella's chambers."

The words shook Cameron from his lusty thoughts.

Ach, but she shouldn't be in Albany's rooms! What was she doing here? And though she appeared calm, he could see her cheeks were a shade too pink and her breath just a little too quick. Both hinted at another reason rather than being lost.

Fortunately, Albany was too distracted to notice.

"There is naught to forgive for such a fortuitous act of fate." The prince swept his arm in a grand gesture. "Pray join me afore the king delights us yet again with another esteemed astrologer's dire prophecies portending impending doom." He delivered the last words in the most scathingly sarcastic tone possible.

"Forgive me, your highness, but—" Kate began to protest.

"No." Albany cut her short. "Stay." His eyes took on a decidedly lecherous glint. "I've thought of ye often, lass, since the day I saw ye upon the road."

Cameron stepped forward, prepared to intervene, when Kate dipped in yet another graceful curtsey.

"Thank ye kindly, your highness." She smiled at him in what appeared to be genuine warmth. "But I dare not stay. Princess Anabella would be horrified should I taint your chivalrous reputation. I must return to her quickly, for fear that I may have already unwittingly caused ye harm, your highness."

At the mention of the princess, Albany unconsciously inched back, his face registering a mixture of surprise and confusion.

Cameron allowed his lips to curve in a smile of admiration.

How had Kate known that the prince feared the woman? Ach, but she was adept at handling the situation. Still, he did not want her to face the man alone. With a firm step, he entered the chamber.

Glancing sideways to see him, Albany frowned uncertainly. "Did the wee lass just threaten me?" He shook his head, and then his tone shifted. "'Tis no small wonder that she caught your eye, Cameron."

At the mention of his name, Kate started and whirled, her eyes locking with his. There was a wealth of emotion in those wide, brown passionate pools of warmth, and it was all he could do to prevent himself from stepping forward to sweep her into a comforting embrace.

But first, he was done with Albany's lewd behavior. Facing him, he fixed the man with a contemptuous eye and warned him in a dangerous tone, "Have a care, my lord. There are things that will never be yours."

With his dark brows drawn into a line, Albany retorted heatedly, "Have ye forgotten who I am? There is not a woman that walks that I cannot have, ye fool!"

Cameron eyed him with rising anger. The man had changed, indeed. The Albany of old would never have uttered those words.

"And why do I come upon this unseemly brawl?" Princess Anabella's cold words snaked through the chamber before he could respond.

They stepped back as she slowly entered the room, her cold eyes swept Albany first and then himself, from head to toe, before settling on Kate curtseying behind them.

"Ach, the folly of youth!" Princess Anabella all but growled.

"Your highness." Kate's voice trembled.

"She came at my bidding, your highness," Cameron stated coolly, moving to stand protectively at her side. She was so tiny. He tended to forget how truly delicate and small she was.

"If ye are too weak to keep your vow for less than a day, Cameron, then I'll lend ye my strength!" Princess Anabella's eyes turned furious as her lips twisted in a thin line.

But Cameron was scarcely listening to the woman. Ach, he had already led Kate down the path of fate. He would do better to hold her close, and protect her now with his entire soul. One look into her eyes, one touch of her skin would provide him with whatever strength he needed. For her, he would change the tides of fate himself.

Slowly, he began to smile.

There was an answering light in her eyes.

"Nay, your highness. Mayhap I have found my strength at last," he said in a strangely light tone, his gaze still locked with Kate's. "I shall take steps to remedy this situation immediately."

Aye, he'd make Kate his for all to see. Julian was right. She would make a stunning countess.

Princess Anabella's eyes narrowed, but further conversation proved impossible as King James chose that moment to arrive. Clad in heavy royal robes trimmed with ermine, he stumbled into the chamber, tripping over the hem and promptly losing his footing.

He would have fallen had not Cameron stepped forward to catch his arm.

The king frowned, weaving unsteadily a moment, before lifting his eyes to meet Cameron's in a sluggish response that revealed that he was quite drunk.

"Your majesty." Cameron bowed his head in respect.

Attempting to focus his gaze, but with little success, King James finally slurred, "Well met the day, fair cousin!"

Princess Anabella expelled her breath in disgust as Mar and Thomas arrived at the door, pausing to watch.

But the king was not looking at them. Raising his hand, he waved it in greeting an inch from Cameron's nose in an almost childlike gesture and with a friendly smile, hiccupped. "'Tis ever a pleasure to speak with ye, Cameron! I would that ye had been born my brother. Never have ye forgotten that there is but one anointed ruler in the land!"

The wine on his breath was overwhelming, and his neglect to use the royal "we" indicated he was exceptionally drunk, hardly in a state to speak of such weighty matters as prophecies. Guiding him to the nearest chair, Cameron suggested, "Perhaps we should reconvene on the morrow, your majesty?"

The king nodded gamely in agreement.

"'Tis a bad omen!" Thomas intercepted quickly, anger clearly written upon his long face. "Aye, a bad omen if we must delay this a moment longer, your majesty! 'Tis in the stars to gain clarity this night, and we must not lose the chance. The black arts canna be trifled with!"

The king frowned, but then nodded in agreement, his head wobbling.

"Ach, ye are but a puppet!" Albany exploded, watching his older brother in outright astonishment. Turning to Mar still standing at the door, he asked incredulously, "Can ye not see, Mar? He's but a fool! Surely, ye can see it now?"

Mar folded his arms, eyed both of his brothers grimly, and sighed. "I would we were once again wee lads hawking on the moors, when we knew only of loyalty and honor as kinsmen. I only came this night to ask ye both to join me at dawn, to hunt as we once did, and to reclaim what we've so clearly lost. Aye, and ye too, Cameron."

Albany impatiently rolled his eyes.

"Mar!" The king began to weep, holding his hand out to his youngest brother. "I've never doubted ye, lad. Your heart has always been true!" Tears coursed unchecked down his cheeks. "Aye, I'll ride! I'll ride on the morrow with ye, 'tis a good plan, lad."

"I fail to see why I must listen to this drunken dithering," Princess Anabella snapped sourly. "If ye'll excuse me—"

"Forgive me, your highness!" Thomas stepped quickly to block her way and bowed low, almost sweeping the floor with his chin. "But the most esteemed astrologer William Hathaway of England has arrived to shed further light on Andrews' prophecy. I pray ye would give him but a moment of your time."

William Hathaway was a short, wiry man dressed entirely in black. He stood hesitantly behind Mar, clutching a large leather-bound manuscript to his chest.

Cameron raised his voice to challenge Thomas. "Is this truly the time? The king is in need of rest." Thomas was clearly up to something unholy.

"I'll allow it," Princess Anabella inserted brusquely. "But for a moment only. Be quick."

Albany growled in frustration.

Gingerly, the astrologer entered the chamber, bowing profusely in all directions until Thomas impatiently grasped him by the arm and pulled him to the desk.

"I'll need parchment," the astrologer whispered timidly as Thomas pushed him down onto the chair.

As the man was settled, Cameron reached down and captured

Kate's hand in his, lightly tracing his thumb over her delicate fingers. Ach, but she was fashioned for pleasure. Already, his thoughts had taken a lusty turn when Princess Anabella's harsh tone once again interrupted them.

"Kate, return to my chambers immediately!" the princess ordered abruptly.

As Kate moved to obey, Cameron laid a restraining hand upon her slender shoulders and murmured, "Aye, 'tis not a vow I will keep, your highness, and 'twas a foolish one to begin with. 'Tis too late. I have already slapped the face of destiny and my only path now is to see it done."

"And what riddle is this?" The princess frowned, greatly displeased.

Before he could reply, Thomas startled them all.

"God's Wounds!" the man swore, all but yanking the drawer from Albany's desk.

Albany looked over in annoyance. "Are ye blind as well, fool? Can ye not see the drawer filled to the brim with parchment? Be quick, I've had my fill of this madness!"

The king gave a long, loud yawn and held out his hand to Mar. "I would hear the poet once more, the one from Pisa. His verse extolling my virtues is a work beyond comparison. Send for him at once, Mar! I would hear his dulcet tones sooth my tortured heart."

But Mar ignored his besotted brother. He still stood at the chamber's entrance, arms folded and feet planted widely apart with his eyes riveted upon Thomas Cochrane.

Thomas slapped the flat of his hand on the desk. His face clouded darkly and then he straightened. With deliberate slowness, he turned to Kate, understanding dawning in his eyes.

Under his touch, Cameron felt Kate tense at once. Ach, but the lass began to tremble, though she gave little outward sign of it, and then he understood.

Kate had taken whatever it was that Thomas was so clearly seeking desperately.

There was no other reason for her to have been in the chamber.

Slowly, Thomas approached to bow before her. "'Tis good to see ye standing by your earl where ye belong, lass," he said with a thin, wavering laugh. "I hope to see ye remain there from this moment on."

It was clearly a veiled threat. "Aye, she will, Thomas," Cameron replied in a deadly, silken tone. "And those who seek to tear us apart will not live long to regret their folly."

"I'm finished with this!" Albany shouted, shoving the astrologer's chair with his boot. "Be gone, ye minion, afore ye become overly familiar with Stirling's dungeons!"

"Come, Kate." Cameron pulled her away, ignoring Princess Anabella's objections and Albany's jealous glares. No, he would take Kate away from Thomas and right quickly. The lass had clearly made a bitter enemy, and 'twas she, now, who was in great danger.

Bowing his farewell to the half-unconscious king, he slid his arm about Kate's waist and guided her from the chamber.

"Cameron!" she hissed as he pulled her down the corridor to his apartments. "I-I mean, my lord! There is a matter most urgent—"

"Not now, Kate," he murmured under his breath. "Wait but a moment, my sweeting."

Shortly thereafter, she stood in his chambers, but the moment they were alone in the dim light of the flickering fire, he could do nothing but look down upon her with acute longing. Aye, he knew she could see the desire burning in his eyes, but there was no need to hide his long-buried emotions now.

Aye, they were already on the accursed path, but he found himself oddly freed to feel, filling with hope. He'd walk through the Fires of Hell itself to protect her. He'd break this curse once and for all. He could not lose her. He *would* not.

With a guttural sound deep in his throat, he pulled her hard against his chest.

Placing her hands on his chest, she looked up into his eyes, struggling to hide her distress. "'Tis said that ye'll wed Lady Elsa—"

"Never," he interrupted, laying a finger upon her lips. "I'll never have any other but ye, Kate. And I'll never let ye go, I swear it."

She stirred in his arms. "But ye are an earl, not a thief!"

"Kate, I am neither." He laughed softly, tracing his finger along the line of her jaw. "Think of me as Cameron, a man who loves ye and never another."

She blinked, holding still under his touch, and then he could no longer restrain himself from capturing her mouth in a hard, demanding kiss.

Her lips, soft and gentle, trembled against his at first, but then she wound her arms around his neck and fully kissed him back, making tiny sounds of intense pleasure. Gripping his hair with both of her hands, she moaned as his lips traveled down her neck in feather-light kisses, and flooded with the fires of passion, his hands slid over her bodice when his fingers unexpectedly brushed against parchment.

Frowning, he tore his lips from hers and glanced down, breathing hard.

With her face flushed, Kate fumbled with her bodice a moment to draw out two letters. "I overheard Thomas ordering Maura to put these in Albany's desk. He swore the prince and ye would be undone when they were found, and—"

Half tempted to fling the letters into the fire so he that he might return to the delightful pleasures of her skin, Cameron graced them with only a cursory glance. He had almost tossed them over his shoulder when the belated realization struck him that the wax seal was strikingly similar to that of Edward IV, the king of England.

He froze.

All lustful thoughts disappeared in an instant.

Holding the letters up against the dim, red firelight for a better view, his eyes locked on the wax seal.

There was no doubt.

Both letters, one addressed to Albany and the other to himself, bore King Edward IV's signature red wax seal.

He stared at them, stunned, as the enormity of the risk she had taken slowly sank in.

"Kate!" He choked. "Swear to me that ye'll never place yourself in such danger again! If ye had been caught—" He shuddered, unable to let himself dwell on it further.

"But if the letters had been found, then ye would have suffered!" She shook her head fiercely, her dark eyes flaring passionately. "I canna bear it if something were to happen to ye, Cameron!"

Pulling her after him to the chairs before the fire, he took a deep breath and broke the seal on the letter addressed to himself.

Edward IV, by the grace of God King of England and Defender of the Faith, to the most Illustrious Cameron Stewart, Earl of Lennox, greetings.

We are in receipt of your great proof of friendship and loyalty as demonstrated by your promise of men and arms for your support in the matter of delivering the throne of Scotland to its rightful Sovereign, Alexander Stewart, Duke of Albany.

We will rely on the armed men to be sent to at the time and place we specify and for this we also entreat you, with your cousin Alexander Stewart, by the nearness of blood which is between you, to proceed with moderation until the appointed time.

We shall not fail in our endeavor to free Scotland from the perfidious reign of James III and when that time of victory has come upon us we will grant you titles and lands in Wales and also Kent as confirmed by the affixing of our seal.

Dated by the hand of Edward IV at London, 4th of May in the 18th year of our reign

"Sweet Mary!" Cameron swore, staring at the missive with horror.

What unholy plan had Thomas concocted? It was far more serious than he had thought if he had resorted to forging such letters.

Aye, there was no doubt that the wee lass had saved his life.

Clearly, Thomas had wanted these letters found this night and if they had been, with the king's current suspicious state of mind, cousin or no, Cameron could well have lost his head on the spot.

With a sense of dread, he kicked life into the dying fire and kneeling close for a better view, tore open the letter addressed to Albany.

Edward IV, by the grace of God King of England and Defender of the Faith, to the most Serene and Mighty Alexander Stewart, Duke of Albany, soon by the grace of God King of Scotland, greetings.

We do not doubt that the recent tidings of your slaughters and plundering expeditions of late in the Borders are subject of rumor only. Such dark suspicions will not stand in the way of the alliance between us to place you upon your rightful throne.

Have patience in our good judgment that we will heed your demands to claim your right to be solemnly crowned King of Scotland but at a time most opportune to insure victory. The continued ambition of those in James' court have plunged Scotland into a treacherous state, full of private war and feudal disorder that is most advantageous to our cause at this time and we will begin this endeavor soon to the lasting prospect of peace between our kingdoms when you take the throne that is your right.

May your Lord Julian Gray feel that he has offended not only us, but also you, by daring to impede our messengers whom we sent to you in the month past. Fortunately, the missive was destroyed before he could lay eyes upon it, but heed our counsel that the frequent interchange of messengers must need halt for a time, or your esteemed venture will be cast into great peril should the discovery of it reach the ears of your brother.

Dated by the hand of Edward IV at London, 4th of May in the 18th year of our reign

Cameron read the letter twice, knowing in his heart that this one was no forgery. It held the ring of truth. Lifting his voice, he called for his man, Sir Arval.

The grizzled Frenchman appeared at once.

"Bid Lord Gray come without delay!" Cameron ordered grimly.

The man bowed and left but not before sending Kate a warm smile.

She sat opposite him, perched on the edge of her chair, a worried expression upon her face. "What is it?" she asked in a fearful tone. "Are ye safe?"

Moving to kneel before her, he gently placed the letters on her lap and took her hands in his. "I owe ye my life, Kate," he whispered, kissing her fingertips. "Read them and ye'll see. I'll hide naught from ye again."

An expression of bashful humor entered her eyes. "Ach, Cameron, ye should know I canna read! Not many can, ye lout!"

It wasn't until she called him a *lout* that he became aware just exactly how much he had ached for her to do so. With his lips curving into a smile, he replied, "Then 'tis time ye learned, my sweeting." Aye, as his countess, she would find it a necessary skill.

She eyed him skeptically, but patiently allowed him to point to the words and read aloud but as the meaning became clear, she gasped, "Ach, Cameron! Ye must run! 'Tis too dangerous for ye here!"

He suppressed a sigh. If only he could run, he would. "I cannot do that, Kate. I must stay and see this through, for the sake of Scotland." Aye, 'twas his duty.

Sliding from the chair to his side before the fire, she cupped his cheek in her hand. "I always thought the nobles only collected coin to spend their days reveling in luxury without a care in the world," she confessed.

He gave a little laugh. "Most do, my sweeting."

She was so close, and the sweet smell of her skin made his blood boil. His feelings for the lass only intensified each day. With a tender look, he pulled her closer and let his lips brush the top of her head in a soft caress before dropping his lips to kiss her cheek gently.

Her expression was serious, and he was ready to ask the cause of her concern when she suddenly hugged him and buried her face against his shoulder.

"Do ye think of … bairns, Cameron?" Her voice sounded muffled against his chest, and she began to pluck the cloth of his shirt almost nervously.

He frowned at the unexpected question, but answered truthfully, "I've thought little of the wee lassies in my keeping, but I have seen them well cared for. I swear they are the king's, Kate, and not mine! I would never deceive ye." He titled her chin up with his finger.

With her brows drawn in a line, she appeared worried, and he wondered if she thought him a liar. He sighed. Ach, he should not have let the misunderstanding that he was a thief continue for so long. "I swear ye can trust me, Kate. I'll never hide anything from ye for the rest of our lives, I swear it."

There was a strange silence between them.

His frown deepened.

"I should return to the princess," Kate said finally, moving as if to rise.

"No, ye cannot go back, my sweeting." He gently grasped her hands, pulling her back down and tucked a strand of hair behind her ear. "What is it that concerns ye so? Have I—"

"Canna go back?" It was her turn to frown. "What can ye mean?"

He sighed. "Ye've heard the letters, Kate. They are of the most treacherous nature, and now we must assume Thomas knows that I've seen them. Ye aren't safe here anymore, lass." He squeezed her fingers tightly as he vowed, "I'll see ye and your father sent off afore dawn to—"

"Ye'll be sending me away?" She snatched her hands angrily

207

from his.

"For a short time only, until this is settled—" he began, but she interrupted him again.

"But I dinna want to leave, Cameron!" Her dark eyes were suspiciously bright.

"I won't send ye far, my love," he promised and then whispered into her hair, "I will not make it without ye, lass. I cannot bear to be apart from ye long."

Somehow, he was kissing her again, a deep, intimate kiss of sweet abandon when Lord Julian Gray strode into the chamber.

Spying them on the floor, the man's long lashes dropped in a mirthful expression as he stifled a yawn and queried, "And what might this most urgent matter be, Cameron, that ye sought fit to drag me from a most pressing matter of my own?"

Rising to his feet, Cameron sent him a dark look of amusement. "The lass can wait, whomever she may be, Julian."

Julian sent him a devilish grin. "Ach, 'tis three of them, Cameron. I canna decide which—"

With a grim expression, Cameron pressed the letters into his hands, murmuring a quick explanation of how Kate had come by them.

Julian read them where he stood, scanning the contents quickly. He showed no emotion until he had finished them both. Waving the letter addressed to Cameron with a snort of disgust, he said, "'Tis not even a clever forgery. The writing is not Edward's."

"Aye," Cameron agreed.

Exchanging a long look with him, Julian bent forward and tossed the parchment into the fire.

They watched in silence as the paper began to smoke before a sudden burst of flames rose to devour it.

"And what of Albany's?" Cameron asked quietly.

Julian gave a rough laugh. Settling into a chair, he helped himself to a goblet of heated ale brought by Sir Arval before continuing. "I found myself in Cumberland afore coming to Stirling and there I crossed paths with an Englishman of the most suspicious nature. He burnt the letter ere I could read it, but I saw the red wax seal well enough."

Cameron clenched his jaw.

He had known there was truth in Albany's missive.

Albany was proving as big a fool as his brother James. Was the dreaming, wistful Mar the only royal Stewart with a shred of honor left in him?

"The plundering of the Borderlands had been laid on one John of Scougal and his band of desperate retainers. For that reason they were executed by the hand of Albany himself," Cameron informed grimly. "Word of it reached court on the day of my own arrival here."

Julian blew his hair back from his face and mused aloud, "So, he murdered others to cover his crimes?" After a moment, he noted, "Have ye not seen how Lord Hume speaks with Thomas at every feast now? The man refused to acknowledge his presence before, and I now have no doubt I will find out on the morrow that the Humes' coin is behind the gold chain that now proudly hangs on Thomas' neck."

Lord Hume headed one of the most powerful Borderland clans. If Albany had broken truce with England by plundering the Borderlands for his own gain, and had then made John of Scougal pay the price, it was no small wonder the fierce Borderland clans would seek vengeance against the prince. They would stop at nothing until they saw Albany beheaded. But such a thing would pitch Scotland into a civil war in its current state, for James was not a loved king. He could no longer count on the nobles to rally to his call.

But if the Borderlanders had the truth on their side, why had they embroiled Thomas in the matter? What were they seeking? And had Thomas stumbled upon yet another secret? Had Albany, corrupted by greed and power, truly begun plotting for the throne?

Were they headed for a civil war already?

"I find it tempting to let Thomas have his way with the scoundrel." Julian voiced the thought crossing his mind as well. "Betraying his own country and executing innocent men are crimes that should not go unpunished for any man and doubly so for one of royal blood."

"Aye, he must be punished, but we must see what the Humes want from Thomas. In any case, I'll see Scotland safe first," Cameron said at last. "We must assume Albany has Edward's backing and plans to wage war. We must band the nobles together, to protect our land, or we will surely fall."

Julian snorted. "I fear Scotland is already lost. The king is an imprudent, feeble-minded puppet. Albany has become a bloodthirsty plunderer seeking his own gain. And Mar is a melancholy lad, mourning for days long gone and only lives now for the hunt. None of them can unite Scotland under a single banner."

Gazing into the crackling flames, Cameron murmured softly, "We have the crown prince."

"A wee lad of six?" Julian retorted in surprise.

"Aye." Cameron nodded slowly. "He can be taught the ways that befit a true king and he may well be the only answer. We can unite the nobles under his name and protect our fair country."

"'Tis a task more suited to a man of your skills than mine." Julian circled the lip of his goblet with a finger, shaking his head. "'Tis not an easy task to unite the clans when they would much rather feud. Scotland grows only more divided by the day. Not an hour past, Archibald Douglas rode from these very gates to raise arms against the Earl of Errol on the news their latest truce has been broken. It only lasted a month this time."

Cameron closed his eyes. Rebellions were rising in Ross, Caithness, and Sutherland. The feuds in Annandale between the Lairds of Caerlaverock and Drumlanrig had recently turned deadly. That the Earl of Angus had now engaged in yet another feud with the Earl of Errol only fractured the country even more.

"Why cannot James stand and lead his country?" Cameron swore under his breath, pounding his fist against the mantle.

They fell silent.

And then Julian held Albany's letter up with two fingers, peering down at Kate still sitting on the rug close to the hearth. "'Tis a dangerous thing ye've done, lass." He whistled under his breath. "Thomas will not let this matter go."

Kneeling by her side, Cameron slid a protective arm about her shoulders. "Will ye escort her to Craigmillar at dawn, Julian? I'll leave on the hunt with the rest, but I would delay Thomas' knowledge of her escape for as long as I may. He'll not expect her to leave so soon."

"Need ye ask?" Julian cocked a brow and drained his ale in one long gulp. Rising to his feet, he bowed. "But I'll not return here until I've been to the Borders to uncover the truth of John of Scougal myself and to see what the Humes seek. But Albany had best pray what I discover is in his favor."

"We cannot shake the throne now," Cameron warned. "We cannot present Scotland as too tempting of a morsel for Edward not to bite, and should he march on us now, Scotland would fall. Already, we are too divided. I need time to speak with the nobles, to open their eyes and gain their support in protecting our land under the name of the crown prince."

Julian pursed his lips grimly. "Aye, ye speak wisely, Cameron. We need a Stewart to rise and lead us through these shadowed times. 'Tis up to ye. James is a fool, Albany is blind, and Mar is a dreamer. No man will listen to any of them."

Cameron thinned his lips grimly.

"Then, Kate, this onion-eyed varlet will return for ye at dawn." Julian bowed to her with a humorous glint in his gray eyes.

"Ach, my lord, will ye never forget my foolish words?" Kate asked, rising to her feet.

Snagging her hand and pressing it against his heart, Julian grinned. "Never, wee Kate."

Cameron watched him leave and heaved a sigh.

The court intrigues of years past were mere games compared to the matter he was embroiled in now. Never had he expected to stumble upon such treachery. But, for the sake of Scotland, he would rise to hold the country together.

Ach, but he must immediately take steps to insure the crown prince would be a lad of honor, worthy to bear the crown. Why hadn't he involved himself in the matter before?

"Enough thinking, my lord."

He glanced over to see Kate's soft, smiling eyes peering deep into his.

Reaching to pull his head down, she stood on her tiptoes to kiss his brow. "Ye can save Scotland in the morning, Cameron," she whispered.

He could feel her breath upon his face, and his skin began to tingle.

"If I'm to be gone soon then let us not sleep." She smiled, lowering her lashes and peering up from under them with a secretive expression.

And then she slowly kissed him. It was a lingering kiss, and he allowed himself to savor every moment. His hands began moving as his lips searched out the hollows of her neck and then his fingers deftly untied her bodice, revealing her slim shape that made his blood run hot.

"Ye shall have no other but me," he growled low in his throat. Aye, he had already tread the path, he might as well take the pleasures that came with it. And nothing would satisfy his desire save to make her his once more.

Carrying her to his bedchamber, he lay down upon the bed. Her hair flowed long and free over the goose-down pillows, and his heart began to pound as he stripped off his shirt and unlaced his breeches.

And then, beginning with her toes, he kissed a trail over her soft, creamy skin until she moaned softly, "End this torture!"

Reaching over, he quenched the candle and plunged the chamber into darkness.

11

WITCHCRAFT

Cameron looked out of the window, eyeing the hazy aura that circled the waning moon with a heavy heart. Behind him, Kate sighed in her sleep, and he silently drew the bed curtains aside, staring down at her for a time with a sad smile upon his lips.

Already, his heart ached with the pain of parting.

Gently, he leaned down and kissed her cheek.

She murmured in her sleep and slowly opened her eyes. Sitting up, she whispered, "Is it time?" Her voice wavered, betraying her emotion.

"Aye, my sweeting." How he wished he could say any other words but those.

She turned her head away, and he could see her swallow in the weak moonlight, struggling to compose herself. Then she faced him once more with a smile, but her eyes were suspiciously bright, and her voice unnaturally cheerful. "'Twill be a difficult ride, my lord. Ye dinna let me sleep long."

He lowered his lashes and smiled to give her strength. Pulling her into his arms, he nibbled her ear, possessively biting a strand of her hair, and let his hands roam freely over her skin one more time.

Playfully, she swatted his fingers but then burst into tears.

"We will not be parted long. I swear it, Kate," he promised, cradling her close.

She tried to speak, but the words caught in her throat.

"'Twill be over soon," he whispered in a soothing tone. "And then I'll take ye to Inchmurrin. Ye'll love Loch Lomond, 'tis the bonniest loch in Scotland, lass. We'll spend our days sailing the blue waters, and ye can show me how to fish."

"Ach, I'm a poor fisherman." She gave a shaking laugh. "I've only sold fish in the markets."

"Relieving good citizens of their coin?" he teased gently.

The jest had the desired effect. She raised her head and sent him a good-naturedly offended look before strangely averting her eyes. "Do ye think of bairns sailing the loch with ye?"

He raised a puzzled brow and repeated, "Bairns?"

"My fondest memories are the days I spent sailing with father and my wee sister, Joan." She gave a hurried explanation.

Briefly, he wondered if she desired bairns, but then she moved to slip into her shift and lustful thoughts quickly displaced all others. He leaned back on the bed, eyeing her appreciatively until she reached over and pinched his nose.

"Ach, but ye make a lass uncomfortable with such lecherous looks, ye lout!" She laughed. "Get ye dressed! Ye canna escort me naked!"

Turning away from him, she walked to the window to stare out into the dark sky.

Dressing quickly, he joined her there, standing behind her to encompass her in a warm embrace. He leaned down to rest his chin on her shoulder, and breathed deeply, simply smelling her familiar sweet skin.

He wanted the moment to last forever, but all too soon, Sir Arval called from the adjoining chamber.

"It is time," Cameron whispered in her ear with great reluctance, and slowly threading his fingers through hers, guided her out of the bedchamber.

"My lord." The grizzled Frenchman bowed a deep greeting. "The Lord Julian Gray has already departed and even now awaits ye at Stirling Bridge." Sir Arval himself was to escort Kate's father soon after, making the same journey to Craigmillar at a slower pace.

Cameron nodded his thanks as Kate flung her arms about the man's neck, giving his cheek a warm kiss. "I canna thank ye enough for the care ye show my father, Sir Arval." She began to curtsey, but he caught her arm in protest.

"Never to me, my lady." The man laughed. Blushing, he repeated, "Never bow to me."

Cameron watched the man go with a smile. Apparently, even the Frenchman had fallen under his Kate's spell.

Choosing his finest mantle and favorite silver brooch, he gently swathed her in the dark velvet and pinned the brooch at her throat in silence. And then with emotion threatening to overwhelm him, he led her through the dark corridors without speaking a word.

Aye, she would be safe in Craigmillar, in the keeping of the Prestons.

Craigmillar Castle lay on a low hill not far away, only three miles south of Edinburgh. The Prestons had long been among his closest allies, but he would not trust even them with the truth. Sir Arval would introduce Kate as his own distant relative and would remain there with her and her father for as long as was needed. Cameron trusted Sir Arval as much as Julian and knew she was safe in his care.

Slowly, Cameron led her across the darkened courtyard, past the guards and down the king's private stairs leading to the lower gardens. The steps spiraling into the darkness below seemed endless at first, but all too quickly they arrived at the bottom of Castle Hill, and shortly thereafter, stood on the old stone bridge spanning the River Forth.

Fog blanketed the river in the chilly predawn air, rising to cloak the bridge in a mysterious shroud. And then the sound of clattering hooves announced Julian's arrival before a whirl of mist suddenly dispersed. The young lord appeared astride his massive black horse, a dark cloak muffling his face.

"Must I go?" Kate turned on Cameron, tears sliding down her cheeks.

"Aye, it won't be long, Kate." He pressed his cheek against the top of her head.

They stood there, clinging to each other as Julian kindly looked away.

Finally, even as Cameron's heart pleaded for her to stay, he forced his lips to form the words, "Ye must leave, lass."

Taking his cue, Julian leaned down to sweep Kate into his lap with an easy arm. "Come, lass. We must be gone while the world still sleeps," the man rumbled softly. Reaching down again, he clasped Cameron's shoulder in a comforting gesture and swore, "I will see her safely there, upon my life."

Cameron nodded.

And then Julian wheeled his great beast, and the dark horse galloped across the bridge, swallowed immediately by the heavy fog.

They were gone.

Cameron drew a long, dragging breath.

He stood there until the sky turned gray, and only then summoned the strength to leave. And as he turned, his eye caught on her small shoeprint in the mud.

Ach, her foot was so tiny.

He smiled, but it was a bittersweet one. With a heavy heart, he slowly returned up the steep slope as the first shafts of the sun bathed the morning fog in a golden glow.

The rosy radiance of the dawn lit the sky as he entered Stirling Castle, but his hand had only just touched the door of the royal apartments when he heard a stifled scream sounding from nearby.

Rounding the corner close to the kitchens, he came upon a short, stocky man kicking a blonde-haired woman groveling on the ground before him.

Within moments, Cameron had the man disarmed and on his knees.

"What devilry is this?" Cameron's voice filled with disdain as he shoved the man back with a booted foot. "Speak, knave!"

"I am but following my master's orders, my lord!" the man stuttered.

"And whom might your master be, scoundrel?" Cameron pressed firmly.

The woman struggled to rise unsteadily to her feet. Already, her left eye was swollen shut and her lips bruised, but she did not appear to be gravely injured.

"Thank ye, my lord," she half-whispered, half-sobbed, bobbing up and down. "Thank ye, my lord!"

Turning back to the man once more, Cameron repeated, raising his voice, "Who ordered ye?"

But the man stubbornly remained silent.

Ordering the nearby guards to take the man to the dungeons, Cameron assured the woman he would have one of his men settle the affair. Looking down upon her with pity, he asked, "Are ye well enough, lass?"

"Aye, my lord," she replied through cracked lips. "Ye saved my life, my lord."

"What cause had the man to beat ye so?" he queried gently.

"'Twas a misunderstanding, my lord." She began to shake uncontrollably. "He thought I was negligent in my duty, but I swear I did what he asked, my lord."

Filled with compassion, Cameron unclasped his mantle and threw it over her shoulders. Ordering another guard to escort her to safety, he returned to his apartments and promptly gave the affair no further thought.

Now, he must ready for the hunt, but 'twas now a hunt in more ways than one.

He would see Scotland on solid footing, and to accomplish that, the influence of one Thomas Cochrane must disappear from court. 'Twould take some doing and likely longer than he wished, but he would see it done.

Splashing water on his face, he eyed the bed with a twinge of longing.

The night with Kate already seemed years in the past.

How long would it be before he held her close to his heart once again?

Donning his leather hunting shirt, he set about preparing for a day of sport in the wilds when his eye fell upon a rosewood box upon the table.

Ach, Albany's letter.

He'd placed it there last night, before he had become distracted by the pleasures of Kate.

Slowly holding the parchment up to the light, he made a grim decision, and by the time he had arrived outside Albany's private apartments, he found himself filled with a deep, abiding wrath.

Kicking the door back, he strode past Albany's men and into the prince's private bedchamber.

He'd not allow Albany's hunger for power leave Scotland wide open for England to attack.

Albany glanced up from lacing his leather breeches. His face flooded with alarm. "What happened, Cameron?"

Cameron silently thrust the letter into his hand.

Albany's eyes fixed on the red wax seal. He went pale, and his hand began to shake. "Are ye accusing me of treason?" He didn't wait for a response. Striding to the fire, the prince threw the unread letter into the flames.

"That missive was planted in your chambers to be found by the king. If I were accusing ye, I wouldna have just let ye burn it,"

221

Cameron said in a cutting tone, observing the man closely.

Albany snorted. Regaining his color, he pompously swaggered to the table and poured himself a goblet of wine. "'Tis clearly the work of the Humes and Hepburns. The Borderlanders seek my head for their own gain. I will deal with them swiftly!"

"No." Cameron's lips crooked in a scathing smile. "I'll not allow it."

Ach, where was the honorable Albany of old? Did no shred of him exist anymore?

"No?" Albany paused, tilting his head to one side. His nostrils flared a little.

"We both know ye've been conspiring with Edward," Cameron responded in a tone of authority. "Ach, but ye've been a short-sighted fool! By abusing your position as Warden of the Marches, ye lost all chances ye might have had for the throne. Half of the country would rise against ye now. Ye'll never gain the support that ye need."

"So, ye *are* accusing me of treason?" Albany angrily growled the question.

With deliberate slowness, Cameron walked to the man, stopping a mere inch from his face. "I'm here to warn ye, Albany," he said in a low, threatening tone. "I'll not allow ye, or the Borderlanders, to deliver us to England. Swear to me now that ye'll halt this nonsense."

Albany blinked a little, and then licked his lips. "Ach, but ye've misunderstood—"

"Swear it," Cameron repeated evenly.

'Twas far more effective than if he had shouted.

Albany paled once again, but nodded in a jerking manner. "Aye."

"Ach!" Cameron gave a sound of disgust. "How can ye think only of your own gain? Plundering the Borderlands ye swore to protect?"

"The Humes have poisoned your mind!" Albany protested through white lips. "They have given false accounts in order to remove me and gain power, Cameron!"

"'Tis likely so," Cameron granted, clenching his jaw. "Just as 'tis true ye did plunder for your own gain whilst planning to wrest the throne from James. Neither ye nor the Borderlanders are innocent! I'm not a fool, Albany!"

Albany swallowed, all but confirming it.

"But it ends now." Cameron took the goblet from Albany's hand and poured the contents upon the floor. "And God help ye if ye break this vow, Albany, for 'tis your blood that will spill the next time, and not wine. I'll not allow ye to destroy Scotland."

He spun on his heel then, leaving Albany standing there, pale and shaken.

By the time Cameron entered the courtyard, it was filled with lords bearing falcons on their arms and ladies astride fine horses with hounds at their sides. Albany was there, sitting on his silver charger, appearing subdued, as Mar impatiently trotted his horse up and down before Stirling's great gates, plucking the string of his bow and searching the gathering crowd for signs of the missing king.

Sitting in the warm sun on the back of his favorite chestnut charger, Cameron took note of the gathered lords while mulling over the best strategies he might employ to rid the court of Thomas Cochrane and unite the bickering nobles.

His gaze fell upon the Borderlander, Lord Hume, sitting silent and sour near Albany.

The man would be his first target.

At that moment, Thomas appeared. Riding alone upon the king's favored mare, the long-faced man was proudly clad in a fine velvet mantle and boots adorned with silver braid. Over his shoulder, he had slung a gold-inlaid hunting horn encrusted with precious stones.

Cameron suppressed a derisive snort. The horn was clearly a gift from Thomas' supporters. The man could scarcely afford such an expensive trinket for himself.

Raising his hand, Thomas announced, "The king desires to confer with his astrologers on troubling matters this fine morning and will not join us, but he bids ye a good hunt and sends me in his stead!"

Mumbles of displeasure greeted this statement.

Angrily, Mar spurred his horse through the gates as Albany maneuvered his horse alongside Thomas, and then snatching the horn from the man's shoulders, sounded the call for the hunt to begin. As the hounds' ears pricked up and the riders sprang forward, Albany carelessly tossed the gaudy thing into Thomas' lap and spurred his horse through the gates.

A murderous expression flickered over Thomas' face, and then as if sensing eyes upon him, the man suddenly glanced Cameron's way.

Thomas froze.

Aye, the man was clearly concerned over the letters.

With a small smile upon his lips, Cameron urged his charger forward, following the hunting party filing from the gates into the narrow streets of Stirling Town. All the while, he was keenly aware of Thomas' burning gaze observing his every move.

Aye, he'd have the man watch him. 'Twould keep him busy from causing other trouble.

Clattering over the bridge to the River Forth with its banks already lined with fisherman, the hunting party galloped into the surrounding woodlands.

For a brief moment, Cameron closed his eyes, recalling his last venture into the woodlands searching for herbs with Kate. A wave of longing rippled through him.

It was tempting to stay there, thinking of her soft skin while listening to the calls of the birds amongst the dew-glistened leaves as shafts of sunlight fell through the trees to the forest floor, leaving a leafy pattern of lacework shadows on the path.

But he roused himself with reluctance, suppressing a sigh.

There were matters of court to attend to before he'd hold Kate once again.

Expelling a breath, he joined the other riders who were forming into smaller groups, only to find his way suddenly blocked by Thomas Cochrane.

"Well met the day, my lord." The man gave a flowery bow.

Cameron remained silent.

The man flushed, but there was a smirk on his face. "Why do I not see the fair Kate by your side, my lord?"

"I've not the time nor liking to bandy words with ye, Thomas," Cameron replied in an aloof manner, drumming his fingers lightly upon his heavy leather saddle. "Tread carefully, for your days are numbered."

The man laughed. It was a braying, high-pitched sound. "Ach, but

I hold the king's heart in my hand, my lord. I am untouchable!"

"Are ye now?" Cameron raised a brow at the man's arrogance. Leaning forward over the neck of his horse, he graced the man with a cynical smile. "Shall we see how long it takes to lose your supporters, ye fool?"

Thomas frowned.

Wheeling his horse around, Cameron cantered to Lord Hume's side, calling out, "Well met the day, Lord Hume."

The withered man drew rein, glancing over his back to eye him suspiciously, but replied readily enough, "Well met the day, my lord."

Ignoring Thomas who was trotting to join them, Cameron immediately brought himself to the matter at hand. "Recent tidings concerning Albany's role in the Borderlands cause me grave concern, Lord Hume. A concern I know ye share."

The man's craggy face tensed ever so slightly, and his gray eyes sharpened. "And the tidings ye speak of, my lord?"

Cameron settled back comfortably in his saddle and replied in a scathing tone, "Letters concerning his office as Warden of the Marches and the plundering of the Borderlands. Whilst crimes must surely be brought to justice, 'twould be a fearful mistake to use such matters for personal gain, do ye not think?"

Thomas turned white, and Lord Hume started as if bitten.

Their guilty faces confirmed that they both sought to benefit from Albany's foolish treachery. 'Twas disheartening. Did no one think of Scotland as a whole?

"Aye, my lord." Lord Hume began to stroke his chin. "A fearful mistake, indeed."

"I'll not stand by and see Scotland torn asunder by greed and treachery." Cameron's dark eyes swept him from head to toe with contempt. "I would have your word that the Borderlanders have no more dealings in such affairs, Lord Hume, and that ye stand with me as a brother to unite this land for the safety of us all."

"The Borderlanders have no such dealings," the man assured with feigned surprise that only made him look guiltier. His was silent a moment and then his expression turned genuine. "And I give ye my word of honor, my lord, the Borderlanders will stand with ye to keep Scotland safe."

"'Tis well, then." Cameron nodded once.

Pressing his lips in a thin line, Lord Hume maneuvered his horse to leave. "Good fortune on the hunt, my lord," he murmured in a subdued tone.

Thomas stretched out his hand, grasping at the man's sleeve, but with a sound of disgust, Lord Hume slapped him away and galloped off.

"My lord!" Thomas called after him indignantly. Then, with his face turning livid with anger, he whirled to face Cameron.

Cameron's lip lifted in a scornful smile. "As I said, soon ye'll be left without an eye to watch your back, Thomas."

"Your noble house shall come to ruin!" Thomas seethed.

"Have a care, ye mason. The king will not shelter ye much longer," Cameron warned in a biting tone before spurring his horse to gallop away.

Cameron spent the next few hours following the winding river through the rippling green grass of the tranquil glens in the company of many lords, strengthening ties and garnering vows of support, all the while keenly aware of Thomas tracing his every move.

But as the afternoon waned, the sudden barking of the scent hounds drew the hunters deeper into the woodlands, and he suddenly found himself alone with a private moment of peace.

Kate would have reached Craigmillar by now.

He closed his eyes, thinking of her sparkling brown eyes and passionate kisses.

Aye, he'd not survive long without her.

But first, he must see stability restored. Only then would he feel safe to keep her at his side.

Stretching in the saddle, he allowed himself to expel a long, deep breath of exasperation.

Ach, but the king had allowed far too much bickering and feuding to occur between the nobles. If England were to engage in war with them now, he was fair certain the nobles of Scotland could not work together long enough to raise an army to defend their own country. They were far more fractured than he had realized. He should have paid more attention himself. How had the country fallen into such a state?

His charger tossed his head, flicking its tail uneasily and Cameron absentmindedly reached down to pat its withers.

It was then that a slight movement from the corner of his eye caught his attention.

Turning slowly, he spied Mar creeping through the underbrush to disappear over a hillock.

Curiously, Cameron urged his horse forward, coming upon the

prince fitting an arrow to the string and pulling it taut.

Leaning forward, Cameron followed the line of the shaft, expecting to find a stag, but instead finding Thomas Cochrane a short distance away.

Before he could respond, Mar let the shaft loose.

But at that moment, Thomas' horse unexpectedly reared, and the arrow whistled harmlessly past the man's ear to embed itself in the tree behind him.

Staring at the feathered shaft in shock, Thomas began to bellow, sounding his horn in a panic, and as hounds and hunters descended upon them, Cameron galloped to Mar's side, holding out his arm.

Cursing bitterly under his breath, Mar leapt up behind him, and they pounded a safe distance away before Mar guided him to his own horse tethered nearby.

Dismounting, the prince complained bitterly, "I swore that Thomas would perish this day and that I would free James from his unholy influence."

"We'll free his majesty, my lord," Cameron assured him. Ach, but he wished himself that the arrow had found its mark. "But I fear 'tis not so easily done, and should he discover 'twas your arrow that flew his way, ye'll be in even more danger."

"More? What sinister thoughts are these?" Mar raised a brow. "What danger could the third son of the royal house of Stewart be in? 'Tis Albany, and his warmongering ways, who lies in danger! Not I, Cameron." He laughed incredulously.

"Aye, 'tis but instinct only, my lord," Cameron confessed. "I would ye were safe in France until I unseat Thomas from his ill-gotten place in court and unite the nobles under one banner."

Mar smiled. "Already my heart is lighter to hear ye aim to do so, fair cousin. Never have I seen ye fail." He looked wistful. "'Tis not a thing I could accomplish. There are those who would claim I sought the throne. But none could accuse ye of that."

Cameron bowed a little and then said, 'Promise me that ye'll not endanger yourself again, my lord. Scotland may need ye yet, for more than hunting and hawking in the royal preserves of Fife."

"I'll not hear those words." Mar set his lips stubbornly. "I will ever support James and his crown."

"Aye, my lord." Cameron bowed in respect. Mar truly was the noblest of the three. But he was foolishly noble. He would never fight his brothers to claim the throne, even if Scotland needed him to.

In silence, they rejoined the others, but it was not long before the horns sounded that the hunt was over, and they returned to the castle high on the rocky crag, bathed in the dying red light of the setting sun.

Swinging wearily down off his horse, Cameron briefly retired to his apartments, changing into fresh attire, before making his way to Stirling's Great Hall for an evening feast.

Bedecked with flowering branches celebrating the victorious hunt, the hall flowed with wine and gossip, with the mysterious shaft aimed at Thomas the most favored subject of all. Few, if any, spoke sympathetically of Thomas. Most speculated that Albany had done the deed. There were even those claiming they had witnessed him in the act.

Cameron had just again extricated himself from yet another telling of the tale when Princess Anabella descended upon him, accompanied by Lady Nicoletta and Lady Elsa.

Lady Elsa's rapt expression gave him momentary pause.

He recognized the look.

Many women had hunted him over the years, wearing that precise same face. He supposed she had taken the rumors of their impending marriage too much to heart. He grimaced. He'd have to speak with the lass soon and find her a husband.

Thrusting her precious dog into Lady Nicoletta's arms, the princess shooed the other women away and drew Cameron into a private corner.

"Ye've been busy this day, Cameron," she murmured in a low voice.

Cameron looked down at her, wondering how much she had managed to piece together.

With lips drawn thin, she asked, "Is Kate safe, lad?"

She only called him "lad" when concerned for his wellbeing. Curious at her sudden interest in Kate, he replied softly, "She is safe, your highness."

The princess gave a rare smile. "The lass is a dangerously deceptive one. I admire that she outwitted Thomas this past night."

Cameron blinked in surprise.

The princess sent him a withering look. "Dinna look so surprised, ye foolish lad. There is naught that goes on in a castle that the womenfolk dinna know."

"I ... see," he replied, astonished.

"Though, 'tis well enough Kate is gone for now," she observed sourly. "I need ye to think on things other than bed-sport."

He felt his cheeks redden, ever so slightly.

She heaved a sigh. "Many times, I have wished ye upon the throne—"

"Hush!" Cameron placed a finger upon her lips.

"James is ill-equipped to be king." She glared at him, slapping his finger away. "He is a fool. He delights only in music and cannot govern the realm. Each year, we suffer more for it. The people grow ever more dissatisfied with their king, but neither Albany nor Mar would make a better one. I fear 'tis only our young crown prince that will save us, lad. We must hold this land together for him at all costs."

Cameron eyed her thoughtfully, wondering exactly how much she knew.

"I know ye share my mind, or else ye wouldna have spent the day as ye did, lad," she said with a peppery smile. "Aye, we'll keep Scotland strong until our crown prince can stand up to lead us."

He couldn't hold back the humph of laughter. Aye, the woman truly was astute. "I am grateful that I am not your enemy, your highness." He couldn't resist teasing.

With a sour look, she led him to the high table as Thomas Cochrane insolently strutted into the hall.

As the king's favorite passed Albany, the prince leaned forward and viciously thrust his dagger to the hilt into a haunch of venison.

Cameron grimaced.

Ach, but the man was a fool in overtly challenging Thomas so. Why did the royal Stewarts all seem to believe they were immune to danger?

Then the king entered in a grand procession, slowly making his way to his canopied chair. He paused briefly behind Mar, but as the youngest prince rose to greet his brother, the king brushed past him, not even granting a cool nod his way.

Mar frowned in disbelief.

The feast began, elaborate course after course arrived, but Cameron found he had little appetite. It was an endless affair, filled with empty words and tasteless fare.

He had all but made up his mind to leave when a sudden gust of wind roared through Stirling's Great Hall.

The candles guttered.

The king paled.

"Your majesty!" Thomas rasped, standing abruptly. "'Tis the sign! 'Tis as the sorceress claimed!"

"Then bring her at once!" The king gripped the edge of the table.

Curiously, Cameron watched as a woman swathed in a red-hooded mantle was brought forth to stand directly before the king, and as she drew back her hood, he caught his breath in surprise.

It was the lass he had rescued that very morning.

With growing suspicion and a great sense of dread, he watched her curtsey low before the king.

"This is Maura, your majesty," Thomas introduced her, bowing before her in respect. "She has walked among us for a time as a lowly chambermaid, seeking to gain a deeper understanding of her visions, my lord."

Cameron held still.

Maura.

He clenched his fist. No doubt, she was the same Maura that Kate had spoken of, the very same woman who had planted the letters in Albany's desk.

Ach, but the beating made perfect sense now.

She had begun to weave back and forth, rolling her eyes into the back of her head. And then in a low, hissing voice, she claimed that a spirit had visited her during the night, imparting the final words of prophecy for the king.

"And those words?" The king's voice rose to an almost hysterical pitch.

She paused for effect, and then answered in a loud, ringing tone, "A lion in Scotland shall be slain by one of his own *kindred*, your majesty." She stressed the word.

"Kindred?" The king sprang to his feet. "Not whelp, but kindred?"

"Aye. Kindred, your majesty." Maura curtsied low.

Albany abruptly banged his goblet down onto the table as Mar rose to his feet in disgust. And as one, both brothers left the hall.

When they had gone, the hall erupted into the sounds of shocked, loud voices and Cameron decided he had quite had enough.

"Shall we leave the table?" he asked the princess at his side.

"Aye." The woman sighed. "I am weary of these fools."

He sent his men to fetch Maura immediately, but they returned a short time later.

She was nowhere to be found.

* * *

A torturous week passed. A week that saw the tense relationship between the king and his brothers grow even more strained, and one that saw Thomas strutting about the castle with a perpetually pleased expression.

Cameron and the princess repeatedly suggested to both Albany and Mar that they should escape to France, but they refused to listen.

By the end of the week, there was still no news of Julian, and even though he knew of no other man that could match Julian's courageous daring, Cameron sent one of his own men to the Borderlands for news.

The only joy that week brought was the secret missive from Sir Arval informing him that Kate was safe at Craigmillar, and had been introduced as his distant cousin, Lucinda MacKenzie. For some odd reason, the name made him smile.

The uneasy days marched on.

Cameron's man returned with the news that the Lord Julian Gray could not be found. Cameron responded by sending more men, but a week later, they returned with the same tidings.

Growing more concerned by the day, Cameron focused on banding the nobles together and relentlessly eroding Thomas' support at court, and for the most part, succeeded quite well in all respects, save one—King James remained Thomas' faithful protector.

And then one evening, as the month of June was nearing an end, Lord Julian Gray finally strode through the door of his private chambers, travel-stained and weary.

"Julian!" Cameron exclaimed with relief, rising to clasp the man's shoulders.

Heaving a long sigh, Julian collapsed upon a chair, running his hands through his fair hair. "I rode to the Borderlands and found even more crimes to lay at Albany's feet. But half were lies spread by the Humes and Hepburns so that they might gain his lands. They care little for true justice even though Albany truly is guilty of murdering John of Scougal."

"Aye." Cameron nodded courteously. He did not have the heart to tell Julian that he already knew it.

Julian read his expression anyway. Rolling his eyes, he snorted in disgust. "Ach, Cameron! Why do I exhaust myself if ye pry the news from others afore I can return?" He grinned, but shot him an exasperated look.

"I sent men after ye thrice, Julian." Cameron handed him a goblet of warm, spiced wine. "Where did ye go?"

"London," he replied grimly.

"London?" Cameron raised a curious brow.

"Edward is indeed eyeing Scotland as a tasty morsel, ready to be eaten. Already, he is planning with the Duke of Gloucester to levy taxes to wage war against us. Ach, ye were right, Cameron." Julian clenched his jaw. "We canna afford to reveal Albany's crimes. Half the country, though weary of James, would rise to defend him, whilst the other half would dance with joy, calling for his execution forthwith. We'd split asunder."

"And deliver ourselves into Edward's hands," Cameron finished for him, tapping his long finger lightly on the arm of his chair.

They exchanged grim looks.

"Thomas is up to some new devilry, but he has few supporters now," Cameron said after a time. "And the king remains in his chambers, speaking only with Thomas and fortune tellers."

"How is it that Thomas yet lives?" Julian growled.

Cameron grimaced. "He does not stray far from the king's side, and when he does, he is heavily guarded. Even I cannot find a way to slay him now."

They spoke long into the night, sipping spiced wine. Gradually, exhaustion and the fire entranced them both.

It was almost dawn, when Cameron leaned his head back against the chair and closed his burning eyes. The last thing he recalled was smiling over Julian's loud snores of exhaustion and then men were shouting.

Both Cameron and Julian sprang to their feet, awake in an instant.

The door to the chamber crashed open.

"My lord!" one of his men gasped as he entered. "Albany has ridden to Dunbar to prepare for war!"

Cameron's lips parted in surprise.

"Why?" Julian demanded harshly.

The man paused, clearly shaken. Licking his dry lips, he continued, "In the dark of the night, Mar was rousted from his bed and accused of consulting with sorcerers and witches to conspire against the king's own life! Thomas Cochrane spirited him away, imprisoning him this very night!"

They stared at the man numbly.

"Where?" Cameron pressed. "Where did Thomas take him?"

"Craigmillar, my lord."

Cameron felt all color drain from his face.

What strange twist of fate had sent Thomas Cochrane directly to Kate?

12

CRAIGMILLAR

Kate leaned against the round tower housing the pigeons at Craigmillar, taking enjoyment in their soft, peaceful coos while soaking in the last warmth of the setting sun.

Already, she had been at Craigmillar for over a month.

After pounding through the mist-shrouded woodlands on the back of Julian's charger, they had arrived at Craigmillar before the noon bells tolled in the nearby town of Edinburgh. And after Julian had introduced her to the kind Lady Preston, he had stayed by her side until both her father and Sir Arval had arrived. Then with a brotherly kiss on the top of her head, the young lord had bade her farewell, and mounting his horse, had galloped off to the Borderlands. She had watched him go with a sense of loss.

But the days passed pleasantly, and while her father recuperated comfortably in a well-cushioned chair before the fire in Craigmillar's main hall, Sir Arval insisted on teaching her how to read and how to ride a horse.

She detested the reading lessons but adored cantering through the surrounding woodlands, around the outskirts of Edinburgh, and amongst the herds of cows and flocks of sheep in the nearby green meadows.

And though her days bustled with activity and more than a little laughter, she grew lonelier with each passing day.

Oh, how her heart ached for Cameron.

Standing beside the cold stones of the tower, her face began to crumple with the sudden threat of tears. Ach, but the mere thought of him was too painful, and she pushed it away quickly.

Carried on the summer wind, the baying of hounds sounded from somewhere far away, breaking her thoughts and reminding her that she was late for the evening meal.

She eyed the castle keep which rose formidably before her in a somewhat forlorn manner.

She could hardly believe that fate had brought her here as a guest, dining on trout and strawberries under an ornate iron chandelier with pure white wax candles. Ach, she should be in the kitchens, serving others the venison, fresh bread, and almond cakes whilst wistfully drooling over bowls of oranges. She should not be eating such delicacies herself. Fate was playing an odd game with her.

With a yawn, she slowly made her way back to the keep.

She had been curiously tired the past few days and a little pale, enough so that Sir Arval had refused to take her riding that day. Instead, he had suggested she should simply rest. She had resisted, but once stretched out upon her feather bed, had soon fallen asleep.

Climbing the stone stairs, she entered the main hall and spied Sir Arval waving from a table next to her drowsing father still sitting by the fire. She eyed him with a twinge of worry. His health was still very frail, and she wondered if he would ever be strong again.

"Did you read the page, *ma chérie*?" Sir Arval greeted her with a challenging twinkle in his eye.

Kate sent him an exasperated look. He knew quite well she hadn't. Ach, why did the man hound her so?

The Frenchman gave a fond growl. "Then you'll read twice as long tonight!"

"'Tis a waste of a good evening," she grumbled, slipping onto the bench next to him.

"And did ye hear of the Candlemaker's daughter?" A voice giggled.

Both Kate and Sir Arval glanced over their shoulders to see a thin, wispy lass carrying a basket of bread. She stopped to speak with a middle-aged woman setting the table nearby.

The women exchanged knowing looks.

"Ach, the Candlemaker's daughter?" The other woman began to cluck. "She's with a bairn now, isn't she? And nae a husband in sight!"

"Aye! She's a fallen woman." The wispy lass gave a superior sniff. "What would ye do, Hilde, if ye carried a bairn out of wedlock?"

"I would die of shame!" The woman fanned her cheeks. "'Tis the worst disgrace!"

Chattering, they moved away.

Kate quickly dropped her gaze.

She was almost certain now that she carried Cameron's bairn, and if she did, then soon, they would be talking about her like that. Hoping she was mistaken, she took a deep breath and stared down at her trencher of waterfowl in fig sauce with a sudden queasiness.

Clearing his throat, Sir Arval leaned forward and patted her hands. "The earl hasn't abandoned you, *ma chérie*," he murmured softly.

Kate jerked back as color stained her face. Why had he said that? Did he suspect she carried a bairn? 'Twas it that obvious?

Discomfited, she tore a chunk of bread and dipped it into the fig sauce, but no sooner had she tasted the morsel then she felt her stomach heave.

Desperately, she clapped her hands over her mouth and pushed it away.

"You should rest, *ma chérie*," Sir Arval suggested kindly.

She shook her head in protest, but the motion triggered a stronger wave of nausea.

She paled. Ach, she truly was carrying a bairn. She already knew it in her heart. There would soon be no denying it. Everyone would know. A myriad of conflicting emotions welled up within her—awe, fear, excitement, and most assuredly shame.

"His lordship will see you well taken care of." Sir Arval was patting her hand. "He is not a man to love lightly, child. He'll protect you and—"

Strangely wanting to weep, she jumped to her feet and escaped up the steps to her small chamber. Leaning against the narrow window, she clutched her stomach, rocking back and forth a little on her heels.

She was no longer a respectable woman. Ach, she was now a fallen woman. And womenfolk would soon be tittering over her and her poor bairn.

The thought was an upsetting one. While she could become accustomed to whispers and outraged looks, her poor bairn would find it far more hurtful.

She closed her eyes.

The road ahead was most certainly a hard one.

She was not a fool. Cameron would never be allowed to wed her and make her a proper wife. And while he would assuredly provide for his bairn, he would never be able to give the child his name—the name of kings.

Hot tears loomed, but she bit her lip, stubbornly refusing to shed them. Having disgraced herself, she should want to die of shame. Yet, she still couldn't bring herself to regret anything. The moment she thought of Cameron's chiseled lips and dark, passionate eyes, she dreamt of tumbling into bed with him again.

Why was she such a wanton fool?

Ach, what would her own bairn think of her?

But even as shame threatened to consume her, a fierce wave of protectiveness rose to overwhelm it.

She was truly having a bairn.

She couldn't deny the little leap of joy in her heart thinking of a bairn with wee fingers and toes, a bairn to hold close to her heart through the long, lonely nights, and a bairn she could tease into giggling with a tickle under the chin.

Her lips curved into a guilty smile. Whatever fortune the future held, she would provide her child with a life filled with as much love and laughter as her own had been. She could simply show the lad or lassie how to cover their ears to ward off the painful words of others.

Feeling suddenly drained, she sank to the edge of her bed and slowly stretched out to rest for a moment, but instead quickly drifted off into an uneasy asleep.

It was some time later, in the inky blackness of the night, that Kate awoke with a jolt.

Slowly, she sat up, disoriented, and then she heard a woman scream from the hall below.

Leaping to her feet, she ran to the door.

Men shouted, and the woman shrieked again.

Without hesitation, she rushed towards her father's chamber but nearly collided with a blonde-haired woman holding a torch aloft.

"Kate?" The voice was familiar.

Kate glanced at her again and then gasped. "Maura?"

"So, ye've been hiding here!" Maura smirked, arching a fine brow.

Angry voices filtered up from below, and Kate pointed to the dark stairs winding below. "Do ye know what is happening, Maura?"

"Aye." Maura's eyes glittered coldly in the torchlight. "Come with me."

Something in her tone made Kate hesitate. "But I must find my father—"

"Ye haven't a choice, Kate," Maura hissed, reaching out and grabbing her arm.

As Maura began wrestling her back, Sir Arval's lean figure suddenly staggered from the stairwell. He stumbled towards Kate, clutching his side, and even in the faint, flickering light, she could see a dark stain spreading beneath his fingers.

Her heart leapt to her throat.

"Kate!" Sir Arval gasped. He only made it several steps before collapsing to his knees and then pitched forward unconsciously to the floor.

With a shriek, Kate lunged toward him, but Maura was strong and yanked her back.

"Ach, 'tis too late for him and your father," the woman informed her coldly.

Seized by fear, Kate whirled and grasped her shoulders. "Father? What do ye mean, Maura? My father?"

Dimly, she heard Maura reply as if from miles away, "'Twas the fool who gave ye away when we saw him sitting by the fire. And 'twas enough to tell us that—"

"Father?" Kate screamed, but several strange men appeared and grabbed her from behind, pulling her down the corridor in the opposite direction. "Father!"

"He's dead." Maura followed with a frown, covering her ears in annoyance. "Ach, be silent! Ye shrill worse than a fishwife! But then, 'tis what ye are—"

But Kate was no longer listening to her.

Dead?

Her father couldn't be dead.

No, not after she'd nursed him back to health—brought him back from the brink of death!

Desperately, she fought the hands that dragged her, but it was futile.

And then for the first time in her life, she fainted.

* * *

Gradually, Kate became aware of voices. One voice was deep and sounded weary. The other was familiar, an annoyingly nasal tone.

Slowly, she lifted her lashes. Her head ached. She was lying on the cold, stone floor. Dazed and stiff, she propped herself up on her elbow, and then a pair of booted feet paused before her. She heard a nasal laugh.

It was Thomas Cochrane.

Dressed in sumptuous green velvet, and with his heavy gold chain about his neck, he hunched over her with his hands clasped behind his back.

With an expression of pleasure upon his long face, he said, "I have been blessed this day. Not only do I have a title to an earldom within my grasp, I will soon have Cameron crawling before me, weeping tears of despair."

Kate stared at him, her thoughts strangely muddled. Why was the man speaking of Cameron?

"Aye, I'll watch him suffer!" Thomas continued, his voice shaking with pent emotion. "As ruler of this land, I'll hound him—"

"Ruler?" the weary, deep voice interrupted him with a disdainful snort. "Playing the puppet master will never be the same as being the king, ye fool! And your time is at an end. James will never forgive ye for what ye've done now."

Turning her head, Kate saw a finely dressed nobleman slouched against the wall, his hands and feet bound. There was a jagged cut on his forehead, and it took her moment to recognize his pale face as John Stewart, Earl of Mar, the youngest brother of King James.

Kate caught her breath in surprise.

"Aye." Thomas smiled, apparently enjoying her reaction. "Even Mar, a prince of the royal Stewart blood is powerless before me. Even now the king mulls over tidings that his cherished brother conspired with sorcerers and witches to slay him."

Mar gave a contemptuous laugh. "He'll never believe ye. At last, ye are undone, knave. Even now, my brother will be riding to Craigmillar to secure my freedom! Ach, ye are but a fool!"

Thomas Cochrane's lips twisted in a scornful smile. "Who is the fool? Your brother is a firm believer in the black arts. 'Tis ye who will die right soon, ye and the witches that I say colluded with ye these past months, pleading with the devil to smite your own brother!"

Mar gave a snort of disgust.

Thomas shrugged. "I never would have harmed ye, Mar. 'Twas Albany I was after, but then ye sought to kill me at the hunt. Ye brought this upon yourself!"

At that, Mar fell silent, and Kate swallowed, shaking her head in bewilderment. She was feeling strangely lethargic and confused. Was she caught in some ghastly nightmare? She closed her eyes, willing herself to wake. But when she opened her eyes again, nothing changed.

She frowned. Where was her father? Where was Sir Arval?

"And ye, Kate!" Thomas sneered, dropping on one knee before her. "I respected ye. We are both commoners grasping for power, and I respected that in ye ... until ye betrayed me by thieving the letters from Albany's desk." Reaching down, he grasped her by the throat and hissed. "And for that, ye'll pay."

As his fingers pressed harder, she struggled for air, clawing desperately at his hands until he shoved her back with revulsion.

Raising his hand, he moved towards her and struck her hard across the face.

Pain exploded in her nose, and she fell back to the floor, striking her head. For a brief moment, she saw sparks of light followed quickly by a thick darkness, and then her vision returned.

Looming over her, Thomas pulled a small, gold-inlaid dagger from his belt. With a gleam of pleasure in his eye, he trailed the blade down the side of her face, down her neck, and to the pearl-laced bodice of her gray gown. Then with a vicious jerk, he half-tore, half-ripped it away, using it to mop the blood streaming from her nose.

Holding the bloodstained cloth against the torchlight, he gave a smile of satisfaction.

Kate numbly looked away, and it was then that her eye caught on the blood-splattered stones.

Suddenly, she remembered her father and Sir Arval.

They were dead.

This had to be a nightmare. It couldn't be true. Her father and Sir Arval couldn't really be dead!

But she did not weep. She could not even react. The numbness rose, taking a firm hold upon her, and she watched impassively as Maura entered the room and held up several of the pure, white wax candles from the hall.

Giving the candles to Thomas, Maura dipped in a quick curtsey. "Wax, as ye requested, my lord."

Pleased, Thomas dangling the candles over Kate and laughed. "Do ye not recognize your own witchery, Kate? Do ye not see the waxen form of the king that ye gave to Mar to perform his unholy deeds? Aye, ye'll both burn at the stake afore I'm through with ye!"

Kate eyed the candles apathetically.

The man was mad, but she strangely didn't care.

"But first we must be off to my house in the Canongate." Thomas shoved the candles back into Maura's hands. "I'll not risk Cameron's arrival here. If I know the earl, he is already well on his way, knowing that we found his precious Kate." At that, he tossed his head back to laugh, a loud, long, jarring sound. "Aye, the hand of fate guided me on the most blessed of paths this day, even delivering the Earl of Lennox into my hand! Ach, Kate, but ye were a splendid find!"

And then men arrived, pulling Mar and Kate to their feet, pushing them down the stairs, and through Craigmillar's hall.

Kate moved as if in a dream, not even tempted to glance at the fire where her father had spent his days drowsing in the chair.

She no longer cared to think.

Saddled horses awaited them in the courtyard as the sun rose in the east, bathing Craigmillar with a pale, pink light. And as Thomas' men hefted Mar over one of the horses, tying him to the saddle, she found herself plucked up and placed in the lap of a grim, muscled man with lank and greasy hair.

She didn't struggle as they sprang away, galloping towards the town of Edinburgh. She merely watched with detached interest as the dark and mighty Edinburgh Castle grew closer, rising high upon the rocky cliffs above the surrounding town and Forth Valley.

It was not long before the horses' hooves clattered on the cobblestoned streets of Edinburgh and up the widening road that led to the dark, walled castle. But before they reached it, Thomas veered suddenly, guiding his horse onto the narrow wynd that snaked through the tall houses of the Canongate.

At length, he reined before one of the dwellings, and raising his hand, signaled them to dismount. Lifting Kate down from the horse himself, he pushed her through a creaking, red door, up a narrow stair, and into a small chamber with high windows on the second floor.

Moments later, another man appeared, prodding Mar forward with the blade of a dirk. Ducking his head, the prince entered the chamber slowly, his hands still bound behind his back.

Fishing within the folds of his cloak, Thomas withdrew Kate's bloodstained bodice and tossed it to the man with the dirk. "Send this to Cameron, with my message." His long face creased into a beaming smile. He turned back to Kate, rubbing his hands together briskly.

She merely stared at him.

"I would think ye a half-wit, Kate, if I hadn't seen the fire in ye afore." Thomas frowned, looking a little disappointed.

"Leave the lass be, knave," Mar ordered from his position near the door. "She has no place in this matter. Set her free at once!"

"Ah, 'tis ye who are the half-wit," Thomas ridiculed the prince, shaking his head in wonder. "Ye canna even understand your own dire circumstance!"

As the men traded insults, Kate dully watched as Maura, carrying the wax candles, entered the chamber and knelt before the hearth. Blowing over the bits of peat and twigs, she coaxed the fire back to life and set about arranging the candles in the small iron pot suspended over it.

Leaving Mar, Thomas joined Maura, tossing a small cloth bundle at her feet.

"In there ye'll find the king's cherished ring and a cutting from his favorite robe. Use them both," he said. "And take some of Mar's hair, 'tis the same shade as James. Be quick! I must return to Stirling right quickly. I've yet to declare both Mar and Kate witches, and there is still much to be done."

Witches? Kate shook her head and frowned.

"Take heart, Kate," Mar called from behind her. "The king will stop this mad man. At last, Thomas has gone too far. No one will ever believe that we are witches, seeking to harm the king!"

Kate merely blinked.

"Ach, she's gone mad." Maura cast Kate a side-length glance as she expelled her breath, and then a momentary expression of sorrow crossed the woman's face as she muttered, "Mayhap, 'tis better this way."

"What say ye?" Thomas lifted his head and marched to where Maura sat on her heels before the hearth. Raising a threatening hand, his eyes narrowed. "Do not think to betray me, Maura! Do ye recall the last time ye failed me?"

Maura clenched her teeth but replied in a sure voice, "I'll not fail ye, my lord. Have no fear."

Thomas remained there for a time, staring down at her, but she kept her gaze focused on the wax she was forming with her hands, and at length he moved away, calling for his men.

"We've the other witches to finish off now," Thomas told them. "Now that we have them confessing their crimes of witchery, 'tis time to begin the burnings. The king canna help but be convinced now and—"

"Ach, ye fool!" Mar tossed his head. "James will never—"

In two strides, Thomas stood before Mar. He struck him across the face with such force that the man's head struck the wall.

"How does that feel?" Thomas asked in a voice riddled with pleasure.

With blood trickling from the corner of his mouth, Mar swore, "Ye are a dead man!"

"Bind his mouth!" Thomas snapped, returning to stand above Kate.

Kate did not move.

After a moment, he heaved a breath of disappointment. "Ach, perhaps she has gone mad." Losing interest, he joined his men, saying, "Then, let us be gone, to see to the conspirators of the devil!"

As they filed out of the small chamber, Kate wearily leaned back against the wall, faintly aware for the first time that her head and nose ached.

Across the chamber, Mar sat with his mouth now bound and four men with dirks flanking him, but the eyes upon which he looked at Kate were kind and full of compassion.

Time passed.

Occasionally, Kate heard the church bells tolling in the distance.

Once, Maura pressed bread and water into her hands, but she had little appetite and no interest in rousing herself from her stupor.

Finally, Maura rose proudly to her feet, holding a small wax doll aloft, and Thomas Cochrane returned to the chamber, bearing a wide smile of satisfaction.

"Well done." He snatched the doll from her hands and wagged it at Mar still sitting in the corner. "When the king sees this witchery, your fate is sealed, Mar."

Mar did not respond. He remained as he was, slumped against the wall.

Turning to Kate, Thomas prodded her with his toe. "Up with ye, Kate! 'Tis time ye joined your fellow witches at the Tolbooth Prison."

Clasping her hand, he pulled her up and threw his cloak over her head.

"Maura, ye'll come with us to bear witness of Kate's crimes against the king," he ordered the woman as he tucked the wax figure into a leather pouch.

"But willna the earl find her there?" Maura protested, pulling Kate down the stairs after Thomas.

"I've paid the guards well. They'll hide her until the burning. The earl will never find her there, not in time," Thomas replied, and then suddenly turned accusingly upon the woman. "Not unless ye think to tell him for some ill-gotten gain of your own!"

Maura hissed, drawing back. "I've never betrayed ye, my lord."

He didn't appear entirely convinced as he readjusted his cloak to mask more of Kate's face. And then with an intimidating scowl, he planted his face inches from hers and warned, "Do not even think to run, lass. There's naught ye can do to escape your fate now. 'Tis to prison with ye, and then to burn for your crimes against the king."

Kate took a deep breath. For a moment, a voice of panic struggled to rise past the waves of confusion and the constant pain in her head, but the effort proved to be too much. Losing interest, she only wondered when she could lie down and sleep.

"Ach, she's been struck dumb as well as mad." Maura sniffed

disdainfully. "She's not responded to me the entire day."

"'Tis no matter for I'll take my joy in Cameron's suffering." Thomas shrugged callously and then set off up Canongate Road, pulling Kate after him. "Come, we must hasten!"

He led them towards the center of the town, past the High Kirk of Edinburgh, and to the Mercat Cross in the center of the market square where a crowd of merchants and bystanders milled about. Long sheets of parchment had been posted on the Mercat Cross and on several of the buildings nearby.

"Ach, 'tis a proclamation of witchery!" a man's voice filtered through the fog in Kate's mind. "It states they practiced the black arts against the king!"

"Who's that? 'Tis another one?" a voice shrilled from nearby.

"Aye, 'tis a witch!" Thomas raised his voice, gripping Kate by the forearm and yanking her forward. "Stand back, I must take her to the Tolbooth straightway!"

A gasp swept over the crowd. Some ignored Thomas to press closer and began to pelt them with small stones.

"God's Wounds!" Thomas thundered, raising his arm to protect his face. "'Twas not I who committed this crime! Stand back, ye ruffians!"

He shoved his way through the increasingly rowdy throng, and at last stood before the Tolbooth Prison, a great gray-stoned building with a massive iron door guarded by several men.

Recognizing Thomas Cochrane, one of the men signaled the others to drive the unruly mob back as he quickly escorted them inside.

"This is the witch I spoke of," Thomas announced, yanking the cloak from Kate's head. "At all costs, she must not be found."

"Aye, my lord." The man bowed. "Upon my life, I will not have her found."

And as Thomas began to speak with him, another man came forward to grip Kate's arm and push her down a narrow corridor. Finally, he paused in front of a dark cell with a straw-covered floor.

There was a rasp of a key in the lock and the screeching creak of a door, and then Kate found herself shoved inside. She stumbled and fell, and a rank stench rose to greet her as she landed in the sour straw. But she was too tired to do anything other than close her eyes.

She was caught in a nightmare.

13

THE TOLBOOTH PRISON

In the darkness before dawn, Cameron strode purposefully to the king's apartments with his cloak billowing out behind him and Julian at his heels. His heart cried out to depart at once for Craigmillar and Kate, but he knew that he must attempt to stop the king's madness, at least until his men were ready to ride. He knew no one else would even try to open the king's eyes. Instead, the other nobles would immediately seek to raise arms and plunge the country into civil war.

As he brushed past the king's guards without breaking his stride, some of the men lifted their weapons as if to challenge his entry, but only for a brief moment before they stepped back and sent him a nod of respect instead.

Cameron drew his lips in a thin line of disapproval.

Even the loyalty of the king's own personal guard had waned.

Was no one satisfied with the king?

It did not bode well for the future.

The cluster of attendants waiting in the darkened antechamber scattered before him, and guided by the faint flickering light, Cameron kicked back the door to the king's privy chamber and entered with a dark, forbidding glare.

King James sat at his table poring over the pages of a large book as the astrologers Andrews and Hathaway hovered attentively but bleary-eyed, behind him. From the melting wax dripping from the tapers to form large pools on the table, it was clear they had not slept all night.

The king took one look at Cameron's menacing expression and paled.

As Julian remained on the threshold, arms bracing each doorpost, Cameron advanced, his eyes filling with icy disdain.

Dismissing the astrologers, the king licked his lips and clapped his hands to order in a thin, wavering voice, "Have cakes and drinks brought for his lordship at once!"

Cameron surveyed the king's table and arched a scathing brow at the silver platters of half-eaten tarts and unfinished goblets of wine littering its surface before speaking in a deadly, cold voice, "I find it appalling that a king can dine on delicacies and study books whilst his own youngest brother is imprisoned and falsely accused of witchcraft."

The king froze.

Expelling his breath in unmasked contempt, Cameron continued in a chilling, even tone, "Aye, I've no more time for polished words and courtly speech with ye. Ye'll stop this madness with Thomas at once! Can ye not see how the people grow dissatisfied with their king? If ye continue walking this path there will not be one left standing with ye!"

The king swallowed and sputtered, "We are your king! Dare ye think to threaten us?

"Aye, I dare." Cameron's dark eyes smoldered. "And if ye do not free Mar at once, I will see ye undone myself!"

The king shuddered but insisted feebly, "But Thomas found evidence, Cameron, evidence that Mar is a warlock, dabbling with the dark powers and consulting ceaselessly with necromancers and, mayhap Satan himself, to shorten the life of his own brother, the king!"

"Ach!" Julian made a disgusted sound from the door.

With pity swiftly waning for the weak-willed man trembling before him, Cameron replied in a cutting tone, "And, like a fool, ye believe every word that Thomas utters? Can ye not see the man lusts only for power and plays ye for a puppet?"

King James licked his lips nervously.

"Look at me!" Cameron ordered in a lethally calm tone. "Look at me, James! Look in my eyes and swear that ye actually believe Mar— our most loyal Mar—is a warlock!"

The king trembled, resisting for a time, before finally lifting his gaze to Cameron's.

A silence so profound fell in the room that the breath of each man could easily be heard.

And then tears welled in the king's eyes, and he buried his face in his hands, gasping, "What have I done, Cameron? What have I done to Mar? And what have I done to Albany—"

"Albany?" Cameron seized upon the name, his dark eyes widening in dismay. "What madness has overtaken ye this foul night? What have ye done to Albany? Speak quickly!"

"An ambush," the king confessed in a voice scarce above a whisper. Desperately, he clawed at Cameron's sleeve. "Save them, Cameron! Save them both! What have I done to my own brothers—my own blood?"

"Ye'd best pray there is still time," Cameron swore under his breath, shaking himself free of the man's grip. He had heard enough. He was done with the man, king or no. He continued, "If they should come to harm, I swear I'll not be answerable for what might happen to ye. And when this day is done, James, ye'll order Thomas held accountable for his treachery! Swear upon your life's blood that it will be so! 'Tis far past the time to purge Scotland of his unholy influence, afore we have no country left!"

The king blanched but murmured weakly, "Aye … aye. We swear it."

But his voice held no conviction.

Cameron sent him a withering glance. There was no doubt in his mind that when Thomas returned, the king would forget his vow. Speaking with the fool was a waste of his time.

"Ach, I'll no longer bandy words with ye, James," Cameron said with a scornful twist of his lips. "I'm away to Craigmillar." He whirled on his heel.

"Do not leave us, Cameron!" the king begged, reaching out to stop him. "We are in danger! The prophecies have foretold it! Stay with us! Julian can go—"

Biting back a curse of contempt, Cameron left the king in his privy chamber, ignoring the man's cries for him to stay.

He was done with the fool. And if any harm befell his Kate, he would see the man undone right quickly! Cameron's throat tightened at the mere thought of her.

Soon, his men would be ready, and he would ride to Craigmillar. Silently, he prayed that Thomas would not find her even as he knew in his heart that his prayer would go unanswered.

Clenching his jaw, he swiftly returned to his chambers, intent on collecting their weaponry with haste.

Julian had followed.

"The king's unstable in his wits," the young Lord Gray growled, examining several slender blades before hiding them in his boot.

Buckling his heavy sword about his waist, Cameron agreed grimly, "Aye, his actions this night have all but plunged us into a civil war, but 'tis a matter to be dealt with later. Now, I must ride after Mar, and 'tis up to ye to save Albany's neck."

"Aye," Julian muttered, concealing another knife in his sleeve. Then with a glint of ill humor in his gray eyes, he added, "Though I'll shed no tears for the man should I be late."

Quickly inspecting his dirk with a cold detachment, Cameron thrust it into its scabbard before replying evenly, "Justice for Albany's deeds in the Borderlands will have to wait. Take him to France, willing or no. I'll have him gone from Scotland. I've not the time for him now."

"Aye, he'll fit well in France," Julian murmured in agreement, fingering the hilt of his sword. "Lies and treason are the way of life there."

Something in his tone made Cameron pause. Raising a calculating brow, he warned, "Ye'll pledge his safety with your own life, Julian."

Julian visibly hesitated but then replied with a reluctant twist of his lip, "If ye insist then, Cameron. I'll see the man safe. Though I would I was riding with ye to Craigmillar to save Kate instead."

At the mention of her name, Cameron's throat constricted.

He turned away.

If Thomas Cochrane had touched a single hair on Kate's head, he was a dead man!

Satisfied with his weaponry, he pulled on his gloves and quit the chamber, heading for the stables at a swift pace.

The lads were leading their saddled chargers out of the stables when Cameron and Julian arrived and they mounted at once, waiting impatiently in the chilly predawn air for Cameron's company of men to form behind them.

Finally, all were ready, and then without a word, Cameron sprang forward, leading them through the gates of Stirling Castle to gallop down Castle Hill and over the stone bridge of the River Forth.

The ride was a torturous one, not only for the mad pace they set but for the thoughts in his heart as well.

Why had he tempted fate? How could he have thought to defy his unlucky destiny? His foolishness may have harmed Kate. He could do nothing now save fight destiny itself.

But fight destiny he would, or he would die in the attempt.

With grim determination, he clung to a fragile thread of hope and spurred his horse on.

Several times, he heard a pack of wolves howling in the darkness before the sky began to lighten. They followed the river as the water steadily turned silver, reflecting the gray sky above. The morning mist swirled as they passed through it, growing only thicker with time.

Finally, the river widened into the Firth of Forth and the black, rocky crags of Edinburgh appeared in the distance.

At a fork in the road, Cameron raised his arm, signaling the men to halt.

It was time for Julian to part their company.

"Ach, 'tis cruel to send me after Albany. The man should suffer an ill fate for his misdeeds!" Julian struck the pommel of his saddle with his fist. "I should be riding with ye!"

Cameron clenched his jaw. "While my heart agrees with ye, Julian, ye know that should both princes perish this evil day an even darker shadow will befall us. 'Tis not Albany ye are saving, but Scotland itself. Ye have no choice. Ye must go at once!"

Julian heaved an exasperated breath.

Pulling off his glove, Cameron leaned forward to clasp Julian's forearm. "May the winds favor your voyage to France, my friend."

After a moment of hesitation, Julian sighed. And then with a dark smile, he clasped Cameron's forearm in return, shaking it a little. "And may ye lay a snare that Thomas cannot escape, my friend."

Cameron's eyes lit with a silent promise.

And then the fair-haired young lord spurred his mighty horse forward, riding low over its neck to gallop after Albany with unparalleled speed.

Satisfied, Cameron signaled his men to ride, and soon after, he was charging across the bright green grass to the gray walls of Craigmillar rising before him. Gripping the handle of his sword firmly, he thundered through the gates of the castle, prepared for the worst.

The Prestons stood on high alert. Men in dark, red plaids stood brandishing swords with shields on their arms. Recognizing him immediately, they ran forward, catching the reins of his charger as he leapt from the saddle.

"Where is Kate?" The demand tore from his throat. "And Sir Arval?"

Guiding him to the keep, they led him down a narrow corridor, speaking all the while.

In the middle of the night, Thomas Cochrane had arrived with Mar, bearing the king's orders to imprison him there. But upon spying Kate's father, Thomas had struck the ailing man severely before searching the castle for Kate. The Prestons and Sir Arval had raised their swords against them, but Thomas had used Mar as a hostage to escape, taking Kate with them. Sir Arval had nearly paid with his life before Thomas had galloped away in the direction of Edinburgh.

"And Kate? Was she harmed?" Cameron asked in a hoarse whisper.

"Nay, my lord. She appeared hale, hearty enough to walk," they swore, pushing open a narrow, iron-studded door and beckoning him to enter. "But Sir Arval and John are both injured sorely, my lord. Nigh unto death."

There were two beds in the chamber, one holding the silent figure of Kate's father, and the other an even stiller form of Sir Arval. A monk in brown robes moved between them, dabbing their foreheads with an herb-infused cloth.

Cameron peered down at their waxen faces. Their breathing was shallow and their eyes closed.

Aye, this was his fault.

"Tend to them well," he ordered grimly. And then feeling ill, he turned away, murmuring under his breath, "Forgive me."

Returning to the courtyard, he leaned his head against the stone wall of the keep and closed his eyes. He wanted nothing more than to scream out of pure rage, but he knew he must remain calm if he were to outwit his cursed destiny.

Taking a deep breath, he focused on Thomas.

The man was an overbearing, pompous fool, and did not know the meaning of stealth. There would be talk of him in Edinburgh.

Taking heart, Cameron lifted his head.

Aye, he would ride to Edinburgh and track Thomas down. He would find his Kate and pluck her from the very fingers of death seeking to encircle her. And never would he let her out of his sight again.

"Hold strong, my heart," he whispered softly to her, and then turning to his men, ordered in a deep voice, "To Edinburgh with haste!"

The mysterious fog had deepened, hugging the ground. And the surrounding woodlands were strangely silent as they made their way to the town of Edinburgh, a scant three miles away. They were almost upon the gates of the town when a horse suddenly appeared in a swirl of mist to block their path.

Cameron's charger reared. Steadying the beast with a calm hand, he raised his voice to hail, "Who goes there?"

"I bear a message for Cameron, the Earl of Lennox," came the reply.

Tilting his head to the side, Cameron dropped a hand to rest on the hilt of his sword and urged his horse forward, saying, "I am the Earl of Lennox. Give me your message."

The messenger waited until he was close before tossing a bundle at him, and then hastily pulling his horse back, disappeared into the mist.

Leaning in his saddle, Cameron caught the bundle before it fell to the ground. Untying the rough hemp twine, he shook the cloth and held it up for a better view.

His heart stood still.

The pearl-encrusted bodice of Kate's gown fluttered in his hand, covered in blood as a slip of parchment spun to the ground.

He turned white.

One of his men leapt from the saddle to pluck the parchment from the mud and place it in his fingers.

With a cold detachment, he read the words aloud: *I, Thomas Cochrane, await ye in Stirling.*

Passionate vows of vengeance sprang from the lips of his men surrounding him.

"Then we ride to Stirling, my lord?" they asked.

Cameron took a deep breath.

Bringing Kate's bodice to his lips, he silently vowed he would find her before slipping the pearl-encrusted cloth under his shirt to rest near his heart.

Thomas clearly did not want him in Edinburgh. Why else would he have his man wait at the gates to send him back to Stirling? He must be getting close.

Crumpling the man's missive, he dashed it to the ground with a savage twist of his lip and ordered imperiously, "We ride on to Edinburgh and speak with every man, woman, lad and lassie until we find those who witnessed Thomas' arrival. I'll enlist the aid of the queen herself. I've not the stomach for playing games with Thomas Cochrane."

As one, they surged forward, clattering through the gates and riding up the Royal Mile to the walls of the ancient castle of Edinburgh where the queen resided.

Commanding his men to begin searching the town at once, Cameron threw back the hood of his mud-spattered cloak and entered the main gates of the castle alone to beg audience with the queen.

She saw him at once.

Margaret of Denmark, Queen of Scotland, was a slender young woman, blue-eyed, fair of hair, and gentle of heart. Queen of Scotland from the tender age of thirteen, she had already given the king two heirs and was even now expecting a third child. She received Cameron in her privy chamber, in the company of her most trusted ladies. Resting her hand on the top of her expanding belly, she viewed Cameron with an expression of alarm.

"What has happened, my good earl?" she asked, her eyes wide.

With regret in causing her distress, Cameron quickly relayed the events leading up to his arrival.

The queen gasped, falling back as several of her ladies rushed to steady her, and her clear blue eyes filled with tears. "Not Mar! Not Mar! We must search for him at once! My men are yours to command, my good earl. Take whatever you need!"

"And when this is done, we will speak further, my queen." Cameron bowed before her, touching his lips to her hand. Aye, he'd see her wee son, James, safely on the throne of Scotland, but first he had to hold the country together long enough for it to happen.

Quitting Edinburgh castle with a host of the queen's men under his command, he ordered them to search for Mar and Kate, leaving no stone unturned.

Striding down the streets of Edinburgh himself, he questioned all who crossed his path. But it was not long before he discovered the fear of witches running rampant through the town. With a growing alarm, he made his way to the Mercat Cross next to St. Giles Cathedral, and found posted on its stones the proclamation accusing Mar of witchcraft.

With a curse, Cameron tore the parchment down.

In a bold script, the words named Mar a warlock, presiding over a coven of witches with the purpose to practice the black arts against the king. And under Mar's name ran a list of others, men and women, with two scheduled for execution on the morrow.

James himself had signed and sealed the proclamation.

Cameron cursed again.

The man had truly gone mad if he would allow the burning of his own subjects over Thomas' lies. With such short notice, it would be difficult to defy the king and stop the executions, but he had to try.

Cameron ordered a contingent of his men to search the Tolbooth prison immediately, for any sign of Mar and Kate, while the others continued to gather information from the streets of Edinburgh. After seeing them on their way, Cameron hastily returned to the castle to speak with the queen and her advisors, pleading with them to defy the king's order and stop the executions. They discussed the matter long into the night, crafting letters to the king and his advisors begging them to put an end to the madness, but they all knew it would take time, longer than some of the prisoners had left to live.

In the early hours before dawn, Cameron was once again searching the streets, and as soft colors painted the sky, he questioned the local innkeepers and halted travelers along their way, seeking any clue that might lead him to Mar and Kate.

It was then, that one of his men found him.

"Tidings, my lord!" the man gasped, holding onto his knees to catch his breath. "A lad waits for us at the Mercat Cross. With his own eyes, he saw Mar led into a house with a red door, and he'll show us the way."

Drawing his cloak about him, Cameron followed his man with great haste, clutching Kate's bloodstained bodice close to his heart and vowing soundlessly, "I will find ye, Kate, stay strong."

As promised, the lad awaited them, and in short order, Cameron and his men stood in front of the house with the red door. Raising his sword, his men followed suit, and they burst into the house, and swarmed up the steps.

The skirmish was short-lived.

Thomas' men were too few and lacked the will to fight. Laying down their weapons almost at once, the men knelt and pointed to a door in the corner of the room.

Still brandishing his sword, Cameron crossed the chamber in two strides and kicked the door back with his foot.

The interior room was dark, lit only by a single taper and the dull glow of a dying fire. It took a moment for his eyes to adjust to see a tall, cowled monk clad in coarse woolen robes hovering over a wooden bathtub filled with water.

And next to him stood Thomas Cochrane, pale and shaking.

With a red tide of anger rising to possess him, Cameron found himself in front of the man, clutching his throat and demanding in a chill, deadly voice, "Where is Kate? What have ye done with her?"

A weak, gurgling sound from the tub interrupted him.

Glancing down, Cameron saw Mar lying silent, still, in a strangely dark water with an overwhelming odor.

"My lord, he ... he was ill with a fever!" Thomas began to explain in a trembling voice. "The monks bled him, to save his life!"

With eyes widening in alarm, Cameron shoved Thomas back. "What have ye done!"

Ach, it was the stench of blood that met his nostrils!

His heart leapt into his throat.

Mar lay in his own blood.

"No!" Cameron cried. Bodily lifting Mar out of the water, he heaved him over the edge of the tub, collapsing with him onto the floor.

But one look at the man's white face signaled it was too late.

Desperately, Cameron sought to staunch the bleeding gashes on Mar's wrists and legs, all the while crying out for his men to assist him and beseeching under his breath, "Mar! Not like this! Not like this!"

And then Mar's lashes quivered feebly, and his marble lips formed his name, "Cameron."

With tears in his eyes, Cameron leaned down, placing his ear close to the man's trembling mouth.

"Promise ... me..." Mar breathed in slow, rasping words. "Save James, Cameron. Promise me ... that ye'll save James."

Cameron closed his eyes.

"Save ... James," Mar repeated, dropping his eyes to see his own blood pooling on the chamber floor. He lifted his lashes again to look upon Cameron in stunned disbelief. "James ... didna do this, Cameron. Save ... him."

And then with a last frail breath, his chest moved no more.

For several moments, Cameron stared in shock at the lifeless form of the prince lying in his arms, and then, rising swiftly to his feet, he struck Thomas a mighty blow across the face.

The man fell down, but after some groveling, regained his feet.

"I'll see ye hanged when this is over!" Cameron vowed, grabbing the man's arm and dragging him roughly into the adjoining room. "But tell me first and I'll ask ye only once. What have ye done to Kate? Where is she?"

Thomas swallowed.

With anger raging in his veins, Cameron pulled him to the table, kicking a chair out of his way and sweeping the cups off to clear its surface.

Forcing Thomas' hand down upon it, he spoke in a cold, measured tone, "Then know ye this, Thomas. Your life depends on Kate's. And this scar will ever remind ye of that fact."

With a single, swift motion, he drew his dagger and plunged it through Thomas' hand, pinning it to the table.

Thomas screamed in agony and the blood drained from his face. "She's at the Tolbooth Prison, to be burnt as a witch!"

Cameron's eyes flooded with alarm.

"We searched the Tolbooth, my lord," one of his men inserted quickly.

Cameron's eyes narrowed at Thomas. "Think ye to lie to me?" he hissed, twisting the blade still embedded in Thomas' hand.

The man screamed again, licking his lips nervously. "I swear, my lord, I swear I am speaking the truth. 'Tis a secret cell. I will take ye there myself!"

"Then do so, at once!" Cameron all but roared the order.

Wrenching his dagger free, he grasped Thomas by the neck, shoved him down the stairs and out into the secluded close.

Drawing his sword, he warned the man, "I will not hesitate to smite your worthless head from your shoulders, should ye think to escape me! Now give wings to your feet!"

With his hand leaving a trail of blood, Thomas began to run, and Cameron swiftly followed.

Black clouds of smoke billowed over the rooftops as they approached the Tolbooth Prison. A frenzied mob of trouble causers and malcontents had gathered outside, armed with stones and sticks.

Screams rent the air.

The burnings had already begun.

Not allowing himself to think, Cameron forced his way to the front to behold a sight that would sicken him the remainder of his days. He closed his eyes, relieved the two victims were clearly men, even as their screams burned through his soul.

It did not last long. As the flames rose to consume them, he turned, his eyes sweeping over the bloodthirsty crowd with revulsion before dropping a contemptuous gaze upon Thomas. "What manner of devil are ye?"

Shoving the man through the mob, they finally stood on the steps of the Tolbooth Prison, and then Thomas led them to the secret cell.

Pushing open the iron and oaken door, Cameron burst inside the cell, crying, "Kate!"

The cell was empty.

14

SKYE

Kate had not slept from the moment she arrived at the Tolbooth Prison. No sooner had she collapsed on the sour straw than two guards entered the cell. Lifting her up, they escorted her to a small chamber where a middle-aged man with thick lips, slanted eyes, and a bulging belly sat at a writing desk. He held a long, feathered quill in his hand.

"Are ye Kate Ferguson?" he mumbled, spitting a little as he talked.

Kate grimaced. The persistent pain at the back of her head had dulled, but it was still strangely difficult to think.

"Are ye struck dumb?" The man lifted a bored brow.

"She's Kate Ferguson," one of the guards answered on her behalf.

The man at the desk grunted, "Witnesses?"

"Maura McKinney, your lordship," Maura said, stepping from the shadows. "I've come to offer my testimony, your lordship."

Scratching his scalp with the tip of his quill, the man yawned. "Swear ye'll tell the truth, lass."

Picking up an ivory cross from the desktop, he held it out to Maura and watched apathetically as she knelt and kissed it reverently. He then tossed it back on the desk in a careless gesture.

Dipping his quill in the inkpot, he ordered, "Ach, be quick. I've two witches more for which to pen testament this night!"

"I swear upon my soul's salvation that I witnessed Kate conspiring with the warlock, John Stewart, Earl of Mar," Maura replied in a hurried, rehearsed manner. "I saw them dancing about a wax figure of the king, roasting it with the intent to cause his majesty harm, and suspending it above a cauldron of boiling water to melt its feet so his majesty would suffer difficulty and—"

The man held up a hand signaling Maura to wait as his quill scratched furiously across the parchment. Then he asked, "Dolls? How many?"

"I saw three, your lordship!" Maura curtsied, her blue eyes round and earnest. "They were making many, your lordship, and devising many tortures to heap upon them to hasten his majesty's demise. Kate bedecked the dolls with thread from his majesty's robes and locks of his own hair."

Kate frowned in confusion. 'Twas Maura who had made the doll. Dimly, she wondered if she should mention it.

The man's head bobbed up and down as he continued writing. Finally, he gave a nod of satisfaction. "'Tis duly noted, lass. 'Tis enough—"

But Maura was not finished yet. Licking her lips, she added, "Aye, and Kate called the Devil's minions last fall to curse her own village with a plague. She alone did not suffer, and when the good folk sought to cast her out, she cursed the harvest as well!"

Kate stared numbly at the woman. Plague? She had lost her own mother and wee sister, Joan, in that illness. Ach, her father still suffered from it! Or had. The memory of his death rose in her mind, but she was oddly unable to weep.

She scarcely heard Maura continue.

"And she practiced her accursed ways in Stirling, taking coin from good womenfolk for potions of love but giving them malicious ones in their stead that caused them to break out in a pox and to lose their hair!"

Lifting his quill from the page, the man glanced at Maura with a snort of impatience. "Ach, 'tis mischief only and not a crime worthy of death as the others! Hie ye off, lass." With a frown, he waved her away and motioned to the guards. "Bring the next witch!"

The guards opened the door and brought in a shriveled, wizened old woman. She shuffled past Kate with her aged face resigned as though she had accepted her fate. And as Kate was led away, someone stepped forward and accused the woman of conspiring with Mar against the king in exchange for the promise of perpetual youth.

It was only after the men had shoved Kate into her dark cell, closing the door behind her, that she felt a vague sense of alarm. Sinking to her knees, she buried her face in her arms.

What was happening?

She began to shake, and her forehead beaded with sweat.

Threads of light from the flickering torches of the passageway filtered through the tiny window in the iron and oak door.

She did not know how long she sat there, watching the shadows play across the rancid straw on the floor. It could have been hours or minutes, before a weak shaft of gray light fell through a small window high on the cold, stone wall behind her, and the door to her cell creaked slowly open.

"Kate!" Maura's voice snaked into the room. "Ach, Kate! Ye must be quick afore we are caught!"

Kate blinked slowly.

"Ach, have ye truly gone mad?" Maura's tone wavered between fear and disgust.

Cold fingers closed around Kate's wrist, tugging her to her feet, and then a hand delivered a stinging slap across her cheek.

"Kate! I've not the time for this now! We must run afore they burn us both as witches!"

With a great effort, Kate focused her eyes on Maura's frightened blue ones.

Pressing her lips in a tight thin line, Maura's nostrils flared. "We've only a moment afore the guards return! Come!"

She didn't wait for Kate to reply. Yanking her by the forearm, Maura pulled her out of the cell and down the corridor, hurrying through a large, rank-smelling chamber with a group of women huddled in one corner opposite a man fettered in chains.

At the sound of approaching voices and booted feet, Maura cursed and darted into a darkened archway, dragging Kate in after her.

As if in a dream, Kate watched three men pass slowly in front of them, mere inches away. And then Maura was shoving her again, peppering her commands with curses as a door in front of them suddenly opened, and they burst outside. A cloud of acrid, brown smoke blew in their faces.

With eyes tearing in response, Kate coughed and stumbled as Maura pushed her through a wild crowd surging around two pillars of fire. Someone was screaming, many were shouting, as a shrill voice intoned, "Do ye repent? Repent and save your wicked souls!"

"Sweet Mary!" Maura cried out behind her. "May the saints forgive me! We have to go, Kate. Now! Dinna look at the fire! Let's go!"

Kate frowned, still bewildered.

The high hum of anxiety permeated the air. Fear and anger were clearly writ on the faces swirling around her. And as Maura tugged her in the opposite direction, she glanced over her shoulder to see the two columns of fire.

One suddenly shifted, and a skeletal, human hand pitched forward to sag at an odd angle before a roaring crackle of flames rose to consume it.

Kate froze, her eyes widening in horror as Maura yanked her back. And then, not wanting to see anymore, she turned away. Beginning to shake all over, she covered her face with her hand, but it was difficult to block out the bitter stench of scorched flesh.

"Hurry!" Maura screeched hysterically, weaving through the frenzied mob and down the High Street of Edinburgh. "Follow me, Kate! Hurry!"

Deep inside, a tiny voice inside Kate screamed that she should not trust nor follow Maura, but her desire to escape the bloodlust of the crowd was greater. Scarcely able to breathe, she stumbled after Maura for what seemed like hours before she felt the familiar sway of a boat and sank down gratefully, cradling her head in her hands. Fighting off tears of shock, she rubbed her burning eyes and closing them, gave way to an overwhelming, crushing weariness.

* * *

Kate awoke to the pleasant warmth of the sun on her skin. She lay on a straw pallet. The sheets were coarse but clean. The room was small with a dirt floor and bits of straw crammed between the crevices of ancient, crumbling stone walls.

The sun streamed through a tiny, open window, and she could hear the bleating of sheep and the sound of laughter outside.

Confused, she slowly sat up, struggling to recall where she was but succeeding only in summoning a series of dim, disjointed memories.

Her father's death at Craigmillar. Sir Arval collapsing against the wall. A hand falling out of the flames in Edinburgh. The endless lurch of a cart jolting along a rutted road. And the blooming, purple heather coloring the endless moors stretching into the distance. And then the steady, soft crooning of an old woman sitting on a bench beneath a tree.

She frowned.

Where was she?

An image of Cameron's dark, passionate eyes flashed through her mind.

She shivered, her heart swelling at once with an ache so deep that she could not bear it. Ach, she could not think of Cameron nor of his bairn.

His bairn! With a ripple of fear, she frantically clutched her abdomen. A larger than expected swell met her searching fingers and she glanced in surprise. Their bairn was safe and had clearly grown. Her lips parted in confusion.

A sound at the door startled her, and she glanced up to see an ancient woman shuffling into the room with the aid of a stick. She gripped a small basket in her crooked fingers.

"Here I am again, my wee lassie," her familiar voice crooned. "'Tis time for ye to eat, and then we'll sit in the warm sun for a wee bit of fresh air."

As she hobbled closer, Kate licked her lips and asked, "Could ye tell me where I am, my good mother?"

The old woman started violently and dropped her basket. "Sweet Mary, have ye finally awakened?"

Kate held still, frowning as the old woman shuffled closer.

With her aged eyes wrinkling in surprise, the old woman's lips creased into a wide smile. "I knew ye had the will to live, lassie. 'Tis good to see ye in your eyes again!"

Still frowning, Kate glanced around and repeated, "Where am I?"

"Ye be in Kiltaraglen, and I am Flora MacLean," the old woman replied with a slight cackle. Sitting down on the edge of the bed, she rested both hands on the top of her stick and heaved a long, loud sigh. "I've fretted over ye so these past two months, ever since ye arrived with your sister Maura. And we've—"

"Maura?" Kate interrupted with a ripple of alarm before adding with belated astonishment, "Two ... *months?*"

Even as she asked, she knew it was true.

She had been hearing this woman's voice crooning to her softly through her dreams, bathing her forehead and patiently feeding her bannocks and fish. She had sat with her on the bench in the warm sun whilst listening to the plaintive wail of the gulls and the roar of the sea.

"Ye've been caught in a muckle dream, lassie." Flora leaned over to pat Kate's abdomen with her twisted fingers. "Ach, I feared the fairies had cast ye in a spell to take your wee bairn!"

Kate glanced down at her belly, covering it possessively with both of her hands. She closed her eyes. Her bairn was safe. Cameron's bairn was safe.

Cameron. Her lips twisted downwards. She couldn't think of Cameron—not yet.

So much had happened, she wanted to cry to relieve her aching heart, but the tears refused to come.

Rising unsteadily to her feet, Flora said, "I'll fetch Maura, lassie. Your sister will be right relieved to find ye've returned to us."

The mention of Maura's name filled Kate with trepidation. Where had Maura taken her to? And for what purpose? Reaching out to stay Flora, she shook her head, asking, "Kiltaraglen? Can ye tell me where that might be, my good mother?"

The old woman clucked a little, shaking her head. "Ach, everyone knows of Kiltaraglen, lassie! 'Tis on the bonniest isle on Earth. You're on Skye."

Skye! Kate felt a thread of hope. "Are we near Dunvegan?" she asked. "My mother's own Aunt Isobel lives there."

"Isobel?" Flora's eyes lit with a warm recognition. "I know the wee lassie right well!"

Kate felt an immense and comforting sense of relief.

"I'll send a lad for her straightway. Dunvegan's nae far, lassie," Flora assured, and then her aged eyes crinkled in bewilderment. "Though 'tis strange Maura dinna mention it afore."

Kate tensed.

Flora's aged eyes narrowed, but there was a kindly smile on her lips. "Ach, then, 'tis nae matter. I'll send word to Isobel straightway to expect ye when ye've gained a wee bit of strength in your limbs, and your heart is lighter."

At that, Kate grimaced. "My heart will never be light again." She had lost too much. She was certain she would never smile again.

"Ach!" the old woman snorted in mirth. "Ye haven't lived long enough to say that, ye wee fool." With a broad smile, she shuffled away. "I'll send Maura to ye. She'll be glad to see ye've come back to us."

Swinging her legs out of the bed, Kate ran her hands apprehensively over her arms, but she had little time to prepare for Maura before the woman burst into the room.

Maura was paler, thinner than Kate had remembered her, and there were dark circles under her puffy eyes. Furrowing her brows, the once proud woman nervously sidled up to Kate. "Are ye well, Kate?"

Kate stared at her.

Maura cleared her throat. "Do ye … remember?"

"Remember what, Maura?" Kate finally asked in a voice edged with pain. "My poor father's death? Sir Arval's? The wax doll and Edinburgh?" She couldn't mention Cameron. His name was too painful.

An utter wave of loneliness swept over her.

Maura caught her breath. "But I saved ye, Kate!" Her blue eyes filled with tears. "I saved ye from being burnt as a witch! Do ye recall that?"

Kate swallowed, recalling again the smoke in Edinburgh and the hand falling out of the fire. She shuddered.

"I am but a wave, tossed here and there by the whim of the wind!" Maura wailed softly, beating her hands against her chest. "How can ye not recall that I saved ye? I brought ye here, and I've tended ye well these past two months, both ye and your bairn!"

Kate turned her face away and covered her ears with her hands, not wanting to hear the woman's voice.

"Ye have to forgive me Kate!" Maura cried, reaching over to snatch her hands away. "Do ye forgive me, Kate? Do ye?" She gripped Kate's shoulders and began to shake them in a silent plea.

Stepping aside, Kate pushed Maura away and choked. "Ach, Maura! My father's dead now, and ye had a hand in it!"

"How can ye say such vile things!" Maura wept, wiping her tears with the back of her hand. "How can ye after I've saved ye and Cameron's bairn!"

At the mention of Cameron's name, Kate flinched. Two months. Did he think her dead?

"I beg ye to forgive me, Kate!" Maura fell to her knees, confessing, "I only wanted to be bonny. I dinna know how it all became so twisted! I only wanted to be bonny!"

Memories flooded through Kate, scenes that she wished had remained buried. Gasping, she covered her face with her hands, but then as if sensing her distress, the babe in her belly moved.

Kate froze.

Her throat caught.

Oblivious to Maura's sobs, her hand dropped wondrously to the soft swell to feel the slight flutter under her fingertips. And then her spirits began to lift and her heart to rise. She was not alone.

"I beg ye, Kate!" Maura was holding desperately onto her ankles.

Kate glanced down.

Suddenly, there was something pitiful about the woman groveling at her feet. She did not know how long she stood there before she finally whispered, "I will always curse the day I met ye, Maura, and I'll ever hate your choices that brought about my father's death, but I dinna hate ye. I *will* not hate ye. I'll always pity ye. But ..." Kate paused and drew a deep breath.

Maura's tortured blue eyes locked with hers.

Pulling herself up to her full height, Kate finished in a resolute voice, "But if ye truly desire forgiveness, never let me hear your voice nor see your face again!"

And then Kate left her there, cringing on the floor, lost and forlorn.

* * *

Flora led her to the bench under the shade of the tree, and Kate closed her eyes, listening to the peacefully familiar sound of rustling leaves sighing in the wind mixed with the calls of the gulls and the roaring of the sea.

Keeping her promise, the ancient woman immediately sent a lad with tidings to Dunvegan, though Kate was startled to find the "lad" was a gray-haired man in his late fifties.

After he departed, Flora joined her on the bench, and the day passed in pleasant chatter. She asked Kate many questions, but wisely refrained from mentioning Maura or enquiring about the father of Kate's bairn. And as the light of day faded, Flora brought fresh bannocks and a wooden bowl of mutton stew, and then she wearily returned to her straw pallet. The soft crackle of the fire mingled peacefully with the old woman's crooning, and it was not long before Kate fell into a deep, dreamless sleep.

The next time Kate awoke, it was to the sound of Isobel's voice.

Rising as quickly as she could, Kate ran into the next room to behold the short, round, gray-haired woman wearing a plaid and stretching her hands out to her with an expression of joy. "Ach, my wee Kate! The sight of ye makes my old heart sing!"

Throwing herself into Isobel's arms, Kate buried her head on her shoulders, wishing desperately that she could weep, but the tears stubbornly refused to come.

"Ach, my dear lassie." Isobel stroked her hair. "What brings ye here like this? And your father? Where is John?"

Kate shuddered and forced herself to whisper, "He's ... gone, Aunt Isobel."

Isobel caught her breath and hugged her fiercely. "Say 'tis not so! How did it happen?"

But Kate could not reply. Threading her fingers in her aunt's plaid, she shook her head instead.

"Then think no more on it now, my wee lassie! Think no more," Isobel murmured into her hair.

Heaving a long sigh, Kate simply remained there, beginning to feel safe for the first time in weeks.

And then a tall, muscular man ducked his head and entered the cottage. His dark hair was thick, shoulder length and bound by a strip of leather. And his brown eyes were alive with a passion that strangely reminded her of Cameron.

Slowly, Kate drew back and stared.

Following her gaze, Isobel smiled at the man fondly. "And this is my Ruan, lass, the Laird of Dunvegan. Ye've heard me speak of him oft enough. Ach, my Ruan could charm otters from the sea."

Ruan laughed. It was a deep, warm sound as he leaned down to plant a fond kiss on Isobel's forehead before nodding kindly at Kate.

Isobel had often spoken of Ruan MacLeod. Having raised the man from birth, Kate knew that she loved him as her own flesh and blood, and from the expression in his eyes as he peered down at the woman, it was clear he felt the same way.

Kate dropped into a quick curtsey, but he stepped forward and caught her arm with a smile. "I've heard Isobel pine after ye oft enough, Kate, and 'tis right glad I am to finally have ye here with us. Think of me as your brother."

Kate forced her lips to smile, but it was more of a grimace than anything else.

And then Isobel's eyes dipped, and her face creased with pleasure. "Ach, ye've a bairn, lass! 'Tis wondrous news! And what of your husband?"

Kate bowed her head.

There was a slight, stilted silence before she replied in a shamed whisper, "I am not wed, Aunt Isobel. I can only ask for forgiveness and beg ye to help us both."

Defensively, she clutched her belly.

Ruan did not miss her gesture, and there was an understanding in his dark eyes as he replied in a deep, easy voice, "Lass, 'tis welcome ye are to Dunvegan, both ye and your bairn, and ye can stay as long as ye please. I'll warrant my own wee son will be right glad of another playfellow, or will, when he is old enough."

Crushing her close, Isobel kissed the top of her head. "Ye needn't speak of it now, my sweet lassie. Just know ye are home and welcome. The both of ye!"

Turning away, she greeted Flora and stood about exchanging bits of news for a time before farewells were said and Kate gratefully kissed Flora's lined cheek, promising one day to return.

And then Ruan led Kate out of the cottage to where three shaggy mountain horses grazed on the green grass. They were massive, shaggy beasts, stamping their feet and Kate hesitantly approached one.

It was vastly different from the horses she had ridden at Craigmillar. The thought brought memories of Sir Arval and her lips twisted downwards, but still there were no tears.

"Allow me to help ye, Kate," Ruan offered, lifting her gently into the saddle to place the reins in her hands before assisting Isobel with the same.

Pushing back the hood of her cloak, Kate closed her eyes and let the sun and wind caress her face. Why couldn't she weep? Her heart was heavy with pain, a pain almost unbearable, but still the tears refused to flow.

And then Ruan lifted his hand in farewell and they were moving. As he guided them north at a slow pace, Kate found herself once again struck with his resemblance to Cameron.

A lump rose in her throat.

Why couldn't she weep, even for Cameron?

With a gloomy sigh of despair, she forced her eyes to the scenery unfolding around her.

They rode along the tops of bushy heath-edged cliffs that swept down to the restless sea and through green, narrow glens. Ahead in the distance rose flat-topped mountains shrouded in mist as moor-birds flew above them with keening cries.

The sun was warm and the day pleasant, and they had just stopped under an edge of rock where the water fell into a deep, amber-colored pool to water their horses when Ruan snorted. His dark brows burrowed into a frown.

"Ach, the wee hellion willna listen to me, Isobel!" He scowled, pointing to a fast-moving rider dashing their way at breakneck speed. "By the Saints, I swear she'll put me in an early grave! I've told her countless times that stallion is nae fit for riding!"

Isobel's withered face creased with laughter. "Your pain has only begun, lad. If I know our wee Merry, she'll teach your son her wild ways, and then ye'll see what true suffering is."

"I willna survive!" Ruan groaned.

In moments, the black stallion reined beside them, rearing mightily on his haunches and shaking his wild mane as a tall, slender lass brought him under control with a quick word and an exhilarating laugh.

From the dark eyes sparkling with mischief and the black braid twisting down her back, Kate recognized her at once to be Ruan's sister, Merry.

After quick introductions, they resumed their journey with Ruan taking his sister to task, but she blithely ignored him, leaving their company often to race the stallion wildly along the moors. But it was with a proud gleam that Ruan viewed her, shaking his head and cursing under his breath with approval more than anything else.

They made their path over the moors, through thick curtains of moss and ferns and alongside burns rushing through deep crevices. The land was wild, rugged, and as the afternoon waned, the mist, light, and shadows played across the hills and surrounding moorlands, deepening the sense of mystery brooding around them.

They passed through several villages with thatch-roofed cottages hugging the black, jagged rocky cliffs, and the sun was halfway down the sky when the rugged outlines of Dunvegan rose before them. Separated from the shore by a narrow ravine, the waters of the sea loch lapped at the base of the moss-covered rocks of the island upon which the keep and its ancient tower stood.

"The only way in is through the sea-gate, lass." Ruan informed her in a deep voice, lifting her down from the mountain horse with an easy arm. "And then ye'll be home."

Kate's throat constricted. Home. She eyed the castle before her, wondering if she would ever feel a sense of home again.

A lad in a boat rowed them to the sea-gate, opening directly onto the water, and Ruan leapt out, assisting them all out of the vessel before guiding them up a long, narrow stair cut deep in the rocks leading to the castle.

They were met by his lady, Bree, a shy, soft-spoken woman with a mass of unruly brown curls, and large, kind green eyes.

Ruan's face lit as he stooped to kiss her cheek and murmur into her hair.

And then Bree turned to Kate and held out her hands. "You are most welcome here, Kate. You look in sore need of rest. Let me show you to your room at once!"

"Thank ye kindly, my lady," Kate whispered and dipped into a curtsey.

"Please call me Bree!" Bree laughed, her green eyes filled with warmth. "I confess that I still cringe every time I hear the word 'lady'."

Ruan's deep baritone laughed as he swept his wife into a close embrace, and then with a smile he stepped away. "I must see to Afraig and my wee son."

"Ye best warn the old woman that I am coming soon." Isobel frowned at the mention of Afraig. "But first I'll see to my wee Kate."

Both Bree and Isobel led Kate up a narrow, winding stair to a small, pleasant tower room with a window looking out to the sea.

"This room will be yours, Kate." Bree smiled, looking around fondly. "'Twas mine when I first arrived here."

"And dinna fret so much, Kate." Isobel squeezed her gently on the shoulder. "Ye clearly have seen too much sorrow this past year, but ye are home now, and ye'll see that soon enough. I'll bring ye some tea and a bite to eat, and then ye can take a wee rest."

They left her alone then, and a familiar dullness descended on Kate as she moved slowly to peer out of the window. A small fishing boat sailed on the horizon, summoning memories of her father at once and a sharp stab of pain.

But then Isobel returned with a soothing tea of chamomile and honey along with a wooden bowl of oatmeal and smoked fish. Sniffing the nutty fragrance, Kate's stomach heaved in a riotous wave of nausea. She blanched, and turned her face away.

"Ach, 'tis a wee lassie ye carry, Kate," Isobel cackled, rubbing her hands together. "'Tis the lassies that turn your stomach more."

Kate forced a wan smile.

The gray-haired woman watched her a moment before surrounding her in a warm hug once again. "Take rest, my wee one. There will be plenty of time for talk later."

Alone again, Kate returned to the window. And as the sounds of pipes began to play, she closed her eyes, rested her head against the wooden shutters, and simply let the forlorn melody wash over her.

Soon, she would think of Cameron.

But not quite yet.

The next day passed and then another. She grew stronger and more alert with each passing moment, and she desperately wanted to weep, to relieve her heart of its heavy burden. But still her tears did not fall.

Bree stubbornly refused to permit her to work and suggested that Kate keep her company instead, but though Kate found the lady kind and gentle, she found it difficult to speak and instead spent her time wandering near the castle.

On the third day, Merry joined her on the moors; silently keeping her company as they slowly rambled through the purple heather, trailed along the rushing amber-colored burns, and breathed deeply of the bog-myrtle perfuming the air.

A week had passed when one afternoon Merry held out her hand. With a lively gleam in her dark eyes, she said, "I've something to show ye, Kate. 'Tis a bit of a walk. Do ye feel well enough to try?"

When Kate nodded, the slender lass led her down a narrow path through a meadow of purple vetch as high as their heads, and down to a rock-strewn beach pebbled with shells. Gulls rode the winds above them, and she could hear the barking of seal lions basking on an islet of black rocks a short distance away. Nearby, a cliff rose, riddled with crannies bearing the nests of rock-pigeons.

As dark clouds gathered on the horizon, Merry turned to her with an inviting smile. "Scream with me, Kate."

Kate frowned and repeated, "Scream?"

"Aye." Merry nodded, turning to look out over the sea. "There were times this past year that I could not sleep after Ruan rescued me from Fearghus. A faceless, nameless fear would come in the night, and I would wake up screaming. But it has all but gone since Ruan walked these beaches with me, teaching me to scream here instead. I still come here to scream in the wind, but not so often anymore." Turning back to Kate, her eyes took on a devilish gleam. "Ye'll have to scream, Kate. I'll not show ye the way home until ye do."

Kate frowned, but Merry was stubborn. Seizing her hand, the tall lass began to scream into the wind.

Kate watched her a moment, and then a wave of dark feelings rose in her soul. Not knowing exactly why, she opened her lips and joined in, at first softer but growing louder and stronger with each passing moment.

As the sea dashed furiously against the rocks on the beach, Kate screamed, endlessly shrieking until her voice was hoarse, and then hot tears began to trickle down her cheeks. Sobbing, she screamed, falling to the beach on her knees. Clutching her swelling belly, she screamed and wept the flood of tears she had been unable to shed even for her mother and wee sister, Joan. And then she felt Ruan's strong arms lifting her, gently placing her on the back of a shaggy, mountain pony.

A short time later, she found herself huddled close to the fire in Dunvegan's main hall, lulled into a calm silence by the dancing flames. She was exhausted, yet filled with more peace than she had felt in ages.

"Are ye feeling better, lass?"

Kate rose clumsily to her feet, but the Laird of Dunvegan stayed her with a kindly smile. "Ach, Kate. Be at peace."

Drawing up a chair, Ruan sat down with a brotherly smile. But his dark eyes were alert and sharp as he said, "If ye've need of my avenging arm, lass, speak and I'll see it done."

She knew he referred to her bairn, and she felt a ripple of gratefulness toward the man.

Ach, she missed Cameron with her entire soul.

Her breath caught in a pang of longing, and for the first time, she let herself think of the man. How she wanted to see his dark eyes once more, touch his chiseled lips, and trail her finger along the dash in the middle of his chin.

Did he think her dead? Ach, did he even know that she carried his bairn? Her heart cried out. There was nothing she wouldn't give to feel his arms encircle her once more.

"There's naught I wouldn't do for ye, lass, and not a lad I wouldn't take to task on your behalf." Ruan's deep voice broke into her thoughts.

Kate sighed, staring into the flames, and murmured, "'Tis not such a matter, my lord." Thinking of those wondrous nights with Cameron, she confessed in a whisper, "'Twas a … thief, an outlaw that … I love still with my entire heart, my lord. But it canna be."

"Give me the man's name, and I'll see what can be done," Ruan insisted gently. "Not every sin is unforgiveable, lass. I would know what caused this man to turn to such a life. Perhaps it can be changed."

Kate grimaced and shook her head. Ach, the Laird of Dunvegan had an easy charm and a disarming smile. She had revealed too much. There was no hope in it. Cameron could only wed a lady. He was an earl and she, only a fisherman's daughter.

Unable to speak, she merely shook her head again.

"Then we'll speak another time, Kate," Ruan said after a bit, reaching down to pat her shoulder in a fatherly way. "'Tis time for the evening meal. Come, join us."

With tear-swollen eyes, she joined them at the table, enticed by the welcoming scent of fresh barley bread. And after managing a few bites of a satisfying soup of cod, turnips, and cabbage, she retired to her tower room.

It had begun to rain.

Leaning her head against the window, she took peace in the soothing sound and let her thoughts dwell on Cameron. Where was he? What was he doing? Was he taking comfort in the embrace of another woman? The thought was an uncomfortable one.

She frowned, but it bothered her more with each passing moment.

And then, she felt her old sense of self begin to return.

A wave of determination rose to consume her.

How could she live if she didn't see the man again?

What was she doing? Why was she pining and staring out of the window? Nothing would come from lack of action. She should hie herself away and hunt him down.

And then she recalled Lady Elsa's words, informing her that he deserved a well-bred lady at his side, one of his own class and not a commoner.

She clenched her hands.

She'd not let another woman kiss his chiseled lips or trace the dash on the middle of his chin. She'd rather be his mistress than nothing at all. Aye, perhaps she truly was a craven, fallen woman, but she loved him, enough to live even a life of perpetual shame.

The bairn in her belly shifted, and she made up her mind all at once.

He, at least, deserved to know his bairn existed. 'Twas only fair.

Feeling more alive than she had in some time, she threw back the door to her chamber and went in search of parchment, blessing Sir Arval for teaching her how to write at least a few words—enough so that she was sure she could at least let Cameron know where she was.

15

THE WEDDING

Cameron stood in the center of Kate's cell. It was empty, save for the rat rustling the sour straw in the corner.

"Heaven save us!" one of the guards gasped, crossing himself frantically. "The lass truly *was* a witch! Satan himself must have ferreted her away—"

Lifting the corner of his lip in contempt, Cameron felled the man senseless with a blow to the head.

The remaining guard nervously licked his lips. "Perhaps she's been taken back to the scribe, my lord," the man offered helpfully. "I'll lead the way right quickly!"

But Kate was not there.

He searched the entire prison but found only a sheet of parchment accusing her of practicing witchcraft against the king. Holding the document aloft, he read the name of the witness aloud.

"Maura."

Cameron's heart sank. Ach, he would ever curse the day that he had rescued the woman! Because of her, Mar was dead and Kate, gone missing. He refused to think that she might be dead.

Crumpling the parchment in his long fingers, he drew his dirk in a single, swift motion and strode down the corridor to where Thomas Cochrane waited outside under his men's safekeeping. Kicking the door back, he intended to confront the man at once, but a crowd had suddenly gathered around the Mercat Cross, and Thomas and his men were nowhere to be seen.

And then, a familiar voice hailed him. "Cameron!"

Turning, Cameron spied King James astride his black charger a short distance away with Thomas Cochrane at his side, sitting on a dappled gray gelding. The pleased and proud expression on the man's long face announcing he was once again under the protection of the king.

Cameron felt sick at heart.

"Cameron!" the king called out, urging his horse through the crowd to peer down at him. "Thomas has found Mar! Dead! He is dead, Cameron! Mar is dead!" His face was pale, distraught.

Catching the king's stirrup, Cameron yanked it savagely. "Aye, and 'twas Thomas' own hand that saw it done! I was there!"

The king blinked in surprise as Thomas pressed forward to join them.

"Mar was ill, my lord," the man's nasal voice inserted. "'Twas an accident, nothing more!"

"An accident?" Cameron repeated in disbelief. "Aye, the only accident 'twas I caught ye in the act!"

"Mar was ill, Cameron!" The king frowned, shaking his head. "The royal physicians opened his veins to reduce the heated frenzy of his fever! And 'twas Mar's own thrashing in the water that broke open the bandages."

Cameron stared at them incredulously.

With a wavering smile, the king staunchly insisted, "'Twas ill fortune, Cameron! Nay, 'twas Mar's own fault, had he not lashed out so wildly in the water, he would be with us still!"

Cameron found himself struck speechless. How could Mar have had so much loyalty to such a fool? Ach, the last words on the man's dying lips had been concerned ones for his own brother. Cameron felt sick.

"His lordship is overwrought, your majesty. 'Twas what caused him to strike at me so, but I harbor no ill will towards him." Thomas murmured to the king, holding up his bandaged hand. "It seems that his mistress has also suffered some misfortune here today."

King James' eyes lit with a guilty relief. "'Tis no wonder he mistook the situation. A man canna think clearly in such times. Aye, this has been a trying day for us all!"

Cameron's dark eyes narrowed in contempt, and he moved away in disgust. It was a waste of time to be speaking with either of them.

As the king called after him, begging for him to stay, Cameron shoved his way through the crowd. He'd find his Kate and see Mar's death avenged, no matter how long it took. And upon returning to his apartments in Edinburgh Castle, he ordered his men to continue the search for Kate.

"Aye, and send men to Stirling and her village as well. Look for any kinfolk she might have fled to." Glancing down at the crumpled document declaring her a witch, he added grimly, "And search for the lass, Maura. Mayhap she'll know something."

When they had gone, he bowed his head and whispered, "I'll find ye, Kate. I swear I'll find ye, and when I do, I'll never let ye go again!"

* * *

Treachery and intrigue filled the following weeks, more than Cameron had thought he'd ever experience in a lifetime.

They had scarcely buried Mar when Thomas Cochrane escalated the accusations of witchcraft. In the name of the king, he had a dozen men and women burnt at the stake, before Cameron, the queen, and the nobles succeeded in stopping the madness.

As the news of Mar's death rippled throughout the land, a steady stream of clan chieftains flocked to Edinburgh, intent on waging war.

The country had nearly split in twain.

And as the king found his reception at court growing colder by the day, he removed himself from Edinburgh Castle and retired to Holyrood House at the opposite end of the Royal Mile, taking Thomas with him.

Through it all, Cameron relentlessly searched for Kate. He sent for Lord Julian Gray and scoured the streets of Edinburgh, interviewing countless numbers of witnesses himself. Several times each week, he rode to Craigmillar hoping that Kate's father had recovered enough to give him some hint of where she might be. But though the man grew stronger by the day, he had lost the power of speech.

Kate had simply vanished.

And so time passed, each night growing only darker and longer, until one particularly torturous night he finally collapsed into an exhausted sleep and had scarcely closed his eyes when he began to dream.

It was a wondrous dream, images of Kate's laughing brown eyes and her soft lips caressing his. It was a dream that he wanted to last forever, but upon waking, the pain of finding her still gone was unbearable.

With a haggard step, he quit his chambers and called for his charger, and as the sun rose on the horizon, he thundered down the streets of Edinburgh bound for Craigmillar once more—as quickly as his horse could gallop.

The Prestons guarding Craigmillar lifted their arms in greeting as he rode through the gates, and Sir Arval himself met him as he entered the keep.

"'Tis good to see ye walking once more!" Cameron greeted the man with a warm clasp on the shoulder. "I've missed ye sorely."

The grizzled Frenchman was thin, pale, and clearly still very weak. "Have you news of Kate, my lord?" he asked with a haunted look.

Cameron closed his eyes.

It was enough of an answer.

"Then that could be good tidings in itself, my lord," Sir Arval murmured in encouragement, but more to himself than Cameron. "For it means she's still—"

Cameron eyed him grimly. He didn't want the man to finish the thought. He couldn't allow himself to think she might be dead. "How fares John Ferguson?" he interrupted.

"Stronger, my lord." Sir Arval bowed gravely. "But the power of speech still fails him."

Taking the steps two at a time, Cameron made his way to John's chamber.

It was heartening to see the fisherman out of his bed, sitting on a cushioned chair in the early warmth of the sun. And as Cameron approached, the man's head tilted and his hand lifted in a gesture of recognition.

As he had oft done the past few months, Cameron knelt beside the man, holding his fingers between his own, to share the latest tidings of his search for Kate.

"I will find her," Cameron swore softly. "Even if I must turn over every stone in Scotland, I will find her."

The fisherman groaned, and Cameron glanced up to see the man's lip twitching in a smile.

It was the first time he had seen the man regain the use of his mouth since his near fatal injury. He bowed his head in hope. Mayhap soon her father would regain the ability to speak and help guide them to where she might be.

They simply sat there for a time, until shouts in the courtyard below drifted through the open window.

There were voices, loud and angry ones.

Cameron's lips drew in a thin line. Ach, 'twas another crisis, no doubt. He was fair sick of them. Gritting his teeth, he rose to his feet and peered through the narrow window to spy Archibald Douglas, the Earl of Angus, bellowing, "Where is Cameron! Find him at once! I must speak to him at once!"

Expelling a deep breath, Cameron moved to the door and was halfway down the stair when the earl nearly collided with him.

"I've just come from Holyrood!" the red-haired, blunt-faced earl roared in greeting. "The fool has made the idiot the Earl of Mar! Earl of *Mar*, Cameron!"

Cameron's lips parted in surprise, and he repeated softly in astonishment, "The king has given Thomas Cochrane his brother's own title and lands?"

"Aye, and I've had enough!" Archibald swore, kicking the wall. "I'll bring Albany back from France this very night!"

Gripping Archibald's arm, Cameron guided him to the hall as the man continued to shout threats of war, and it took some doing before the Earl of Angus was finally convinced to put such thoughts aside for a time and wait.

The shadows were long when Cameron wearily mounted his charger and returned to Edinburgh, but he did not immediately return to the castle rising high on the hill.

No, he had words he must say to the king.

Reining before the wide, green expanse of grass, he entered Holyrood House, heading at once for the royal residence in the gray-stoned abbey guesthouse.

The king was not there, but the monks guided him to the gardens. And moments later, Cameron strode down the hard gravel paths to where the king and Thomas stood under a rowan tree, clad in sumptuous, ermine-trimmed robes.

"Cameron!" King James' face lit with pleasure. "'Tis well to see ye here! I would our feud would end—"

With anger seething in his veins, Cameron interrupted him coldly, "Did ye truly bestow the earldom of Mar upon this venomous serpent?" He allowed his dark eyes to rest upon Thomas for the briefest of moments.

The man's long face reddened as the king swallowed visibly.

"Have ye no shame, James?" Cameron eyed the king with icy contempt. "I've told ye the truth of Mar's death, yet ye ever turn a deaf ear on me! How can ye bequeath his lands to the very man who murdered him?"

"'Twas the fever!" The king licked his lips. "Ye've misunderstood, Cameron!"

Cameron graced him with a smile riddled in disdain. "I do not envy ye, James. Ye truly are cursed. Ye'll spend many a long, sleepless night convincing yourself that Mar's death was an accident. Aye, such torment will be a fitting punishment."

All color drained from the king's face.

"And I'll never forgive ye for Mar," Cameron grated in a low tone, permitting his eyes to mirror his disgust. "I'll see ye undone for it."

At that, the king's nostrils flared. "Is that a threat, Cameron?"

"'Tis a warning." Cameron let his voice turn rough. "Tread carefully, or ye'll lose what little ye have left quicker than ye think." He turned to leave.

"Wait!" the king lurched forward, grabbing his arm. "Walk here awhile!"

Shaking him off, Cameron murmured, "I've no appetite for your company."

He had taken only a step before Thomas cried out, "My fellow earl, ye may think ye are untouchable with many friends, but I'll see ye banished from court for such insolence towards the king!"

With a smile of the deepest scorn, Cameron turned halfway to reply, "Ach, I know ye to be a fool of the highest order, Thomas, and

I'll aid ye in punishing yourself. Ye'll not walk this Earth much longer."

Spinning abruptly on his heel, he left them standing there, mouths agape.

He returned to Edinburgh Castle then, to comfort the distraught queen and to persuade the nobles to remain united in keeping the country free of civil war. He wanted nothing more than to rid himself of James and Thomas Cochrane, but not at the risk of losing the entire country to chaos. He could not place Albany, another murderer, upon the throne, and the crown prince was yet too young. The resulting battle over his regency would be even more dangerous.

The night was nearly over when he returned once more to his chambers.

He lay on his bed, but sleep eluded him.

Painful memories pierced his heart, memories of Kate's sparkling brown eyes, her cheerful laughter, and the way her nose wrinkled when she smiled. Memories of the nights they had made passionate love, the feel of her soft skin and warm lips against his.

Rising to his feet, he paced before the window, his long fingers clutching the gray cloth of Kate's bodice that he kept close to his heart.

The candle on the writing desk flickered.

Moving to stare at the parchment resting there, he lightly traced his finger over the accursed document accusing Kate of witchcraft. It was his last bond to her existence. He could not bring himself to destroy it. Not yet.

"Where are ye, Kate?" he whispered as he had countless times in the past few months. "Where are ye?"

He gripped the tattered bodice tighter and closed his eyes.

Ach, fate ever sought to torment him, but he would not give up. He would never stop seeking her.

And then slowly, a deep, abiding anger welled up inside him.

It grew stronger with each passing moment, until striking the desk with his fist, he raised his voice and cursed destiny itself, "No matter how hard ye try to wrest her away from me, I'll only hold on tighter!"

As if in answer, the candle flickered in a sudden draft.

After a moment, he leaned forward and blew it out, preferring the complete darkness. It suited his mood.

Moving to the window, he threw open the shutters. The waning moon illuminated the rooftops of the surrounding town and glistened on the waters of the Firth of Forth far below. It would have been a peaceful scene if not for the suffering in his heart.

Wearily, he ran his hand over his face.

Each day was an endless torture, another day of woe. Would the torment ever end?

Again, the anger rose, stronger this time.

Ach, if he could, he would slap destiny in the face.

He began to pace like a caged animal when a new thought struck him.

Aye, he *could* slap destiny in the face. He could wed his Kate this very night.

The thought caught hold, giving him strength.

Striding across the chamber, he flung the door open, shouting to his men in the darkened antechamber, "Send for a priest at once!"

He'd marry her this very day.

And as an afterthought, he added, "Send for Princess Anabella straightway!"

Aye, he'd have his marriage witnessed as well, witnessed so never again could the king force him to wed another.

The sky had begun to lighten, signaling the arrival of the sun, and as he waited, the faint glow on the horizon flowered into an array of dazzling colors, heralding in the new day.

A shaft of sunlight fell upon the parchment on his desk, and Cameron found himself peering down at the wretched document once more. With a sudden flare of anger, he caught it up and viciously ripped it into shreds. Kicking the fire back into life, he watched with a measure of satisfaction as the feeble flames rose to consume it.

The priest arrived then, a man clad in brown woolen robes and with tonsured gray hair. He listened to Cameron with kind, green eyes before sitting at the desk to scribe a document proclaiming Kate Ferguson as Cameron's wife, the Countess of Lennox.

The man's quill was still sliding across the parchment when Princess Anabella arrived with Lady Elsa and Lady Nicoletta at her heels. The three women stared at him in outright alarm.

"What is the meaning of this?" the princess demanded harshly. "What ill has befallen us?"

With a stoic expression, Cameron replied, "I would have ye bear witness to my marriage."

Princess Anabella blinked. She glanced about the chamber, clearly bewildered. "Marriage?"

"Aye, this day I wed Kate," Cameron answered through the sudden knot rising in his throat.

There was a stilted silence.

Then the princess asked gruffly, "What madness is this?"

"Call it madness if ye will." Cameron clenched his jaw. "But never will I wed another."

His voice caught, and he fell silent.

The priest dipped his quill in the ink, the tip scratching loudly in the silence. And then, sprinkling the wet ink with sand, he rose to his feet and bowed to Cameron. "I am ready, my lord."

"Then we will begin," Cameron murmured, his voice filled with emotion.

"Wait, my lord!"

Cameron glanced back to see Lady Elsa nervously stepping forward.

With fluttering fingers, she dipped into a timid curtsey. "Allow me to stand as a proxy for Kate, I beg of you, my lord. My last words to her were ... harsh and unkind." Her lips trembled and, dropping her eyes, she added in a voice barely above a whisper, "And I would seek forgiveness for such cruelty."

Cameron hesitated, but her eyes were sincere, and grimly nodding his permission, he knelt before the priest as Lady Elsa timorously joined him in a rustle of silk.

It did not take long. It was over in minutes. And then Lady Elsa rose to move away.

But Cameron remained as he was.

Aye, he'd wed his Kate. But would he ever hold her in his arms again?

Hot tears choked his throat as a wave of grief rose to overpower him.

A low sound of despair escaped his lips as he sagged against the edge of the desk. And then with a great, shuddering gasp of air, he began to weep. Violent, harsh sobs tore from his throat, racking his entire body.

Hushed, hurried voices sounded about him, but he paid them no heed and soon was alone. He wept as if his heart would break. Aye, his heart had broken. He could not live without her. He could not live without his Kate.

Finally, Cameron drew a long, ragged breath and fell silent with a sense of loss beyond tears.

And then he heard Lord Julian Gray's familiar deep voice drawl, "Ach, but ye look ghastly, Cameron." Julian approached and gave his shoulders a rough shake. "Rise up, ye fool!"

Cameron did not respond.

"Get ye on your feet, lad!" Julian groaned as he half prodded, half lifted him to stand upright before handing him a goblet of wine. "Drink this first. Ye'll need it."

Cameron stared at it woodenly.

"Drink it!" Julian jiggled the goblet a little, shoving it into his hands.

Cameron bolted it down in a single draught and then turned to leave when Julian blocked his way. With a grim look, Cameron murmured, "Step aside, Julian. What more do ye want from me?"

"I want ye to ride, Cameron," Julian replied grimly, but there was a look of compassion in his gray eyes. "We leave at once. Ruan MacLeod has sore need of ye in Dunvegan. 'Twill do your heart good to leave this accursed place. I swear I'll find your Kate, lad."

Cameron closed his eyes.

Ach, what evil cloud had descended upon Scotland that now it had even touched upon Ruan and Skye?

But Julian did not allow him to even think. Tossing a cloak over his shoulders, the young lord pulled Cameron out to where the horses were already saddled. And then they were galloping madly down the cobblestoned streets of Edinburgh.

Aye, Cameron thought dully, 'twould do him good to leave this accursed place.

Julian set a furious pace, riding low on the neck of his horse as they galloped west until the Firth of Forth turned into a river. Taking a northerly road, they ran their horses over the swelling and falling moorlands, across fields of upland flowers, and through stands of birch growing on the shores of the narrow, winding lochs.

For days, they rested little and spoke even less, stopping only when the horses were in a lather, until they finally stood on the western shores where the waves shattered the cliffs hanging over the sea.

A boat took them to Skye then, sailing up the coast under an immeasurable expanse of blue sky as sea-birds drifted in the wind over their heads. And though it took hours, it seemed only minutes before they saw the Three Maidens, the three isolated pillars of rock standing in the sea just beyond the mighty cliffs that signaled they were close to Dunvegan. And shortly after, the familiar walls of Dunvegan Castle appeared, rising high on its green-and-purple islet, close to the wild shores of the sea loch.

They had no sooner arrived at the sea-gate than Cameron leapt from the boat, with Julian at his heels. And he had taken only a few steps up the stone passageway before Isobel hurried down to greet him.

"Cameron!" The woman's eyes lit with pleasure. "I've missed your silver tongue, lad!" And then taking one look at his face, she gasped, "What has happened?"

Bowing politely over her hand, Cameron replied grimly, "I came the moment I received Ruan's summons, Isobel. Is he well?"

Isobel frowned. "Summons? Ruan didna send for ye, lad! What are ye speaking of?"

Cameron held still.

And then Julian sauntered to his side and draped a casual arm about his shoulders. "Ach, perhaps I was a wee bit mistaken. But now that we are here, let's at least greet the man, Cameron!"

16

DUNVEGAN

Kate hovered over the small writing desk in her tower room, biting the tip of her quill in frustration.

She eyed the letter she had been struggling with for several days and cringed.

Sir Arval would have been right disappointed in her.

Composing her own letter had proven to be much harder than she had thought. Blotches of ink splattered over the parchment, blotting out half of the words. Ach, she didn't even recognize half of them herself anymore. The entire letter-writing effort had been a laborious and disappointing affair. She wished she had paid more heed to what the kind Frenchman had attempted to teach her at Craigmillar.

Sighing, she rose to her feet and opening the wooden chest next to the bed, carefully laid the parchment atop a fine plaid that Bree had given her the evening before. It was a fine garment, a symbol welcoming her into their clan, but she could not bring herself to wear it. Not yet.

She didn't want to let Cameron go. Ach, why did the father of her bairn have to be an earl with royal ties? As if sensing her thoughts, the baby kicked. She smiled. Cameron's bairn was a strong one, constantly kicking her through the night.

She heaved a wistful sigh.

If only Cameron truly were a thief, they could have wed and shared a humble home with their sweet bairn. She knew Lady Elsa was right; he could only wed a lady of high birth. But the very thought of that tore Kate's heart asunder. How could she bear that?

There were moments when she wondered if the letter was better left unfinished.

Perhaps she was better off not knowing.

"Ach, Kate, it does ye no good stewing over matters ye canna control!" she wryly criticized herself, and with a sad smile, placed a protective hand over her expanding belly and left her tower room. Holding onto the rope that spanned the length of the stair, she carefully navigated down to encounter Bree walking her way.

The Lady of Dunvegan wore a blue, woolen gown with a brown and yellow plaid flung over her shoulders. Balancing her dark-haired son on her hip, she waved as the bairn giggled, and grabbing a fistful of her brown curls, began to yank.

"Roderick MacLeod! If you have your way, I swear I'll be balder than your grandfather soon!" Bree frowned at her son, but her voice was rich with laughter. Extracting his chubby fingers from her hair, she sent Kate a look of amused exasperation.

Smiling, Kate reached forward to pinch the bairn's cheek playfully.

Roderick giggled and clapped his hands.

"And where are you off to, Kate?" Bree lifted a suspicious brow. "I'll not have you in the scullery scrubbing pots again!"

"Ach, but I'm not one to stay idle, my lady." Kate's eyes twinkled as she caught the bairn's hands and waved them back and forth. Soon she'd have her own babe to play with. The thought made her throat constrict, and it was a moment before she could continue. "I'm fair restless. I canna sit still."

"Then keep Merry company instead!" Bree suggested with a laugh.

Kate smiled, shaking her head in wonder. "I wish I could, but I fear I canna ride wild stallions on the moor nor shoot an arrow with such skill!"

"Yes, she's quite an uncommon—" Bree began when Isobel and Afraig appeared at the end of the passageway.

With their hands on their hips, the two old women began to bicker, rolling their eyes and huffing.

Bree's lips twisted in a wry smile. "It seems as if I'm needed, Kate. Ruan and I figured that today it would be time for another battle. They've been unusually friendly to each other the past four days."

Kate suppressed a giggle. She'd already heard enough from Isobel to know that although the women engaged in continual spats, their respect for each other ran deep.

Bree was halfway down the corridor when she shot a warning over her shoulder. "And, I had better not find you in the scullery, Kate!"

Kate smiled. Both Bree and Ruan were beyond kind. Smoothing her skirts, she headed to the kitchens anyway.

She was restless. She had to keep her hands busy. The Lady of Dunvegan had only ordered her not to scrub pots. She hadn't said Kate couldn't help prepare the mid-day meal.

Stepping under the arched doors, Kate made her way to the long, wooden table where the cooks bustled over platters destined for the laird's table in the great hall above.

They eyed her warily.

With a cheerful smile but critical eye, she sniffed the waterfowl and inspected the fish and mutton. Leaning close, she pulled off a sliver of the roasted mutton lying in a bed of herbs and tasted it. "Ach, that needs a touch more rosemary, my good man. And the waterfowl is too dry! Ye'll have to add a sauce and perhaps a pinch of cinnamon."

One of the men gave a slight growl and turned away.

The other lifted a red, bushy brow in amusement. "I do agree with ye, lassie. I told him so myself!" Pushing a dish of almond cakes across the table, he shot her a good-natured grin. "And what of these almond cakes, do they meet with yer approval, ye wee beastie?"

Kate smiled at him warmly. Selecting the smallest cake, she popped it into her mouth. It tasted wonderfully sweet. Closing her eyes, she breathed. "I've just tasted a bit of heaven!"

At that, both men laughed. Time passed quickly as she watched them work and chattered, and it seemed only a moment later that they stood back, dusting their hands in satisfaction to announce the meal ready.

Reaching for a platter, Kate volunteered brightly, "I'll just take the mutton up to the table now!"

The bushy-browed man caught her wrist, "Ach, no, ye wee beastie, Ruan would be right sore with us! He was fair angry we let ye into the scullery yesterday. Ach, 'twasn't as if we could stop ye, and 'twas only as he knew ye to be right hard-headed that we escaped harsher words!"

Wrinkling her nose in a smile, Kate brushed him aside and grabbed the mutton anyway. "I've no fear of the man! And ye'd best add a wee bit more sauce to the waterfowl afore I return. 'Tis not fit to serve as it stands!"

Ignoring their protests, she swept through the arched doors, pausing a moment to look out of the window facing the sea. A warm beam of sunlight fell on her skin, and a soft gust of wind blew through the opening to ruffle her hair.

A boat had just docked at the sea-gate.

She watched it for a moment with a twinge of nostalgia, and then closed her eyes and took a deep breath. She had lost so much. Her wondrously carefree childhood fishing on the lochs. Her mother and sister. Now, her father as well.

And Cameron.

Would she lose him, too?

Would she even ever see him again?

As if sensing her distress, her babe moved as though to remind her that she was not alone, and she whispered softly in reply, "Ach, wee one, even if I never see him again, I'll keep him safe, locked deep in my heart. And I'll remember enough of him for the both of us."

Aye, she could never forget the man. He was forever burned in her soul.

Choking a little, she murmured, "God keep ye well, Cameron."

And then stubbornly raising her chin, she marched with the mutton towards the stairs only to collide with Isobel scurrying down them as quickly as her old bones allowed.

"What are ye doing, Kate?" her aunt asked with a lovingly fierce frown. "Ruan willna want ye to serve him, lassie! 'Twill please him less than when he found ye in the scullery yesterday!"

"I canna be so idle, auntie," Kate said with a sunny smile. "It does me good to keep moving! I canna simply sit!"

Her aunt continued to frown, but her eyes were darting through the windows to the boat at the sea-gate. "Give me a moment and then we'll talk, lassie! I canna have Afraig discovering who our visitors are first!"

And with that, she rushed down the passageway.

Kate laughed, shaking her head, and swept up the stairs. She almost felt she belonged in the place. Another month and perhaps it would feel like home. Mayhap tomorrow, she would wear the plaid that Bree had given her.

At the top of the stair, a sudden draft blew the aroma of the mutton into her face, and a riotous wave assaulted her stomach. She grimaced. Aye, this bairn was proving trying at times. 'Twas still difficult to eat most days, and some days it was nigh impossible.

"Ach, ye wee one, you must help your mother now," she fondly reprimanded her belly.

Dunvegan's main hall bustled with activity. Tables lined the length of the room. And standing before the fireplace was the laird's table with the MacLeod coat of arms hanging above it. Nearby, stood the heavy iron locked chest protecting the castle's treasure—the famed Fairy Flag of Dunvegan. Kate eyed it curiously, wondering how she might get to see the wondrous thing when several boisterous children began to chase around her, catching her skirts.

Laughing, she stumbled a little, lifting the platter of mutton over their heads.

"Be watchful, ye wee hellions!" Ruan shouted, swatting them away with a good-natured chuckle, but upon spying Kate holding the mutton, he quickly scowled and snatched the platter away. "Kate, what are ye doing, lass? Why dinna ye sit and rest a wee spell?"

"I canna simply sit, my lord," Kate protested with a smile. Again, a delicate waft of rosemary and mutton rose to attack her nostrils. She gagged.

"Sit, Kate!" Ruan ordered with a frown, and then one of the lads ran back to whisper excitedly in his ear. The Laird of Dunvegan's dark brows lifted in surprise. "He's here? Now?"

Taking advantage of his distraction, Kate escaped back to the kitchens.

"Is this to yer liking, my lady?" the bushy-browed cook teased, handing her the platter of waterfowl now swimming in sauce. "And I've added the pinch of cinnamon as ye requested, your majesty."

"'Twill do, my good man." Kate laughed. She experienced only a small wave of queasiness as she returned to the bustling hall.

But this time, the tall, cloaked figure of a stranger blocked her path as he stood speaking to Ruan softly at the high table.

"Ye look ill and beleaguered, lad!" Ruan frowned, clasping the man's shoulder in a familiar gesture. His face was flooded with concern. "What happened? Surely, ye've nae been wed again?"

Suddenly and with a vengeance, the wave of nausea returned.

Desperately covering her mouth with one hand, Kate lunged for the table, intending to place the wobbling platter there as quickly as she could with the other. But it was too heavy and the tart fragrance of the sauce caused the bile to rise in her throat. Dropping the entire thing, she fell to her knees and retched violently.

She became aware of the man's fine leather boots only after she had soiled them.

Horrified, she clamped her hands over her mouth.

A long-fingered, ringed hand swam into view, and a familiar deep voice offered politely, "Allow me to assist ye…"

Ach, but she missed Cameron so sorely that she was now hearing his voice!

Heaving a sigh, she glanced up, preparing to seek forgiveness for ruining the man's fine leather boots.

Dark, passionate eyes met hers. The chiseled lips. The dash in the middle of his chin.

Cameron Malcolm Stewart, Earl of Lennox, Lord of Ballachastell, Inchmurrin, and a score of other holdings towered over her, his hand still outstretched, his dark eyes stunned and his carved lips parted in shock.

And then Kate's mind went blank.

Dimly, she heard Ruan ask, "Ach, what is it, lad?"

But Cameron's attention had focused only on her.

Dropping to his knee by her side, he lifted his hand as if to stroke her cheek but paused halfway, whispering, "Kate? Is … it really ye, Kate?" His voice caught.

Ach, but he looked fair awful, much thinner and grimmer. Dark stubble graced his chin. She'd never seen him so unkempt and disheveled, yet even still she thought him the handsomest man that she'd ever seen. Slowly, her finger rose of its own accord to trace the dash in the middle of his chin.

Capturing her hand, he pressed her fingers against his lips and closed his eyes.

"Do … ye know the lass, then?" Ruan's astonished voice sounded above them.

But still Cameron had eyes only for her. Lifting his lashes, he caught Kate's face between his hands and whispered, "I've been searching everywhere, Kate! There's not a stone in Edinburgh that I haven't overturned to find ye! I thought … I feared ye were … dead!" His voice broke.

Tears slid down her cheeks, happy tears. Tears of relief. How could she have ever doubted him? Cupping her hands over his, she slid her lips sideways to kiss his palm, and then finally found her voice. "I've been trying to write ye a letter, Cameron, but 'twas sore difficult! Ach, I've only just awakened from a stupor not even a fortnight past! 'Twas Maura who brought me here to Skye, though I still remember little of it."

"Maura?" Cameron's dark eyes widened.

"Aye, she rescued me from the Tolbooth." Kate shuddered. "She sought forgiveness for my poor father's death, and Sir Arval's—"

"But they both still live, my sweeting!" Cameron's lips curved in a compassionate smile. "Though your father struggles to regain the power of speech still, but I am sure—"

Kate gasped. "Alive? He's alive? My father's alive? And Sir Arval?" Her words came out in a shriek.

"Aye, my wee Kate!" Cameron laughed.

Suddenly, Kate thought her heart would burst from sheer joy.

Closing her eyes, she tipped her head back and laughed, and then lunging for Cameron, threw her arms about his neck, fairly knocking him over.

"What a wondrous day!" she cried in a voice thick with tears. "Ach, this must be a dream! 'Tis too wondrous to be real!"

She felt Cameron's deep laughter rumble through his chest, and then he rose to his feet, taking her along with him.

Belatedly, she recalled her bulging belly. Blushing furiously, she hung her head and babbled hurriedly, "Ach, Cameron, I understand that ye can never make me an honorable woman, but 'tis no matter! Our bairn will know only love, and I'll show the wee one how to ignore the harsh words of others. After all, 'twill only be words, and words can be ignored easily enough, and simply because the words are uttered, it doesna make them true—"

But it was clear that he wasn't listening. He stood still, staring at the prominent, smooth curve in complete shock.

"Surely…'tis nae…*your* bairn, Cameron?" Ruan choked, his brows rising to his hairline. "Kate, ye said the father 'twas an outlaw, a thief!"

The comment roused Cameron at once and with his chiseled lips curving into a smile, he murmured, "Aye, so 'twas, Ruan."

With his dark eyes locked on Kate's, Cameron gently caught her wrist and pulled her into the circle of his arms. And as his gaze possessively traced the soft angles of her body, his long fingers dropped, lightly caressing the swell in wonder.

Suddenly, she was very shy.

"I never dreamt I'd be taking ye to task over this! Of all men to walk this fair Earth!" Ruan's deep, puzzled laugh cut in. "But ye should make this right, lad. 'Tis not—"

"Ach, there is no need." Another familiar voice chuckled. "It has been made right in the eyes of all, Ruan."

Startled, Kate ducked around Cameron's shoulder to see Lord Julian Gray lounging against the wall, with his arms folded and his gray eyes dancing with mirth.

"My lord!" she smiled warmly, stepping away from Cameron to curtsey, but he quickly caught her elbow.

"There are few ye bow to now, my sweeting," Cameron murmured in her ear, and then sweeping her back into his embrace, he kissed the top of her head.

As Kate frowned in confusion, Julian approached and swept into a low bow before saying, "My most beloved Countess of Lennox, 'tis your favorite onion-eyed varlet come to greet ye!"

Kate's brows knit in a mixture of hurt and confusion. Placing a hand protectively over her unborn child, she chided, "Ach, my lord. 'Tis not a matter for jest—"

"'Tis no jest." The corner of Cameron's lip lifted in amusement. "I wed ye not a week past. 'Tis signed, sealed, and witnessed. Lady Elsa stood for ye, lass, and spoke your vows."

It was Kate's turn to stare in shock. "Ach, but I fear ye've gone mad, Cameron—"

"'Tis true, my lady," Julian interrupted with a light-hearted laugh.

"But...but... I wasna there!" Kate sputtered, bewildered. "And I'm the daughter of a fisherman! How can this be?"

"There is little in this world that I canna have if I want it,"

Cameron rumbled in her ear.

Kate stared, and then her brown eyes sparkled in challenge. "But ye didna ask me, Cameron. I may have said no! And I've told ye afore that my kisses canna be bought!"

With his dark eyes filling with tender amusement, Cameron grasped both of her hands and slowly sank down on one knee before her. Looking deeply into her eyes, he spoke in a hushed tone. "Kate Ferguson, I died each day we were apart, and I cannot live through another sleepless night without ye by my side. I love ye with my entire heart and soul, ach, ye carry my heart in your hand, lass. I'm nothing without ye."

Kate's nose wrinkled into a smile.

But Cameron wasn't finished. His eyes hardened. "And I swear I will protect ye, from destiny itself if need be. Never again will ye be caught in games of power. I'll see ye safe from the evil designs of men—"

"Thomas wasna your fault, Cameron," Kate interrupted, patting him on the cheek and then added, "But 'tis not the time to speak of him!"

He winced a little but nodded in agreement. "Never again will I let ye out of my sight. I want nothing more than to walk by your side on this fair green Earth for the remainder of my days. Kate, will ye do me the honor of becoming my wife?"

Scarcely able to believe her ears, Kate leaned down and rubbed her nose against his, replying breathlessly, "Aye, I'll wed ye, ye lout!"

With his lips curving into a smile, Cameron rose to his feet and swept her close once again, before turning to Julian. "Why didn't ye tell me that Kate was here, lad?"

"Cameron, I wasna certain myself!" Julian shook his head a little incredulously. "Ye led me on a merry chase, Kate. I've been searching for weeks. 'Twas finally a fortnight ago that I teased a rumor from a lass near your old village, claiming ye to be Isobel's kin. I rode with ye, Cameron, intending to ask Isobel in the hopes that it might be true, but I knew Ruan could help ye in any case. Edinburgh was fair slaughtering ye."

Cameron swallowed and wordlessly clasped the man's shoulders.

"Then 'tis an occasion to celebrate!" Ruan clapped his hands before muttering to Lord Julian Gray, "Aye, and I'll have an explanation of how this came to be. I'm fair mystified. I would know the story of this outlaw and thief."

And then everyone surrounded them at once, clambering for details and the latest tidings until Bree finally shooed them all away.

"There will be time for talk later." The Lady of Dunvegan smiled warmly before turning to Kate and Cameron. "Cameron, why don't you take your bride out for a bit of fresh air and let us prepare for a celebration?"

Cameron did not hesitate, and again, Kate felt the strange wave of shyness wash over her as he slipped his arm about her waist and guided her out of Dunvegan's hall and into the sunlight. At the sea-gate, he gently lifted her into a waiting boat before jumping inside to row it himself the short distance to the shore.

Watching him from under lowered lashes, she couldn't help but admire the ripple of his muscles. Ach, his fine linen shirt was unbuttoned, open at the throat, revealing his collarbone. She swallowed. Never had she seen a brawnier man. How could he be her husband, her lawfully wedded husband?

She fanned her reddening cheeks.

And then she saw his dark eyes upon her, eyes filled with amusement but also with an answering gleam of desire.

Blushing deeper, she cleared her throat and asked, "What of Mar? Is he well?"

At once, Cameron flinched.

Kate sighed.

It was clear enough not all the news was good.

The boat came ashore, and as he tenderly lifted her out, he began to share the details of what had happened.

She listened in horror, and with fingers entwined, they slowly walked down a winding path. And when all of her questions had been asked and answered, they simply strolled in silence, listening to the comforting song of the birds and the bleating of nearby sheep.

Arriving at the top of a hillock scarred with weather-beaten rocks, they paused to view the solemn grandeur of the moors spread out before them, covered in a rich, royal purple mantle of blooming heather.

Reaching down, Cameron plucked a wildflower and playfully tucked it behind her ear. And then lowering his head, he pressed a kiss against her neck, and murmured, "Am I truly awake, lass?"

Stepping into the circle of his arms, Kate leaned her head against his shoulder and sighed. "I feel safe here, Cameron. I never want to leave."

His arms tightened, and his voice took on a fierce tone. "And I'll see ye stay here forever, Kate, if it be your wish. I swear it."

They remained that way for some time, standing on the moors, and then Cameron slid a ring from his smallest finger and slipped it onto hers. "When we return to Edinburgh, I'll have the goldsmiths craft ye whatever ye desire, my sweeting," he promised, "But until then, wear this."

It was beautiful, a heavy, intricately carved gold ring housing a large dark red ruby.

With her eyes sparkling in pleasure, she replied, "I've no need for another, Cameron. This is the bonniest ring that I've ever seen."

He began to laugh then, a soft sound of deep amusement. "My sweet Kate, ye are now one of the richest women in Scotland. Ye'll have many rings, countless jewels, and—"

"Ach, why would I need so much when I only have ten fingers, Cameron? I canna wear a ring on each one!" she interrupted, wrinkling her nose in a smile.

Threading her fingers through his, she pulled him to a path leading down the face of the gentle slope and through a green wooded hollow of larch and pine. A small burn cut through their path, and as she made ready to step gingerly across, he caught her up in his strong arms and carried her over, setting her down gently on the opposite, grassy bank.

The look in his eye made her heart pound, and then his lips descended to gently brush her cheek before sweeping down to plant a soft kiss on her swelling belly.

With her eyes misting in tears, Kate tugged at his hand, pulling him through the springy turf, white with sandwort, to the edge of the sea.

Steep basalt cliffs rose in the distance as she guided him along the beach where tidal pools of anemones lay nestled between big, black boulders and shattered bits of pink coral. Reaching a flat, wide shelf of rock overhanging the sea, she sat down upon a rock, kicked off her shoes and dipped her feet in the cool water.

"Join me, ye lout," she teased, patting the spot next to her. "Stay here and rest awhile."

With his chiseled lips curved into a smile, he did as she bid. His dark lashes lowering once more to sweep over the curve of her belly, and there was a smugness, a pride in his eyes that made her blush.

As if aware of his intense gaze, the bairn shifted.

"Feel your wee one, Cameron!" Kate grabbed his hand, pressing his palm against the soft flutter.

His lips parted with wonder, and his tender look made Kate's heart feel as if it would burst. Throwing her arms about him, she hugged him fiercely.

And then, he caught her close to his heart, holding her tenderly, pulling her back against his chest and resting his chin on the top of her head. They sat there for some time, idly watching the white clouds race across the azure sky, casting fleeting shadows on the ground below.

And it was only when the sun began its descent, catching a sail of a ship on the distant horizon that Kate stirred in his arms.

"We should return afore Auntie Isobel starts fretting," she said with reluctance.

He didn't move, but he laughed a little. "I've known Isobel my entire life. 'Tis a strange twist of fate that I wed her niece," he said softly.

Reaching up, she ran her hands through his raven hair.

Gently, he took her hands in his and rising to his feet, lifted her to hers before leaning down to kiss her with such tenderness and raw feeling that she could scarcely breathe. And then sliding his hand down to hers, they returned hand in hand to the castle perched on the edge of the sea.

A lad was lighting the torches in Dunvegan's main hall when they arrived. Fresh garlands of flowers graced the walls, and the tables were laden with platters of venison and rowan berries, bannocks, smoked haddock, and game pie. The soft strains of a lute played as the clan members streamed into the hall to greet Cameron and Kate, and to offer their congratulations.

And then Isobel appeared to slide her arm about Kate's waist. "I'll be stealing your bride for a wee bit, Cameron," she announced with a proud smile.

But Cameron drew Kate closer instead. "I do not wish to let her go, fair Isobel," he teased lightly, but with a sober undercurrent in his tone. "I fear this is all a dream."

Patting his cheek, Kate slipped away, following Isobel down the passageway to where Bree awaited them in her private chambers.

A fine gown of soft blue wool lay on the bed, along with a garland of heather and wildflowers. Ignoring her protests, Bree and Isobel soon had her dressed, and they then placed the wreath upon her head.

Clasping Kate's hands between her aged ones, Isobel's eyes grew misty. "Ye look just like your dear mother, my wee Kate. 'Tis proud I am to see ye."

At the mention of her mother, Kate gulped, and her own eyes began to tear.

"Oh, you are such a beautiful bride, Kate!" Bree laughed, joining in the weeping to wipe her own tears away with the back of her hand. "Come, 'tis time for the celebration!"

They led her back to the hall, and as the pipers began to play, she stepped into the light amidst the cheers of the clan. And then Cameron was there, looking down at her with unmistakable pride to guide her to an honored seat at the laird's table.

Time passed quickly, and speeches were made as the food was served.

Kate sat at Cameron's side, charmed with his attentiveness as he insisted upon carving her the choicest cuts of meat, offering her the tastiest tidbits on the tip of his dagger.

And then the dancing began, and as Kate's feet began to tap under the table, Lord Julian Gray appeared before them.

"My dear countess, my lord earl, I wish ye only happiness from this moment on," he said, bowing low.

"'Tis only because of ye that this day happened, lad." Cameron rose to clap him on the back as Ruan appeared at the fair-haired lord's side.

"And ye, Julian?" Ruan asked with a curious brow. "'Tis time ye found a lass and wed yourself, lad."

At that, Julian tossed his head back and laughed. "There is not a lass that walks this Earth who can keep my interest for more than a month, Ruan, and well ye know it!"

Ruan and Cameron exchanged amused looks, and then with a

snort, the Laird of Dunvegan snagged his lady about the waist and twirled her into the circle of dancers.

"We shall see what fate has in store for ye, Julian," Cameron remarked lightly, before turning back to Kate. "Shall we dance afore ye wear out your slippers under the table, my sweeting?"

With her eyes sparkling with pleasure, Kate sprang to her feet and slipping her hands into his, allowed him to sweep her away.

The torches had long since burned down in their sconces when Kate finally stopped dancing and returned to the table to catch her breath.

"If only my poor father were here," she said wistfully as Cameron joined her side.

"We'll have another wedding in Edinburgh, my sweet," he promised, his lips curving into a smile. "We can have as many as ye like. I'll never tire of wedding ye."

And then taking her hand in his, he bowed to the merrymakers in the hall and led her away, amidst cheers and hooting laughter.

"Ach, such fools!" Kate wrinkled her nose in a wry smile. "They've clearly gone mad if they canna see I'm over half gone in carrying your bairn!"

He didn't reply but merely followed as she led him up to her tower room.

The first thing Kate noticed as she stepped into the small chamber was the clean smell of lavender, light and sweet. Lighted tapers graced the small writing desk, and garlands of flowers bedecked the bed. The window was open, and though the moon had not yet risen, the stars were bright enough to illuminate the dark shiny surface of the loch.

Suddenly, she was shy once again, and then Cameron closed the door and swept her into his arms. He simply stood there, holding her close, before moving to sit down on the edge of the bed. Drawing her upon his knee, he looked into her eyes with a half-smile playing on his lips.

Slowly, she reached up to twirl a strand of his hair around her fingers, but then she was suddenly nervous. "I'm not meant to be a countess, Cameron. Ye've made a mistake."

"There's naught that could suit ye better, my sweeting." The soft sound of his voice sent a sudden shiver down her spine.

She closed her eyes. Aye, the deep, silken voice that she had so longed to hear would now ever be at her side. 'Twas fair impossible to believe. Bashfully, she confessed, "I canna believe you're mine to keep."

"'Tis I who cannot believe such a bonny, sprightly creature as ye will ever be mine," he whispered softly, burying his face in her hair.

She smiled, and then recalling her letter, slipped off his knee and opened the wooden chest next to the bed. With a rueful expression, she handed him the tortured parchment. "I tried writing ye a letter, Cameron. But I fear even I canna decipher the words anymore. Sir Arval will be right disappointed in me."

Cameron laughed in the deep rumbling tone that she had missed so much. "He'll be so glad that ye've been found, Kate, that he'll forgive ye anything." Lightly, he traced the line of her jaw before sighing. His countenance suddenly darkened. "I fear I must return to the unruly kingdom of Scotland straightway on the morrow, to Edinburgh and the queen. But you will not have to see Thomas again. I no longer serve the king and his court."

"I'm coming with ye, then," Kate said quickly. "Ye canna hie me off to some castle ever again. I won't have it."

"Aye, I swear it, lass." Breathing heavily, he clasped her to him. "I'll never let ye go, Kate. Never. And I swear I'll never allow any man to harm ye again."

She rested her head upon his chest a moment, simply enjoying the scent of him, before reaching up to pull his head down and kiss his soft, chiseled lips.

The kiss was sweet, gentle, and filled with an unguarded tenderness.

And then Cameron pulled back. Lifting a finger to stroke her cheek, he whispered in a tone that sent another shiver down her spine, "I love ye so much, Kate, that the mere thought of losing ye is a mortal wound to my very soul."

Her heart sang, but as his eyes darkened with passion, he smothered any words she might have said with another deep, soulful kiss.

She melted against him, brushing her palms over his muscular chest and deepening the kiss. He moaned softly—or was that her? And then he shifted, his lips searing a path of fire on her skin. Shivering, she lifted his face to frame it with her hands and then kissed him with a kiss that ignited the fire of desire.

With a low, rumbling groan, he pulled back. Again, she saw the passion raging in his eyes and she knew it mirrored her own, and then he gently fell back with her onto the bed. And as the moon rose in the balmy, summer night, they shared their fierce, surging love.

17

THE COUNTESS

Cameron woke with the sun. He had slept little. Not because of their tender, passionate lovemaking—after which Kate had promptly fallen asleep—but because deep in his heart, he harbored the fear he would wake to find it was all a dream.

He lay as he was, cradling Kate in his arms and cherishing each moment, watching the circling birds through the window and listening to the seals barking in the distance. Never had he felt such a deep, abiding peace. He wished it would never end.

Kate stirred in her sleep, moving her hand to rest lightly on her belly, and Cameron smiled.

Slowly, and with deep reverence, he moved to kiss the soft curve, skimming his fingers over his unborn bairn in a light caress. The babe moved under his hand, and his eyes misted with emotion. The great feeling of protectiveness that washed over him was beyond anything he had ever experienced.

And then his peace disappeared with a single thought.

Childbirth was a perilous venture.

And his wee Kate was so small.

He frowned. Surely, fate would spare her further misfortune. So far, her life with him had been a harsh and turbulent one. Wasn't that enough?

He fretted for a time until he noticed that her long, thick lashes had lifted and that her sparkling brown eyes were observing him with curiosity. "And why do ye look so grim, Cameron?" she asked.

Sweeping her dark hair aside, he lowered his lips and kissed the nape of her neck, unable to confess his dark thoughts.

But Kate's sharp eyes had missed nothing. "Do ye still believe that ye are cursed?"

He swallowed.

She buried her face against his chest, and her thin shoulders began to shake.

Alarmed, he attempted to push her back so that he might console her, but she only snuggled deeper, and he realized then that she was laughing.

"Ach, Kate!" He sat up, annoyed but vastly relieved. "Ye fair frightened me!"

Propping herself up on her elbow, she wrinkled her nose and made a face. "If it is a curse ye are worried over, fool, then save your fears!" Her dark eyes danced. "I am, after all, a witch. Curses mean naught to me!"

Amazed that she could jest over the matter, he eyed her in wonder and then slowly returned her smile. Aye, life with her would be warm and real.

She would make an exceptional countess.

Fiercely, he caught her close, pressing her against his chest and burying his face in her hair.

"Cameron, ye fear too much," she whispered, rubbing her cheek against his chest. "I never dreamt I would be accused of witchcraft, nor did I dream I would wed the finest earl in Scotland. If such things are possible then none of us can know our future. Let us simply live and take joy in the day!"

He nodded into her hair, knowing a small part of him would always fear he had cursed her, but he knew that he'd rather live with the fear than live without her.

Rising from the bed, he stepped into his breeches and groped for his shirt, shrugging it over his shoulders when the slip of Kate's bloodstained bodice fluttered to the floor.

"What is that?" she asked as he stooped to pick it up.

Slowly, he held it out.

She recognized it at once, and a look of dismay crossed her face.

"I kept it always, close to my heart," he confessed softly.

"Then keep it no more!" she pursed her lips. "Ach, burn the dreaded thing, it has no place in our life now."

But a sudden thought crossed his mind, and he shook his head, tucking it away into the folds of his cloak. "I have other plans for this, my sweeting. But I will see that ye never lay eyes upon it again. Come, 'tis time to start the day."

He watched her dress and then holding her close, shared a tender kiss before descending the tower stairs to find Julian already gone with the dawn, bound for Edinburgh.

Cameron sighed, knowing that he must do the same.

They stayed longer than they should have before finally exchanging farewells and promises to visit soon. Then Cameron gently led Kate down to the sea-gate, lifted her into the boat, covered her warmly with a fine woolen plaid, and ordered the men to depart.

As they set sail, Merry appeared on the shore astride her black stallion, and as the boat glided north, the young lass raced with them for a time, galloping along the shores and across the blooming, purple moors with her dark hair streaming out behind her.

But when the boat approached the shadow of a mighty cliff, she reared the beast on its hind legs, and waving a cheerful farewell, wheeled around to fly in the opposite direction.

The sea was calm and akin to smooth glass as they sailed past islands and precipitous cliffs. The flat tops of MacLeod's Tables rose in the distance.

Kate rested her head upon Cameron's shoulder as they sat in the warm sunshine, watching the peaceful rolling moors slip by them. Sailing past Duntulm Castle standing on its lofty mound with its windows looking sheer into the sea, they turned south down the coast to the narrows of Raasay.

And it was then that Kate asked if she might bid farewell to Flora.

"I wouldna be here, Cameron, if not for her," Kate said, sharing the details of the woman's care.

"Then I am forever in her debt, my countess." Cameron kissed Kate's fingers, permitting his eyes to smile.

Reaching Kiltaraglen shortly thereafter, they sailed into the loch mirroring the rosy-tinted hills and the darker, shattered peaks of the Cuillin behind them.

Cameron leapt ashore and with an easy arm, lifted Kate down, setting her carefully upon her feet. And then hand in hand, they slowly walked up the path leading to Flora's small cottage on the hilltop.

When they arrived, the old woman was sitting on the bench beneath the tree.

"Kate, 'tis good to see ye again, lassie." Flora hobbled to her feet, placing both wrinkled, clawed hands on the top of her stick. "Isobel sent word that ye might come."

Kate rushed over to wrap the old woman in a warm hug as Cameron followed at a sedate pace. He waited until they had exchanged their greetings before bowing over the ancient woman's hand.

"I am forever in your debt, kind lady," he addressed her in a respectful tone. "Is there aught ye desire? Name it, and I'll see it yours."

Flora laughed, shaking her head. "There is little I need, laddie, and there is little I desire anymore … aye, nae even youth."

"Surely there must be something?" Cameron insisted politely. "Ye have saved the life of my wife and child. A man can owe no greater debt."

"Ach, well, if ye insist." Flora's lips split into a wide smile. "I've always wanted to taste an orange, my lord. I've heard they are as sweet as honey. I saw one once, a few years ago, but I didna taste it."

Cameron smiled. "I'll see that ye have your fill of them and more besides, good mother."

Aye, he'd see her well supplied with all of the delicacies of the king's table. Eyeing the state of her cottage, he decided he would send men to repair it as well. Aye, he'd see that she wanted for naught for the remainder of her days.

As Kate and Flora began to chatter, he strolled about, taking notes of things he would have done before returning to hear Kate say, "And if ye see Maura, let her know that both my father and Sir Arval live still. I would have her know the truth so that she may find some peace in her tortured heart."

Flora patted Kate's hands. "Hold kindness dear to your heart, sweet lassie, and dinna let the travails of life rend it from your soul."

And as Kate kissed her withered cheek in farewell, Cameron bowed politely.

Though he was less inclined to be so forgiving of Maura, he did feel the stirrings of pity for the woman.

It was too dark to resume their journey by the time they reached the bottom of the hill, and so they stayed the night at the local inn instead. And after dispatching a man to arrange fitting transport for Kate's journey to Edinburgh and another to see to Flora's needs, Cameron joined Kate in a lavender-scented bed and for the first time in months, slept well.

They rose with the dawn and set sail once more. Kiltaraglen dwindled into the distance as the boat ploughed through the sea, wave by wave.

And as the afternoon sun finally pierced the pearly haze that had shrouded the sea since morning, they entered the narrow channel of Loch Alsh where the castle of Eilean Donan perched on its rocky islet with moss and golden seaweed clinging to the black rocks at the base.

The elderly Lord MacKenzie and his white-haired lady met them as they disembarked and led them to the castle where they stayed until Kate's velvet-curtained litter arrived several days later.

"What is this?" Kate asked, wrinkling her nose at the luxurious litter slung between two white palfreys. "I'm not the queen, Cameron!"

"I'll take no chances with ye, lass." Cameron lifted a challenging brow. "'Tis not safe for ye to ride a horse while carrying a bairn."

She protested only a little after that, but soon he saw her safely ensconced in pillows and plaids. They exchanged their farewells with the Mackenzies and set off, traveling at a slow pace, up slopes fragrant with thyme, through stands of birch trees quivering in the breeze, and along the blooming moors.

They halted early each day, spending nights in ivy-covered inns, neighboring castles, and more than once in one of his own holdings before finally crossing the mountains to see Stirling Castle perched below them in the distance.

And as they once again crossed the old stone bridge spanning the River Forth, Kate called out for the horses to halt.

With a bright smile, she held out her hands. "Let's walk awhile, Cameron!"

Cameron gently lifted her out of the litter, an answering smile curving his lips.

"'Twas not so long ago that I thought ye an outlaw." Kate laughed, pulling him up Stirling's cobblestoned streets. "And ye let me think it, ye lout!"

"Even then, I could not bear to lose ye, lass," Cameron replied softly, viewing her from under lowered lashes. Reaching down, he stole a kiss.

She blushed a little, batting him away before she said, "We should hie ourselves off to the almshouse straightway. Even though I know Lady Kate cares for it now, we should see whether she's doing it properly, shouldn't we, Cameron? I've been fair concerned over it. What if she's lost interest and wee Donald is suffering?"

"I do believe the lady has been preoccupied of late," Cameron replied with a sly twist of his lips. "But I have heard from the monks that 'tis the wee Kate Ferguson they fear. I doubt your Donald has come to harm."

She walked a few steps before cocking a bewildered brow at him. "How would ye hear from the monks now? When did ye have aught to do with the almshouse?"

"I sought ye there a time or two when ye still thought me an outlaw." Cameron's lips twitched into a broader smile. "And Father Gilbert mentioned your meddlesome ways upon each occasion then."

"Meddlesome?" Kate's brown eyes lit with indignation. "Ach, the woolens were of poor quality, Cameron!"

Frowning a little, she fell silent but quickened her pace until they once again turned down the tree-lined lane.

The almshouse bustled with activity. The roof had long ago been repaired, and the men were halfway complete with the building of a new addition. A group of children played under a tree with several barking dogs as a group of women surrounded a large, black cauldron. They were chatting with the elderly gray-haired monk stirring it.

As Cameron and Kate arrived, the monk glanced up, and his blue eyes smiled. Handing the ladle to one of the women, he hurried over to greet them.

"My lord, my lady, 'tis well to see ye again. Ye'll find all in order here."

"Ye've done well, Father Gilbert." Cameron surveyed the place,

337

nodding in satisfaction.

The monk dipped his head in respect and replied, "As have ye and Lady Kate, my lord, 'tis through your generosity that these good works can continue." He then smiled at Kate. "And, my lady, ye'll find the woolens to be of the highest quality as ye requested."

It was then that Cameron saw the understanding dawn in Kate's eyes. Misty-eyed, she rounded on him and punched him in the shoulder. "Ach, ye lout! 'Twas your hand all along!"

With a soft laugh, Cameron caught her wrist and pulled her close. Planting a kiss on her cheek, he murmured, "Then go see that the lady has done all to your satisfaction, my wee Kate. There's no limit to what this Lady Kate may desire done."

They stayed some time there, and while Kate found them all—including the wee Donald—quite well taken care of, she found plenty of changes to make and began rattling off orders until the poor monk was overwhelmed, and Cameron feared she would exhaust herself.

Pulling her away at last, he retired with her to the castle on the hill overlooking the river below and rested until the pale moon rose on the horizon. That night, they once more slept in the chamber where their love had begun, and he again stayed awake until the wee hours of the morning, but this time to savor the feeling of peace as Kate slept deeply, with her head upon his shoulder.

They left early the next morning, bound for Craigmillar, passing swiftly through the woodlands, the tops of the trees blurred by mist. Cameron had sent messengers ahead to prepare Kate's father and Sir Arval for the journey on to Edinburgh, but it was an unexpected surprise when both men, sitting astride fine horses, met them three miles from the castle.

The change in Kate's father was astounding.

The man dismounted with only a helping hand from Sir Arval and walked to meet Kate halfway as she ran to her father's side. She wept as though her heart would burst, and there was not a dry eye among those witnessing the reunion.

After several hours had passed, the party neared Edinburgh, and it was not long before Cameron once again saw the dark castle rising high on the crag above him.

He sighed.

Treachery and intrigue awaited him there, but this time he vowed that he would overcome it.

Lord Julian Gray stood in the upper courtyard to greet them, clad in a fine velvet cloak and with both a dirk and a sword belted about his slim waist.

At his side, hovered Lady Nicoletta and Lady Elsa.

"And what is this?" Cameron's dark eyes swept over Julian's weapons.

"'Tis Albany in France." The man sighed a little. "And tidings he may be the target of an assassination plot."

Lady Nicoletta rolled her eyes in a gesture that Julian did not miss. Turning upon the sultry woman, the fair-haired lord cocked a challenging brow. "Ye've been naught but discouraging of this entire venture to protect the prince, Nicoletta. Enough so that now I'm wondering what drives ye. Do ye want this assassination to succeed?"

Lady Nicoletta's eyes flashed dangerously. "And who are you to accuse me of such perfidious desires, lordling? If such tidings are true, then the queen should send a man who knows how to use a dirk for more than spearing a partridge while dandling a lass upon his knee!"

"Ach, are ye jealous?" Julian's eyes narrowed in surprised speculation. "I didna think ye fancied me—"

"Fancy *you*?" Lady Nicoletta eyed him in outright disdain. "Who would fancy a man who has kissed every woman in Scotland, if not in France as well?"

"Life is simply one person going as another arrives," he answered with a flippant shrug.

They moved away, continuing to spat, as Lady Elsa stepped forward to bow low before Kate.

"I would you forgave me my jealous words of ill will, my lady." The woman's fingers fluttered nervously. "I was—"

"'Tis more than forgiven, my lady," Kate interrupted, hurriedly pulling Elsa to her feet.

"You may not call me that, my lady," Lady Elsa whispered with a shy twist of her lips. "You must call me *Elsa*."

Kate grimaced, but her dark eyes were smiling. "Ach, I'm little learned in such fine ways. Ye'll have to teach me!"

"I would be honored and delighted, my lady." Lady Elsa's face flooded with a genuine warmth, and then she turned to Cameron and bowed again. "'Tis good to see ye well, my lord."

"And so with ye," he replied, inclining his head politely and then added, "I have not thanked ye as I should have for standing in for Kate at the wedding."

Lady Elsa smiled wryly. "'Twas not the wedding I had wished for, my lord," she confessed ruefully.

340

"Forgive me, kind lady," Cameron answered softly.

"There is naught to forgive, my lord," she replied in a wistful tone. "Now that I see you both here together, I would I could wait for love ere you wed me off."

"I swear ye'll only marry the man ye wish," Cameron promised.

He then led Kate across the upper courtyard, into the castle with its high gray-stoned walls and up a stairway to his apartments before leaving her in the company of ladies waiting with the gowns and jewels that befitted her station.

He retired to his own chamber, to make ready for meeting the queen, but it did not take him long. Soon, he stood again before his desk, peering down at the writ upon it declaring Kate to be his wife.

At once, the memory returned of the parchment accusing her of witchcraft, and he slid his hand into his pocket, removing the bloodstained bodice. Moving to the window, he stared down in the direction of Holyrood.

Aye, he'd leave Cochrane a message that would strike fear into his soul. He'd see justice done, not only for the sake of Kate, but in memory of John Stewart, Earl of Mar.

Sir Arval's voice shattered his thoughts, announcing the queen expected both Cameron and his lady to join her for supper.

Tucking the bodice away, he stepped into the adjoining chamber but paused upon the threshold.

Kate was already waiting for him, standing straight and proud before the crackling fire. He'd always thought Kate bonny, but the stunning creature in front of him took his breath away. The finest gown of blue satin fell over her prominent belly in graceful, loose folds. The bodice gleamed with pearls, and the jewels about her neck twinkled in the firelight.

Ach, she truly was born to be a countess—to stand among the leading nobles of the realm. With grace in her every movement she walked towards him to slip her arms about his waist.

The scent of her hair filled his nostrils, and he let his hand caress and tickle her neck. "We'd best go afore I find an excuse not to go at all, my sweeting," he teased in a low, soft voice.

As they stepped into the queen's privy chamber, Queen Margaret rose to greet them, the long sleeves of her green satin gown sweeping almost to her knees. Her blue eyes locked on Kate's prominent belly and lit with interest even as her own hand dropped to rest upon her own unborn child.

"I did not know you were expecting a child, Cameron." The queen smiled warmly.

"He didna know it himself, Margaret," Princess Anabella snorted as she swept into the room, but her grim eyes were twinkling as her gaze swept Kate from head to toe. "Now ye look the proper countess, Kate."

Kate curtsied deeply to them both.

"Now that we are cousins, I will expect you often in my company." The queen nodded to one of her ladies standing in the corner holding a large bundle wrapped in silk and said, "Give the countess her gift."

The woman set the bundle on the table and carefully lifted the silk covering away to reveal a gilded cage housing two yellow canaries.

Kate's eyes sparkled in delight, and in moments, she was

chattering with the queen quite comfortably. And as the evening progressed, and talk turned to the business of childbirth, Cameron rose to his feet and excused himself.

He exited the queen's privy chamber with a smile upon his lips. The three women had scarcely noticed he had left.

But then his countenance darkened, and drawing out Kate's bloodstained gray bodice, he held it up against the torchlight.

His dark eyes narrowed, and covering his face with his hood, he left the castle bound for Holyrood.

* * *

Thomas Cochrane had stayed late in the king's apartments in Holyrood, speaking with his majesty on possible ways that they might regain control of the country. It was Cameron now, who held the nobles of Scotland in his hand. Both the king and he were at a loss of how they might wrest even a shred of power back.

Since encountering Cameron on the day of Mar's death, Thomas had feared for his life. A fear, of late, that grew tenfold by the day. He ordered guards to accompany him at all times now, even within Holyrood itself. And he'd taken to posting men outside every window and each door of his apartments, in order to guarantee the safety of his private chambers.

He hurried down the corridors, six armed men at his heels. Taking the steps two at a time, he nervously glanced ahead and spied his guarded door with some sense of relief.

He was almost safe.

He rushed past the bowing men and fairly flew into his apartments, leaning against the door with a loud sigh.

He was in his sanctuary now, a place so well protected that no one could penetrate it.

Taking another deep breath, he rubbed his hands together briskly and glanced about the chamber.

Aye, he felt safe here. This was one place where danger could not reach him.

It was then that he noticed something on his writing desk.

Curious, he grabbed a torch from a nearby sconce and approached. But each step slowed as he recognized Kate's gray, pearl-encrusted bodice pinned to his desk by the very blade that had pierced his now-scarred hand.

He swallowed.

With violently shaking hands, he pushed back the tattered cloth with a finger to see words scrawled upon a slip of parchment, words that—even unread—made his soul quake with fear.

He closed his eyes.

It was several long moments before he could open them again and force himself to read the words. Barely suppressing the scream rising to his white lips, he whispered them aloud: *May God have mercy on your soul, for I shall not.*

EPILOGUE

The smell of snow was in the air as Cameron wheeled his prancing charger around again to inspect his men for the fourth time.

"All is ready, my lord." Sir Arval maneuvered his steed to block his path. "I do believe fifty men, three litters, and five midwives is quite enough to make journey. 'Tis only sixty miles, my lord."

Cameron's dark lashes dropped in suspicion. "Did Kate send ye here?"

Sir Arval smiled, a little bashfully. "Yes, my lord. She swore she would walk to Inchmurrin herself if you didn't permit us to finally leave. She's readied the children and has sent for her winter boots—"

"Ach, there she is." Cameron's dark brows furrowed as Kate appeared at the gate of Edinburgh Castle, accompanied by two fur-bundled lassies and a maid carrying a third. They were the king's children, the daughters he had acquired through his previous marriages, but of late, he had come to feel almost as if they were his own. Kate's first action as countess had been to send for them, and the girls had fallen in love with her instantly.

Who couldn't help but fall in love with the lass?

Even the queen was quite taken with Kate. Her majesty had wept at the news of their departure from court. And even though they had promised to return in the spring, she had sworn it would not be soon enough.

Catching sight of him, Kate waved, stubbornly lifted her chin, and boldly stepped forward.

He was at her side in an instant. "Kate, I'm not quite ready. Ye should wait by the fire a wee bit longer, my sweeting!" he said, removing his black, fur-trimmed cape to throw it over her fine green woolen one.

"Cameron, I'll never see Inchmurrin at this pace!" She stamped her foot impatiently. "Our bairn will be born afore ye allow me to leave, and I've still a month to go!"

Bundled in two cloaks, she looked like a soft plump seal, but he knew better than to say it. With his lips curving into a private smile, he pulled his mantle about her closer, tucking it under her chin and protectively over her belly.

"Come, lassies." Kate held her hands out to the young girls at her side. "Are ye ready to walk to Inchmurrin? 'Tis not far."

"Ach, Kate." Cameron smiled, giving in. "If ye insist then, we'll leave."

Her brown eyes sparkled as she threw her arms about his neck, her dark hair spilling from under her hood. "I so very much insist that we leave this very moment, ye obstinate mule! My father has been waiting for me nigh on a fortnight now!"

Sliding his pair of soft leather gloves over her fingers, he lifted her into one of the litters before tossing the giggling lassies in next to her. And as the snow began to fall silently, gently coating the streets of Edinburgh, he began the journey to return home with Kate, to his ancestral lands.

The ride was a joyous and uneventful one. He led his men and the litters through snow-dusted moors, majestic glens, and dark green groves of pine until Ben Lomond rose in the distance and they stood on the bonny shores of Loch Lomond.

And as Inchmurrin stood tall and proud in the early winter dusk, gleaming on the southwest point of the isle, they stopped, and Kate leapt from the litter to pull him down from his charger. Then she covered his face with a wealth of kisses.

"Cameron, there canna be a bonnier place on this Earth," she finally said with sparkling eyes. "And as soon as spring comes, I'll have father teach us how to fish!"

* * *

It had been a pleasant, cozy day. It was the height of winter, and the winds were cold and bitter.

Kate sat before the fire with her quill scribbling endlessly over sheets of parchment as Lady Elsa sat at her side, stitching clothes for the bairn with her ever-busy fingers.

Cameron shook his head in amazement.

The two women were inseparable now.

He tried not to hover too much and did his best not to fret. Last week, he'd been concerned the bairn would arrive a wee bit too early. This week, he was certain the bairn was late.

As the evening shadows grew long, they made ready to sleep when Sir Arval arrived in a cold, swirling gust of wind.

"Ach, 'tis such bitter weather! But I am so glad ye came, Sir Arval," Kate cried out in a warm greeting, holding out her hands.

"Yes, it is a bone-chilling cold, my lady!" Sir Arval kissed her hand, drawing a beautifully scripted letter from a leather pouch slung over his shoulder. His lips spread into a wide smile. "Is this letter a jest, my lady?"

Kate's dark eyes swept over the parchment with a frown of disappointment. "I thought ye would be so pleased at the improvement—"

"Then, you truly wrote this? Not another?" The man's eyes beamed with pride.

Kate laughed as her father entered the room, leaning on the arm of Princess Anabella.

"Aye, my wee Kate wrote it," the fisherman said, with only a slight slur to his words.

"Kate spends her entire day with a quill in her hand," the princess added with a crisp nod of approval. "She's quite stubborn, Sir Arval, but I am sure ye know that already. Have ye news of the queen?"

"Aye, your highness." Sir Arval nodded. "She was delivered of a fine, healthy boy and the king has named him John Stewart."

A silence descended upon the room, and Cameron turned away, recalling again how John, the Earl of Mar, had spent his last dying thoughts upon his brother James. Aye, it was an unspoken apology. The king would never have given his newborn son his brother's name for any other reason.

Cameron clenched his fist.

It was not enough.

"I ... think I should lie down a wee spell." Kate's uncertain voice broke the silence.

All eyes turned upon her at once.

"Is it time, lass?" came her father's soft query. There was a smile upon his lips.

"Aye, father." Kate began to laugh and then promptly sucked her breath in pain. "I do believe it is!"

They had planned for this moment well. The princess and Sir Arval descended upon Cameron at once, drawing him to his privy chamber, as Lady Elsa and the midwives ferreted Kate away.

Princess Anabella plied him with fine Rhennish wine while Sir Arval tempted him with platters of tarts and roasted partridge, but he would have none of it. He paced before the fire, sending a page for tidings every ten minutes until sweat poured from the lad's face and another page would take his place.

"'Tis far too perilous!" Cameron slammed his fist in his palm for the tenth time. He struggled to control his fears, but memories of his previous wives' experiences in childbirth ran rampant through his mind.

"Ach, Cameron, Kate is a strong woman." The princess finally stood before him, cupping his face in her hands and giving him a grim shake. "Nay, Kate is a remarkable lass, lad. And I've no doubt in my mind that she'll rise to become the most powerful woman in Scotland one day. Aye, I know when I've finally met my successor."

The pride in her voice succeeded in distracting him for a moment, but only for a moment.

Kissing her hands, he drew away and resumed his pacing and swearing. "No more bairns! She'll have no more bairns. I'll not live through this again!"

And then, against their bitter protests, he slipped up the stairs to poke his head into the bedchamber to see for himself how Kate was faring. She appeared tired, but between the labor pains, she sent him a warm smile and a cheerful wave that gave him strength.

He would have stayed longer, but the midwives threatened to have him locked in the dungeons if he did not return to his privy chamber. And so he waited, until the agony was unbearable and stole up the stairs to check on her once again.

On his last trip, he paused at the door to hear the lusty cry of a newborn babe and kicking it back, he saw his Kate squealing with laughter, clutching the bairn to her breast in joy as the long beams of the newly risen sun filtered through the windows to bathe both of them in a soft, morning glow.

"Cameron! Come and see your wee lassie!" Kate wrinkled her nose in the smile he loved so well.

Cautiously, he approached.

Kate glowed, her cheeks were rosy, and the bairn she cradled was pink and plump.

He closed his eyes, unable to believe they had avoided disaster. Never again would she do such a dangerous thing!

And then he heard the fateful words.

"Ach, Cameron, one bairn is simply not enough! Let's have a dozen more!"

He gulped, and then his world began to spin.

The last thing he heard before darkness embraced him was, "Ach, his lordship is going to faint. Catch him!"

The End

Excerpt
from

THE DARING HEART

**Book Three of the
Highland Heather and Hearts
Scottish Romance Series**

Lord Julian Gray's dark lashes flew open.

He became aware of the sharp blade pressed against his ribs the exact moment the door to his bedchamber crashed open.

'Twas not the way he preferred to awake from a deep sleep.

The Italian assassin he had been trailing the past week stood framed in the door, observing him with the deadliest of expressions. He was a lean, dark-haired man possessing an air of refinement. His nose was long and thin, and he peered across the chamber at Julian with one hand holding a torch aloft and the other firmly clasped upon the hilt of his sword.

The bed jiggled a little as the blade in his ribs dug a little deeper into his flesh, and a woman's husky voice whispered softly in his ear. "Play nice, if you wish to live."

"Explain yourself, knave!" the assassin at the door roared at the same moment.

Julian's gray eyes narrowed.

Under the covers, the blade slid along his chest, and he caught his breath.

Ach, but he could recognize his own blade anywhere.

The canny vixen had stolen his own dagger from under his pillow!

Startled, he cast a quick, side-length glance at his bedside assailant, and his lips parted in surprise.

Even in the flickering torchlight, he could see the lass was a feast for the senses! Honey-colored tresses cascaded over a creamy naked shoulder. Her lips were wide and full, her nose pointed at the tip, and her lashes fluttering over stunning hazel eyes.

She pressed the tip of the dagger deeper, dangerously close to piercing his flesh.

There was a rasp of steel as the assassin crossed the chamber and pulled out his sword, cursing, "I'll have your head, knave!"

"It's too late, Orazio!" The hazel-eyed lass threw herself over Julian's bare chest. "We are wed, and the marriage has already been consummated!"

Julian choked.

His reward was a twist of the blade. This time, he was *certain* it drew blood.

Orazio drew a sharp breath. "Liselle! What have you *done?*"

"Did you find her?" a hauntingly familiar voice asked from the hallway outside.

Julian blinked in astonishment as Lady Nicoletta, lady-in-waiting to Princess Anabella of Scotland, appeared in the doorway, her full lips drawn in a tight, worried expression.

They stared at each other in shock.

"Lord Julian Gray!" Nicoletta was the first to regain control.

Julian licked his dry lips. "Nicoletta? What are ye doing in France?"

But Nicoletta was not listening to him. Running to the side of the bed, she placed her hands firmly upon her hips and glared at the lass still draped over Julian.

"Liselle, get out of that bed at once! Lord Gray is a man of the most disreputable ilk. You'll have naught to do with him!"

Julian snorted in a wicked amusement, but after one look at Orazio, quickly changed it into a cough. Adopting an insulted manner, he began to protest, "Ach, 'tis not true, Nicoletta! Ye've always misunderstood me!"

Orazio's dark brow swept up in astonishment. "Do you know this man, Nicoletta?"

"Does it matter?" the lass at his side asked pointedly. "He is my husband. The deed is done!"

Nicoletta gasped, clutching her heart. "Husband?"

Julian opened his mouth to object but shut it quickly when the tip of the dagger poked him again.

"Julian, did you truly wed our sister?" Nicoletta asked in a strangled voice.

Julian caught his breath. The wee, malevolent beastie spilling his blood drop-by-drop was the sister of the deadliest and most famed Italian assassin? As was Lady Nicoletta?

He really had no choice.

The man glowering above him, weapon drawn, was intent only upon securing his sister's honor. He could read it in his eyes.

"Aye!" Julian growled with a flash of annoyance.

The blade beneath the covers bit him deeper.

He clenched his jaw.

Ach, but he was going to discipline this wee terror the moment they were alone. Clearing his throat, he confirmed firmly, "Aye, I wed … Lady Liselle … last night."

But Orazio's eyes had narrowed suspiciously. "I would see both of your hands first, Liselle. And then let the man speak."

With a smirk, Liselle arched her back and slowly lifted her hands out from under the covers. Dropping one hand to thread her fingers through Julian's fair hair, she lightly skimmed the palm of the other over his naked chest. "We've been properly wed, haven't we now?" she asked Julian in a low, husky voice.

Under the covers, a new blade needled his flesh.

Had the lass found his dirk as well? And was she using her knees?

Ach, but her skills were impressive.

At that, Julian paused, and for the first time in his life experienced a ripple of genuine interest. He subjected the mischievous lass to a second, deeper look. She had the most unusual eyes he had ever seen. They were green, flecked, and ringed with gold.

And the expression in them was charmingly malicious.

He stared at her in wonder.

How had she slipped into his tightly locked chamber—avoided the traps he had set just the night before at each door and window? And how had she slipped into his bed and used his own dagger against him?

But most importantly, just what exactly had the wicked sprite embroiled him in?

More coming soon!

ABOUT THE AUTHOR

Like many of us on this planet, Carmen Caine/Madison Adler is from another world. She spends every moment she can scribbling stories on sticky notes that her kids find posted all over the car, house, and barn.

When she is not working as a software engineer, she is busy ferrying her kids to various appointments, writing lyrics for her husband's songs, taking care of the dog Tigger and his heart condition, attempting to tame her three insane cats, scratching her three Nigerian Dwarf Goats behind the horns or coddling her flock of thirty bizarre chickens from around the world.

The "Glass Wall" is the first book of her new paranormal series about Ancient Beings, Tulpas and different dimensions.

Carmen would love to have you as a friend www.facebook.com/Carmen.Caine

Carmen Caine also writes contemporary fantasy under the pen name of: Madison Adler.

OTHER BOOKS

Madison Adler/Carmen Caine writes fantasy under the name of Madison Adler and Medieval Romances under the name of Carmen Caine.

The "Glass Wall" is the first book of her new quirky paranormal series about ancient beings, Tulpas and different dimensions:

"The Glass Wall" (Now Available)

"The Brotherhood of the Snake" (Spring 2012)

"The Inner Circle"

"The Egg"

Her Scottish Medieval series, "The Highland Heather and Hearts Scottish Romance Series" covers the span of years ranging from 1478-1488:

"The Kindling Heart" (Now Available)

"The Bedeviled Heart" (Now Available)

"The Daring Heart" (2012)

"The Loyal Heart"